Conten

Heroes

by southplains

Adam

$\mathcal{I}$ have always been amazed by Joe's propensity to be in the wrong place at the wrong time. As a youngster, you could tell him to stay outside the corral, then you'd turn around and he would've climbed under the fence and would be on his way to crowd the feet of a nervous horse. Tell him to stay in the buggy to keep his church clothes clean and before you knew it he'd found the only mud puddle in Virginia City and had managed to transfer the whole thing to the front of his shirt.

Now that he's grown, he's not only kept but honed that talent for always being where he shouldn't, and like I said, his aptitude for it amazes me.

No. 'Amaze' is not the right word, exactly. The way he turns up everywhere except where he should be, or at least where we expect him to be—well, it exasperates, frustrates, infuriates me.

And today it horrifies me.

For the past three minutes—it seems a lot longer, but there's a clock on the wall opposite me, and believe me, I know exactly how long it's been—I've been lying on my belly on the plank floor of the bank with my hands clasped behind my head. I'm wedged between Hoss and Pa, who are lying in the same uncomfortable position I am. A few feet away are Mr. Ludlow, the bank president, and Arlen and Jonah, two of the clerks. Beyond Jonah is Mrs. Hayword; my heart goes out to her as she tries to choke back quiet sobs. The poor woman is terrified, but there's nothing I or anyone else can do for her at the moment.

On Mrs. Hayword's other side is Ralph Layton, pale and perspiring, his eyes squeezed shut. I make a mental note to myself not to rely on Ralph in case we have to do something drastic. Right now he looks like he'd shatter if somebody whispered 'boo' in his ear.

I hope he doesn't do anything foolish. Not that I don't understand Ralph's fear. He has good reason to be afraid. They are amateurs, these men robbing the bank, obviously nervous, looking as if they want to bolt and run as much as we do. It has been my experience that placing a gun in the hands of a nervous man can sometimes be more dangerous than giving one to a flat-out mean one.

Very carefully, I raise my eyes to watch the men holding us at gunpoint. There are five of them—three out here watching us and two behind the counter. The two behind the counter are hastily dumping money into gunny sacks. All of them are shouting at each other, and the way their fingers are twitching against the triggers of their guns unnerves me. They have our guns, and we are at their mercy.

Yes, I understand Ralph Layton's fear. I'm afraid, too. But I push my fear down and hold it there so that I can think clearly. We've got to be careful. You never know in which direction a nervous man might leap.

The Best of

BONANZA

World

The Best of
BONANZA®
World

BW BOOKS

2011

THE BEST OF BONANZA WORLD
A collection of favorite stories posted on the Bonanza World website.
www.bonanzaworld.net

All elements of "BONANZA" are copyright © and trademark ™, ® 2011, Bonanza Ventures.
All rights reserved.

This collection is officially licensed by Bonanza Ventures. All stories in this collection are works of
fiction and are copyright © 2002-2011 Bonanza Ventures. All rights reserved.

"Map of the Ponderosa" copyright © 1959 National Broadcasting Company, Inc.,
copyright © renewed 1986.

Photograph of Ponderosa ranch house at Incline Village courtesy of Vicki Christian.

All Bonanza photographic images copyright © and courtesy of Andrew J. Klyde
Collection/Bonanza Ventures. Used with permission.

Editor:
Emmy Peters

Editorial Contributors:
Englishgirl
Adamsdarling
Wrenny
JeanieC

Cover art design:
Jenny Proust

Illustrations:
Ann-Cathrine Loo

Thanks also to our anonymous assistants and proofreaders.

DEDICATIONS

In memory of four talented actors,
Lorne Greene, Pernell Roberts, Dan Blocker and Michael Landon,
the embodiment of the Cartwrights,
forever remembered and loved by their fans

and

In memory of David Dortort,
Bonanza creator and executive producer,
who imagined it all and brought it to life,
our eternal gratitude

and

In memory of Joan Markowitz,
Madam of the Ponderosa,
and great friend to all of us at Bonanza World

We're in a sticky situation, but if we all do as we're told we might end up living through this. If we all lie still and quiet and keep our heads, chances are these men will take the money and run, and we'll be left with the chance to get up off the floor and walk away. Later we can work on capturing the robbers and putting them behind bars where they belong, but for now we need to work on staying alive.

Some might not think lying still is the most heroic action to take, but there's a time for heroics and there's a time for common sense. Right now, heroics would be a pretty sure way for all of us to end up dead. So we lie still on the floor, all of us, praying that they'll just take the money and go.

The gunmen have drawn the blinds, but one of the windows still has a narrow slit between the blind and the windowsill, and the bright afternoon sun manages to find its way through it. A shaft of sunlight streams across the floor in front of my face, and dust motes swim in a nonchalant dance, indifferent to the human concerns around them.

My eyes drift again to the gunmen. I know better than to antagonize these men. And yet, when I realize that one of them is staring back at me, I can't bring myself to drop my gaze. I look him solidly in the eye even though I have to crane my neck back to do it. I know I'm inviting trouble, but I can't help wanting him to know that he's not going to get away with what he's doing.

That's when I hear Joe's laughing voice out on the sidewalk outside the bank, and everything shifts.

Dear God, he's coming in. He doesn't have a clue about what's going on here inside the bank, and he's coming in. I hear Hoss groan a soft oath into my right ear. With horrified fascination, I stare at the door along with everyone else. Joe has paused outside the door, and he's shouting good-naturedly back and forth with someone across the street. Through the curtained glass I can see the silhouette of his head and torso as he gestures in loud and idle conversation even as he sidles closer to the door.

The gunmen's jitteriness increases tenfold as they watch him.

Their attention is swinging back and forth from us to the door, and so are their guns. They are hissing warnings at each other, concerned that their plan is falling to pieces now that someone is coming in from the street, and panic is starting to wash over their faces. For the first time in my life, I find myself wishing that Joe had gone to pass his time in the saloon while he waited for us.

Out of the corner of my eye, I see Pa furtively unclasp his hands from behind his head. I, too, prepare to move, although I still have no idea what we can do to avoid the catastrophe looming our way. It is happening too quickly, and we are unprepared. We had no intention of having to face death on this fine day. Hoss and I hadn't even intended to come in, but we had gone to Hubert's Saddlery to drop off a saddle that needed repair, and when we passed by the bank, we saw that Pa was still inside. We decided to wait for him and went inside, tipping our hats at the small group of men waiting in the lobby.

"Mr. Ludlow will be with you in a few minutes, gentlemen," Arlen was telling them. But as it turned out, they were no gentlemen, but criminals intent on robbing the bank. We were unsuspecting and unaware at the wrong moment, and these men took advantage of that.

And now they are in control of our very lives as we lie at their feet.

Outside, Joe chuckles at something, and I hear him call a name. Seth.

Keep him out there, Seth. For God's sake, talk him into having a drink. Anything. Just don't let him come in.

But although Joe keeps up his good-natured shouting across the street to his friend, he makes no move away from the bank door. Once more Pa shifts, and this time one of the gunmen notices. He instantly places the end of his gun barrel against Pa's head. All my own thoughts of making a break for it freeze inside my skull.

"One more move and you're a dead man," hisses the man holding the gun, and my father stops moving.

"Lewis! Keep fillin' them bags!" the man at the window orders, but he keeps his eyes on my brother's sun-rimmed shape. I watch the man's fingers tighten on his trigger as he aims his gun at the door.

"Just let him come in," I say quickly. I am immediately ordered to shut my mouth, but I continue on, talking as fast as I can. "He doesn't know you're here. Just let him come in, and he'll lie down on the floor with the rest of us." Dear God, I hope I know what I'm saying. Joe, reacting with caution rather than leaping into action—it's a long shot. But he's coming in, regardless of what anyone can do to stop it. All I can do is try to calm the nerves of these nervous gunmen so that they don't shoot him out of sheer reflex.

"He won't give you any trouble," I insist, and I hope my own doubt does not show on my face.

They look quickly at each other, trying to decide what to do. Their nerves are keeping them balanced on the edge and I can feel my breath shortening into shallow pants, for I know they can't be counted on to hold their fire.

Joe calls out something else, and then he reaches for the door-knob. He's still laughing, and I can see that his head is still turned out toward the street. I look back at the gunmen; they are tensing, ready to shoot—too ready. I turn my head to stare at the turning doorknob as the whole world slows down into tiny, precise crystals of time, and then I swing my gaze back to Pa. His dark eyes meet mine. Gun aimed at his head or not, he is no more inclined than I am to lie still while my kid brother walks into a barrage of bullets. On my right, I feel Hoss's big body go rigid, and I know he, too, is going to make a move.

Our choice of lying still and compliant has been taken away from us. Whether we move or not, whether we take action or not, something is about to happen, and it won't be anything good.

Each fragment of time is magnified and spread out in the oddest way. I become aware of every movement in the room—

every tiny flinch of the gunmen's fingers on their triggers, every drop of sweat trickling down Mr. Ludlow's face. On the wall across the room, the second hand on the clock moves with infinitely slow precision. At the same time, my sense of hearing seems to be peculiarly distorted. I can hear the robbers yelling at us to stay down, but it's as if their voices are coming out of a deep tunnel, muted and indistinct. Yet I can hear the tick of the clock; it is inordinately loud, as is the click of the door latch as it opens.

The moment seems to stretch out forever, and Joe's smiling profile comes clearly into view as the door swings open. His face is still turned toward the street as he waves again. One lean leg stretches out into the room; he turns his face toward us and his smile slips into confusion as, in a twinkling of time, he tries to make sense of what he's seeing. Beside me I hear Pa shout a warning at him. Then the room explodes as both Pa and Hoss lunge for the two gunmen nearest them.

I move, too. I'm on my feet faster than I thought possible, plowing into the third gunman. I hear the breath rush out of the man as my head thuds into the softness of his belly. He drops his gun; I grab it and ram a knee into his stomach, not waiting to see him fall before I whirl and bring the gun up.

The entire world is one of shouts and screams and gunshots. I have no time to think. My only option is to shoot, and that is what I do. I shoot as fast as I can, even though I know I'll never be able to get off as many shots as I'll need.

Joe is staggering back against the door as it swings shut behind him, his eyes huge in his face, his hand whipping his gun from his holster. He screams my name, and I turn to my left just in time to see one of the gunmen raise his gun toward my face.

I'm too late. I know that. Even though I try anyway, I know I can't get a shot off in time. I wait for the impact of the bullet, and I'm surprised when the gunman suddenly rocks back. Someone else's gun has found him first. When I look back to my right, I know it was Joe's. He is already shooting again.

Across the room, Hoss is pounding the daylights out of one of the men. I swing my gun in the direction of a robber who is drawing on Pa, and I pull the trigger. The man goes down. He's still holding onto his gun, though, and he turns it toward me. I shoot again, but my balance is off, and my aim goes wide. Then something icy hot slices across my left side, and I fall back.

My head spins, and suddenly I'm on the floor again without even being sure how I got here. There are more shots. I raise my gun to fire, but somebody kicks me hard in the hand. The pain is intense; I know right away that my hand is broken, but as my gun goes spinning across the floor away from me I scramble and reach out for it anyway. It is quickly kicked out of my reach.

Another shot, close by me. I look up to see Joe spin and then slam back into the door as if somebody has picked him up and thrown him against it. He looks mildly surprised, his eyes wide and his mouth slightly open. His gun slips out of his hand and he slides slowly down to sit on the floor, leaving a streak of red to mark his trail down the door.

Oh, God, oh, God, oh, God. Everything—everything has gone wrong. I start crawling across the floor toward Joe, but some-body's boot lands hard in my belly, flipping me over to land on my back. I try to draw in a breath and find I can't. I can hear roars of outrage coming from Hoss, and then muffled, sickening thuds—and then nothing. Nothing from Pa, either. Are they still there? I want to look, I want to find my family, but I'm lying on my back and the ceiling of the bank is heaving over me like an undulating sea.

I fight against the pain in my hand and belly and side, and I roll over to lie with my cheek pressed against the floor. I try again to breathe, but it's as if my lungs have forgotten how to function.

Is Pa gone? My brothers? I wonder whether I should wait for the world to stop spinning or just hope that it will fade away.

Joe

I'M NUMB. All over, I'm numb. I'm pretty certain I've been shot, but I never even felt it. Is that possible? To be shot and not have any pain?

I'm not real straight on anything that just happened.

Up until the last few seconds, though, my memory is pretty clear. I had finished loading the wagon with supplies at the mercantile, so I went to the saddlery to catch up to my brothers. Mr. Hubert said they'd left already, so I knew they were probably at the bank waiting on Pa. Impatient, I headed that direction.

Normally I would've been happy as a bedbug to just sit in the saloon and have a couple of beers while they got their business done, but today was different. I'm taking Janie Williams to the dance in town tonight, and I promised her I'd pick her up at seven o'clock, so I'm anxious to get home and get all shined up. It's taken me weeks to convince her pa to let her go, so I don't want to mess things up by being late. Adam has been harping on me for years about my habit of being late. He says a lack of punctuality gives people the impression that you don't care. At least as far as women are concerned, I instinctively know he's right.

So because I don't want to be late tonight, I started getting jumpy. I decided to try to hurry my family along.

My buddy, Seth, had hollered at me as I crossed the street, and we traded some friendly insults as I walked up to the bank. The last thing I yelled at him was that I'd see him at the dance.

I knew things weren't right as soon as I opened the door to the bank and saw everyone on the floor, but there was no time for it to register on my brain. The shooting started as soon as I stepped inside; seemed like everywhere I turned there was a gun. I saw someone point a gun at Adam's head, and I thought I was going to choke on my own fear. I didn't have time to choke on anything, though—I was too busy shooting the man to keep him from killing Adam.

Then I saw that there were more gunmen back behind the

counter—I didn't know how many. They were shooting, and I was shooting back, and then—and then the back of my skull met the door, and for a minute I thought I was going to black out from the force of it. But I didn't. Instead, my legs went all rubbery and I just kind of sank to the floor. I wanted to stand back up but I couldn't. My legs just wouldn't work right.

I am fast with a gun. It's something I enjoy working at in my spare time, even though Pa frowns on it. He doesn't see any reason for a law-abiding man to work at being a fast draw. Says if I'm not careful it will get me into more trouble than it will ever get me out of. But I've always enjoyed the feel of the cool weight in my hand, the satisfaction of hitting a target dead-on center. I like practicing, shooting until I can do it faster and faster.

I guess I need more practice, though, because today I wasn't near fast enough.

I look down now at the right side of my chest and I can see a hole in my jacket. It's small, no bigger than what I could fit my finger through, but dark red blood is slowly soaking up through the green fabric, and I know it's true: I've been shot, despite the fact that I feel no pain.

I feel so strange. There's still shooting going on, but I can't bring myself to care. I hear Hoss shouting, and he's angry, but I'm not sure why. I want to tell him to simmer down, but I don't have the energy. I can't seem to find him anyway. And then he stops yelling, so I stop looking for him. It's hard to keep my eyes focused on anything. Then the shooting stops, and all of a sudden I just feel tired; all I can think about is how good it would feel to just close my eyes. I feel myself sagging forward.

But then Adam starts up. I can hear him even over all the racket that's going on in that bank lobby. He's yelling—at *me*, although I can't imagine what I've done wrong, and he sounds so mad that he forces me to straighten up and open my eyes. I can sometimes get away with ignoring Hoss, but anytime I've ever tried it with Adam, I've only gotten myself into deeper trouble. So I raise my head to try to find him.

And there he is. He's lying on the floor, and he's got his arms wrapped around his middle, and there's blood seeping between the fingers of his left hand. It scares me, all that blood; it looks so much worse than the small amount on the front of my jacket. I stare at it, wondering how bad he's hurt, but he's still yelling at me, so I force myself to focus on his face. He's looking right at me, and he's yelling my name, over and over.

He's yelling, but I can't seem to attach any meaning to his words. I concentrate less on watching him and more on listening to him.

"Look at me, Joe. Joe, look at me!"

I am looking at him—aren't I? But, no, I guess I'm not, because I realize that my eyes have dropped again to around the vicinity of my legs, which are stretched out in front of me like I'm getting ready to take an afternoon siesta. With an effort, I raise my head until I can look my brother in the face. He looks scared, really scared, and that bothers me; Adam so seldom lets it show when he's afraid. I wonder how bad off he is, and I start to ask him how bad he's been hit.

Before I can say anything, one of the gunmen swings the butt of his rifle hard into Adam's head. I suck in a choked, startled breath as the force of the blow sends Adam rolling over the floor away from me. He ends up with his back to me, and he doesn't move again.

Anger surges up within me, and I try to get up to help my brother, but my body refuses to cooperate. I come nowhere near standing up. Instead, I end up toppling over. I'm lying on the floor, my back still up against the door, and the back of my shirt feels sticky and warm. I can still see Adam lying on the floor across the room, but he's fading off into the distance, as if I'm moving away from him.

The last thought I have is that I'm going to be late picking Janie up after all.

Ben

MY THOUGHTS ARE in scattered disarray as I come to, but even so, I remember where I am. I continue to lie still, both to calm the hammer pounding in my head and to prevent the gunmen, if they're still here, from noticing that I'm awake. I've got to take stock, to figure out what I can do to get my boys and myself out of this unholy mess.

The bank robbers are still here, all right; they're arguing loudly amongst themselves about what to do next. I don't know how long I've been out, but it can't be long. The smell of gunsmoke is still strong in the air, and in the background I can hear poor Mrs. Hayword's quiet sobs coming in little broken hitches. Arlen is whispering to her, trying to calm her. Heavy boots tread rapidly back and forth across the floorboards.

I do not hear my sons, and it is that which makes me abandon my intention of lying still. I raise my head and open my eyes, and the first thing I see is Hoss's large bulk lying next to me, his chest moving steadily up and down, and I release a small breath of relief. I can't help wincing, though, when I see his face. He has been brutally beaten, and the marks on his face indicate pistol stocks, not fists. But he is alive.

Anger rises up strong and bitter within me as I look at him, and then fear immediately takes its place as I remember the rest. I look for my oldest son, and I find him lying just behind Mr. Ludlow's desk. At first I am afraid he is not alive; the blood in my veins ices over, and it is hard for me to draw in a breath. Adam is lying on his left side, his pale face toward me; he is curled into himself, and his right side is drenched in blood. Then he moves, just the tiniest bit, and lets out a soft moan, and suddenly I am once more among the living myself.

My oldest son is alive, but he is in trouble. The front of his shirt and both his hands are covered in blood.

"Adam." My boy's name rushes past my lips of its own volition, and my initial instinct to lie quietly disappears as I struggle to sit up. One of the gunmen immediately screams at me to stay down, and he points his gun in my direction, but his threats are lost on me. When a father sees his son lying helpless and bleeding, the fear for that son consumes him; there is no room for anything else. So I glare at the gunmen and shake my head.

"I'm going to see to my son."

"The hell you are. You're going to stay put like I told you, or I'm going to put a hole right through you."

I shrug my shoulders. "Then do it if you think you have to." I am not bluffing; I will let him shoot me before I will lie still and watch my child bleed to death. For an instant the man's face hardens, and I think he is going to pull the trigger. But there must be something in my eyes that causes him to change his mind, because he suddenly snorts in disgust and spits at the floor.

"Go ahead, then. But if you try anything, I'll cut you in half."

I ignore the pounding in my head and scramble across the floor to Adam before the man can change his mind, although his attention has already been diverted from me by one of the other gunmen.

"Bartell, people are running down the street toward the bank. All that shootin'...we gotta get outta here!"

The man who had just threatened to shoot me grits his teeth. "Don't you think I know that? Just stay at the window and shut up." He looks toward the back of the bank. "Lewis, how's J.D. doing?"

"He ain't good. Bleedin' like a stuck pig. I'm tryin' to get it stopped."

Good, I think. At least one of them is down. My thoughts are racing as I fumble with Adam's shirt, pulling it up to see the damage. The amount of blood sends my heart into the pit of my stomach, but as I wipe at it with my neckerchief, I see that the wound itself appears to be a shallow one. There is a bloody crease across Adam's side, a furrow a quarter-inch deep that the bullet plowed out as it whipped by him. I shudder, thinking how close my boy came. Still, the bleeding is bad, and he's not out of the woods yet. None of us are.

"Henry's gone. The kid got him."

The kid. Flashes of what happened pass through my mind. I press against the wound in Adam's side, and I look around for Joe, but I can't find him. The last time I saw him he was shooting from the doorway, but my line of vision to the door is blocked by the desk. Did he make it out of the bank? I pray that he did even as I crane my neck, trying to see, but a small noise from Adam gains my attention.

"Pa?" Adam's voice is hoarse and uncharacteristically squeaky, but I've never heard it sound more beautiful. I look into his eyes as they flutter open, and I try to sound unafraid when I speak. One of the first things we learn as parents is that our children's feelings feed off of our own. Even though my sons are now men, I know that, in times of crisis, they still look to me for reassurance, whether they see fit to admit to it or not. I try hard now to give Adam that reassurance.

"I'm here, son. You're all right. Just lie still."

"Got hit..."

He sounds almost apologetic, and I give him what I hope is an encouraging smile.

"Yes, but we're going to take care of that." I look back at Hoss, and I know I need to check on him more closely now that I know Adam is alive. I am torn between my sons, and I know the first thing I must do is to determine which one is in the most immediate danger. I lean down to Adam. "Can you hold my neckerchief against your side for just a moment? I need to see to Hoss." I take his hand to guide it to the neckerchief, but he flinches hard and sucks in a breath.

"It's broken," he gasps, and I see immediately what he's talking about. His hand is already turning blue and purple, and he pulls it in close to his side as if to protect it. He maneuvers his left hand up to hold the cloth against his wound. "Go to Hoss," he whispers. "I'm all right. I'm a little winded, but I'm okay."

'A little winded' is a ridiculous understatement but I have no choice, and Adam knows that. Whether or not my oldest is truly all right, and I don't think he is, I have other sons who need my help. I nod, and leave him to crawl back to Hoss, who, to my relief, is starting to groan and move around. Gently, I stroke his battered face, and my anger surges back as I look at him. My middle son does not go down easily, and his very strength sometimes works against him by inviting more violent assault than a normal-sized man would draw. He has certainly taken more punishment today than most men could endure.

But he is coming to. The relief of that added to the fact that my oldest is alive means that my blessings, few as they are on a day gone so wrong, have just doubled.

Hoss blinks, and I can see the pain in his expression. "Take it easy, son," I tell him. "Everything's all right."

Clarity comes into his blue eyes along with fear, and he begins to struggle to sit up despite my efforts to keep him from doing so.

"Adam and Joe—"

"Adam's here. He's hurt, but I think he's going to be all right, for now anyway. I still have to find Joe—"

"Joe's shot, Pa. They shot him."

The pain in Hoss's voice has nothing to do with the beating he's received, and my insides go cold. I was hit on the back of the head and saw nothing of what happened to Joe, but the look on Hoss's face terrifies me.

I don't wait for him to say more. Instead, I immediately get to my feet to find my youngest son.

"Get down!"

It is Hank again, standing in front of me, waving his gun in my face. I glare back at him.

"My son—"

Hank throws Adam a quick glance. "You saw to him already," he says curtly. He nods toward Hoss. "And that one, too. So sit down and shut up."

"No," I say, frustrated that I'm having to explain myself, "my third son. He came in later...after you had us lie down on the floor."

Hank looks surprised. "You mean the kid that waltzed in here and messed everything up?" He laughs, but it is a sound without mirth. "Mister, your boys sure have a way of bringin' trouble down on their heads." He shakes his head. "Go ahead, but make it quick. Looks to me like you're wastin' your time on him, anyway."

He steps to the side and indicates the door, and my knees almost buckle. A streak of red has been smeared down the length of the door, an abhorrent guidepost to where my youngest son lies unmoving on the floor. I'm not even aware of moving, but suddenly I am on my knees in front of him, running my fingers over his white face.

"Joe," I whisper, but I already know he can't hear me. Over the humming in my ears, I can't even hear myself. I slide my hand down his neck and the faint beat of his pulse throbs almost imperceptibly against my cold fingertips. I choke back a groan of relief and turn my attention to the small, bloody hole high up on the right side of his chest. I pull his jacket and shirt apart to see the damage, ripping at the fabric, and then I pause. The wound is deceptively innocent looking, but I look again at the blood streaked across the door and I know that I haven't seen the worst of it. Sure enough, as I roll Joseph's body toward mine, I can better see the destruction the bullet has wrought. The exit wound is slightly below and just to the right of his shoulder blade. Blood is still flowing freely from it, and the hole is three times bigger than the one in his chest.

I rip the sleeve from my own shirt and wad it up against the wound, but the fabric is quickly soaked. I close my eyes in dismay, but then I become aware of Hoss arguing loudly with Hank, and I look over my shoulder. Hoss is standing and he's trying to convince the gunman to allow him to help me with Joe, but Hank is having none of it. He looks like he is ready to end the argument by shooting Hoss point-blank, and I quickly call Hoss down.

"Joe's alive, Hoss," I tell him. "Just do what they say, son." I see that Adam has gotten himself into a sitting position, and I nod warningly at him. "You, too, Adam. Just sit tight."

My voice sounds so confident and sure. It surprises me. I have never been less sure in my life. I sit here, holding my youngest child's head in my lap, and I wonder how long he can last. I wonder if any of us will last. But I will fight with my last breath to try to save my sons and, for the moment, that means keeping my oldest two calm.

I look over and, for the first time, I see Jonah, the bank clerk, lying on the floor. His eyes are open and vacant, and I know that he is dead. I wonder how his young wife will be able to bear the news. It won't matter to her that he died bravely, trying to overpower these men who have come into our town, our bank, to take by force money that our friends and neighbors have sweated blood for years to accumulate. All that will matter to her is that Jonah will be dead and cold in his grave, his young life extinguished in seconds by men who decided it was easier to simply take than to work.

I look down at Joseph's head cradled in my lap and I know that it is very possible that I, too, will be grieving before the day is done. I press harder against the wound in Joe's back and I begin to pray in earnest.

Hoss

I'M SCARED. Real scared. To see the look on Joe's face when that bullet caught him...well, I don't have words for the way he looked. It was as if in that tiny little bit of time, he was already gone. Just that quick. The time it takes for a bullet to travel a few feet is more than enough time for a brother to leave for good.

Pa's sittin' on the floor over by the door holdin' him, and I can't see much around Pa's back—just the curls on Joe's head layin' against the crook of Pa's right arm, and Joe's legs stretched out on the other side of him. Seein' Joe's legs makes me even more scared because they're still. Joe's legs are never still. Whenever he's been in bed sick, or even when he's asleep, lots of times his legs will keep shiftin' around like they know he's got other places he wants to be.

But not now.

"Pa?" I call. Pa ain't said anything for a long time, and I got to know.

I got to know.

Pa doesn't answer. I glance at Adam, still over by Mr. Ludlow's desk, and I see him look toward Pa and then shut his eyes, like he's hurtin' too bad to hold 'em open. Adam's hurtin' all right; I know that. He's sittin' up now, although he probably shouldn't be, and he's still got his left hand clamped tight against his side, and it don't look like the pressure is doin' much to stop the bleedin'. But I don't think it's just the pain in his body that's makin' him shut his eyes. He saw what happened to Little Joe same as I did.

"Pa," I call again. My voice hitches a little, and this time Pa slowly raises his head and looks back at me. He knows what I'm askin' just by calling his name. But the grief written across his face steals my breath from my lungs, and for a moment I believe Joe is already gone. Then Pa manages to put a tiny, sickly sort of smile on his face and he shakes his head at me.

"He's here. He's fighting," he says quietly, and even though the relief of it makes me weak, I am scared because he has nothing more encouraging to tell me. He turns his face from me to stare at Adam. "How are you doing, son?" he asks, and I know already what Adam will say.

"Fine as frog hair, Pa," Adam says, and I have to admire the way Adam makes it sound true. If it weren't for my brother's pale skin and all that blood, I might even be inclined to believe that he really is fine.

"Shut up! If you three don't quit your yammerin', I'm gonna shoot the lot of ya right here." The one they call Bartell is waving his gun at us, and I look up at him, wishin' I could get a chance to wrap my hand around his throat. He's the one that shot Little Joe, and I swear to myself that he ain't gonna get away with it. He motions to the others to watch us, and then he goes to look out the window again. He stands there and I watch him for a long time, wondering if I will ever get a chance to make him pay for what he's done.

A tiny sound from Adam makes me forget about Bartell for the moment. I look at my brother, and I know I can't keep sittin' here. Adam ain't doin' good. He looks sick, and his body is wavering back and forth like grass fluttering in the breeze.

I don't care what Bartell does. I ain't gonna sit and just watch it all happen. I don't know what I can do for either of my brothers, but if we're gonna die today, we ain't gonna do it scattered across the room from each other.

I stand up and Hank yells at me to sit back down. I act like I can't hear a word; I start walkin' toward Adam, and Hank yells again and the other gunmen start yellin', too. I hear the soft clicks of gun hammers being cocked, and I know there's a good chance I might be beatin' Joe and Adam to heaven, but that's okay. I'm used to clearin' the way.

I keep movin'.

Adam

I'M SICK. I don't know what's brought it on; the pain, maybe. At any rate, my stomach is churning. My side stings like nobody's business and my hand is throbbing and my head is spinning, and I know I need to lie down again, but I don't want to. Pa's got enough worry on his mind with Joe; he doesn't need to know how awful I'm beginning to feel.

But Hoss knows. Like always, he knows, and he's up and striding toward me, his chin jutted out in the way it does whenever he's decided that enough is enough. The gunmen are snapping to attention and screaming at him, but he keeps coming anyway.

I stiffen; I've already noted where the four remaining gunmen are positioned, and I wonder if I have it in me to try to jump at least one of them before they gun my brother down. Something like divine intervention steps in though, because Bartell shouts at them to hold their fire.

"Let him go," Bartell shouts. "We got bigger fish to fry than worryin' about them. In fact, get 'em all up against that wall together. Easier to watch 'em that way, anyway."

Hank spits a wad of tobacco at Hoss's feet. "All right, big man, you heard him. Get your brother here out of the way and then get back over to that wall. The rest of you, get over there."

While Mr. Ludlow and the others scurry to do what they're told, Hoss speeds his pace and in seconds he's beside me, hunkering down next to me.

"That was a stupid thing to do," I tell him in a low voice, and I sound angry because I *am* angry. I'm angry because I can't control what is happening, so I fall back on trying to control what happens to my brothers. It's a ridiculous reaction, and I know it, but I snap at him anyway. "You know better than to mess around with men like this. They'd think nothing of killing you, especially not at this point."

But Hoss doesn't seem to notice that I'm upset with him. He smiles, but the worry in his blue eyes waters the smile down. "Yeah, well, I was gettin' a mite lonely sittin' over there all by myself. Can you walk?" He lays a big hand gently against my back.

I know Hoss is perfectly capable of carrying me, and I'm feeling bad enough to let him. But then I notice Pa staring hard over his shoulder at me, and I know I've got to keep up appearances for his sake. The eldest child in a family carries certain responsibilities that his siblings will never know, and keeping up a facade of strength during times of stress is one of them.

"Yeah, I can walk," I tell Hoss, and I let him help me to my feet. The floor pitches and I would drop flat on my face, but my brother has a tight hold on me, and I do little more than hang onto his shirt as I stumble across the room. Before I know it, I'm leaning against the wall next to Mr. Ludlow, and then he and Hoss ease me down until I'm sitting on the floor.

"I'll be right back," Hoss murmurs, and then he turns and heads toward Pa and Joe.

"What the hell do you think you're doin'? Just stop right there and get back against the wall," Bartell growls from the window, and raises his gun.

Hoss stops, but he makes no move to come back. "I'm goin' to move my brother out of the way of the door," he says, nodding toward Pa and Joe. Moving Joe probably won't help him any, but I know why Hoss wants to do it; he wants us all together, where we can protect one another, at least to some extent. The look on Bartell's face tells me that he's not going to allow it, but Hoss comes up with the one reason he should.

"There's two ways outta here—the front door and the back. You're gonna have to go through one of 'em, and right now my brother's body is blocking the front. Seems to me you'd better make sure the coast is clear if you get the chance." He speaks matter-of-factly, and I am amazed at how calm and collected my brother has remained through all of this.

It is a laughably simple argument and yet a logical one, and Bartell gives a short nod. "Fine. Get him outta the way then. But after that, you pin yourself against the wall and you stay there, you got that?"

Hoss nods brusquely and hurries over to Pa. He bends and picks Joe up as if he weighs nothing at all, and Pa quickly rises to help even though Hoss doesn't need any. The disparity in my brothers' appearance has been noted all their lives, but it has never struck me harder than it does at this particular moment. Still and quiet in Hoss's big arms, Joe looks small and fragile, almost childlike. Hoss's face has taken on a hard brittleness, as if it wants to crack, and I notice that he refuses to look down at Joe while he crosses the floor back over to us.

I look back at the door as they move away from it and my stomach rolls again, and this time it's not just because I'm hurting. I grit my teeth to beat back the nausea. Joe's blood is already drying on the white-painted wood, an uneven, dark streak snaking down the length of the door, an obscene testament to the way the peace of a warm summer's day can be shattered by a group of men we don't even know. A small puddle of blood has collected on the floor where Pa sat holding Joe in his arms; even now it is being tracked across the wooden plank floor by the gunmen as they move from one window to the next. There is something about the sight of my brother's blood on the bottom of their boots that enrages me so fiercely that I find I can hardly breathe because of it.

I watch as Pa and Hoss lower Joe to the floor in front of me.

"Leave his jacket on, Hoss. He's shivering." Pa takes off his own coat and stuffs it under Joe's head as a pillow. Joe never moves; worse, he doesn't make a sound. That shakes me more than I'd ever admit, because Joe isn't one to keep quiet when he's hurt. When he's really in pain, he lets out little whimpers and grunts and groans, kind of like a wounded pup.

Not now, though. He lies stretched out on the floor, absolutely still and silent except for that slight, periodic shivering, while Hoss and Pa press bandanas and their bare hands hard against his back, desperately trying to stop the bleeding. Viciously, Hoss rips one of his shirt sleeves off to use in an attempt to stop the blood. He looks up at me and starts to shake his head, but then remembers Pa and catches himself.

No, don't shake your head, Hoss. Not like that, not with that desperation in your eyes. You look like a drowning man reaching for a hand that's not there. Only it's not you that's drowning; it's Joe, and we're all reaching for him, and I don't know if any of us will be able to save him.

I shudder, and then the sound of tearing cloth draws my attention. Mrs. Hayword is ripping the bottom ruffle from one of her petticoats. She thrusts it at Hoss.

"Here," she says, "use this as a bandage."

Hoss nods a quick thanks and reaches beneath Joe's jacket to press the cloth against his back while Pa holds the boy up on his side. After a few minutes Hoss withdraws the scrap of petticoat again; the pristine white cloth has been soaked through with red, startling in its brilliance, like a hunter's kill in a field of snow.

I know my own dismay is reflected in the eyes of my father and brother. So much blood. I hear cloth ripping again. Mrs. Hayword tears strip after strip from the creamy froth peeking from beneath her skirts. Hoss keeps taking them, keeps pressing hard against Joe's back while the rest of us watch. I see my kid brother's life leaving bit by bit; it gleams on those immaculate petticoat ruffles, as brilliant and dazzling as his short life has been, and in my mind I'm going over everything that happened, wondering what I could've done to change things. The day's events play out again and again in my imagination. I could've jumped faster, shot faster, done something...anything.

"Bleedin's slowed down," Hoss finally mumbles, and I look up, slightly startled by his words. I realize now that I had not expected to hear them. Pa sighs a heavy breath of relief and nods, and I wonder if it's true or if they are only trying to convince one another, and perhaps me. But they wrap a strip of petticoat around his torso and bind it tightly so that it holds the makeshift bandage in place, and sure enough, the amount of blood that insists on seeping through has lessened. Pa pulls Joe's shirt and jacket back into place, and they settle him as comfortably as possible on the floor with his head pillowed on Pa's coat. Pa's hand lies gently against his cheek and lingers there for a moment before he scoots back a couple of feet to settle against the wall between me and Mrs. Hayword. I realize, as my father does, that they've done everything they can for my brother, at least for the moment. Hoss sits against the wall on my other side, and I notice that they are more or less propping me up between them.

And here we sit, helpless, while my kid brother in all likelihood lies dying at our feet. All of our eyes are on him, like we're afraid he'll leave if we look away.

Apparently I've made some sort of sound, because Pa and Hoss both look sharply at me.

"How are you feeling, Adam?" Pa's slightly unsteady voice is soft and concerned, and I want to lift some of the worry from his shoulders, but suddenly, the effort of trying to put on a stoic front is just too much.

"Like hell," I answer honestly, and for once the lapse into mild profanity doesn't even cause my father's brow to rise. He simply pats me on the leg and shifts so that more of my weight is leaning on him.

"Everything is going to be all right," he promises, just as I've heard him promise a thousand times throughout my life. Usually he's been right, too—but not always. I know it's nothing good to dwell on, but thoughts of times he's been wrong crowd into my head. When Hoss's mother was struck by that arrow, Pa told me everything would be all right—and it wasn't. The same thing happened in those first moments after Marie fell from her horse—only by then I was old enough to realize that Pa's words were meant to keep himself from collapse as much as they were to comfort his sons.

And now I look at Joe, and I know as well as Pa does that if we don't get him into a doctor's care very soon, he is going to die. Pa can make all the promises he wants, and it's not going to do a bit of good in the end.

I swear again, and Hoss and Pa look at me, and I can see the worry increase on their faces.

I am suddenly so angry—angry at the robbers, angry at Joe for not waiting for us at the mercantile like he said he would, or at least at the saloon the way we would normally expect him to do, angry that Seth didn't keep him talking for five more minutes. Dear God, I find I'm even angry at little Janie Williams. Joe mentioned several times earlier today that he was anxious to get back home because of her, and I know that's why he came to the bank. He wanted us to get a move on so that he wouldn't be late for the dance.

"He was in a hurry to get out of town because he couldn't wait to pick Janie up," I say. "A dance. That's what he's dying for. A dance and a girl. I hope she's worth it." My voice drips with bitter resentment.

Hoss is surprised and irritated at my outburst. He looks at me as if he thinks I've lost my mind. "What are you talkin' about? This ain't nobody's fault except those yahoos with the guns. It ain't Joe's fault, and it sure ain't got nothin' to do with little Janie."

I rub my good hand hard over my eyes and leave it there, my anger dissipating as quickly as it surfaced. Hoss is right, of course. I can't imagine why such an irrational thought ever jumped into my mind, much less out of my mouth. Ridiculous. It's the pain, I suppose. Has to be the pain. And the worry over Joe, of course. My emotions are running rampant over my good sense, and it occurs to me that my conduct is astonishingly like that of the brother who lies on the floor in front of me.

The thought draws a mirthless chuckle out of me. When I take my hand from over my eyes, Pa and Hoss are still watching me, and I can tell how concerned they are.

I look at Pa and, inexplicably, soft laughter continues to bubble out of my throat. To my dismay I realize that tears are forming in my eyes, which again is behavior more like Joe's than my own. I must be worse off than even I realize.

Pa reacts to my odd response by pulling my head gently into his shoulder, and I give a shuddering sigh and go quiet. I lean on Pa and I try to watch the gunmen, but mostly I watch Joe. I feel so very tired; I want to shut my eyes and sleep until this is all over, but I'm afraid that if I do I'll wake up to find my kid brother gone.

Ben

MY FEAR THREATENS to overwhelm me. Two sons badly wounded, and I have no idea how to get them the help they need. Outside I hear Roy Coffee calling to the robbers to give themselves up. Bartell answers by shooting through the window at him.

It becomes more obvious every minute that action will have to take place, and it will have be initiated from within the bank; otherwise there is no telling how long we will be holed up here. I look at the terrified customers and bank officials sitting against the wall next to me, though, and I wonder if they are up to doing what must be done.

Against my side, I can feel Adam taking hard, heavy breaths. He is in worse shape than he has led me to believe, and I am inclined to think that his injury is not as superficial as I first thought. We need to take a better look at him. His dark head is still buried in my shoulder; I look over it at Hoss, and give my middle son a pointed nod. Hoss nods back, knowing what I need him to do. He leans away from Adam so that he can get at his side.

"Just gonna check your wound again, older brother," he says quietly, and lifts Adam's shirt. If Adam even notices, he gives no indication.

From where I sit on Adam's right I can't see the wound, and I don't want to disturb Adam by shifting my position, so I watch Hoss's expression carefully. He leans down and studies Adam's ribcage as he pushes his shirt up out of the way. His mouth tightens in a grim line, and I know the news is bad even before Hoss looks at me and gives his head a slight shake.

"Bleedin' again," he says softly.

"How bad?" I ask, and I'm thankful for now that Adam doesn't appear to be listening.

"Bad," he sighs, and holds up a palm wet with red blood.

I mentally kick myself for not noticing the seriousness of the wound earlier. Adam had assured me that he was all right, but still, I should have known. A father should always know, shouldn't he?

"I thought it was just a crease," I say to Hoss. "I thought the bullet passed through—"

Hoss nods as he squints at his brother's side. "It did. I can't figure out why he's losing so much blood. Maybe it nicked a vein or somethin'—"

"Quit pokin' at it, and stop talking about me like I'm not here," Adam mutters. I would feel relieved that he has entered the conversation except for the fact that he doesn't lift his head from my shoulder and his voice is slurred. His hand, now swollen and blue, lies limply in his lap, his left arm across it as if to protect it.

Mrs. Hayword, bless her heart, hears our subdued conversation and offers more pieces of petticoat. I shoot her a look of gratitude before I tend to my boy. Her tears have long since dried, and I make a mental note to tell her husband how bravely she behaved during all this. He's bound to know by now what is going on—the entire town must know—and I can only imagine what he must be going through.

Hoss and I press against the wound, just as we did for Joseph a few minutes ago; I try to keep the panic out of my movements, but it's hard. Adam's blood, like that of his youngest brother, is flowing too freely, and I don't like the ashen tone of his skin.

"Adam, let's get you lying down," I say, and I'm not surprised when he tries to refuse. I pay no attention, and we soon have him lying beside Joseph. The two of them suddenly look so young and helpless that a fleeting memory of them both as children passes through my mind. Terror of losing them surges through me, and I shake my head to clear it.

Adam's prone position seems to help, and Hoss and I eventually get the bleeding slowed to a more manageable level. We use yet another strip of petticoat to fashion a sling to hold his injured hand close to his body. We are careful as we move the hand, and Adam doesn't complain, but I see him wince and I know how much he's hurting, which makes me wince as well.

"It's all right," I tell him again, even though of course it isn't. But what else does a father say when he has nothing else to give?

I look around in desperation. The four remaining gunmen are still agitated; although they've stopped paying as much attention to us, one of them, the injured one, stays hovering near and watching us warily, his gun barrel still pointed in our direction. Two of the others are at the windows, taking care to stay out of the sights of the guns now pointed at them from across the street. The fourth man is posted at the back door, dividing his attention between the alley and us.

This standoff could go on all night. We can't wait. Adam, and Joe in particular, can't wait. There has to be a way out for us, but I can't see it. God help me, I can't see it.

I think about all the years I've protected my sons, sheltered them, given them love and advice and tried to make sure they become the sort of men a father and a country can be proud of. I think of the times I've nursed them back from both injuries and grief; I remember the times we laughed together, and the times we cried together. I think about the agonizing loss of their mothers, and how I, myself, was brought back from the brink of despair by the love and needs of my small sons. I think about nights spent in front of a welcoming fireplace while the winter wind swirls around the house, my sons and I happy and secure in the arms of each others' company.

Is it all to end like this, then? Late on a sunny afternoon, with me helplessly watching while two of my sons die on a dusty bank floor?

Hoss

IT AIN'T RIGHT. I watch my brothers sufferin', and it's all I can think—it ain't right, what these men have done today.

I don't like to see nothin' get hurt. Not animals, not people. But right now, with my brothers lyin' in front of me, I know I won't hesitate to hurt these men if I can get my hands on them. I stare at the one holdin' the gun on us, and it's like he knows what I'm thinkin'. His eyes narrow and he raises his gun up slightly to point it more in my direction.

I glance at Pa beside me, and I see his eyes dart from one gun-man to the next; I know he's tryin' to think of some way out. If Joe and Adam weren't hurt, we'd likely bide our time and wait for the right moment to make our move. These men can't stay on their toes forever. Sooner or later they'll make a mistake.

Only we ain't got that kinda time. My brothers need help, and they need it now.

Little Joe ain't moved yet, and I wonder if he'll ever move again. I swallow the sick feelin' that rises up in my belly, and I push that thought out of my head and I look at Adam. He's shifted until he's lying right up next to Joe, his left shoulder pressed up against Joe's right. Adam's eyes are closed, but I know he's awake. He's awake, and he's listenin', and he's tryin' to be ready the best he can if somethin' happens.

Ever' so often the robbers fire a shot out the window. They ain't listenin' to whatever Roy's hollerin' from out on the street, that's for sure.

I lean closer to Pa and whisper, "Pa, we gotta do somethin'." It's a foolish thing to say; I know I'm not tellin' him anything he doesn't already know, and I ain't got no ideas on how to get out of this mess. But Pa looks at me and gives a slight nod, and the flash in his dark eyes lets me know that whatever happens, the Cart-wrights won't go down with a whimper.

We'll go down fightin' with everything we got.

Joe

SHOTS FIRED. Not a volley of shots; just one or two every few minutes. I try to block them out, but I can't.

I'm waking up, drifting up from a thick bank of fog, and I feel as though I've been asleep for a long, long time. My head feels as clogged with cotton as my mouth does, and it's hard to think. I struggle to clear my head, and I remember the shooting, but not much else. My body is stiff and cold, as if I've spent the night laid out on a slab of rock, and I shift to ease the discomfort.

The movement causes new pain to burst through my right shoulder blade, and a groan slips out of my mouth before I can stop it. It's pain like I've never felt before, white-hot and unbearable, and if staying awake means dealing with it, then I'm going back to sleep.

"Joe?"

Adam's voice, soft, questioning. Worried. I turn my head slight-ly toward the sound of it, but my eyes won't open the way I want them to, and after the first try, I don't care if they open or not. The pain in my back intensifies with such raging viciousness that I try again to climb back into the fog.

"Joe." Adam's still there, but I'm already turning away from him.

"Pa! He's trying to wake up."

No. No, I'm not. I'm not staying here, not like this. Dear God, the pain is threatening to eat me alive....

"Son? Joseph, listen to me. You need to wake up. Joe, come on, it's important that you open your eyes and look at me."

No, Pa. What's important is that I escape whatever it is that's chewing my back apart. I'll just sleep for a little longer, Pa, and when I wake up again, it will be better....

"Little Joe!"

Hoss...for pete's sake, you don't need to yell, brother. Can't you see that I'm hurting, that I don't feel well? I thought I wanted to wake up, but I don't. It's too hard.... I'm going back for more shut-eye, but I'll be back....

"He ain't breathin'...he ain't breathin'!"

What the heck are you talking about, Hoss? 'Course I'm breathing. I'm just needing some more sleep, that's all. The pain is just so bad...so bad....

More shouting from Pa and my brothers, but I don't try to make out what they're saying. I'm drifting away from them, and the pain is better already. Soon it's gone altogether, and their voices are a distant murmur. 'Bye, Pa. I'll see you later, brothers. I got places to go, trails to ride... I see Cochise standing and waiting for me, his head and tail up, his nostrils wide with the anticipation of a flat-out run through open grass. And on his back...on his back is a lovely woman with green eyes and hair the color of secrets and shadows. She's smiling at me, and she's holding out her hand as though to beckon me near. I smile back and I start moving toward her.

I've always been a sucker for a pretty face. Just ask my pa and brothers, they'll tell you. But this woman...I don't know, there's something about her...

"Joe!"

"Little Joe!"

Not now. Go away, brothers. I've got better places to be....

I'm jogging through a field of impossibly green grass toward Cochise and this beautiful woman, and all I can think of is how I want to be close to her... Something hovers just at the edge of my memory, something warm and comforting. I'm jogging now in my hurry to go to her, but she's shaking her head. She's smiling, but she's shaking her head, and she's turning Cochise and riding away....

No, don't go! I'm running hard now, trying to catch her, but Cochise is loping through the grass, carrying her away. She looks back over her shoulder at me, and she's saying something. I can't hear her voice, and yet I know what words her lips are forming.

Go back, Joseph. Go back.

No. Don't leave me. Please don't leave me.

I'm still running, stumbling in my hurry to follow, and I'm sobbing, begging her to wait for me, but she's fading away....

I stumble and my chest hits the ground hard—so hard that it knocks the breath right out of me. My eyes flutter open with the shock of it. And just like that, I'm slammed back into the pain. And I find that it's not the ground that's hit me in the chest. It's Hoss. He's bent over me, face red, tears streaming down his cheeks...and he's hitting me. Hitting me, right in the chest! Adam and Pa are trying to pull him off me, and they've got tears on their faces, too.

They astonish me, those tears. Something has happened, and I've missed it.

Pa and Adam are straining to pull Hoss off of me, although poor old Adam doesn't look like he'd be able to flick a gnat off a horse's hind end right now. They're both telling Hoss to leave me alone, but Hoss isn't paying them any mind. He's too busy yelling at me.

"I ain't gonna let you do this, Little Joe. Do you hear? I ain't gonna let you!" And he raises up one of those big fists and cocks it back to get ready to whack me again, even though Pa is hanging onto his arm for dear life to keep him from doing it.

And all of a sudden, I get mad. What's he thinking, this big galoot of a brother, pounding on me when I'm already hurt? I suck in a noisy, shuddering gasp of air and throw up my left arm to keep him from hammering that fist into me one more time—and he stops dead.

The look on his face would make me laugh if I thought I had enough gumption to do it, which I don't. His mouth drops open, and I swear, if I could gather the energy to reach up and shove him, he'd fall over like a dead tree in a strong wind.

Pa and Adam look much the same. Then they begin to smile the most ridiculous looking smiles, like they want to laugh and cry at the same time. But not me; I don't feel like smiling. A strange sadness washes over me. I suddenly feel as though I've lost something precious, like I've left something valuable beyond price back in that dream with the emerald-green grass.

The pain is pushing hard against me, and for just a moment, I consider running away again, back into that gauzy dream, back to the lady with the angel's face. I can still find her, I know I can.

I shut my eyes, ready to hurry back to that green, green field.

"Joseph? Look at me."

It's her! My eyes snap open.

But disappointment threatens to overwhelm me. It's not the lady with the dark hair and green eyes. This woman's eyes are brown and her hair is auburn, and after I blink a few times I realize that it is Mrs. Hayword. I remember getting a brief glimpse of her when the shooting started. She was lying on the floor, screaming....

She smiles at me. I've always liked Mrs. Hayword. I hate to disappoint her now, but I have to hurry...I have to go back. My eyelids flutter shut once more.

But Mrs. Hayword is insistent. She taps gloved fingers against my cheek, and I feel obligated to look at her again.

"Joseph, pay attention now. I spoke to Janie Williams this afternoon."

Janie.

"She told me all about how you're taking her to the dance tonight. She's very excited about it, Joseph. You don't want to disappoint her, do you?"

No, I don't. I like Janie very much, and I've been waiting for this night for weeks. But it's obvious that I'm not going to be dancing anytime soon.

"No dancing tonight," I whisper. "Janie's not...gonna be happy."

Mrs. Hayword smiles. "I'm sure she'll be very understanding, Joseph, but you're going to have to explain things to her. If a gentleman can't keep a commitment, it's up to him to tell a young lady why, isn't it?"

She's right. I have to stick around to talk to Janie again. In that instant, I know I can't just walk away. It wouldn't be right to leave like this, to leave Janie. To leave Pa and Hoss and Adam.

So I gather my strength and prepare to work through the pain. I know I can do it. My Pa and brothers are close by, and I know when my strength runs out I can lean on theirs.

And when I picture the lady with the green eyes again, she's smiling and nodding and telling me I've done the right thing.

She'll wait for me. She'll wait as long as it takes.

Adam

HOSS IS CALLING me seven kinds of a fool as he's trying to get my wound to stop bleeding again. My hand is throbbing, and I turn my face away from Hoss so that he won't see how much it hurts.

Joe is asleep again, but this time it is a natural sleep, disturbed though it is by the pain his injury is causing him. Pa is bent over him, holding his hand and murmuring softly to him. I hope the gunmen don't order Pa to move back to the wall, because I know he won't do it. Death itself wouldn't pull him away...I shiver as the phrase slips through my mind.

"You didn't have no business movin' around like that," Hoss grouches at me, but then he stops and just shakes his head. He knows why I had to move, and he knows, as I do, that it's something we'll likely never be able to talk about.

Joe was gone. We all know it. We watched him take that last, soft, shuddering breath, and then—nothing. We watched his young face change in that vague but unquestionable way that happens when life is no longer present, and then...and then something happened that I simply do not understand.

When Joe stopped breathing, panic and heartache instantly dealt us all a hard, unforgiving blow. While Pa and I sat stunned, Hoss's grief exploded into something wild and uncontrolled. When he doubled up a fist and started pounding Joe in the chest, we tried to stop him, but there is no stopping Hoss when his emotions overtake him. I myself have been on the receiving end of Hoss's fists, but I've never seen him touch our kid brother like that. I know it was raw anguish that lead him to do it, but my heart broke anyway as it happened, and I know Pa's did, too. We tried to stop him, we begged, we pleaded, but Hoss is too strong.

And then, the miracle.

I don't understand it, but it happened, and I know it's something that I will remember even after I've grown to be an old, old man.

Everything is going to be all right. I hear my father's words again, and I wonder if they are simply a statement of belief in miracles. A faith in Providence stepping in and changing something as abominable as a man's fist striking his dead brother into a thing of blessed reprieve....

I shiver again and allow Hoss to push me back down onto the floor as he presses new bandages against my side, and I watch Mrs. Hayword tear yet more strips of petticoat from beneath her dress to hand to him. Some women these days choose to go about with a bare minimum of petticoats; thank goodness Mrs. Hayword is a more fashionable type. More of Providence's work there, I expect. I watch her, and I wonder how she knew just what to say in those few seconds while Joe had that peculiar expression on his face. Though Hoss had inexplicably brought him back, somehow I knew he was hovering between this life and the next, as though he couldn't make up his mind about where to go.

But when Mrs. Hayword brought up Janie Williams' name, I watched something shift in my brother's eyes, and I knew in that moment that the fight was won.

I wonder if Mrs. Hayword's husband knows what a treasure he has in her.

"You look awful."

Surprised, I turn my head toward the soft voice. Joe's eyes are open again and, although they're glazed with pain, they regard me steadily.

I conjure up a smile for him. "You look great," I say, and my little joke is rewarded by a weak, almost silent version of that cascading chuckle for which my kid brother is famous. He cuts it off short because of the pain it causes, but the sound of it comforts me anyway. I look up at Pa, and the corner of his mouth twitches up at me.

We have much to be thankful for on this treacherous afternoon. We're here, all of us alive, huddled on the floor and bizarrely insulated from the gunmen by nothing more than a brace of family solidarity and the robbers' growing concern over their own immediate futures. They still have one man holding a gun on us, but even he is becoming overly preoccupied with what is transpiring outside the bank. He did little more than cast a few glances our way even while Hoss was pounding on Joe's chest, and his own injury is beginning to wear on him. I watch him for a moment, wondering if this is the weak link that will give us our chance.

Hoss gives the binding around my torso a last tug. Then our attention is drawn by Bartell shooting out the window again.

"That's what I think about your offer, Sheriff!" he shouts. "A fair trial," he smirks at his partners. "He must think we're really stupid."

"Well, maybe we are," Hank barks back. "This was supposed to be quick and easy. Get in, get out, that's what you said. Now we're stuck in here with a whole damn town waiting to gun us down if we step foot outside."

Hank glances at us, and ice forms in the pit of my stomach.

"What about them?" he says.

Bartell shakes his head. "What about 'em?"

Hank shrugs. "Hostages. They ain't gonna shoot through their own to get to us."

Bartell stares at us, and then slowly nods. "Yeah, maybe you're right."

One of the fears that has been twining through my mind since this all started now takes firm root. In my experience, hostages used as shields have a fairly poor survival rate, especially when nervous men are involved.

"One of these ones that are shot up, then," J.D. calls to them, his eyes pinned on us. "Less likely to give trouble."

Bartell grunts an agreement. "Yeah, all right, let's do it. This ain't gonna get no better."

I gather myself, pushing Hoss's hands away to sit back up again; if they have me or Joe in mind, it is not going to be Joe. The rough handling would be enough to finish him off. I'll be the one.

But Mrs. Hayword is quicker than I am.

"I'll go," she says, and stands up.

Hoss stands, too, as if to shield her. "No. You don't want no woman slowin' you down. I'll go. I won't give you no trouble."

Bartell bursts out laughing. "Oh, yeah, right, big man. I ain't that stupid. No, I think I like the idea of bringin' a woman along. More sympathy from the posse that way. And I think more than one hostage is an even better idea."

"Then take me," Mr. Ludlow says, and I look at him, surprised. He rises to his feet, shoulders back, chin out, and he has never looked like a larger man to me. My father immediately shakes his head and moves to get up. I know he won't hesitate to sacrifice himself.

I stare at Mr. Ludlow, still surprised. He's been so quiet during this entire episode, staying low, trying not to draw attention to himself. It's a funny thing, how bravery sometimes chooses unexpected moments to make an appearance. It is the most extravagantly generous offer that can be made, one's own life for that of another, but it's one I cannot possibly accept. I struggle to get to my feet despite Pa's sharp "Adam!" and Hoss's big hands attempting to gently press me down again.

"All of you, sit down until I say to move!" Bartell roars. "None of

you got any say in this, so shut your traps or I'll shut 'em permanent-like."

We all ease back to the floor, but J.D. rolls his eyes and winces as he flexes his bullet-creased arm. "It don't matter who we take. The woman, the little fella on the floor—it don't matter. Let's just do it and get the hell outta here."

"Yeah, yeah, okay," Bartell mutters, and fires a last warning shot out the window.

The uncertainty of just who they will use is the last straw for me. If I knew it would be just me, I'd be inclined to try to just go with it, rather than risk more people getting hurt in the gunfire that will be sure to ensue if we try to resist. But that's just it—there is no way of predicting who they will grab in the end and I cannot, in good conscience, sit by while an older man or a woman or perhaps even my kid brother gets pulled into the line of fire while these men try to make a run for it.

I look at Pa, then at Hoss, and their eyes meet mine. They know it's time. I look down at Joe, whose eyes have grown hard and clear, and he shows me with a nod that he knows, too. He shifts and I see his muscles tense. The kid is hurt so badly, and he's scared, but he trusts his family to see him through this. I reach out with my good hand to pat him on the shoulder, and I quietly say what I've heard Pa say to all of us, over and over, throughout all the hardships in our lives.

"It'll be all right."

Such a simple phrase, possibly even meaningless, but Joe's face shows gratitude for it, nonetheless. Pa gives his hand a final squeeze, and then we prepare to move. Hoss nods in the direction of Mrs. Hayword and the others, and they, too, know what is about to happen. Mrs. Hayword raises her hand and her fingers listlessly stroke the strand of pearls encircling her throat. I watch Mr. Ludlow and Arlen the bank clerk each take a deep breath and sit up straight.

On the other side of Arlen, Ralph Layton blanches and slowly drops his face down onto his raised knees. I know now, as I knew in the beginning, that he will be no help, but I feel only pity for him. It must be a terrible thing to be so frozen with fear that you can do nothing but wait for death to come for you. It's coming for us all now, and it may even catch us, but my father didn't raise his sons to meekly stand and wait for the slaughter. We will rise to meet it, and we will fight it.

Pa is closest to J.D., the one who has been posting watch over us. Pa gives us one last look, and then he lunges for the man, hitting him in the knees. Bartell and Hank both turn, surprised, and run in our direction, raising their gun barrels as they move. I'm unaware of my own pain as I rush toward Hank. I see Hoss moving toward Bartell, and I can't see how either Hoss or I will make it before they gun us down.

For the second time on this long, long afternoon, time slows down, hanging like a trembling water droplet on the edge of a leaf just before it crashes to earth. Shouts, screams, shots firing, bullets whining, all at an impossibly lingering pace—I see so much, hear so much—and it is a cruel perception, for I also see how hopeless it is. Bartell is drawing a bead on Hoss even as Hoss tries to reach him; Pa is struggling with J.D., and my foolish little brother has managed to somehow scrape himself off the floor and is stumbling toward Lewis at the back door. He shouldn't have been able to do it, but somehow he has. He can barely manage to move, much less fight someone for a gun, but now Arlen has jumped forward and interceded for him, flying toward Lewis in an attempt to stop him from shooting Joe. The thought occurs to me that, in all likelihood, both Arlen and Joe will be lost.

And me...the black mouth of Hank's gun muzzle yawns before me; in another instant, it will devour me whole.

Did Hoss bring Joe back just to have us go before him? Is that how this will all end? So be it, then. Joe never liked being by himself much, and I don't expect that he would feel any differently about traveling alone to heaven. We'll go, if that's how it has to be, and we'll all go together.

But now I see a flash of buttery yellow skirts out of the corner of my eye. In this oddly slowed passage of time, they furl and ripple around Mrs. Hayword's trim ankles like the waving of a flag, and I feel a deep regret. Oh, Mrs. Hayword, please get back. Stay down. But she doesn't. She grabs at the pearls around her neck, and she jerks them loose.

They glimmer and flash in the light as they fly, those pearls, and I watch their journey even as I brace myself against the impact from the guns. Like bullets from angels, the pearls scatter and bounce across the dusty plank floor. It is all I see, because I suddenly slip and go down hard on the floor, the jolt to my broken hand sucking my breath away.

Around me, though, other men fall—Bartell, Hank. Hoss, too, all slipping on those tiny orbs spreading across the floor. The floor shudders with the weight of their bodies crashing against it. Guns clatter against the wooden planks and go skidding away. It's ridiculous, really. I'd laugh outright if the situation wasn't so serious.

Bartell staggers to his feet only to slip and go down again, and Hoss manages to get close enough to grab for his lower legs. The man goes down like a tree. In front of me, Hank is reaching out across the floor for his rifle. I kick out hard and my boot catches him solidly in the elbow. He yelps and then reaches for the gun once again, but I've already got it, awkward though it is in my left hand. I am close enough to him, however, that I could likely hit him regardless of my aim, and he knows it. He backs up, his hands already rising in surrender.

I sit up slowly, panting hard. I'm not going to stand up. I don't think I've got it in me to try. But it's all right. It's finished. Off to my right, Mr. Ludlow is helping my father finish off J.D., and at the back door Arlen has a gun digging into Lewis's ribs. Joe lies slowly writhing on the floor a few feet in front of them, but he looks at me and makes a pitiful attempt at a smile.

"Layton!" I bark. Ralph still sits against the wall, arms wrapped around his head as if to protect himself. At the sound of his name, he cautiously raises his head.

"Get the door," I tell him, and I'm appalled at the tremor in my voice. The light in the room is slowly going dim, and I know I'm about to be pretty worthless. "Tell Sheriff Coffee it's over," I say. Ralph stares around the room, and then at me. "Go!" I shout, and he scrambles to do as I say.

I hear the sound of metal hitting wood, and I realize it's the gun leaving my hand and hitting the floor. Suddenly my cheek is resting against the floor, and then Pa is there. One solitary pearl glides past my face as Pa kneels to look into my eyes.

"Just hang on, son," he says, and rests a quiet hand on the back of my neck. "Everything will be all right."

And I know he tells the truth.

Hoss

THEY'RE ALL SHAKING our hands and calling us heroes. It's been three weeks, and the word still makes me as dadburned uncomfortable as it ever did. I watch my brothers' cheeks redden every time somebody brings it up, and I know it bothers them as much as it does me.

Naw, I don't think we're heroes. We only did what we had to do, and we didn't do it for reasons that had anything to do with heroics or glory. It had to do with saving what's most precious to us—each other. That's it. That's all.

I'm in a hurry. The package we've been waitin' on finally arrived from San Francisco today. I've got the little box in my hand, all purtied up with a pink ribbon that Mrs. Schuster down at the mercantile tied on for me. I rush down the street to Doc Martin's, and everybody looks up when I blow through the door.

"Did you get it?" Adam reaches out and snags the box before I can even answer. I frown at him. For somebody that was never any good using his left hand, he's sure gotten a lot quicker with it while his right one's been in a cast. He's standin' too close to Joe's bed, though, and little brother ends up swipin' it right out of his hand.

"Hey, watch it," I caution. "You'll mess up the purty bow on it. Mrs. Schuster worked right hard on wrappin' it up nice."

Joe pulls a face, but he holds the box more carefully. "Did you look at it before Mrs. Schuster wrapped it?"

"Yeah, I looked at it—"

Adam grabs the box again and holds it up over his head and

squints at it as if he can see through the box. "Did the new ones match the original?"

"What? Yeah, they matched all right—"

"The color? The size?" Adam is lookin' at me now, and I don't much like the snappy questions he's aimin' at me 'cause I'm not exactly sure how to answer 'em.

"Well...yeah, they matched. I think."

"You think? You *think*?"

How come Adam can make me sweat with just two little words?

I grab the box out of his hand and push my chest out at him.

"Look, you told me to go get it and I done that. You didn't tell me I had to stand and stare at it all day."

He glares at me and swipes the box back. Joe lunges for it, which makes Doc look up from his paperwork and yell at him.

"I know I said you could go home tomorrow, Little Joe, but that doesn't mean I can't change my mind. If this is the kind of shenanigans you intend to pull—"

"You listen to him, Joe," Mr. Ludlow tells him, and shakes a pudgy finger at him. "You don't want to pull those stitches, young man."

"He's right, Joe," Arlen adds, and I have to grin. For once, Adam and I have plenty of help in keeping Joe where he's supposed to be.

"Okay, okay," Joe mutters, and he lies back obediently, the pout on his face lifting only when Adam grins and hands the box to him. We both know Joe doesn't want to do anything that might extend his stay—poor kid's been holed up here at Doc Martin's ever since the robbery. Doc refused to allow him to be moved, and truth be told, we felt better havin' him right under the doc's care. There were a couple of times when we thought we might still lose him. And even after he started gettin' better, there were times when we caught him starin' off into the distance, like he was workin' hard at rememberin' somethin' important. It bothered me when he looked like that. Bothered me a lot, and I can't put my finger on why, exactly.

Adam was in pretty rough shape, too, of course, and Doc Martin kept him under his thumb right alongside Joe. Adam actually stayed on extra days even after Doc gave his okay to go home, just so Joe wouldn't be by himself. 'Course, he didn't let on to Joe about that. Joe woulda seen it as babysittin' and he never woulda stood for it.

But now they're both on their way to bein' mended, although it looks like I'll be doin' their chores for a good long bit yet.

The door bursts open again. It's little Janie Williams, and the excited glow on her cheeks makes her even purtier than she normally is. Yep, I can sure see what Joe sees in that gal.

"They're coming!" she says breathlessly. "Your pa is walking them down the street right now. Did you get it?"

"Right here." Joe holds up the box. Janie sails over to the bed and plants a kiss on his cheek. From the look on both their faces, I expect that kiss would be a lot different if me and Adam and the others weren't around.

"Do the new ones match the original?" Janie asks.

I feel my smile leave my face. "Dadburnit, why does everybody keep askin' that?"

Janie looks at me, her eyes wide. "But it's important, Hoss."

"He *thinks* they matched," Adam explains.

"They matched close enough!" I explode. "And anyway, there's nothin' we can do about it now. They're almost here."

It's true. Pa and Mr. and Mrs. Hayword are right out front, and now here they come through the door, laughing and talking and shouting hellos. Soon the room is filled with happy noise that makes Doc grumble somethin' about 'convalescence', but nobody pays him any mind. Mrs. Hayword has hugs and kisses for all of us, and when she kisses Joe on the forehead, he brings the little pink-ribboned box out from beneath his blankets.

"This is for you," he says soberly, and the room goes quiet, although we're all still smiling.

She's surprised, I can tell. She looks around the room at all of us, lastly at her husband who looks for all the world like a proud new bridegroom, and she very slowly and carefully begins to undo the ribbon. Beside her, Joe fidgets, and I have to laugh. He was never the sort to unwrap a present any way but fast.

Finally the box is opened, and we all watch her face.

"Oh. Oh, my," she whispers, and tears well up in her eyes as she pulls a strand of pearls from the box.

Joe is looking anxious. "Pa and Hoss gathered up all the ones they could find in the bank, but some slipped between the cracks in the floor, and Hoss crawled underneath the building and found a couple more in the dust, but the rest—"

"We found as many as we could, but the rest were lost and had to be replaced with new ones," Pa finished. "I entrusted the job to a jeweler I know in San Francisco. I—I hope it is satisfactory." Now even Pa is looking anxious. We all know what that necklace meant to Mrs. Hayword. It belonged to her grandmother, and she wore it almost every day before—well, before that day at the bank.

"Satisfactory?" Mrs. Hayword smiles even as a tear slips down her cheek. "Dear Ben, it is beyond satisfactory. It is beautiful. John, would you?" She turns her back to her husband, who gently clasps the necklace around her neck.

Adam clears his throat. "We know it can't really replace the original, but—"

She shakes her head. "Nonsense. It's better than the original. Old pearls from my grandmother mixed with new ones from friends I care very much about. I love it. Thank you all so very much. I'll treasure it forever."

Dang, that Mrs. Hayword is sure a practical sort of woman. A lot of ladies would've mourned the loss of those pearls for a long time, but I reckon she's the sort that knows what's really important. I look at Mr. Hayword watching his wife, and I know he knows what's important, too.

"Looks like a party in here!" It's Roy Coffee, pokin' his head in the door and grinnin'. "Well, if this don't beat all. A room full of heroes, right here in Virginia City."

There's that blasted word again. I grimace at Roy and he winks back at me. He knows how it bothers me to hear it. I reckon that's why he keeps insistin' on sayin' it.

Naw, we ain't heroes.

Not that there aren't heroes in this world. I've seen 'em. But they don't always come in the shape or size you'd expect. Sometimes they wear yellow dresses and pearls and they think of ways to win that no man could come up with.

I remember something Joe's mother used to tell us. It's something I've held onto all my life, especially during times when I've been scared, and I reckon it's something that Mrs. Hayword knew all along.

"Courage is simply fear that has said its prayers."

The Murder of Little Joe Cartwright

by Christy Gleason

Late Saturday morning, Adam Cartwright walked into the house after finally finishing his own morning chores, as well as those of his two younger brothers, Hoss and Little Joe. He didn't object to doing Hoss' chores—he was away with their father, Ben, on a trip to Sacramento, rather precluding him from completing them himself. But Little Joe was supposed to be doing his own chores, and he hadn't yet managed it in the three weeks the rest of the family had been gone. Adam's temper— often on a short fuse where his little brother Joseph was concerned—was fast reaching the explosion stage.

It's a darn good thing Pa and Hoss are due back next week, Adam thought to himself with a scowl. Any longer and there'd be one less family member to come home to.

He rounded the corner of the great room to sit down for

breakfast and found his little brother already at the table, wolfing down hotcakes like he hadn't eaten in at least a century. Adam's eyebrows lowered and he came around and glared at his brother.

"Where have you been?" he snapped. "And why are you eating?"

Joe looked at him in surprise. "I'm eating because it's breakfast time. And I've been in bed. Where else would I have been at this time of day?"

"Certainly not in the barn, doing your chores. Wouldn't want to run afoul of your brilliant plan for making me do all the work while Pa is gone."

Joe flashed his brother his most winning smile. "But you're so darn good at chores, Adam. Honest, no matter how hard I try, I can't do 'em as well as you. You're just awful talented that way." He speared a couple more flapjacks and tucked in ravenously. "You should have got here earlier, Adam. These flapjacks are the best Hop Sing ever made, and that's saying something. Too bad they're all gone."

"You ate them *all*?" Adam asked in astonishment. "What'd'you do—build up an appetite sleeping late?"

Joe smiled beatifically. "I'm a growing boy."

"You won't be growing much more, once I get my hands on you," Adam snapped, grabbing Joe's plate and taking the remaining hotcakes for himself.

"Hey...!" Joe exclaimed.

Adam lifted an eyebrow in his brother's direction, effectively silencing him. On occasion, Little Joe grasped precisely when to quit when it came to his oldest brother.

"Say, Adam..." he started as he watched Adam begin to eat.

Adam didn't even look up. "I don't want to hear it. You're not getting a day off today, and that's final."

Joe looked wounded. "That's not what I was going to say," he pouted. "When have I ever asked for an extra day off?"

"Yesterday."

"Well, I meant before that."

"Day before."

"Oh. Yeah. Well, what I was going to ask was, could I maybe work around the house today, instead of outside? I know there's all sorts of stuff that needs to be done around here."

"Like what? Holding your bed to the floor?"

"Well...like..." He broke off.

"Crocheting doilies?"

Joe glared at his brother. "I ain't a sissy! I just don't wanna work outside today, that's all."

Adam sighed and for the first time actually looked up from his breakfast. "Joe, what is all this about? Normally no one can keep you inside even under doctor's orders. And now you're actually volunteering to spend the day attached to the feather duster. What's going on?"

Joe squirmed in his seat, and Adam closed his eyes, taking a big breath. He knew that look, and it meant that whatever was going on it was worse than he had suspected.

"Out with it, Joe."

"Well, see, you don't know about this, but I went to town last night..."

"Of course I know. And perhaps you'll recall I specifically forbade you to."

Joe looked astonished. "You know?"

"Yeah. Can't imagine how I figured it out. The fact that you said you were tired and turning in early couldn't possibly have tipped me off. By the way, if you're going to stuff pillows into your bed to simulate a body, next time you might want to try using more than one. Just a suggestion."

Joe smiled feebly. "Good idea, Adam. Gee, you're smart."

Adam rolled his eyes. If Joe was buttering him up, whatever was going on had to be bad. "So...contrary to my express orders you went to town, and..."

"See there's this new saloon girl..."

Adam's eyes shot heavenward once more. "Oh, here we go..."

"She's awfully pretty, Adam."

"They always are with you, aren't they?"

Joe beamed. "Yeah, I sure can spot 'em!"

"So what's the problem? Besides the fact that a sixteen-year-old boy was in the saloon without permission."

Joe ignored the last comment. "Well, strange as it sounds, it was just when she was settling down on my lap that her husband walked in...."

Adam fingers suddenly became lifeless, and his fork clattered loudly to the table. "Her husband! She's married and she's working at the saloon?"

"Yeah, ain't that somethin'? So, with one thing and another, he came over to me and happened to mention that he didn't much care for seein' his wife loungin' around on my lap."

"Imagine that."

"Uh-huh. So he told me what he planned to do to me."

"Which was..."

"Well, he started by telling me that he was going to turn me inside out and use my kidneys for target practice. After that...well...it got sorta unpleasant."

Adam groaned. "Big man is he? Sort of brawny and robust?"

Joe squinted a thoughtful eye. "I'd say he was about nine-feet tall, and eight wide. Of course, that's just an estimate. Might have been bigger."

"Oh wonderful..."

"Well, of course, you know me..."

"I do. That's why I'm worried."

"...I thought fast, and when he asked me my name so he could inform my next of kin of my untimely demise, I told him my name was Tim Cullins."

"Where'd that name come from?" Adam asked with great interest.

"Oh, it's just an alias I keep handy for times when..."

Adam held up his hand. "Never mind. I don't want to know. The point is, does this happily-married gentleman know who you are or not?"

"Well, like I said, I told him I was Tim Cullins. Only..."

"Here it comes..."

"See, I was sitting at the table with Seth and Mitch, and they started laughing when I said my name. Probably thinking about the situation last time I used it, now that I think about it. But this bruiser, he might be a tad brainier than you'd expect from someone that size, 'cause when they started laughing, he got this sort of suspicious look on his face."

"And then?"

"I legged it."

"I see. So you're not sure at this point whether he knows who you are or not. Is that the gist of it? And if he does know, you're afraid he's going to come looking for you. So you want to hide out until the heat has died down."

"Yeah, that's pretty much it."

"Tell me. Do you do this sort of thing just to irritate me? Or is that simply an added bonus?"

Joe smiled weakly at his brother, but was saved from responding by the sudden strident pounding on the door. A voice called out from the front of the house.

"I know you're in there, Cartwright! Get out here right now and meet your death like a man!"

Joe jumped up from the table and squeaked in terror. "You gotta hide me, Adam! Quick!"

The pounding came again. "Get out here, you little pipsqueak, or I'm coming in after you!"

A look of anger crossed Adam's face. He didn't appreciate hearing someone threatening to murder his little brother. He considered that to be solely his purview.

"Stay here out of sight," he told Joe grimly. He headed towards the door and flung it open. His first thought was that Joe had rather underestimated the size of the man. Clearly he was at least sixteen feet tall. Adam blinked a few times, and got himself under control. Well, maybe he was exaggerating. Twelve feet, perhaps.

"May I help you?" he asked politely.

"I'm looking for the pipsqueak."

"I see. If you could be a tad more specific, it might hurry things along."

"Just how many pipsqueaks are there around this place?"

"You'd be surprised."

"Well the one I want is named Cartwright but he goes skulking around under the name of Cullins, stealing men's wives."

"Aha. Well, that particular pipsqueak would be my brother Joe."

Joe, listening intently from the dining room, looked outraged as he heard Adam giving him up to the giant. He was about to stride out and confront his brother, when he remembered that, under the circumstances, that might not be the best course of action. He stayed put, but resolved to point out to Adam the error of his ways once this was over—with fists, if need be.

"Well get him out here. I have plans that involve him. To begin with, I am going to tear off his head and make him eat it!"

"That does sound like fun," Adam admitted, "but I'm afraid you're a little late."

Goliath glared. "What do you mean?"

"It means that I beat you to it. I murdered him myself when he got home last night."

"What!"

"Yes. He hasn't been doing his chores, you see. And then when he snuck off to the saloon against my express orders...well, I'm only human, after all."

The man looked at Adam doubtfully. Although he was larger than the pipsqueak, he wasn't very big himself. Could he really have killed the boy?

"How did you do it?" he asked. "Did you torture him?"

Adam's eyes became misty and faraway. "Oh yes," he said

dreamily. "Don't want to do these things too quickly, you know. It wants drawing-out. You have to remember, you've only known him since last night, and just think about everything you want to do to him. I've known him for sixteen years! Sixteen very l-o-n-g years."

The look on Adam's face as he said this convinced the man, and his face sagged in disappointment. He felt a little foolish riding all the way out here, simply to turn around and head back empty-handed. "Well, may I have the body, at least?" he asked hopefully. "Not quite as good, of course, but there should be some satisfaction."

"Gosh, I'm sorry, but it's too late. I got rid of it. It was cluttering up the place."

"I don't mind digging it up."

"Oh, I didn't bury him. I was going to, but it's sort of warm today, and that seemed like an awful lot of work. So I just tied some rocks to him and chucked him in the lake. Saved heaps of time."

"Oh." The man looked crestfallen.

"Sorry to ruin your plans," Adam apologized. "If I'd known you were coming, I'd have waited to do him in. We could have had a nice little party. But..." He shrugged.

"Well, it can't be helped, I suppose," the man sighed in regret. "Guess I'll be getting back to town. No hard feelings, though, Mister. Stop by the Bucket of Blood sometime. I'll buy you a beer." He held his hand out, and Adam shook it with great dignity.

"You wouldn't mind keeping this just between us, would you? I'd just as soon the story didn't get back to my father. I'm planning on telling him that Joe's off on a hunting trip, and when he doesn't come home, Pa'll assume Joe got eaten by a bear. "

Goliath looked at Adam admiringly. "Good idea. It's important to have a cover story ready, I find."

"Yes, you can't leave these things to the last minute. Loose ends can be so messy. Well, I'm afraid I'll have to say goodbye. I have a great deal of work to do."

The man nodded and Adam turned and closed the door behind him.

Joe peeked out from around the corner and beamed at his brother. "Way-to-go, Adam! That ought to take care of the problem."

Adam shot his brother a pained look. "Do you really think he's going to buy that story for long? Would you believe it?"

"Sure I would. Why couldn't you have killed me?" Joe argued. "You're a good shot."

Adam snorted. "Well there's certainly no denying I have reason. But let me rephrase. Do you honestly believe that anyone with even a modicum of brains would believe it? I wouldn't be surprised if he figures it out before he's half-way back to town. I hate to say this, but I think you need to take off for a little while."

Joe looked delighted. "You're saying I can take a vacation?"

"Well, not a vacation, exactly," Adam replied acidly. "A vacation is a temporary freedom from work. But freedom from work sort of defines your life, doesn't it? So let's just say you'll laze around somewhere else for a change."

"I could go to Carson City! I hear they have a new saloon over there with some great card games going on."

"You just never learn, do you? Well, be back before the stage arrives Thursday afternoon. If you're not here when Pa and Hoss get back, there'll be questions raised that I'm guessing you'd just as soon not have answered."

Joe grinned. "Sure thing, Adam. Have a good time while I'm gone." He shot up the stairs to pack, fortunately missing the glower that Adam sent his way just before he stalked out the door to do the work of three.

MONDAY MORNING FOUND Adam in the barn fixing the hayloft ladder. With every pounding of a nail, his annoyance grew as he reminded himself that Little Joe was supposed to have done this particular chore the day after their father had left, and, as usual, Adam was ending up doing it for him. He was just promising himself the distinct pleasure of snatching Joe baldheaded when he finally returned, when he heard the ringing of horse hooves in the yard.

For a moment he thought Joe had come home early, and then, getting a grip on himself, he realized it had to be a visitor. Joe never made it back from a vacation on time—let alone early. Clearly he had company. Half-expecting the return of Goliath, Adam wondered briefly if the man rode his horse, or his horse rode him. He exited the barn to satisfy his curiosity on the subject and was surprised and pleased to see Roy Coffee, Virginia City's sheriff, dismounting.

"Morning, Roy," Adam called out from behind the man.

At the sound of Adam's voice, Roy whirled around, his hand hovering near the butt of his gun, a look of wariness clouding his face.

Adam grinned. "What's got you so jumpy, Roy? You look like you've seen the Devil himself!"

Roy didn't smile. "I don't know what I'm seeing anymore, Adam, and that's the truth."

Adam looked concerned as he walked over to the lawman. "You feeling all right, Roy?"

"No Adam, I ain't."

"Well, come in the house and sit down then."

Adam attempted to lead the Sheriff into the ranch house, but Roy remained glued to his spot. Adam looked at him with growing concern.

"What's the matter with you?"

"Adam, answer me a question."

Adam shrugged. "Sure, if I can."

"What were you doin' in the barn when I showed up?"

An eyebrow rose quizzically. "Fixing the ladder."

"Really. Now t'me that seems like the sorta job a junior oughta be handlin'—not yer Pa's right-hand man. Not the feller who's runnin' the ranch while Ben's gone."

Adam's face showed a mixture of annoyance and chagrin. "And don't I know it. Joe was supposed to have done it over three weeks ago—but you know Little Brother."

"Yeah. Yeah, I do at that. Well, why not have him do it now?"

"Joe's gone," Adam replied curtly, his irritation at his brother still holding sway.

Roy fixed him with a stare. "Gone where?"

Suddenly a warning alarm began ringing in Adam's head. Why, he asked himself, was Roy out here bright and early, inquiring about Joe? Thinking quickly, he suspected that The Gargantua of Virginia City had been spreading tales about his little brother. He resolved not to tell Roy anything until he determined exactly what it was Joe had been accused of.

Adam crossed his arms over his chest and leaned casually against a porch support. "Why are you asking about Little Joe?"

"Where is he?"

"I told you. He's gone."

"I'm gonna need a better answer than that."

Adam's eyes became remote. He was very fond of Roy—but his family's well-being came before everything else. "Well you're not getting one."

"In that case, I'm'a gonna have t'ask you t'come into town with me, Adam."

Adam shook his head. "Sorry. I got work to do."

"I'm afraid I'm gonna hafta insist. There's some odd rumors flyin' 'round town. Now you gonna come quietly, or am I gonna hafta handcuff you?"

Adam's mouth dropped open. "You can't arrest me for not answering a question!"

"No. No, I sure can't at that. But I can arrest you fer murder."

"Murder!"

"I'll need you t'come along with me now Adam, nice and quiet-like."

"Wait a minute! Wait a minute! Just who am I supposed to have murdered?

Roy looked at him steadily for a moment before finally answering. "Little Joe Cartwright."

"LOOK, THERE'S NO denying he *deserves* to be murdered, but..." Adam broke off. "Uh, wait a minute. Strike that last comment..."

Judge Ketchel pounded his gavel vigorously and glared down at Adam. "The prisoner will be silent!" he demanded. "Now, having heard from Sam Kendall that the prisoner readily admitted to the crimes of torture and murder of one Joseph Francis Cartwright..." Adam glared over at the skulking giant who had self-righteously repeated Adam's ridiculous claims on the stand, "...and having heard from Sheriff Roy Coffee that no trace of a Joe Cartwright, nor a Tim Cullins could be found in Carson City..." Adam shot Roy a wounded look of betrayal, "and twelve men of Virginia City having rejected the prisoner's testimony that the presumed deceased was, in fact, in Carson City under an assumed name and in all probability playing poker, drinking beer, and kissing ladies of ill-repute, and furthermore having found him guilty of all charges," Adam sent a menacing glower at the jury, "this Court has no recourse but to sentence Adam Cartwright to be hanged by the neck until he is dead." The judge looked directly at Adam. "And may God have mercy on your soul."

"If God has any mercy, he'll leave me for eternity alone with Joe in a room filled with sharp objects," Adam snapped.

"Silence!" Judge Ketchel demanded once more. "Adam Cartwright shall be taken to the Virginia City jail, where he will remain while a scaffold is erected in the Town Square. There, tomorrow at three o'clock in the afternoon, he shall be hanged. This Court is adjourned."

The judge rose and left the room hurriedly. Roy dragged a

somewhat unwilling Adam to his feet and tugged him out the door. Truthfully, Adam decided as he dodged the menacing glares and shouts of "Brother Killer" from the men, and the weeping and cries of "Dear Little Joe" coming from the young ladies, this was getting a little old.

"I'd really like to go home, Roy," he commented as Roy locked him up once again in the jail where he'd spent the previous two nights.

"Reckon you would, at that, Adam," Roy replied, "but ain't likely to happen."

"You know, if you'd just looked a little longer for Joe, you'd have found him."

"Yeah. Floatin' in Lake Tahoe, I s'pose."

"ROY!! How many times do I have to explain this to you?"

"You can explain 'til yer blue in the face, Adam, but it ain't getting' you nowhere. I offered to testify as a character witness for you, and tell the Court how annoying Little Joe can be on occasion, but you done refused. What more can I do?"

"You could go look for Joe, that's what you could do!" Adam retorted coldly.

"I ain't a-gonna do that, Adam. Now, you know I always thought real highly of you, and I'll do what I can to make your last hours pleasant. I'll get you a good meal from the hotel, and I even brought you a new feather pillow. That's all I can do."

Adam's shoulders sagged and he sat down on the cot in despair. "Just promise me one thing, Roy."

Roy looked at the young man with sympathy. "Name it."

"When Joe comes back, kill him for me."

Roy snorted and left the deputy watching the prisoner while he left to get Adam's final supper.

THE STAGE RATTLED to a stop and with a great deal of thanksgiving, Hoss and Ben exited, each holding their hands to the small of their backs.

"Pa, I ain't never riding a stage again when Jake's drivin', and that's a promise. I swear he deliberately hit every hole between here and Sacramento."

Ben laughed and clapped his son on the back. "Well, let's hope the ride back to the Ponderosa is a little smoother. And then we can sleep in our own beds tonight."

"And don't think I ain't lookin' forward to it, neither. I been dreamin' about my bed since we left."

"Well, the sooner we start home, the sooner you can crawl into it. Now if we can just find your brothers," he added, as he scanned the oddly-empty street for any sight of his other two boys.

"Probably at the saloon drinkin' a beer 'steada meetin' us like they's s'posed to be," Hoss answered acidly. "Hey Charlie," he called out as he saw a casual acquaintance ambling down the sidewalk. "You seen Adam or Little Joe?"

Charlie, no particular fan of the Cartwrights, grinned back. "Ain't no sign of Little Joe, and that's the truth. Now Adam. You'll find him right smack down in the Town Square. Sorta the town guest of honor, he is." Charlie laughed and walked away.

Hoss and Ben looked at one another in confusion. "What was that supposed to mean?" Hoss asked.

"Adam must have done something special for the town so they're giving him a prize!" Ben's chest swelled out with pride in his eldest.

Hoss, a bit tired of Adam's constant accomplishments, snorted inelegantly. "Yeah. Prob'ly saved some golden-haired, lisping child from certain death by a run-away horse, if I know him. Somehow always knows how to be in the right place at the right time. Let's go have a beer."

"Now Hoss. You know Adam doesn't do that sort of thing for the admiration he receives. Come on. I want to see him receive his reward."

He hurried off towards the center of town, a less-than-enthralled Hoss trailing behind. They rounded the final building and before their eyes saw Adam standing on the platform of a hangman's scaffolding, a noose dangling beside his head. They stared in shock.

"Just what is going on here?" Ben roared. He and Hoss broke into a run towards the condemned man.

"Hi Pa," Adam replied casually. "How'd the business go in Sacramento?"

"Don't you 'Hi Pa' me, young man! Just what are you doing up there?"

Adam glanced at the hangman's noose. "They're giving me a moment for my final words. I was trying to think of something clever."

Ben bounded up the steps, Hoss right behind him. He looked at Roy. "Why is my boy going to be hanged?"

"I'm sorry to hafta break this to you, Ben, but Adam here done murdered Little Joe. Nothin' else we can do."

Ben turned and glared at Adam with such vehemence that Adam found himself wishing he'd foregone the final words. Hanging had to be easier than looking at Pa when he was in one of his moods. His foot unconsciously began tapping the trapdoor beneath him experimentally, in hopes it would open beneath him and save him from his father's wrath.

"Why do they think you murdered your brother?" Ben asked, his voice deceptively quiet.

Adam winced at the tone, his tapping becoming a stead tromp on the trapdoor. "It's a long story..."

"ADAM!!!"

"Ben, he admitted to it hisself. Now, I'm sorry you came back in time to witness this, but I got a duty to the law. Adam's been sentenced to be hanged, and I gotta hang him. I'm sorry."

Ben looked in astonishment at the sheriff. "I don't know why you think Adam murdered Joe, but just stop this hanging until we can think this thing through."

"Ain't no thinking it through Ben. He's been tried, convicted, and sentenced. Now Jerry, you get that noose over Adam's head."

The deputy obeyed as Ben and Hoss stared in disbelief. Adam looked steadily at them and took a deep breath.

"Pa, promise me one thing..." Adam said.

"Name it," Ben replied huskily, unwilling to admit that he was soon to see his oldest boy die.

"Promise me you'll take care of my books."

Ben stared at his son blankly for a moment. "What did you say?" he finally roared. "Adam Cartwright, books do not matter at a time like this!"

Adam drew himself up to his full height and glared at his father as the deputy tightened the noose. "There is no time," he replied coldly, "that books do not matter."

Ben stared again in shock, and then looked up at the sky, raising his hands heavenward. "God, why did You smite me with half-witted children?" he bellowed.

"Now Pa," Hoss objected. "Me and Joe ain't half-witted."

"Shut up," Adam snarled at his brother.

"Well, you notice we ain't got a noose around our necks," Hoss pointed out.

"If I had my way, Joe would, and I'm beginning to feel the same way about you." Adam snapped.

Roy interrupted the family squabbling. "It's time now. Hoss, take yer pa back down."

Ben and Hoss, still disbelieving that any of this was actually true, began to object. Just then, a low murmuring was heard among the crowd. It increased in volume until nearly all the townspeople were involved. Those on the gallows turned to look at the object of interest.

Ben stared in incredulity for a long moment before his loud voice rang out. "Joseph Cartwright, you get over here right now!"

Joe stepped out of the crowd, a cold beer held in his hand. "Hiya Pa, Hoss. Sorry I was late meeting your stage. Say, Adam, what'cha doin' up there?"

The entire town looked from Joe to Adam and back again. Roy

cleared his throat, and stepped forward removing the noose from Adam's neck while muttering words that no one could quite make out in a vaguely apologetic manner. Adam sent him a pained look and turned his back so that Roy could untie his hands. This done, Adam, looking directly at his little brother, asked, "So Joe, just where have you been?"

Joe looked up in astonishment. "You told me to lay low for a while. So that's what I was doing!"

Adam crossed his arms. "Where?" Adam said again. "You were supposed to be in Carson City."

"Oh yeah. Well, I was gonna go there, until I remembered this gal I met in this saloon in Reno, and I decided to head that way instead. Why?"

"You went to Reno?" Adam asked coldly.

"You went to a saloon?" Ben asked coldly.

Joe smiled weakly. "Well, I had some time to kill and..."

Adam jumped down from the scaffolding and landed on his feet directly in front of Joe. "Kill. Now that's an interesting word you just used there, Brother."

Joe backed away. "What's that mean, Adam?"

Adam moved forward.

Joe backed away once more. "Stop that, Adam! Why are you acting this way? What are you going to do to me?"

Adam moved forward once more. Joe saw the look in his brother's eyes, and, dropping his beer to the ground, turned and ran for Cochise.

A Gem Without Price

by Debra Petersen

I knew that new jewelry store in town, Maxim's, was gonna be trouble right from the start. It's a shame too, 'cause Virginia City really needed something like that. A lot of folks around here have been goin' pretty far away to find an engagement ring or a pocket watch, and having a place with a nice selection of those things should have been all to the good. But then there were the other things, the heavy necklaces and big gaudy rings meant for the newly rich mining millionaires to give their ladies. Those kind of things are just an open invitation to robbers. I knew as sure as I'm sittin' here that somebody was gonna try to knock off that place. I just didn't know everything else that was gonna go down when they did it.

The day it happened didn't start out no different from most others. The morning had been pretty quiet, and round about eleven I was takin' my usual stroll around town just tryin' to pick up on whatever might be happenin' and generally keepin' an eye on things.

When I got to the Mercantile, there was Ben Cartwright, talkin' over the counter to Manny, the clerk.

"Howdy, Ben," I said. "Haven't seen you or the boys around town for a couple weeks or so. Everything all right?" He looked over at me and raised a hand in greeting.

"Hello, Roy. Good to see you. Yes, everything's fine. We've all just had our hands full, repairing winter damage to the fences and such, rounding up the cattle to move to new pastures, branding the new calves...you know what this time of year is like."

I nodded. I heard the same story from Ben, and from the other ranchers, just about every spring.

"Are the boys in town too?" I asked.

"Just Adam," Ben replied. "He had some sort of private business to attend to. I'm not sure where he's gotten himself off to." He smiled. "Hoss and Joe are spending their day off visiting a new neighbor...who just happens to have two quite attractive young daughters. I think they were planning a picnic or something of the sort."

That gave me a chuckle.

"Roy, how would you like to come out for dinner sometime this week?" Ben continued. "We haven't seen enough of each other lately and it would be a good chance to catch up on things."

I was just openin' my mouth to say I'd be happy to when we were interrupted by young Billy Lawson who appeared at the door, panting hard.

"Sheriff Coffee, you gotta come quick!" he gasped. "Something's happenin' over at Maxim's Jewelry Store! Hurry!"

Well, I didn't waste no time. In about a half a second I was out the door and heading down the street with Ben close at my heels. We hadn't gone but maybe twenty steps when we heard shots being fired. People were runnin' down the street away from the store, coverin' their heads or ducking into alleyways between the buildings. Tiny puffs of dust rose in the street, marking where the bullets fell. As the gunfire continued Ben and I drew our guns and took up position right across from the door to the store behind a wagon that was parked there.

Someone else had found refuge there too. Charles Bailey, a quiet young fella with curly brown hair who was a clerk at Maxim's was standing there tremblin' all over. I laid a hand on his shoulder, hopin' to calm him down some.

"What's goin' on here, Chuck?" I asked him.

He took a deep breath and did his best to give me the story. "Mr. Tyler, the manager, was in the back room with a messenger who had brought a shipment of special items for the store. I was waiting on a customer. There was some noise and shouting from in back, then I heard two shots. All of us in the front room kind of froze when we heard that. A few seconds later four men with kerchiefs over their faces and guns drawn came busting out of the back room, shouting for everybody to get down on the floor. I had just showed my customer out and was standing right next to the door, so I managed to slip outside. One of the men took a shot at me as I ran, but, thank God, he missed. Then they started shooting out through the windows. I think they were trying to clear the street to make a path for their getaway."

"Any idea who these men are?"

"The biggest one, the one who was shouting the orders, was called Jerome by one of the others. That's all I know."

Four men with a leader named Jerome. That meant the Casey brothers. And that was not good news.

"How many people are in there? Besides the gunmen, I mean."

"Well, there's Louis, the other clerk, and the couple he was waiting on. Then there were a couple of other people who were just browsing. I think that's about it."

"Thanks, Chuck," I said, giving him a quick clap on the back. I turned to Ben Cartwright. "I'm goin' out there, Ben," I said to him. "You keep me covered." He nodded and focused his attention on the storefront.

I stepped around the wagon and into the middle of the street.

"You in the store!" I called out. "Jerome Casey! This is the sheriff! You or your brothers harm any of those people in there and it's gonna go hard with you. Come on out with your hands up and nobody will get hurt!"

For a long minute nothing happened. Then there was movement at the door and a man who fitted the description I had received of Jerome Casey emerged, the kerchief pulled down from his face, pushing another man roughly in front of him while he held a gun to the man's head. I heard a gasp from behind me. Taking a quick glance back at Ben I saw that his face had gone suddenly pale. Truth to tell, I felt a lump rising in my own throat.

The man with Casey's gun at his head was Adam Cartwright.

"Oh, God," I heard Ben murmur under his breath. "What in the world was Adam doing in there?"

I just happened to know something about that. Last time I spoke to Adam he said somethin' about wantin' to check out this new place. He was thinkin' about a new pocket watch for his pa's next birthday. But I didn't see how knowin' that was gonna help Ben any, so I didn't say anything.

Now, Ben Cartwright's boys have always been like family to me. They're all fine young men, of course, but I have to admit that I have a kind of special regard for Adam. As a lawman I have good reason to appreciate that fierce sense of justice he has. I've seen it in action often enough. Adam has been helpful to me, probably more than anyone in this town except maybe his own father. I have to confess that seein' him in the hands of that desperado with his life being threatened like that kinda sent a shiver through me. I could only imagine what it was doin' to Ben.

Casey stepped forward, keepin' Adam close and his gun cocked. From the way Adam carried himself and the look in his eyes you might have thought that he was the one holdin' a gun on Casey, not the other way around. He's always been a cool customer, but I've never been more impressed with that fact than I was at that moment. He looked over at his pa, and it was clear that he was tryin' to reassure him that he was all right.

"Sheriff," Casey called to me, "it seems to me like I'm the one with the high card here. Now the way I see it is this. You are going to let me and my brothers ride out of here without any trouble. And we'll take this fella with us, just to be sure you don't play us any tricks. Unless you want to see his brains splattered all over the street, that is."

"You won't get very far. You know that, don't ya?" I challenged him.

Casey gave a nasty laugh. "I guess as long as we get out of town all right, we can take care of ourselves after that. I'll take that chance anyway."

I wanted to shake my head. Why do criminals always think so much of themselves—assume they can get away with things? Course it's a good thing they do. Us lawmen would have a lot harder time of it otherwise.

I took a minute to consider. At that point there didn't seem to be much choice. Sometimes you just gotta give in for the moment to give yourself a chance to come back later. This seemed to be one of those times.

I nodded...reluctantly. "Get your ugly faces out of here then."

Ben had come up to stand directly behind me. "Roy..." he said in a choked voice, and I could sense his desperation.

"Take it easy, Ben." I tried to keep my own voice calm. "They ain't about to hurt him. Not as long as they think he can be useful to them. And this ain't over. You know that. It ain't over by a long shot."

A few minutes later Jerome Casey and his brothers were mounted up and heading out of town, taking their loot and their hostage with them. Ben Cartwright stared after them with a look in his eyes that I don't think I'll ever forget.

The other clerk and the other customers in the store were unharmed. One of them, a young fella, told us that Casey had been ready to take his pregnant wife for their hostage, but Adam goaded him, saying she'd only hold them up in their escape, and that's how he wound up being the one chosen instead. Ben shook his head at that, as if to say that was just what he might have expected of his son, but it didn't exactly make him happy.

The manager and the messenger he had been meeting with were found dead in the back room with bullet holes in their heads. There was also a paper listing the pieces in the special shipment of jewelry that had been stolen. The total value came to over $75,000.

Of course we got a posse together and went after the gang as quickly as we could. There were five men besides Ben and me who were plenty eager for the job. One of them was Charles Bailey.

Their trail proved to be kind of hard to follow. At one point there was a fork in the road and the hardness of the ground made their tracks hard to pick up. It was Ben who noticed a few small shreds of paper on one side of the fork and recognized them. Seems Adam liked to carry a small notepad in the inside pocket of his jacket, and it looked like he had somehow managed, right under the nose of his captors, to tear off a few small pieces from it and drop them as an indication of the direction they had taken. We found the same signal at several other points where there was a question as to the right path. Wasn't there a fairy tale where someone left a trail of crumbs to mark their route? Strange as it might seem, that's what I was reminded of.

After several hours of hard riding the trail led us up a rocky slope that passed the entrances to a couple of old abandoned mines. Finally, just as the sun was about to set, we rode through a gap between two rises of ground into an open space surrounded by hilly ground on all sides. In the middle of it there was a good size wooden shack that had once been used by miners. And there were the gang's horses, tied up next to it.

There was light coming from inside, but the silence was almost eerie. You could just feel that they were layin' low in there and waitin' for us. We pulled our horses up behind some rocks at the edge of the area and dismounted, tryin' not to make too much noise. The men stood there lookin' at me while I tried to decide how to proceed.

The first thing I wanted to do was to find out exactly where Adam was and see what the situation looked like in general. I thought Charles Baily would be the best one to try to do that, so I whispered in his ear and he took off toward the shack, keepin' low to the ground, intendin' to try to get a peek in the window. He hadn't covered more than about half the ground when we heard the sound of shattering glass, and a second later a gunshot came from the broken window. Chuck Bailey gave a little cry of pain and lay there, still. He didn't move again. The rest of us drew our guns, took shelter behind the rocks and began firing back. The exchange of fire went on for several minutes, then died down while everyone reloaded their weapons.

And then, suddenly, the situation just blew up in our faces— literally! There was a tremendous explosion and the shack blew apart with jagged pieces of wood falling all around us. We fell to the ground, covering our heads while the rain of debris lasted.

Ben was the first to scramble to his feet. "Adam!" he shouted, and ran right into the ruins, with the rest of us not far behind. The badly burned bodies of the four Casey brothers were sprawled there close together in the middle of the destruction, but there was nary a trace of their hostage. Ben looked around the scene with frantic eyes and continued to shout his boy's name. Finally, from somewhere under the floor there came a muffled sound. Ben fell to his knees and his hand scrabbled through the dirt and debris until he found the handle to a hidden door in the floor. He threw it open, uncovering a small cellar.

And sure enough, there was Adam, curled up in the cramped space, his hands tied, looking up at us with eyes that squinted against the fading light.

"Hello, gentlemen," he said in a raspy voice. "May I have something to drink, please?"

We had him pulled up out of there and untied before you

could say lickety-split, and somebody handed him a canteen. He took a long drink, then poured a little water into his hand and splashed it over his face. He was dirty and thirsty, but he didn't seem to be hurt. Ben embraced him so fiercely that I was afraid for a minute that he might choke him, but somethin' to my surprise, Adam didn't seem to mind.

"Sheriff, take a look at this!" one of the men said. He handed me a soft leather pouch that had also been pulled out of the hole. I opened it, and there were all the pieces of jewelry that had been stolen...all but one, that is. There was one piece missing...a necklace with one very large pearl...a pearl of great price you might say.

I shook my head. The loss of that necklace wasn't gonna go down well with the group that owned Maxim's or with the insurer.

I looked over to where Ben stood with his hands still gripping his son's shoulders, speaking into his ear so quietly that no one else could hear. "What the devil!" I thought to myself. "We recovered the most valuable thing...the thing beyond price. That's what really matters."

I guess that's about it. One happy grace note to what was, at bottom, a sorry situation. Seven men dead all told. And for what? Nothin' that was worth it, that's for sure.

There are still a couple of mysteries about that day. The ruins of the shack were gone over with a fine tooth comb, but we never did find that missing pearl. You might have thought it would have survived the explosion, but.... Was it somehow lost in the getaway? A search was made along the trail we followed that day, but nothin' was found. The only thing I can figure is that it somehow fell out of the pouch and was picked up by some poor passer-by before we got around to looking. We prob'ly never will know for sure. As I expected, the insurers weren't very happy about it, but there wasn't much they could do except pay off the owners.

But the biggest mystery is what caused the explosion. Since

the shack was used by miners it's not surprisin' that there might have been some amount of explosives left there. But how did it get set off? Did they mean to use it against any pursuers and did one of them get careless with it? Again, we'll never know for certain.

It still isn't sure whether the store will ever be opened up again. I don't know myself how I feel about that. I still think that kind of place is an invitation to trouble. But then, I could sure use a new pocket watch.

Here in the West

by Sharon Kay Bottoms

How could I even think of leaving? Nothing back East could compare with these majestic, snow-capped mountains that tower above a lake more dazzling than sapphire—a perfect gem, fit for a monarch's crown. The vanilla fragrance of pine bark—the scent of home—wafts on the breeze that riffles the reflecting water into gentle waves. Overhead I hear the fluttering call of a mountain bluebird, more uplifting to my heart than the grandest operatic aria. The peace and serenity of this place surpasses that which I've found anywhere else, and I've seen enough of this country to be a fair judge. Yet only a few days ago I was prepared to toss it all aside. Oh, I've left home before— once for an extended span of years, as well as for briefer journeys, but I always knew I'd come back. To leave now, for the reason I was contemplating, would have been more permanent—perhaps even eternal. And yet I almost made that mistake—and not for the first time.

The day began in such ordinary fashion. A trip to town for supplies—routine, matter of fact, even boring. Still, having my brother by my side always made for good companionship, even if the conversation was less than scintillating. He's not much for discussing politics or literature, and his idea of art is pretty much limited to the form of a shapely lady, draped in a bit of gauze, that hangs above the bar of the Silver Dollar. Or a horse running bareback and free across an open meadow. It doesn't matter, though; he's my brother, and it's good just to be with him. There is no one in whose company I feel more comfortable and content.

We conducted our business with dispatch—usually the case when I'm with him—so I suggested we celebrate with an especially fine dinner at the Washoe Club, accompanied by a glass of shimmering ruby *Il Vino di Ponderosa* from grapes grown by our neighbor, Georgio Rossi, on land that once was our own. I thought that might be the selling point to tip the balance, but no such luck. "I'd rather have a cold beer," my brother said, and I could scarcely deny him when he'd done most of the work of loading the supplies, while I transacted business at the bank. Now I wish I'd been more insistent on having my own way; then we wouldn't have been where we were when we were and—mercy, what muddled babbling! And I said his conversation was less than scintillating? He's as profound as a professor, compared to me at times.

The fare at the Silver Dollar left much to be desired, in my opinion, but at least it came free with the price of the beer. Of course, we had to have a second one to wash down the intentional saltiness of the food, but neither of us considered that a problem. The cuisine may not have been what my educated palate would have preferred—all right, it definitely wasn't—but rarely have I enjoyed a meal more. He was in fine form that day and kept everyone around in stitches with his recitation of gossip he'd picked up at the mercantile.

We were still laughing as he backed through the bat wings of the saloon just ahead of me. His laughter broke off abruptly, as his eyes widened with surprise. Then they went blank, and my brother sank down to the planked walkway in front of the Silver Dollar. My gun automatically slid from my holster as I cried out his name—both actions pointless. Though I hadn't heard a second shot, the shooter himself lay sprawled in the street, no longer a risk, and my brother had passed into some misty realm beyond reach of my voice.

I dropped to his side, frantically working to stanch the blood that streamed through my fingers and dripped down through the cracks in the boards to the dirt beneath, all the time screaming his name louder and louder. Through a fog I saw Sheriff Coffee charging down the street, roughly pulling the man who had shot my brother to his feet. I spared one glance at him as Roy hand-cuffed him. No one I knew, but that wasn't too surprising. My brother—both of them, for that matter—knew more people in the territory than I did, for good or ill. He's just got a way about him that draws people to him, but which of them would want to hurt him? It was inconceivable.

"Adam, Adam, let me have him," I heard someone say in my ear. Paul Martin. He's here? Not out delivering a baby some-where, like last time? I stared at him in disbelief, although it wasn't until he spoke again that I realized I was doing it. "Adam, move your hands, son," the doctor said softly, but firmly. I looked down and saw my hands, still pressed against the spurting wound, in the doctor's way. I lifted them, bloody palms out and held high, as if I were the culprit the sheriff were taking into custody. It was a trick of the mind, of course, but that's how I felt, as if I were the one responsible for my younger brother's plight. Call it the curse of the eldest if you will; I always feel responsible where my brothers are concerned.

Somehow we got him down to the doc's office and onto his examining table. Then I was banished to the waiting area and left alone with my thoughts. Such strange thoughts. I couldn't help remembering the last time I'd seen a bullet drop a brother. Different this time, thank God. Last time—out by Montpelier Gorge—I had only myself to rely on—and only myself to blame. No guilt this time, except that confounded curse of the eldest, and plenty of hands to help. A good thing, too, since I don't think I could have hefted Hoss up the way I did Joe. Yes, it was a good thing that Joe was the one shot out there and Hoss the one struck down here in town.

I pressed the fingers of both hands into my temple, trying to squeeze the lunacy out of my thinking. It was as if I couldn't shake the maddening thought that it was inevitable for brothers to get shot. Why? The first response that trickled through my addled brain was the one I'd voiced to dear old Sheila Reardon: because out here in the West, it's a jungle—for animals, savages. The question isn't whether a brother will get shot; it's when and where.

Just that quickly I was back where I'd been during those dreadful days of fighting for Joe's life, and I told myself again, as I had then, that once this was all over, I would head East on the first stage—dragging my brothers and Pa with me, if possible—and find a place where we could all live like decent human beings...or, at least, just live.

Roy came in sometime while I was entertaining those tortured thoughts, and I was able, for a few minutes, to displace them with the questions I fired at the lawman. Who was that man? What did he have against Hoss? What could anyone have against Hoss? Or was he merely a pawn in a plot to hurt some other Cartwright? Goodness knows, we've faced that before!

The truth, when I finally gave Roy a chance to speak, only emphasized how crazy life really is here in the West. The shooter wasn't even aiming at Hoss—or anyone else. My brother had been back shot by a drunk firing at random to express the exuberance of his high spirits—emphasis on the spirits. And now my brother lay in that next room, with a wound that could well prove mortal, because some fool didn't have the sense to know when he'd poured enough rotgut down his miserable throat. Inside my head the siren call of that stage headed East began to crescendo, and I was determined to answer it.

Another voice tried to argue against the siren, telling me that there was violence back East, too. It reminded me of places like the Five Points in New York City, where no man could walk safely after dark. The siren, however, insisted that a wise man could easily avoid such places, as he can steer clear of the Barbary Coast out here, but Hoss wasn't shot in some dark alley in a seedy part of town. He was struck down on Main Street in Virginia City. And all he did to put himself in danger was finish his lunch a little early—or late; take your pick. A single moment made the difference, and here in the West peril can strike at any moment, without warning and beyond any wise man's ability to predict and prevent.

When the door to the examining room finally opened, I leaped to my feet. I suppose Paul must have sensed my anxiety, for he hurried to say, "He'll be all right. Touch and go for a while there and he lost a lot of blood, but he's strong. He'll make it, Adam."

Roy slapped me on the back in congratulations. "Just knew it. Ain't nothin' as puny as a stray bullet gonna keep that boy down."

I nodded perfunctorily, although we all know that even the smallest derringer ball has power enough to slay the biggest of men, if it hits just right. "Can I see him?" I asked.

"Soon," Paul promised. "Give the chloroform a chance to wear off."

"Anything I can do for you, son?" Roy asked as he moved toward the door.

"Get me a stage schedule," I muttered and immediately bit my tongue. Whatever my plans might be, this wasn't the time or place to announce them.

Roy and Paul exchanged a worried glance, as if they both thought the stress had knocked out my underpinnings. Roy spoke softly and slowly, as he might have to a man whose sanity he had reason to question. "I had in mind something like sending word to your pa, Adam."

I pursed my lips, mostly to keep from saying anything else to raise their eyebrows, and nodded.

"I'll do it right away," Roy assured me and left.

With a comforting pat to my shoulder, Paul went back into the room with Hoss, and I sat down to wait. The minutes dragged by, but I don't think too many of them actually passed before the doctor told me I could go in. Eager as I was to see my brother, I entered cautiously, hesitant to disturb him. He, on the other hand, grinned broadly, as only he can, and reached toward me. "Hey, Adam," he said.

I felt a smile start to tickle my lips as I heard the same words with which Joe had greeted me when he finally woke from his fever dreams after that ghastly wolf attack. I took Hoss's hand, pleased to feel the warmth of his grasp, even if it wasn't as strong as usual. At that moment I knew, as I'd known the minute Joe had spoken to me, that I wouldn't be going anywhere. I felt a little foolish about my wild swing of mood, more typical of Joe than me, but now that I've had a few days to mull things over, I understand something about myself that I didn't before.

Twice now I've determined to seek refuge back East, and I don't doubt that should Pa or Hoss or Joe be violently assailed another time I'll hear that siren call again. I'll be tempted to answer it, I'm sure, but I know now that my refuge is not back East. It's here—here in the West—and while the songbirds back there may trill a prettier tune, the call of the mountain bluebird will always echo loudest in my ear.

The High Trail

by Wrenny

Joe Cartwright and Harry Simpson trotted their horses along a high mountain meadow, each leading a string of two other horses. The air was markedly cooler up here than it had been down in the dry desert they had crossed yesterday on their way home from the horse auction. Both men's spirits were lifted by the coolness of the day, the beauty of the surrounding mountains and by the fact that they would be home by late tomorrow afternoon.

Just in time for one of Hop Sing's special dinners, thought Joe. *That is, if brother Hoss doesn't eat it all before I get home.*

"Joe, I'm sure glad you talked me into taking this short cut. It would have been three more days of riding if we had stayed on the main road and gone around these mountains instead of through them."

Joe's green eyes twinkled, and he squinted slightly against the bright sunshine as he looked over at his friend and smiled.

"Yeah, well, my brother, Adam, showed me this old Indian trail a few years ago. I didn't want to mention it 'cause I didn't know how you'd feel about taking your new stock through a bit of rough country, but when we started nearing the cutoff, I couldn't stop thinking about how much time we could save heading this way. Glad you agreed."

"I know our pas are already worrying since we didn't get back night before last night like we planned," Harry chuckled. "Not to mention how Mary must be feeling about now. She's probably fretting up a storm!"

"Who? That little ole gal of yours? Why I bet she's been so busy making plans for the wedding and fixing up that little house you two are going to live in that she's scarcely given you a thought since we left!" Joe laughed.

"Sheesh, Joe, you sure know how to hurt a guy. Mary wouldn't forget about me," said Harry with an exaggerated look of sadness on his face.

"Oh come on, Harry, I know you're missing her, but just think. You've got the rest of your lives to be together. With that chunk of land your folks are giving you to raise horses on, you're all set. Why I bet you'll have yourself a houseful of kids before you know it and all the work you can handle. Enjoy this bit of freedom while you have the chance, pal."

Harry's expression lightened. "Oh, great. I feel a lot better now, Joe. Thanks for showing me a bit of reality! Next time just leave me in my dream world, okay?"

"All right," Joe laughed out loud.

Riding along the mountain trail as it rose higher and higher toward the summit, the two friends were quiet as they concentrated on keeping to the path that wasn't always showing clearly through the overgrowth.

Sometimes it took a keen eye to determine which way the path continued, and Joe was very much aware of how easy it would be to become lost up here for someone who had never been shown the way.

At the top of the meadow up ahead, Joe remembered a crossroads of sorts. More like a cross paths since not many people knew about these old trails.

At the crossroads, Joe led Harry and the horses off to the right, just east of the path and down to a little creek bottom to give everyone a well-deserved water break.

Joe and Harry slid off their own mounts and led their strings to the cool gurgling stream.

"We'll take a short break here for a while and give everyone a rest. This is pretty much the summit, so other than a few gullies and hills, it's mostly downhill from here," Joe said as he stretched his fatigued muscles and then kneeled down for a drink.

"I'm all for a rest. I'm 'bout worn out from this trip," replied Harry as he also got down on his belly to slurp up the cool flowing water.

When Harry had drunk his fill he stretched out in the meadow grass. Lying on his side, he gazed at the horses he had purchased, as they cropped at the grass hungrily.

Joe chuckled at his friend who looked just as comfortable as could be.

"Joe, we done good," Harry said wistfully as he admired the horses. "I'm sure grateful to your pa for letting you come along with me to that horse auction."

"Oh, you would have done just fine without me along, Harry. You know horses. Heck, you might even be almost as good a judge of good stock as me...maybe," Joe smiled over at Harry, who craned his head back to give Joe an answering grin.

"Well, I may be 'almost' as good as you at picking 'em out, Cartwright, but I know you saved me some money. I ain't got nearly your experience with the finer points of bidding at an auction. Knowing how much the beasts are worth, when to keep bidding, when to quit. All that kind of thing."

"Guess I have learned a bit about auctions. Been going with my pa and brothers since I can remember," Joe said from under his hat that he had tipped over his eyes as he rested, lying back in the grass.

"So you think your pa's sent the Cavalry out to find us yet Joe?" asked Harry.

Joe snorted. "Hmpff. Wouldn't surprise me. Let's see, how long did we wind up spending in Barnesville? We got there on Tuesday, the auction was supposed to be on Wednesday morning, but then..."

"But then the rains of biblical proportions started, and we got to spend an extra two days in the garden spot of Nevada where a horse auction is the social event of the year," Harry finished Joe's thought.

"Yeah, and not that you would have noticed, but there wasn't one gal in that town that wasn't either married or old enough to be my ma," Joe complained as he yawned.

"Yep, that was some kind of hard rain. Always sort of surprises me how quick a river can rise up like that. Good thing we got acrossed when we did or we'd a been holed up on the other side, hunkered down like drowned rats instead of dry and warm at the hotel. Feel sorry for those hands that had to wait with all them horses on the other side. I know lots of them didn't get to that river 'til Wednesday morning and it were plum too late at that point. That river was about out of its bed by then. No way to push them horses they wanted to sell across it without risking losing a few. And on top a all that, the flooding knocked out the telegraph afore we had a chance to get word out about the delay. That telegraph operator said it'd take a couple of months to get all those poles back up again. Joe, do you s'pose our families got word about all that rain causing all that trouble? Holding up the auction and all? Joe...?"

Detecting a soft snore coming from his traveling companion,

Harry suddenly noticed Joe had been quiet and still for a while.

Smiling, Harry thought to himself, *Well, a little siesta sounds like a good idea to me.*

It was only another ten minutes or so before a raven cackled above Joe's head, startling him from his slumber.

Sitting up, Joe looked around, placing his hat back on top of his head. He saw Harry in the same position he himself had been enjoying a moment earlier.

Stretching his muscles, Joe glanced up the hillside. *Might be a pretty view from up there,* he thought and stood to walk up and have a look while his friend snoozed.

Following the east/west path, he kept going a few hundred yards after the intersection with the north/south trail they had just left. The hill crested here and afforded a panoramic view of the valley below.

As Joe stood soaking up the view and stretching some more, his eye caught a movement down the hill to the west, just under some trees. Pushing his hat, which had been balancing at the back of his head, forward so the brim blocked the glare of the sun, Joe narrowed his eyes in an effort to see what it was. Down the hill in a copse of trees just off the road, he could now make out the rumps of three horses, their tails lazily swatting the flies trying to land on them.

Joe was curious about who would be up here. This road led down to Stewartstown, but it was a good fifteen miles away. The road Joe and Harry were traveling on, heading north, only led down into a river valley, to more roads and ranches, including the Simpson's spread as well as the Ponderosa just beyond that. As far as Joe knew, no one lived up on this mountain.

Advancing down the gently sloping hill, Joe was wary, but did not pull his gun from his holster. He could now see there was someone leaning against one of the trees, resting with his hat covering his face.

Not wishing to startle the person, Joe opened his mouth to begin to shout a greeting. Just then he thought he heard the pounding of horses' hooves in the distance and he turned his attention back to the path where two riders could now be seen, pushing their horses hard. The men were dressed in dirty clothing and Joe could see the horses were foamy with lathered up sweat, breathing with obvious effort from running full tilt up a mountainside.

When they reached the group of trees where the first man had been resting, they reined in the worn out mounts. As they started to dismount, the taller of the two riders looked over at Joe in disbelief before immediately taking his rifle from its scabbard, raising its sight to his eye, and firing off a shot in Joe's direction.

Joe's reflexes helped him in his immediate dive to his left. Pulling his gun in the split second after he hit the ground, Joe fired off a shot just before he rolled quickly to a pile of large rocks, scarcely high enough to conceal him from bullets still being fired at him. His aim was true and he heard a shout of pain.

Breathing hard and shaking slightly from the sudden rush of adrenaline, Joe tried to make sense of what had happened as well as come up with a plan for what he would do next. He suddenly remembered Harry and hoped his friend would not rush into the deadly situation Joe found himself in without using extreme caution. His hopes vanished in an instant as Harry came running over the hill, rifle in hand.

There was very little cover between Joe and Harry; immediately, Joe heard shots fired from the trees below him. Harry managed to return fire once and Joe quickly tried to provide cover by shooting four more shots in quick succession at the trees, but in the next second, he heard a yell and turned just as Harry's body fell to the ground. Joe could see he was still alive as he writhed in pain and groaned loudly.

"Harry, no!" Joe screamed.

Without thinking of his own safety, knowing he could not wait to think out a plan, he ran toward his injured friend, crouching as low to the ground as possible. More shots rang out, hitting the dirt around Joe until one finally found its mark.

The world exploded in a sea of pain for Joe as the bullet flew through muscle and flesh in his upper right arm, exiting the front with a spray of bright red blood. He crashed painfully to the ground near his friend and fought to remain conscious.

The edges of his vision were fading away, but Joe held on, closing his eyes against the pain. He forced himself to slow his breathing. Harry was no longer moaning, but lay silently a few feet from Joe.

It felt like an hour had passed but Joe knew it had to be closer to only a few minutes before he heard the sound of boots on the gravely dirt just downhill of where they lay.

When the crunch of dirt sounded to be right beside him, he could sense that someone was standing over him, blocking the sun. A boot forced its way under his rib cage and was about to roll him.

As he tightened his grip on the pistol in his hand, Joe opened his eyes and rolled over onto his back before the startled assailant could kick him over. In a split second, Joe had the gun pointed at the man standing over him.

The man jumped back in surprise.

"Drop it!" Joe said, never taking his eyes from the face of the man standing over him.

He was tall and thin with dark eyes and by the looks of him, he hadn't had a shave or a bath in weeks.

The command had not sunk in as the man still held a rifle in his hand, pointed at the ground. The audible click from Joe cocking the pistol he held brought the man back from his shock enough that he immediately threw his weapon on the ground.

Now Joe started to sit up, but he still kept his full focus of attention on the man standing there. The movement was difficult since the pain in his arm was now demanding ever-increasing amounts of Joe's attention as well. Knowing his life depended on keeping the pain at bay, Joe kept his voice as calm and even as possible.

"Take two steps backward, and then turn around and face the other way."

The man studied Joe for a moment, watching his eyes for any sign of weakness that could be exploited for his escape. He saw none in Joe's steady gaze.

Doing as commanded, he took two steps backward, then turned away from Joe.

Joe breathed deeply but made every attempt to keep the groan he was holding inside to himself. There was no movement from the trees, and Joe assumed that the other two men were dead or incapable of shooting since no shot had been fired.

Glancing quickly over at his friend's still body, Joe looked for any sign that Harry was still alive. The injured man lay completely unmoving and Joe became extremely worried. Watching carefully, Joe thought he could see a rise and fall of Harry's chest as he breathed, but couldn't be sure this was not just wishful thinking.

Keeping his gun trained on the tall man, Joe moved to get up from the ground. It proved to be too difficult to contain a stifled moan that escaped his lips this time and the man turned his head slightly to get a look at Joe's condition. Joe grit his teeth against the pain and hissed, "I said to turn around!"

A small evil grin appeared on the man's face as he complied with the command, but he still said nothing.

Though his wound was not as serious as it might otherwise have been had it hit him in a more vital area of his body, Joe was still losing blood and the pain was still as bad as any gunshot wound could be.

A plan. Gotta come up with a way out of this! Joe thought desperately.

Helping his more seriously injured friend seemed to be a high priority, and he needed to figure out what to do with his prisoner. There wasn't a whole lot of time left in the day as Joe figured it would be nightfall in only a few more hours. If he hadn't settled on a plan by then, his desperate situation could turn deadly in a hurry.

The prisoner needed to be dealt with first, Joe reasoned, since doing anything else while the man stood there would have been a huge risk.

"Start walking down to those trees. And keep your hands out where I can see them."

"What're you gonna do now boy? Seems you've got yourself in a bit of a spot here," the man growled in a mocking tone as he slowly started walking.

Joe was in no mood to have a conversation with this man who had caused all his problems.

"Just shut up and walk," he replied.

Chuckling softly at some private joke, the man slowly made his way toward the bodies of his companions.

When they were getting close to the trees, Joe knew what he needed to do. With the man still facing away from him, Joe reached down and picked up a good-sized rock from the ground.

He knew his pa would not approve, but Joe felt that since his life and Harry's were at stake, he would have to do what he had to do. With a burst of energy, he took three fast strides right up behind the man and hit him hard with the stone.

The man flung forward and hit the ground with his shoulder.

Falling to the ground, weak from the pain, Joe panted from the sudden exertion. "That ought to hold you for a little while," he whispered.

Joe honestly hoped he hadn't killed the man, but knew he needed the man to be rendered harmless for as long as possible, and this seemed like the surest way he could think of to do it, short of shooting him down in cold blood.

Looking around now, Joe saw the bodies of the two other men close to the trees. Flies were already buzzing around, breaking the stillness of the air. The five horses had scattered a short distance away when the gunfire had begun, but were now slowly eating their way back to where the bodies lay.

Joe got up shakily and slowly walked up to one of the horses, talking softly so as not to spook them. The one he reached first had been one of the horses that had been waiting when the gunmen had arrived. The saddlebags were full of supplies and there were two canteens of water slung over the saddle horn.

Quickly untying the bedroll from the back, Joe then pulled the rawhide strips off the saddle. They were the perfect length to tie up the prisoner, and he set to the task quickly since he had no idea how long the man would remain unconscious. He bound the man's hands tightly in front of him, then his ankles.

As soon as this was done, he went back to the horse and rummaged through to find a clean cloth of some sort to bind his still bleeding wound.

Finding none, Joe thought, *Figures. Dirty as those guys were, they probably wouldn't know what a clean shirt was if it stood up and introduced itself.*

Using a knife, Joe cut his left sleeve from his own shirt, then ripped it into a strip long enough to go around his wounded arm and tied it off tight.

Working as quickly as he could, Joe often glanced up the hill toward where Harry lay, hoping for any sign of life. He was getting very tired, but knew he had no time to waste. Grabbing the bedroll he had earlier thrown on the ground along with one of the canteens, he began his trek back to Harry.

When he reached his friend, he quickly checked for a pulse. It was there. Joe felt a wave of relief flood his exhausted body and suddenly he felt he had just a bit more energy.

Harry had taken a bullet in his left side. From what Joe could see, it looked like it went clean on through, but there was an enormous amount of blood on Harry's shirt, and Harry had still not come around.

Uncorking the canteen, he put it to Harry's lips. Harry swallowed instinctively, but still did not stir. Since he had no clean cloth, Joe cupped his hand and spilled a bit of water into it then gently patted Harry's cheeks and forehead with the moisture.

Joe looked around desperately. He needed something to use for a bandage for Harry's wound.

Thinking about it, Joe remembered he had an extra shirt in his saddlebag.

"Cochise!" Joe cried out at his revelation.

Cochise was over the rise of the hill and down by the creek bottom and Joe could not see his horse.

An ear-piercing whistle split the air as Joe tried to signal to his horse.

He listened intently to the silence around him for a few moments, and then whistled again. Very soon afterwards, he heard a distant whinny, followed shortly after by the sound of hooves trotting along the soft ground. Joe looked at the crest of the hill expectantly, and was soon rewarded with the sight of his black and white paint horse gazing down toward his human companion.

"Good boy, Cooch," Joe smiled.

Once Cochise arrived, Joe worked quickly. He pulled a shirt from the saddlebags and ripped it into long strips. Wadding up a hunk of the cloth, Joe held it in place by wrapping the strips of shirt around Harry's waist.

Standing up, feeling a little shaky, Joe got his jacket off the back of his saddle and tried to put it on. His left arm was no problem, but it was much too painful to try to get his injured right arm into the sleeve, so he just draped it over his shoulder.

He glanced up and saw the other five horses come over the hill, wanting to be with Cochise.

Getting Harry down to the trees was the next chore Joe knew he needed to tackle. The sun was just beginning to set and he knew night would fall quickly. The trees would provide at least some shelter, and he needed to get down the hill to be closer to the prisoner as well.

Knowing he couldn't drag Harry the distance down the hill, Joe decided he would need to use his horse.

He positioned Cochise on the low side of the hill Harry was

lying on, then got behind and lifted his friend from under his arms.

Ignoring his own pain as best he could, Joe grunted and pushed Harry up onto the back of the horse, belly down over the saddle.

"Thank God you're unconscious, Harry," Joe said. "Hope I'm not causing more damage than was already done."

Breathing hard from the exertion, Joe led the horse and his friend down the hill. While it was only a short distance, Joe still needed to stop a few times to make sure Harry didn't slide off onto the ground.

When Joe got to the trees, he glanced over at the outlaw he had knocked out and tied up a short while ago.

Still out, thought Joe and this realization caused him to relax slightly.

Once Harry was lying on the ground with a warm blanket over him, Joe gathered up as many dried sticks and hunks of wood that he could find without straying too far.

He soon had a blazing fire going.

With the arrival of twilight upon them, Joe now turned his attention to the bodies of the two gunmen who had been killed during the shootout. He wasn't quite sure what he should do about them. He certainly did not have the necessary energy to bury them, even if he had a shovel, which of course he did not.

Moving the bodies far off from the immediate area would also require more effort than Joe wanted to expend and besides, Joe thought morbidly, animals would surely be attracted by the smell of blood, and...

Joe didn't think even these men deserved such an end.

Joe finally decided to simply drag them a short distance behind the trees where the light of the fire would hopefully keep animals at bay, yet they would be out of Joe's direct line of vision and out of his thoughts. The effort of simply dragging them a few yards was difficult enough and when he was done, it was full dark and Joe lay down by the fire, panting from his labors.

Besides being completely and utterly exhausted, Joe realized he hadn't eaten since breakfast that morning.

Rallying a bit of energy from deep within, Joe got up once more. As he passed by the prisoner Joe had to look hard into the shadows cast by the fire upon the man's worn face to see if he was awake or not.

Satisfied that the man was still out, Joe walked over to where Cochise stood, ground tied in his place. The other horses instinctively milled nearby, keeping close to the trees for protection.

As Joe approached, the horses Harry had bought startled and bolted a short distance away. Joe spoke softly and went right to Cochise. The horse belonging to the outlaws were all close by as well and Joe suddenly realized he had still another chore to attend to before he could rest his body.

Seven of the eleven horses were still saddled up and apart from Cochise and Harry's horse, both of which were trained to ground tie, the others were wandering around with reins dragging and being stepped on.

Joe just couldn't stand the thought of these animals breaking a leg or injuring their necks by tripping over their reins and knew he needed to care for the animals. One by one, he slowly approached each horse, taking the bridle off after removing the saddle. For Cochise and Harry's horse, Joe got a pair of hobbles on each to prevent them from running off after having their tack removed.

All this seemed to take an eternity in Joe's mind and he was in agony from the throbbing in his arm when he finished.

Joe was especially glad to have found four full canteens of water. *At least I won't have to go all the way back over the hill to get water*, he thought thankfully.

Finding some hardtack biscuits and some jerky in one of the saddlebags, Joe came back to the fire and practically fell to the ground beside it. Glancing over at Harry and seeing that his friend appeared to be resting quietly, Joe allowed his eyes to close for the first time in hours. He felt as if he could sleep for days.

Joe's next thought went to his prisoner. He snapped his eyes open and looked across the fire to see the prisoner staring back at him.

THE DOOR OF the ranch house opened and Ben Cartwright immediately rose from the table.

"Hoss... Adam...That you?"

"Yeah, Pa," Hoss called to his father as he and Adam set their hats on the pegs by the door.

Ben sat slowly back down in front of his uneaten supper.

"Hop Sing," Ben shouted toward the kitchen. "Hoss and Adam are back."

His two sons sat down at their places at the table and waited for the Chinese cook to bring the warmed up dinner back in.

Normally, Hop Sing would have had some choice words for anyone daring to be late for a meal he had prepared, but when he saw that Joe had not returned with his brothers, he simply set the food down and quietly retreated to his duties in the kitchen.

"No luck?"

"'Fraid not," said Adam. "Mr. and Mrs. Simpson are pretty worried themselves. They haven't heard a word from Harry. They figured just like we did that those storms probably held the boys up, but that doesn't stop them from being concerned all the same."

Pa frowned at the beefsteak on his plate.

"Paw, if you don't mind, I think I'd feel better if I rode out after supper and see if I can't meet up with them on the trail. Make sure they're all right," Hoss said. "If I know Joe, he'd a taken that high mountain trail we showed him a few years back. If somethin' happened to one of 'em, the other wouldn't want to leave him behind...or maybe they got lost. Those tails can be a might rough up there. Joe could a gotten turned around and mixed up pretty easy."

Hoss pushed his peas around on his plate, and then continued.

"All I know is, I hate sittin' around waitin' for him to show up, dadburnit. I'd feel a whole lot better if I was doin' somethin'. I can check those herds in those upper meadows on my way if you think I'm being a might foolish and want me to have a better reason for riding up there than checking on my little brother, but..."

Ben held up his hand and interrupted his son. "Hold on, Hoss. It's fine for you to check up on Joe. He's overdue and frankly I've had a bad feeling about it since I got up this morning. I'm plenty worried too. You go as soon as you're ready. Adam, you and I will ride into town this afternoon and see if anyone at the telegraph office has any word from Barnesville."

"Right, Pa," said Adam.

The three men finished their supper in silence. Hoss gathered what he needed for spending a night or two on the trail while Adam readied the horses.

"Well, Hoss, bring us back some good news, alright?" Pa said.

"Sure will, Paw," Hoss replied as he turned Chub out of the yard and trotted off toward the mountains.

Adam put his hand on Pa's shoulder as they both watched him ride out.

"Don't worry, Pa. You know Joe. He probably met some pretty girl along the way. He most likely doesn't even realize we would be worried by now."

"I'm sure you're right Adam," said Pa, but his furrowed brow betrayed how he still felt, despite the attempt to ease his fears.

"MIGHT NOT BE such a good idea, you going to sleep, boy," the man snarled. "I ain't in such a good mood what with this headache you gave me, and all."

"Well, I don't much care what kind of mood you're in, mister,"

Joe replied. "You're not in a position to do much of anything about it anyway."

Fear coursed through his body like lightening as he looked into the man's hate-filled eyes, but it had passed quickly. Now he felt mostly angry at this man who was responsible for the bad situation Joe and Harry found themselves in at the moment. Joe allowed himself a fleeting wish that he had killed the men with the blow to his head, but immediately pushed the dark thought away.

Glancing over at Harry, Joe saw him move slightly. Grabbing up a nearby canteen, he crawled to Harry's side.

"Harry....Harry? Can you hear me?"

Joe gently nudged Harry's arm. Slowly his injured friend blinked his eyes, then opened them, looking at Joe with a pain-filled expression of confusion.

"....Joe...what.... what happened?" He barely had enough strength to give voice to his question.

"Harry, just lay still."

Joe gave him a few gulps of water. "Everything's going to be alright. We ran into some outlaws and they shot you. I've packed your wound with some clothes, but we need to get you to a doctor as soon as we can."

Joe put the back of his hand to Harry's cheek and noticed it was warmer than it should be.

Harry blinked at Joe, still looking confused.

Joe adjusted the blankets he had wrapped over Harry.

"I've never... never been shot before. Hurts. Bad."

"I know," Joe sighed and was grateful that Harry had now closed his eyes.

Feeling a throbbing in his arm, Joe chanced a look at it. His makeshift bandage was blood soaked, but holding. He couldn't tell if the wound was still bleeding or not. All his exertions had not done him any good, he knew.

The last faint smudges of light reflected on the few wisps of clouds high above them faded and a definite chill could be felt in the air now that there was no longer the warmth of the sun to keep it away.

Joe tossed another stick on the fire. It was going to be a long night ahead of him and Joe now began to consider how he was going to manage to keep himself awake. Though he would have given anything right then to lie down and sleep for hours, Joe knew it could be deadly for both him and Harry.

Filling a small coffee pot with water from one of the canteens, Joe threw some grounds into it. The coffee would help, but he knew it was going to be a battle to keep from drifting off.

For a long time, the prisoner had stayed quiet, watching Joe the whole time.

"You know, boy, the minute you go to sleep I'll likely be making my move."

Joe jumped at the sound of the man's voice despite being acutely aware of his presence.

"Yeah, well you won't be getting the chance," Joe said as he glanced back at the man.

"Heh, you ain't got enough strength in ya to stay awake. I been watchin'. You about done in now and the night's jest beginnin'. You might's well untie me now and let me ride outa here. I promise I'll leave ya be and jest go on my way. What do ya say, boy?"

As much as Joe longed to believe the man, he knew better than to gamble his life on whether the man would honor his word or not. Anyway, it didn't take an astute judge of character to know that the man was pretty much as dishonorable as they come, so it didn't take Joe more than half a second's musing to disregard anything coming out the man's mouth.

Joe just gave a low chuckle that lacked any semblance of humor and poked at the fire with a stick.

"No, you're going back to that town you robbed the bank in today to stand trial."

The man looked only slightly surprised that Joe knew about the holdup.

"So you found the money, huh? Tell you what, friend. Since my partners are layin' over under that tree, they won't be needin' their share. Whad'ya say you and me split it, fifty-fifty? We didn't stop to count it, but I reckon there's about twenty thousand dollars there. Why just think whatcha could do with half of that. Come on, boy. Untie me."

Joe wanted the conversation to be over. He was sick of the man's attempts to get Joe to let him go.

"How many people did you kill in the robbery?" he asked, staring the man in the eye with a cool expression.

The man swallowed hard and narrowed his eyes.

"Now what makes you think we done killed anyone?"

Joe looked over at Harry who was mercifully sleeping deeply.

"Just a hunch," he said softly. "'Sides, it doesn't matter one way or another. Tomorrow I'm taking you back. I'm sure the sheriff will have a good idea whether you killed anyone or not. But I'm guessing you did and I'm betting you'll hang for it."

Suddenly the man began struggling against his bindings, a look of panic having settled on his face to replace the self-confident sneer of moments before.

"I ain't goin' back there—you hear me!" he shouted. "You're going to be sorry you ever crossed my path, sonny!"

The constant pain and burning in Joe's arm made him very much aware that he was already quite sorry.

The man sputtered on in an angry tone of voice for a time, but Joe just focused his attention on his coffee. He got up and walked slowly over to the shadowy area where the saddlebags were lying in a heap. Hunger demanded that Joe search through each of the saddlebags for more to eat than beef jerky and hard biscuits.

He didn't find anything else to eat but he did find a bottle of whiskey. Carrying it over to where Harry lay, Joe saw the prisoner was staring at him calmly once again.

"Joe..." Harry was waking up again.

"Harry, I found a bottle of whiskey. You want a drink? Might help take the edge off the pain."

"Yeah, 'kay," grunted Harry.

Joe poured some of the golden liquid into a cup and helped Harry drink.

"Easy. Just a sip," Joe cautioned. He didn't want Harry going off on a coughing spell and opening up his wounds.

"Hey Joe. How's about sharing some of that drink," said the outlaw from the other side of the fire.

Joe glared at the man, again wishing he would just go to sleep. Harry looked over in confusion at the tied-up prisoner.

"Who is he, Joe?" he muttered.

Joe's eyes went back to Harry and immediately his expression softened.

"That's one of those men who got us into this mess, Harry. Don't you worry about him. Just rest now."

Within a minute, Joe could see that Harry had returned to sleep. Joe longed to join his friend but knew it was impossible.

"Come on, Joe, just a little drink."

Turning his attention back to the dirty man across from him, Joe gave the request some thought. Letting the man get drunk might be a way to make him less of a threat to Joe and Harry. But Joe wasn't about to stand over the prisoner, holding the bottle while the guy drank himself under, and he couldn't very well untie him to let him drink under his own power.

No, Joe knew he was in for a long night.

His arm was throbbing now and Joe thought the pain might actually help him. He knew that if he didn't have the burden of keeping watch, the pain would most likely prevent him from sleeping anyway.

But a distinct heaviness in his eyelids told him another truth. The loss of blood combined with the pain had made him more tired than he could remember being for a long time, and Joe thought he was going to have a very hard time staying conscious.

Time passed slowly for the two men who passed it staring at the fire. It was a cloudless night and a crescent moon shown brightly among the millions of stars. The night air had turned quite chilly and Joe kept the fire burning high.

The prisoner had tried to get Joe to engage in conversation, but Joe had no interest in hearing anything he had to say, so he kept his end of it short, usually only grunting a one word answer to the many questions the man threw at him.

The man eventually grew tired of Joe's stalwart refusal to let him know anything about himself and he closed his eyes, surrendering to sleep.

As Joe stared into the fire, he turned his thoughts to his family. He knew Pa would be worried by now, but he wasn't sure that his father or brothers would have set out to find him yet.

Just a few more hours till the sun comes up, thought Joe. *Then what?*

Joe's arm pained him bad and began to feel tight against the bandage from the swelling.

The fire burned bright and slowly Joe became mesmerized by its dancing, flickering flames. The heat it projected felt warmer and warmer. In a few moments, it became uncomfortably warm. Soon, Joe felt like the fire was inside him and his vision became fuzzy. Standing, Joe tried to move away from the burning that felt like it would consume him.

All at once he realized that his legs could not hold him up and the image of the hazy fire began to whirl as Joe collapsed to the ground.

Fever, fatigue and pain at last sent Joe into an oblivious unconsciousness.

When Joe at last brought himself back up to the surface, the first thing he became aware of was cold. He was shivering uncontrollably, causing him to grit his teeth so he wouldn't bite his tongue. He tried to will himself to stop shaking, but his body would not respond to his brain's commands.

Immediately after this awareness, he knew great waves of pain from his arm. Sweat trickled into his eyes despite feeling so very cold, the salt making him squint against the sharp stinging.

Can I possibly feel any more miserable? thought Joe, and with that thought immediately came a wave of nausea. Joe groaned in response to the latest assault on his fevered body.

As seconds ticked by, another part of Joe's brain began to become aware of his surroundings.

It was dark.

Very, very dark.

The sky full of stars he'd seen before passing out had been replaced by a cover of clouds that Joe could have sworn was threatening snow.

In the darkness, Joe could not see even a few inches in front of him. All was deadly quiet as Joe strained his ears to hear any nearby sounds. But the whispery rustling made by the shaking of his body was all he could make out.

While he was decidedly sluggish in his awakening, in reality only a few seconds had passed before Joe suddenly, and with a jolt of adrenaline recalled the situation he was in.

In the blink of an eye, he became hyper alert, senses heightened by the perceived danger he now found himself facing.

"Oh boy," he muttered in a whisper to himself.

As Joe's senses strained for any sort of information, Joe became aware that the fire was not completely extinguished as he had at first assumed. Propping himself up on his good arm, he could see the soft red glow of embers where once the roaring campfire had been.

Must have been out a couple of hours, Joe thought. *Must be getting close to morning.*

Crawling over as close as he could to the embers, Joe gathered a handful of dry leaves he felt at his side. Laying them gently over the amber bits of spent wood, he gently blew air over them until flames began to lick at their dryness, and then blaze.

Now able to see slightly better, he found his small pile of sticks and twigs nearby and began feeding the fire. Within seconds, a decent blaze was burning and Joe looked around him.

The first thing he noticed was that the prisoner was gone.

Once more, a jolt of fear went through him, all his senses on high alert.

Turning his head, he looked over to where Harry was lying and immediately crawled over to his injured friend. Laying his hand first on his shoulder, Joe could feel the man's body trembling.

Next he moved his hand to feel Harry's cheek, immediately noticing the heat of fever burning there. Joe pulled the blanket that was barely covering Harry up to his chin, taking care to tuck it securely around his trembling body.

"Harry? Harry," Joe whispered his friend's name, hoping per- haps Harry was near to consciousness. Joe didn't necessarily want to wake him. While Joe was very concerned about Harry, he was also feeling the need to have a friend right about now to lend some moral support.

Harry moaned softly and mumbled something unintelligible in his feverish sleep.

Joe gave up his attempts at waking him.

Gazing over the flames into the inky blackness as he lay on his left hip facing the fire, Joe tried to acclimate his vision to see into the dark.

A movement caught his eye and he stared intently into the shadows where he had sensed it.

The horse tossed its head once more and Joe let his held breath out slowly.

He sat up and felt his vision spin briefly. He shut his eyes tight and then opened them again, willing the world to stay still.

Joe now realized he could see slightly better and just then also became aware that he could hear birds singing in some distant trees.

Dawn's almost here he thought, and just then he noticed an- other movement out of the corner of his eye.

Slowly, Joe reached down and pulled his gun from his holster.

Did I reload last night? he wondered.

The pain from his arm, combined with the fever, wouldn't allow him to think clearly back to before he had passed out and he didn't dare take his eyes off the area where he had seen the movement in order to check.

Guess I'll find out soon enough.

The light of day was barely visible, but it was enough for Joe to make out shapes better than he could even a few minutes earlier.

Again, he caught a glimpse of movement and now he could make out a large shape on the ground over by the tree where he had left the saddles after removing them from the horses.

Getting up to his knees, Joe knew he needed to move slowly, to avoid passing out again, but he also knew he needed to move quickly.

Now standing, Joe felt his head swim and his vision take on a yellowish gray quality that was not due to the gradually increasing daylight.

He took slow deep breaths and his head and vision returned to something like normal.

Holding his revolver as steady as he could in front of him, he walked toward the shape on the ground. As he got closer, Joe could tell it was his prisoner. The man was frantically trying to rummage through some of the saddlebags. He was having a tough time of it with his hands tied together as they were, but as Joe got close, the man apparently found what he was searching for.

Joe was now close enough to see that the man had gotten hold of a knife. As he approached, Joe leveled his gun at the man.

"Drop it, now!" he yelled.

The man didn't even look up, but continued cutting through his bonds.

"I said drop the knife!" Joe shouted once again.

This time the man looked up, but didn't drop the knife that had by now cut through the rawhide binding his hands.

Had Joe just awakened from a full nights' rest, he might have avoided the attack or been able to fight back, but just as fast as a cat pounces on a mouse, the outlaw was on Joe in a heartbeat.

Joe reacted enough to pull the trigger of his gun, but the man had plowed into him at waist level at the same moment and the bullet hit a tree, sending bits of bark and wood flying.

His gun flew out of his hand at the impact of the body slamming him into the ground. Joe managed somehow to grab the wrist of his attacker. Their arms quivered and moved back and forth as if in a crazy dance, first towards Joe's body, then away as Joe used all the energy he could muster to keep the knife from slicing into him.

The man grabbed Joe's injured right arm and held it tightly. Joe had no strength in this arm to resist and before he could somehow summon the inner reserves that he now desperately needed, Joe was suddenly plunged into a deeper pool of pain than he could have imagined existed.

While the pain before had been bad enough, it could momentarily be pushed away. But as the knife slid slowly into his shoulder, just below his collarbone, he could no longer keep the pain from consuming him as a forest fire consumes a dry pine tree.

Joe let out a scream of agony that he barely recognized as his own voice before the world and everything in it went away completely.

His adversary grinned wickedly in the dim morning light. He pulled the knife out swiftly and wiped it on his filthy pants as he noted a large dark stain take over Joe's lighter colored shirt all across his chest.

Knowing a posse could be catching up any time now that it was the break of day, he never bothered to make sure that Joe was dead, but instead, quickly walked over to where Harry lay.

Harry's eyes fluttered open slowly.

"Joe? Joe what's going on?" he asked weakly.

"I'll tell you what's going on, boy," said the outlaw menacingly. Noticing a bottle of whisky laying to the side where Joe had left it the night before, he picked it up, uncorked the top and guzzled down 4 or 5 swallows of the golden hot liquid before shoving the cork back in.

He stood, whiskey bottle in one hand, bloody knife in the other, and now began to approach Harry.

"Now you ain't gonna give me no trouble and no hard feelings, eh boy?"

Harry moaned and tried to roll over, away from the menace that was now swaying slightly from the whiskey. He could only manage to move a small bit before pain and exhaustion from his wound overcame him.

The last thing he did before the man reached him and began to kneel down by his side was to look over towards Joe.

"Joe!" he cried. "Help me! Please, Joe..."

Joe was falling down a deep well. He could see the dim light above him as he fell, a circle of lightness bold against the dark tunnel.

He felt weightless and detached, but was aware that he would be hitting the ground at any moment and it would all be over. He couldn't survive such a fall, he reasoned, but at least the pain would end.

He just couldn't seem to remember how he had gotten into this situation.

Just then he heard someone calling to him. The voice echoed off the walls of the well and sounded desperate—pleading and begging for him to help.

Pa? No, it wasn't his Pa, but whoever it was needed him.

The circle of light was very small now and Joe closed his eyes for a second. When he opened them, he was no longer in the well, but lying on his back, looking up at he dull gray of the morning sky.

The pain was unbearable and Joe just wanted to run away from it. He brought his knees up and pushed himself over on his side. His right arm and left shoulder were on fire and he felt incredibly weak.

A voice broke through the fog in his mind and he once more heard his name being called. He also heard a chilling, evil laugh.

Once more, Harry called out for Joe. He had no idea where his friend was or why he wouldn't answer.

Through his pain he looked up at the man approaching him.

Harry was having trouble focusing, as if the pain had painted a window of fog in front of his eyes. Soon enough though, the man was kneeling at his side and Harry could see he was holding a knife.

Harry let out a moan as the knife made contact with the skin on his neck. He heard laughter, but the pain when the knife blade began to cut into his neck barely registered above what Harry already felt from the bullet wound in his side.

Seeing terror and pain fill Harry's eyes made the man with the knife rock back on his heels slightly, swaying from the effects of the whiskey he had consumed. He laughed again, wishing he could make this kid die more slowly, but an annoying thought in his head reminded him that the posse could show up at any moment and he needed to move a little faster.

He leaned forward, enjoying the smell of blood that made its way to his nose over his own stench and that of the whiskey. He put the blade on Harry's neck once more as Harry made one more weak plea for Joe to help him.

As Harry shut his eyes and turned his thoughts to his sweetheart, Mary, and to his parents and sisters, he heard the deafening bang of a gun being fired, followed immediately by the feeling of a huge weight pinning him to the ground.

He snapped open his eyes and saw the man lying across his chest, making it almost impossible for him to breath.

He turned his head to the side, desperately trying to suck air into his constricted lungs. Squinting to improve the focus of his pain shrouded vision, he could see a shape, low to the ground a few feet away. He made an effort and could now see that the shape was Joe.

He was on his knees, arms hanging limply at his side, his gun dangling from his left hand about to slip from his fingers and fall to the ground.

Joe's chin was at his chest, as if his head were much too heavy to hold up any longer.

Harry could see that Joe was hurt, his shirtfront covered with blood.

"Joe..." Harry gasped as much from the shock of seeing his friend in such a horrible condition as from the weight on his chest. As Harry watched in horror, Joe swayed slightly, and then fell face down in the dirt.

Harry shut his eyes and felt the sting of tears as he realized what a desperate position he was now in.

His friend had saved his life and now appeared to be dead. And as horrible as that made Harry feel, the thought that he wouldn't live much longer himself pushed away that brief interlude of grief. A few more pain filled moments passed until Harry slipped into the beckoning darkness that descended upon him. His last thought was of the face of his smiling fiancée, Mary.

HOSS AWOKE WITH a start.

What was that? he thought as he pushed himself up on his elbow. It was cold and the light of morning was coyly approaching, slowly pushing away the night.

He couldn't recall what had caused him to wake so abruptly. He listened intently, but the sounds from his horse Chub, nearby, gently nibbling at some grasses was all he could hear.

Rubbing his eyes, Hoss then sat up.

Guess I'd better get some coffee on, now that I'm up, he thought.

The fire from the evening before had died out but he quickly got some sticks together and brought the small blaze back to life. Picking up the small coffee pot, he lifted the lid and peered inside.

Enough for a cup, he mused. He set the pot carefully on a small grate he had brought along on the fire and slowly made his way over to Chub.

BORDERS

Millions of Books, CDs, and Videos available

30% off
Borders Bestsellers

Cafe Espresso

Valos Coffee

Express Orders ready to ship immediately

Free Gift Wrapping

1361 South Alma School Road
Mesa, Arizona 85210
(480) 833-2244
Fax (480) 833-1015

Monday-Saturday: 9a.m. - 11p.m.
Sunday: 10a.m. - 9p.m.

Shop online
anytime
at www.borders.com

BORDERS.com

"How you doin' this mornin', boy?"

He gave his horse a large handful of oat mash then went about saddling up his mount.

As he walked back over to the now steaming coffee pot, he heard the unmistakable crack of a gun being fired, off to the north and up the mountainside.

"Joe…"

His brother's face came suddenly to Hoss as he paused in that split second after hearing the dreaded sound.

With amazing speed, he dumped the coffee on the small fire, mounted Chub and headed off in the direction of the shot.

Moving up the mountain at a brisk pace without overburdening Chub, Hoss talked to the overwhelming feeling of dread that now gripped his heart.

Joe's fine, probably just shooting at a rabbit fer breakfast, that's all. Heck, could be anyone out here, probably ain't even Joe and Harry.

He kept up the litany of thoughts aimed at distracting his rapidly rising feelings of near panic that he kept reminding himself were based on nothing at all tangible.

Judging by the sound of the shot, he knew he didn't have far to go. The gunshot he had heard couldn't have been more than a mile away at the most, but he hadn't heard another sound since then.

Soon he came to the crest of the mountainside and could see where the two trails crossed just up ahead.

While it was much brighter now, the light level was fairly low because of the heavy cloud cover.

"Come on, boy." Hoss urged his horse forward, looking at the ground for signs of tracks and also looking around him, searching for hints of any activity nearby.

When he came to the crossroads, he stopped and dismounted. As his foot touched the ground, Chub suddenly let out a very loud whinny that shook his body and startled Hoss. The sturdy gelding was looking intently to the right, ears perked, then flicking back one at a time, obviously listening for something only he could hear.

Hoss listened too, and let his gaze go in the same direction as his trusted friend.

What is it, boy? Hoss didn't want to verbalize his thoughts for fear of disturbing the silence.

Then he heard it. A chortle from another horse. His eye suddenly caught the movement, down by the trees to the east.

Hoss mounted up in the blink of an eye and nudged Chub down the hill. In a moment he could make out the glow of a dying campfire and in the next moment, he could make out shapes on the ground.

"Oh God, Joe..." He dismounted the second he was near enough and ran to the still body of his younger brother lying face down in the dirt.

As gently as he could, he took Joe by the arm and shoulder and rolled him over.

Joe made no move and Hoss was horrified at the site before him. Joe's entire shirtfront was completely covered with blood.

His face had a large bloody scrape embedded with bits of dirt from his forehead to his chin.

Hoss held the back of Joe's head and gently laid it on the ground.

"Joe?" he whispered. There was no response.

Don't be gone, Joe. Please don't be gone, his mind screamed.

It took a moment to calm his inner voice enough to realize he had to check for a pulse. He shut his eyes for a second, took a deep breath then put his fingers to Joe's neck.

Nothing.

Hoss' mind screamed again and he battled it back once more, knowing he had to remain calm for his brother's sake.

He moved his large fingers around, pressing a little harder, desperately searching for a sign that his best friend in the world was still alive.

There.

A tiny bumping under the skin. Very faint, but he felt it. The relief was so intense that Hoss reeled slightly on his feet as he squatted over his brother.

He got up and ran for his canteen, wetting a bandana as he hurried back to his brother.

Looking up, he saw for the first time Harry lying to his left with the body of another man lying across his chest.

Hoss changed direction and quickly made his way to the men. Laying the canteen and bandana down, he grabbed the shoulder of the man on top and pulled him off Harry.

Hoss knew he must be dead. The bullet hole in his back was huge and the amount of blood was startling.

Harry moaned softly as the man was pulled off his chest and he could finally take a breath.

"Harry, where are you hurt, boy?" said Hoss.

"Joe?" Harry opened his eyes slightly.

"No, Harry it's me, Hoss. Hoss Cartwright."

The morning's events came back to Harry.

"Hoss...Joe, he's dead. I'm sorry Hoss, so sorry...." A tear spilled from Harry's eye as he closed them again.

"Harry, no, Joe's still alive. He's hurt bad, but he's still alive. Harry, what happened here?"

"Sorry, Hoss. Joe was my friend. He saved my life. I'm so sorry, Hoss."

Hoss could see that Harry was out again and wasn't able to understand what he was trying to tell him.

Hoss reached down and pulled the blanket back from his body. He noted the apparent wound in Harry's side and the blood soaked makeshift bandage covering it.

Putting his hand on Harry's forehead, Hoss felt the warmth of fever. He was relieved that it wasn't higher but now began to consider how grave his situation was. There were two badly wounded men, both of whom needed his attention at the moment.

He covered Harry back up and picked up the canteen and ban-

bandana and went back over to Joe.

As he gently dabbed at the scrapes on Joe's face, Joe moaned and began to move his head from side to side, trying to regain his consciousness.

Hoss stopped working on Joe's face and began to unbutton Joe's shirt. The smell of blood sickened Hoss' stomach slightly, but he continued working and soon had his brother's chest exposed.

He quickly saw the source of all the blood. A jagged gash, clearly made by a knife and not a bullet wound as Hoss had assumed at first. Blood was still oozing from the opening.

Hoss jumped up and ran to his saddlebag, opening it and pulling out a small towel he had brought. He also grabbed his clean spare shirt and then he pulled his bedroll from behind the saddle. Kneeling at Joe's side once again, he pressed the towel to the wound.

How am I gonna get you boys home alive?

Hoss' mind desperately searched for ideas on how to help the two critically injured young men.

Before he could arrive at any solution that he felt could work, Joe blinked his eyes and suddenly opened them.

"Joe! It's me. Just take it easy, little brother."

"Hoss." Joe breathed the name softly, his eyes barely focusing on the large man leaning over him.

"Cold. Hurts." His eyelids fluttered, glazed green eyes rolling up into them.

"Joe? Joe! Stay with me. I need your help here!"

Hoss knew that Joe would never refuse a request for help from his brother and sure enough, his idea to keep Joe from slipping away worked. Joe blinked again and looked up imploringly at the big man.

"Ohhh..." he grunted at the pain. "Don't know how much help I can be to you, Hoss."

With his hand still firmly pressing on the wound, Hoss reached the canteen with his other.

"Here, drink some of this." Joe gulped like he had been in the desert for a week, until Hoss moved it out of his reach.

"Cold," Joe said again and began to shiver.

"We'll get you fixed right up in a sec, little buddy," Hoss said as he began ripping up his shirt to wrap around Joe's shoulder. As Hoss worked, he talked softly to his brother, trying to keep him awake, finally covering him up with his bedroll.

Sitting beside Joe, Hoss took his hand. Haltingly, Joe recounted what had taken place on the mountain since the day before.

"Joe, we gotta come up with a plan to get you two outa here. You both need a doctor and I don't know how long either of you can last out here in the weather." He looked up at the gray sky.

"It could start to rainin' anytime but I'm just gonna go on hoping it don't."

"I can ride." Joe said matter-of-factly.

Hoss laughed. "I know you think you can, but you'd bleed to death before we got two miles down the trail. That knife wound needs stitchin'."

Joe knew he was right. He felt weak as a newborn lamb and didn't know if he even had the energy to get to his feet, let alone mount a horse.

"Need to build a travois," Joe sighed.

"Yep, that's what I'm thinking too. Either that or I ride fast as I can for help, but I shore don't want to leave you here alone, so I'd best get going on buildin' that travois."

Wishing he'd thought to bring along a small hatchet, Hoss worked as quickly as possible, cutting branches from trees with his knife that were long enough for his purpose.

It was almost noon before he finished one and he stopped to see how the injured men were. Both were unconscious again. They had both been awake from time to time throughout the morning as Hoss had taken time occasionally to make sure they drank enough water. Now before he took a break to eat a fast bite of lunch, he first went over to Harry.

Feeling his face with the back of his hand, Hoss became alarmed at how hot the young man felt.

Pulling back the blanket, he peered under the bandage to see the wound was red edged and enflamed.

"Dang," Hoss swore under his breath. He wet a piece of cloth with cold water and draped it over Harry's forehead.

"Just hang on, Harry. Please, just hang on."

Checking quickly on his younger brother, he found Joe also to be a bit feverish, but roughly the same as earlier.

Hoss kept his thoughts focused on getting the second travois made faster than he had done the first. He knew this would be difficult, given that he now had to venture further away from the camp to find branches and brush that would work. It took several trips, but Hoss finally dragged the last of the branches into the camp.

It took another hour or so to rig together an uncomfortable looking method of transport, but Hoss was happy to have the hard work behind him. The horses had wandered all over the nearby meadow and were still happily cropping away at the wild grasses and flowers they found there.

Hoss went and slowly approached the nearest one he came to. Slipping a bridle over its head, the horse easily took the bit.

As Hoss now headed toward the camp again, the horse suddenly halted in its tracks, its head held high, ears alert, listening.

Hoss listened, but heard nothing at first.

"Come on, boy," he clucked to the horse.

The horse took two tentative steps, but then stopped again, gazing intently into the distance.

Hoss frowned and listened once more, looking in the same direction as the horse. Then he heard it.

A faint, low rumble that quickly grew louder.

Hoss immediately realized it was a group of riders, coming hard up the mountain.

Within a few moments, they rode up to where Hoss still stood. The group was made up of about ten men and Hoss noticed that a few wore metal stars pinned to their jackets.

As the men rode up, they immediately pulled out their guns and trained them on the surprised man before them.

One of the riders shouted, "That's one of the horses them murderers used. I remember the brand, clear as day!"

Hoss glanced at the rump of the horse he had been leading, noticing the shape of a sideways S with a bar under it.

"String him up!" another rider cried.

Hoss had barely had time to understand what was happening when a few of the men jumped down from their mounts and ran over to him, taking his gun out of its holster and grabbing him roughly by each arm.

The loud report of a gun being fired sounded from another of the men who was still mounted, causing Hoss' would be executioners to jump and look up suddenly.

"Now I'm in charge of this here posse, and I say whether or not we hang anybody."

Keeping his rifle pointed skywards, the man slid off his horse and walked slowly over to where Hoss was still being held.

"You don't look much like an outlaw," the man said as he eyed Hoss closely.

"That's 'cause I ain't an outlaw. Look, you a sheriff or just some yay-hoo with a badge?" Hoss replied.

The man narrowed his eyes and a frown became apparent under his unkempt and bushy moustache.

"The sheriff was one of them that got hisself killed yesterday during the bank holdup. John over there," he gestured to an older man still standing by the horses, "he done lost his son. Now somebody's got to pay for them lives. Jimmy says you got a horse that was ridden out of town by one of those murderers. Sounds like could a been you what done the murderin'."

Hoss was past his initial fright over the posse and he was now enraged by the display of outrageous and deadly stupidity with which this group of men reasoned he was guilty of murder based on his possession of a horse.

Pulling his arms out of the grasp of the men holding them, Hoss shouted "Now you listen and you listen good. My name is Hoss Cartwright."

A few of the men looked at each other, recognizing the name.

"My brother and his friend were ambushed by the men you all are looking for. They were injured but wound up killing those outlaws you were after. If you don't believe me, just go on up that hill into the next clearing and you'll find the bodies. My brother and his friend need help and they need to get to a doctor, so if you fellers are done pretending you're serving justice, get out of the way and let me do what I need to do to help them."

With that Hoss started back up the hillside with the horse in tow. Before he had even gone a few paces, he looked up and saw a figure just ahead of him.

"Drop your weapons!" came a weak shout.

The men from the posse stared, their guns, still trained on Hoss' back, slowly lowered to the ground.

"Joe!" Hoss cried.

Joe stood before him, sweating, with a pale a blanket draped over his shoulders, the bloody bandage peeking out from underneath. In his left hand he barely held a gun and it swayed unsteadily in his weak grasp.

Hoss surged forward and went for the gun, easily knocking it from Joe's hand and in the next second, scooped Joe up in his arms as he collapsed.

As Hoss carried him back up the hill, Joe mumbled "...heard a shot. Thought you were in trouble."

"Thanks Joe. I think between you and me, we got it under control now. Just rest easy."

After he settled Joe back down, he turned and saw all the men had followed him and were wandering about the campsite.

The man with the moustache was leaning over the bodies he found down by the trees, turning their faces to get a look at them.

"Coop, come over here," he shouted to one of the men. A big

man with dark hair walked over.

"You remember seeing these guys in town the other day, over at the saloon when you and me were havin' a beer?"

"Yeah, they shore look like em, Enoch."

"Hey Enoch," came a shout from over by the pile of saddle-bags. "Looky what I found." The man who had shouted was holding fistfuls of money in the air.

Hoss never even glanced up at the man holding the stolen bills; his only concern was for his injured brother.

This fact was not missed by the would be sheriff named Enoch. Any lingering doubts about who Hoss claimed to be quickly vanished with the mounting evidence that the three dead men were the ones they had been chasing.

"Anybody have a clean neckerchief?" shouted Hoss to the men milling about.

He took the one that was silently offered and as gently as possible removed the blood soaked towel that had become useless as a bandage on Joe's shoulder, replacing it with the new bandana.

"We've got to get these men to a doctor. I made a couple of travois. If some of you men would go over and hitch 'em up to a couple of those horses... Use the branded ones. Them others are breeding stock and I don't know if they're broke yet or not."

The group of men that had seemed listless suddenly came to life with their new purpose. Hoss saw them move into action, a few going over to attend to Harry while the others saddled up the horses. Hoss felt a small measure of relief come over him now that he had help.

Joe's eyes blinked open and he tried to focus on his big brother's face.

Never realized how much energy it takes just to open your eyes... or to breathe Joe thought.

He would have said it out loud, but thought that would take more than he had in him at the moment.

Hoss continued caring for Joe's shoulder and hadn't noticed Joe's eyes open, but when Joe let out a grunt of pain, Hoss looked to his face.

"Hey, sorry about that buddy." Hoss said gently. "Glad to see you're still with us."

Joe just stared into his brother's eyes, drawing strength and comfort from the love he found in the deep blue depths.

"Now don't you worry about a thing. Old Hoss'll get you home and into your own bed in no time, so you just relax and take it easy and let me do all the work."

Joe was so tired. He closed his eyes and surrendered to the darkness where he felt no pain.

WHEN JOE OPENED his eyes, it was bright. Sunlight so bright he squinted his eyes against it and groaned.

Someone immediately dimmed the brightness by closing the curtains and when Joe looked again, his heart leapt at the sight of his Pa leaning over him.

"Pa..." Joe breathed.

"Yes, son. I'm here."

Joe tried to sit up but the immediate and brutal pain that shot through his shoulder reminded him why he was in bed during a bright sunny day. He felt a warm hand on his forehead and another grasp his own hand. He heard words, spoken softly, soothing words, but the pain made it too hard to make himself concentrate on what the words were.

"Owwww," he moaned.

"Harry..." he said as soon as the burst of pain faded enough for him to speak again. He looked up at his Pa's face and saw an expression of sadness and concern. Worry was etched into his face and Joe now noticed how tired his father looked as well.

"Shhh... Joseph, please just lie still. You're not well enough to be moving around."

"Harry..." Joe repeated his implied question. He tried to read the answer to the question in Pa's eyes, but there was too much concern and exhaustion on his father's face to read anything more there.

"Pa, I...I need to know if Harry's all right. Please Pa, you've got to tell me."

"Joseph, please stay calm. I'll answer you if you just give me a chance. Harry is alive. When Hoss brought you both in two days ago..."

"Two days...!" Joe gasped.

"Yes, two days, Joe. When Hoss brought you in, you were both in pretty bad shape. The doc came out and sewed you both up as best he could, but it's been a fight to bring you both back after the amount of blood you both lost and the long exposure to the cold and damp weather. You were both fighting off a fever. Yours broke last night, but Harry, well Harry's still ill. He's still here; we thought it best not to move him just yet. His folks and Mary have been here constantly too, taking care of him. Joe, I was so worried about you."

"Is Harry going to make it, Pa?" Joe asked.

"Joe, I don't know how to answer that. I've been concentrating on you getting well. I'm afraid that's all I've been able to focus on these past two days. The doc is due out here again this morning. We'll see what he has to say then. Meanwhile we need to get some broth into you."

Joe felt exhausted and didn't know how he would stay awake to eat anything. In what seemed like the blink of an eye, Pa returned to Joe's bedside with a steaming cup of broth.

After finishing the broth, Joe slept again and when he woke, it was late in the evening.

Pa was sitting in a chair by his bed, snoring softly.

"Pa?" Joe called softly.

Ben was awake in an instant, smiling down at Joe. He immediately put a hand on Joe's forehead to check for fever and was relieved that it was only slightly warm.

Smiling, he asked "How you feel, son?"

"Tired. Sore. Pa, how's Harry? Did the doc come by?"

"Harry's fever broke finally, Joe. Doc thinks he should recover just fine."

Joe sighed with relief.

There was a soft knocking at the door, then Hoss and Adam came into Joe's room.

"We're just going to turn in and thought we'd see if you needed anything. Hey, Short Shanks! Good to see you with your pretty eyes open for a change!" Hoss said, suppressing a strong urge to scoop his brother up and give him a huge hug.

Joe smiled as brightly as he could at his older brothers. "I'm sure glad to be here to open them. Hoss, I don't think I had a chance to thank you. If you hadn't come along when you did, well, me and Harry probably wouldn't have made it."

"Aw, Joe, you know when you and Harry didn't get home when you were supposed to, well, I just figured you'd take that high trail. Just wanted to make sure you didn't get lost."

"I almost lost more than just my way up on that trail," admitted Joe. "I'm really glad you came along and found us when you did, Hoss."

Hoss was quiet for a moment while he got his emotions under control—before he had to hide the tears in his eyes at the thought of having almost lost his brother forever.

"I am too," Hoss answered quietly, looking with sudden interest at a nail in the floor. "There's a lot of things in life it wouldn't hurt none to lose, little brother, but you ain't one of them."

"Thanks, Hoss," Joe whispered as he slowly let his eyes shut. He slept deeply and at peace, knowing he was home again. He knew he was safe and the danger was passed for both Harry and himself.

But more importantly, he knew that, no matter what trail he took in life, there would always be someone to make sure he didn't lose his way home.

The Hostage

by Camera_Chic

"No, take me." Joe moved forward, closer to the man in the red shirt. There was a protest from Adam, and Joe almost looked towards his brother, but he forced himself not to. Out of the corner of his eye, he saw the man who was tying Adam's wrists pause. The man in the red shirt looked down at him, and Joe tried to keep from trembling as he met his eyes. The rest of the man's face was obscured by the neckerchief he wore over his nose. Joe moved a bit closer. "Take me instead," he repeated.

The man almost seemed to laugh. "Why?" he asked.

Joe thought of all the things he could respond with, but finally said, "I'll make a better hostage." He looked at his brother, and tried to explain why with his eyes. Adam had protested when the robbers first came into the bank and pushed Mrs. Clark to the floor. The robbers had told everyone to get down, but she was frozen in fear. Two of them had punched and kicked Adam, and he tried to only defend himself, and not cause a bigger fight. Joe had seen his brother fight before, and he knew. There were several women and a couple of children in the bank, and Adam's concern must have been for them. But now, it was Joe's turn to be concerned for his older brother. They wanted a hostage to help get them out of town, and Joe knew they would probably injure his brother further. How much further, he was afraid to imagine. Adam was already pretty bruised, and he had a nasty cut over his eye. Joe couldn't let them take him.

The man walked up to him, and once again Joe wished he was tall like his brothers. When he was 15, they said he would probably be taller by 16. Growth spurts, and becoming a man, and things like that. It didn't happen though. He didn't even really need to shave yet. The man grasped Joe's chin, and tilted his head back. "I'm not taking a kid."

Joe pulled away from him. "I'm not a kid, I'm 16," he replied, a little hotly.

The man laughed and shook his head. "No way, kid." He started to turn away, but Joe reached out and grasped his arm.

"I won't resist in any way; I'll go quietly with you until you're far enough away. Please..." Instantly he regretted the 'please'; it was a little childish.

"Joe, no!" Adam once again protested, but his action had the opposite effect.

The man said, "Very well, we'll take the kid instead," smirking in Adam's direction. One of the other men knocked Adam to the floor as the man grabbed Joe's arm and pulled him closer to his brother. "Anything you want to say?" he asked, and shoved Joe to his knees next to Adam. He began to tie his hands behind his back.

Adam looked up at him, and it was the first time Joe could remember seeing anything close to tears in his brother's eyes. "Joe...no," Adam whispered. "They might..."

Joe nodded. "I know," he whispered back, and then the man

pulled him to his feet. Joe couldn't break his gaze away from Adam, and as the men led him towards the door, he wondered if he would ever see his brother again.

Outside, Joe could see the ends of shotguns and rifles pointed at him, and he closed his eyes, hoping they wouldn't shoot. He felt the man behind him tighten his grip on his shoulder, and he grimaced. "I'm not going anywhere," he hissed.

"Hold your fire!" Joe heard Sheriff Coffee yell, and he let out a sigh of relief and opened his eyes. He glanced quickly through the men standing around the bank, and noticed almost immediately his father and brother standing near the sheriff. He tried to smile slightly at them, hoping to relieve the fear that had taken over their faces, but it didn't seem to work. He was glad at least that he had been able to see them.

The man pushed Joe towards the horses tethered a few yards from the bank, keeping his gun pressed against Joe's head. Joe was lifted onto one of the horses, and he did his best to hook his feet through the stirrups. They were too long, and his feet nearly didn't reach them. One of the men grabbed the reins, and then all of them rode away from the bank. Joe was afraid that if he turned to look back, he would either fall off the horse or burst into tears, so he stared straight ahead at the top of the horse's head.

Too soon they were out of town. As they veered off the road, Joe couldn't help but think that Hoss would have no problem following their trail. He figured by now Hoss and Ben had entered the bank and untied Adam, and hopefully had made him take care of the cut. Joe hoped there were no other serious injuries. The men had been pretty angry with him, even though he had done nothing wrong. "That's no way to treat a lady," was what he had said when they threw Mrs. Clark to the floor. The man in the red shirt had become furious, and snapped at him, "Don't be telling me what to do!" before commanding two of his men to beat Adam while he and the last man took all the money. Joe was hoping if he did everything they told him, they might at least not beat him the same way. He figured he had a better chance than Adam.

As they started up a steep incline, his horse slipped; and even though it quickly caught itself, the movement was enough for Joe to lose his balance and topple onto the ground. He rolled onto his knees, gasping a little as the wind had been knocked out of him. There was the sharp sound of a gun hammer being cocked, and Joe looked up.

"Trying to get away?" the masked leader asked, pointing his gun at him.

Joe shook his head. "No, sir, the horse slipped and I fell off. I'm sorry..." He tried to sound as apologetic as he could, even though his nature fought against being polite to someone who had hurt his brother the way he had. He was trying hard to not give them a reason to kill him, but as he looked up at the man in front of him, he was afraid that he wouldn't have to.

"Stand up," the man said.

Joe managed to stand, rather unsteadily, as the man in red rode towards him. He looked up as he came to a stop. "Turn around," the man said.

Joe slowly turned. He had hoped to remain alive longer than this. It all seemed so useless; there was so much more still that he had to do. He waited, holding his breath, as the leader commanded the others to ride ahead. It became quiet again, and then the man asked, "Why did you want to switch places with him? You knew what was going to happen, didn't you?"

Joe nodded as tears pricked his eyes. "I knew. He's my brother," he replied quietly. The silence was deafening, and seemed to drag on forever. He almost wanted to ask him what he was waiting for.

"Start walking, back the way we just came. I'm sure you'll run into someone soon." The man called out to his horse, and then the sound of hoof beats retreating could be heard.

Joe turned, afraid to believe what he had just heard. He saw the man riding away in the distance, and then let out a laugh of joy. He almost couldn't believe he was still alive! He turned and started walking back down the hill, tugging against the ropes that bound his hands. About 15 minutes later, he heard horses in front of him, and he started to run towards them. "Pa!" he yelled as he recognized the riders. "Hoss, Adam!" The dozen or so riders came to a stop, and Joe ran towards his father. "Pa!" he called out again. His father hugged him tightly and then pulled him away, looking him over to see if there were injuries, before holding him close again. Joe felt the ropes fall away, and he gladly hugged Ben in return.

"Are you all right?" Ben asked, finally releasing him.

"I'm fine now, Pa," Joe smiled. He glanced up as he felt his brother's hand on his arm.

"What happened?" Hoss asked.

"They let me go," he replied.

"How far ahead are they?" Sheriff Coffee asked.

"Not far, maybe a mile or so," Joe replied.

Ben looked at Adam, who nodded. "I'll take him home, Pa."

"And put something on that wound," Ben said to him, and then he and Hoss mounted their horses again and followed after the posse.

Adam went back to his horse, and helped Joe into the saddle before swinging up after him. He turned back towards town. After a few minutes he said, "Don't ever do that again. Do you know what Pa would have done if something had happened to you?"

Joe thought for a moment, and then replied, "What would he have done if something had happened to you?"

Adam sighed, and then said quietly, "They might have killed you, Joe."

Joe nodded. "I know. But I couldn't let them kill you, Adam."

Adam didn't say anything for a long time. Just as Joe was about to glance back, Adam spoke. "You're some brother," he said, and Joe could hear the emotion in his voice. Joe settled back against him, and watched the scenery as they rode home.

You See, It Was Like This

by Lizk

*A*dam sat on the low table in the center of the room facing the cold fireplace, his chin on his hands, his face grim.

In front of him his younger brother paced back and forth. "Oh, boy... Oh, boy. This isn't good, Adam." Little Joe stopped his nervous pacing to turn apprehensive eyes toward his brother.

"Just quiet down and let me think, Joe," Adam responded impatiently. He chewed on a finger, his own anxiety heightened by his brother's agitation.

"But what are we gonna tell Pa?" Joe began to pace once again.

Adam opened his mouth to respond then shut it. The truth was he didn't know what they were going to tell Pa.

It had seemed simple enough at the time. Pa had asked them to stop by Widow Hammburg's and deliver a package on their way into town. That's all they had to do. Adam wasn't exactly sure how it had gone so wrong...

THE HAMMBURG PLACE was typical of most homesteads in Nevada. It had the usual two-story clapboard farmhouse, this one painted white with red shutters, an even larger barn, chicken coop, corrals, and other outbuildings. A large porch wrapped around two sides of the house and rose bushes graced the front and climbed up the posts on either side of the front steps. They were Widow Hammburg's pride and joy, those rose bushes, and she provided flowers for all the hotels, restaurants and fancy mansions in town as well as for special occasions such as weddings, funerals and holidays. Widow Hammburg and her roses were synonymous.

The rose bushes were in full bloom this fine morning as Adam and Joe rode into the Hammburg farmyard. They dismounted, tied the horses to the hitching post and Joe reached for the package they had to deliver. Together they started up the front steps, but Adam paused to take in the loveliness of the roses, breathing deeply of their fragrance. He liked roses, though he wouldn't have admitted it to his brothers. Their classic beauty and heady scent reminded him of a fine oil painting or a classical symphony; they seemed to belong to the refined part of life. Even here in this homely setting, their velvety splendor added a touch of elegance that made the old farmhouse beautiful.

Little Joe stopped to look back when he realized Adam wasn't next to him. He gave Adam a quizzical look, but Adam simply smiled and bounded up the steps to stand next to him. No, his admiration for the rose wasn't something he cared to share with his brothers.

Elvira Hammburg answered Joe's knock. The sprightly widow was around fifty with white hair tucked into a neat bun at the back of her head. Her plump figure, dressed in blue flowered calico and wrapped with an abundant white apron, made her look grandmotherly, though she had no children of her own. She smiled and her face lit up when she saw who her visitors were.

The Hammburgs and the Cartwrights had been good friends for years and Adam and Joe both had fond memories of the widow's warm cookies and cold milk. Jonas Hammburg had passed on several years ago, but Mrs. Hammburg had continued right on supplying milk, fresh vegetables and, of course, the roses to the citizens of Virginia City and Gold Hill.

"Adam, Joe!" she exclaimed warmly. "What a lovely surprise! Please, come in, come in," she said, opening the door wide for them.

Adam smiled fondly at her. "No, thank you, Mrs. Hammburg, we just stopped by to deliver this package for Pa." He nodded to the tidy, twine-wrapped package in Joe's hands.

Joe held the package out to her. "Here you are, Mrs. Hammburg," he smiled charmingly at her. "All in one piece."

"Oh, thank you," she said taking the package. "Your pa did say he was sending over some periodicals for me to read. It's so sweet of him." Mrs. Hammburg beamed at the men. "But really you must come in and set awhile."

Adam started to protest again, but Mrs. Hammburg held up her hand. "Now, Adam Cartwright, I won't take no for an answer! You haven't visited me for an age, and besides my niece is here from Sacramento and you really must meet her."

At the mention of the niece Joe's face brightened in interest and he jumped in before Adam could refuse again. "Well, Mrs. Hammburg, we certainly couldn't be rude and not meet your niece."

Mrs. Hammburg chuckled and laid a hand on Joe's cheek. "Oh, you are a sweet boy, Little Joe!"

"Joe, we really need to be getting into town," Adam reminded him. "Perhaps we can meet your niece some other time." He smiled politely and tried again to excuse themselves to Mrs. Hammburg.

"We got plenty of time, older brother." With a grin, Joe followed Mrs. Hammburg into the farmhouse. Adam could only roll his eyes and follow him.

Both men removed their hats as they entered the comfortable front room of the house, the center of which was occupied by a low, round table completely covered with paint samples and wallpaper swatches. Bending intently over them was a petite girl of about eighteen, with abundant chestnut hair, green eyes that had a hint of mischief in them, and a pixie face that went well with her diminutive size. She straightened and smiled as her aunt entered with her guests.

Mrs. Hammburg bustled over to her niece and led her forward. "Adam, Joe, this is my niece, Beth, here all the way from Sacramento for the summer," she announced proudly. "Beth, this is Adam and Little Joe Cartwright."

"Uh, just Joe, ma'am," Little Joe corrected.

"How do you do?" Beth asked politely.

"Pleased to meet you, Miss..." Adam paused, not knowing how to finish.

"Oh, there's no need for that, Adam." Mrs. Hammburg waved away his hesitancy, "too much polite just makes people stiff and starchy."

"I agree," Joe stepped in smoothly, taking Beth's hand and bowing slightly over it, "and I am very pleased to meet you, Beth."

Beth flushed lightly, but her green eyes sparkled "Thank you, Little Joe," she said as she reluctantly withdrew her hand.

"Just Joe," Joe reminded her.

"Joe." She dimpled at him, then lowered her eyelids. Adam chuckled to himself amused at how quickly and smoothly his little brother had moved from civility to familiarity with Mrs. Hammburg's niece.

"Well," Mrs. Hammburg said briskly, "it's much too nice of a day for us to be standing in here. Beth take the gentlemen out onto the veranda while I get us some lemonade and cookies."

"No, Mrs. Hammburg, really we can't stay." Adam tried once

again to cut their visit short, but Mrs. Hammburg was already on her way to the kitchen, and ignored him. He turned to Joe. "Joe, you know we can't stay, we have business in Virginia City."

"Older brother, you need to learn to relax a little." Joe nudged Adam in the ribs as he passed by with Beth on his arm. "The business will wait." He turned and smiled at Beth as they sailed out the door.

Adam sighed and shook his head as he followed them. He was clearly outnumbered and knew when to admit defeat gracefully. Besides, Joe was right, the business in Virginia City wasn't pressing, and he knew Mrs. Hammburg would appreciate the visit. He glanced over to where Joe was helping Beth into one of the low wicker chairs situated around a small table at one end of the porch. He also knew his chances of getting Little Joe out of here now were little to none.

Mrs. Hammburg came out carrying a tray with glasses, a pitcher of lemonade, and a plate full of gingersnap cookies. Graciously he took the tray from her and followed her over to join Beth and Joe. Setting the tray on the table, he held Mrs. Hammburg's chair for her, and then leaned back against the porch railing. The spicy fragrance of the roses filled the entire porch, and he glanced over at them. "Your roses are lovely this year, Mrs. Hammburg," he remarked filling in the space left by Beth and Joe's complete absorption in each other.

"Why, thank you, Adam!" Mrs. Hammburg said delighted. "If you like these I should show you the ones in back, they're even more lovely." She jumped up quickly and, setting down her glass, motioned to him, heading once again for the door before he had a chance to protest. Adam merely shook his head in amusement and followed her. He knew from experience that Mrs. Hammburg wouldn't stop for an answer.

She stopped abruptly at the door and turned to look where Beth and Joe were deep in conversation, oblivious to the fact the she and Adam were leaving. She pondered for a moment then smiled at Adam. "We'll just leave those two to get acquainted," she said conspiratorially, then winked broadly at him, before bustling into the house and through to the back door. Adam smiled and shook his head at her, before following after.

Mrs. Hammburg had been right. If the flowers out front were beautiful, these in back were absolutely stunning. Laid out in neat rows were Bourbon, Tea, and Portland roses, as well as several that Adam didn't recognize. Their gorgeous colors ranged from vivid pink to pale blush; sunshine yellow to deep red. It was a sea of color that made Adam draw his breath in sharply in awe.

"Mrs. Hammburg, these are magnificent," he said with deep admiration as he followed her down the first row of luscious blooms.

She smiled. "Thank you, the result of lots of hard work," she said, then gently touched a delicate pink blossom, "and a lot of love."

"I can see that," Adam responded quietly. They moved slowly down the rows, Mrs. Hammburg identifying each rose as Adam stopped to smell and touch the perfect blossoms. It was some time later before they found themselves back at the foot of the steps leading into the house.

"My, I completely forgot about Beth and Joe," Mrs. Hammburg exclaimed.

"I'm guessing they didn't notice," Adam assured her laughing. "Thank you for showing me your roses. They truly are exquisite."

Mrs. Hammburg laughed merrily. "No, thank you, Adam, you've been very patient with an old woman's passion."

"It was my pleasure, Mrs. Hammburg, truly." He held the door open for her as they entered the house. She stopped and turned to him, looked intently into his eyes for a moment, then gently patted his cheek.

"You're a good boy, Adam, I think you really mean that." She smiled then gave him another light slap before sweeping on through the house.

Adam had been right, Joe and Beth didn't seem to have noticed their absence when he and Mrs. Hammburg returned, but

Beth looked up with a wide smile when her aunt settled next to her in the chair.

"Oh, Aunt Elvira! I have the best news!" she announced. "Joe says that he and Adam would be glad to take your orders into town today. Isn't that wonderful?" She turned and cast a beaming smile on Joe, who returned it with a rather besotted grin.

"Oh, but, Beth, we can't ask these gentlemen to do that, it's too much." Mrs. Hammburg demurred, though Adam could see a hopeful look in her eyes, and he wondered warily just what his younger brother was getting them involved in.

"Nonsense, Mrs. Hammburg," Joe responded emphatically "We'd be glad to help out, wouldn't we Adam?"

Adam leaned back against the porch railing and crossed his arms. "Of course, though it would be nice if I knew what it was I was volunteering for." His voice was pleasant but it held a warning hint that he was hoping Joe would catch. They still had business in Virginia City and needed to cut their visit short if they expected to get it done that day.

Joe caught the hint but went irrepressibly on. "Don't worry, Adam, we'll be going into Virginia City, we just need to take Mrs. Hammburg's deliveries in for her. Since we're headed that way anyway, it won't be any trouble at all, will it?" Joe sent Adam a look and tilted his head slightly toward Beth. Adam caught the look, and the hint, and sighed inwardly.

"No, not at all." He gave Mrs. Hammburg a smile, though inwardly he was growling at Joe. "We'd be glad to do it. Only, I thought Billy and Cole Simmons usually took your deliveries in for you?"

"They do, but they're both down with a fever, and I was really wondering how I was going to get everything into town. It's important they go in today. I've got some extra special Comte De Chambourds for the International. But are you sure it's no trouble?"

"Not at all, Mrs. Hammburg!" Joe jumped in. "No trouble at all. We're glad to help, and if Beth here would just come along to make sure we get everything to the right place," Joe turned to look in Beth's eyes, and his voice softened. "Everything will be perfect."

Beth flushed under his gaze. "I'd be glad to help," she replied, smiling.

Mrs. Hammburg clapped her hands delighted. "Well, that's all settled then!" She beamed at Joe and Beth.

Adam debated pointing out that they probably knew Mrs. Hammburg's customers better than Beth did, so there was no reason for Beth to go with them, but he realized that didn't really matter. Joe's purpose was to spend more time with Beth. Beth seemed perfectly agreeable to the plan, and Mrs. Hammburg was absolutely delighted with the arrangement, that much was obvious.

He felt a little left out, being the only one of the group who could see several flaws in the scheme, but since it wouldn't be that much trouble, and Mrs. Hammburg could truly use the help, and as Beth and Joe could hardly drive into town by themselves he let things stand as they were. Quickly he stood and motioned to Beth and Joe.

"Well, since, as Mrs. Hammburg says, it's settled, I think we'd best get to it."

"Oh, yes and thank you so much!" Mrs. Hammburg stood and bustled her way quickly down the steps. "Come along and I'll show you the wagon, and the deliveries, and..." She turned and smiled at Adam who was close behind her. "I'll introduce you to my mules!"

Mrs. Hammburg's mules were truly a pair, but they seemed gentle enough, as Adam hitched them to the buckboard and Joe and Beth loaded the vegetables, milk and roses to be delivered into town.

"This is Clare and that one is Clem," Mrs. Hammburg told him, patting Clare fondly as the mule stood patiently waiting for her turn to be hitched. "They're both my babies. Aren't you, you sweet things?" she said in the singsong voice usually reserved for infants. She turned to Adam. "Now, there's two things you need to remember about Clem and Clare. If you do you'll get along fine." She let go of Clare as Adam took her and backed the animal into place next to Clem. "Now, first off the poor dears don't like to be tied. It annoys them something awful, and they get so worked up. Don't ya, sweetie." Mrs. Hammburg patted Clem's nose and he snuffed. "But don't worry they'll stay put as long as one of you is with them."

"We can't tie them?" Adam's voice was skeptical, and he threw Mrs. Hammburg a glance as he buckled Clare's harness to the traces.

"No, no, they don't like to be tied. They've always been that way; Josiah never could work it out of them, that's why it always took the both of us to go into town. One of us would stand with the mules while the other one delivered the goods. But with the three of you, you shouldn't have any trouble at all. They'll stay put iffen you're watching them. Of course, if you don't they'll wander."

Adam sighed. He wondered if Joe had known about this little quirk of Mrs. Hammburg's mules. He looked at Joe who simply shrugged and placed the last basket of flowers in the buckboard. "You mentioned two things," Adam reminded her.

"Oh, well the other one isn't all that much." Mrs. Hammburg hesitated. "It's just that they don't like yelling. Sets 'em off sure as anything." She laughed suddenly. "I mind the time Josiah had them all hitched and ready to go and Clare stepped right on his foot! Oh my, did he yell then. Those two mules took off like their tails was on fire!" She chuckled again at the memory. "Took us the rest of the morning just to catch up with them." She smiled brightly at Adam. "But I know you aren't the yelling type. Now if it were Ben..." she chuckled again. "Your pa certainly has a voice on him, don't he?"

Adam couldn't help giving Joe another look and they both smiled. Pa was well known for his stentorian voice. Adam gave Clare a slap and turned to Mrs. Hammburg.

"Well, there, that should do it. Do you have a list of your deliveries?"

"Oh yes, in the house." She turned quickly, and started for the barn door, then stopped and glanced back. "Little Joe, you and Beth bring the wagon upta the house, I'll get the list for Adam. Come along, Adam. They can take care of it." And without stopping to see if Adam was following she hurried away.

Adam threw a bemused look at a grinning Joe before he followed Mrs. Hammburg to the house.

The trip into town was uneventful. Beth and Joe chatted away like two old friends and Adam drove, listening with half an ear to their talk, but mostly just enjoying the sunny day and his own thoughts. The mules were well mannered and obedient, a fact Adam appreciated, having run across some that weren't, to his regret.

As they approached Virginia City, Adam pulled out the sheet of paper Mrs. Hammburg had written her clients down on. Adam did a mental plan of the stops they needed to make. There were a couple of private houses that needed milk, then a large order for Walter's General store. He stopped the mules in front of the Harveys, and looked past Beth to Joe.

"I guess you and Beth can stay here with the mules, I'll take the milk into Mrs. Harvey." He didn't anticipate any objections and there were none. Joe simply nodded and he and Beth kept right on talking. Adam was starting to feel distinctly invisible. "Joe, keep an eye on the mules. I can't tie them," Adam reminded him. Joe's only answer was a wave of the hand. "Joe?"

Joe looked over at him, annoyed. "All right, Adam, keep your shirt on. I'll watch the mules, they ain't goin' anywhere with Beth and me sitting right here."

Adam jumped down and swung around to the back of the buckboard. "Just see that they don't."

Joe snorted "Okay." He looked at Beth. "You have to excuse Adam, Beth, he likes to remind me who he thinks is boss around here," he told her loud enough for Adam to hear. Beth giggled, and Adam glared at his brother, but let the comment pass as he grabbed the jars of milk for Mrs. Harvey and headed for her door.

The next two deliveries were quick and easy, but there was a substantial delivery for Clementine Hawkins. Adam had a feeling it wasn't going to be all that quick; Widow Hawkins liked to talk. He considered making Joe do this delivery, but one look at his brother's rapt attention to whatever it was Beth was telling him and he realized it would be easier to just do it himself.

He pulled up in front of the boarding house and curled the reins around the whip stand. Hopping down once again, he looked at Joe. "Joe? The mules?"

"Yeah, Adam, good grief you don't have to tell me every time!" Joe responded irritably.

Adam said nothing, just pulled the basket of pink roses from the back and headed for the front door.

Widow Hawkins was indeed glad to see him. She pulled him into the house, insisting that he sit while she got a vase for the flowers. Vainly he'd tried to explain he had several other boxes for her, but she just waved it away, informing him that he could get them in a moment. By the time he made his escape and returned outside to get the rest of the order some time had passed, and he hurried down the walk. He stopped short at the gate. Beth and Joe were nowhere to be seen and the mules were halfway down the street.

"Joe," Adam muttered, his lips tightening dangerously as he strode down the street after Clem and Clare. Fortunately, the gentle mules let him catch them easily, but he was fuming at Joe. He looked up and down the street, and finally caught sight of them around the back of Widow Hawkins. Beth was admiring the widow's peony bush, and Joe was admiring Beth.

Irritated Adam led the mules back to the front of the board-ing house and stopped next to the front gate. Remembering Mrs. Hammburg's warning, he realized he wasn't going to be able to yell for his brother, nor leave the mules. Not sure what to do, he stood holding the mules his temper flaring. Joe had gotten them into this, now Adam was the one left taking care of it. It was so typical.

"Adam, why aren't you bringin' in the rest of the things?" Widow Hawkins appeared at her door. "I've not got all day you know," she told him pertly.

"I understand Widow Hawkins." He threw another desperate glance at the corner hoping to see Joe and Beth coming. Nothing. There was no other choice. "But I was wondering if you could help me for a moment."

"'elp you, now what do you mean?" Clementine came down the walk toward him.

"Well, I was wondering..." Adam hesitated, mentally calling his brother every name he could think of, but smiling a tight smile. "I was wondering if you could stand with the mules for a moment, while I take the rest of your order in."

"Stand with the mules!" Clementine looked at him as if he was daft. "Why don't you just tie them?"

"Well you see, Widow Hawkins, I can't tie them, they won't stand."

"It's all right, Adam, I'll take them." He heard Joe's voice behind him; he turned to see Joe smiling his most charming smile at Widow Hawkins. "Good morning, Widow Hawkins, beautiful morning isn't it?" Joe touched the brim of his hat. "Do you know Beth Lewis, Mrs. Hammburg's niece from Sacramento?"

Adam should not have been surprised at the easy way Joe had stepped in, charming Widow Hawkins, and seeming so unconcerned by the fact that he had forgotten what he was supposed to be doing. This wasn't the time to go into it with him, Adam knew so he merely gave him a look and held out the mules' reins to him. Joe took the reins and winked at him, then turned back to Clementine and Beth, while Adam quickly lugged the rest of the widow's order into the boarding house.

Adam was unable to say anything when they were once again on their way, either, not with Beth sitting between them. He had to content himself with pointed glares at his brother, which Joe steadfastly ignored. Joe surprised him by getting down at the International Hotel and walking around the back to help him grab the produce for the hotel restaurant.

"Sorry, about that Adam. Beth had heard about Widow Hawkins's peonies and wanted to see them. It won't happen again." He whispered under his breath, then handed Adam the basket of vegetables.

Adam was only slightly mollified, but decided to let it go. "All right, just make sure it doesn't." Quickly, he deposited the basket inside the kitchen door and went back for the two other boxes, and the large basket of roses destined for the hotel. The delicate scent of the roses soothed him, and he buried his nose in them, drinking in their fragrance before passing them over with a dimpled smile to Heather Carr, the Hotel cook's assistant.

Beth and Joe were again deep in conversation, but still where he left them when he returned. Adam was relieved to note they were almost half done with the deliveries. They had only Belmar's Café and Cass's General Store to go in town before heading toward Gold Hill and the mansions lining the mountain.

He stopped behind the Café near the kitchen door and glanced at Joe, but refrained from reminding him about the mules, knowing it would only irritate his brother. Once again he lifted a heavy box out of the buckboard, feeling a pull in his shoulder muscles that would no doubt remind him tomorrow of the unusual duty they had done today.

Mrs. Belmar met him at the door with a surprised smile on her face. "Why, Adam Cartwright, what a pleasant surprise," she said, holding the door for him. She looked over at the wagon, noticing Little Joe and Beth, then back at Adam and the heavy box full of vegetables. "Where's Billy and Cole?" she asked, following Adam into the kitchen and indicating a low table where he could place the box.

Adam heaved a sigh of relief as he set the box down, and turned to Mrs. Belmar. "They're both down with the fever. Joe and I stopped by Widow Hammburg's to deliver a package for Pa, so we offered to do her deliveries for her."

"Well, how very kind of you, Adam," Mrs. Belmar commended him.

"Thanks, I've got a couple more boxes for you." He turned to see Beth and Joe entering the kitchen. "Joe!"

"Hold on Adam, the mules are fine, I just wanted to introduce Beth to Mrs. Belmar." Joe assured him.

Adam grit his teeth, shook his head at Joe, and rushed out the back, Joe right behind him. The mules were standing quietly where they had left them.

"See, Adam, they didn't go anywhere. I was only going to be a second and I knew you were headed right back out. Widow Hammburg told Beth that Mrs. Belmar was the best cook in the territory and Beth's been wanting to meet her," Joe explained. He clapped Adam on the shoulder and grinned at him. "Older Brother, you really need to learn to relax."

Adam turned to face his younger brother. "Joe, you're the one that volunteered for this little job. You're the one who insisted that Beth come along. You're the one who assured Mrs. Hammburg that it would be no trouble at all. Well, so far that's been true, for you at least, because ALL the trouble has been mine! I've driven the buckboard, I've carried in the boxes, I've had to CATCH the mules after you couldn't even stay with them, so they wouldn't wander off." Adam stopped to catch his breath than continued as calmly as his elevated pulse would allow. "And you're telling ME to relax! Joe..." Adam stopped not sure of what else to say, when all he wanted to do was wring his little brother's neck. "Joe..."

"Oh, come on, Adam, it hasn't been that bad." Joe smiled the beguiling smile he'd used on Adam since he was old enough to understand its value.

Adam blew his breath out between his teeth. "Joe, just stay with the mules, while I get the rest of Mrs. Belmar's order for her." He brushed past Joe without looking at him, grabbed the last box for Mrs. Belmar, and didn't move over for Beth who almost collided with him in the doorway. She leapt to the side quickly, and watched him wide-eyed as he surged past her with set face and narrowed eyes.

"Is he okay?" she asked Joe in a whisper as she moved in close to him, her face anxious.

Joe shrugged. "Oh, sure, he's all right. It's just the way he is sometimes. But I think we'd better stay with the wagon from now on." He helped Beth up then jumped up beside her.

Adam didn't speak when he returned. He climbed to his seat, and set the mules forward at a trot. He knew he was overreacting, but couldn't seem to help himself. Something about this whole situation had gotten on his nerves, and having Joe and Beth beside him laughing and chatting, was only making it worse. He pulled the mules up in front of Cass's store and went through the same process he'd already done what felt like a thousand times before already today. He now knew why he had never had any desire to be a delivery driver.

He hopped down and pulled a basket out of the back, decided it was pointless to speak to Joe, so merely trudged his way into Cass's store. Sally Cass was helping a customer and he didn't see Mr. Cass so he set the box down on an empty table and went back out for the next load.

Joe and Beth had gotten down from the wagon and were standing near Clare's head, talking quietly to one another. They didn't look up as he approached the wagon and Adam had that invisible feeling again. He muttered to himself as he grabbed the box of butter and cheese and hefted it over the edge of the buckboard, then turned and lugged the box into the store.

Sally had finished with her customer and joined him as he set the second box beside the first.

"Hi, Adam, how come you're delivering today?"

"It's a long story, Sally, where do you want these?" He knew he sounded gruff, but couldn't help himself.

"Over there, please," she said softly, pointing. Her eyes looked hurt and Adam sighed. Sally was a nice girl and he was sorry he'd snapped at her.

"I'm sorry, Sally, I didn't mean to sound cross, it's just been a rough morning," he apologized as he moved the boxes to where she'd indicated.

"That's all right, Adam, I understand." She smiled. "Everyone has bad days."

He returned her smile with as much of one as he could manage. "Thanks, I've got one more box for you, and then that should do it."

"Fine, just put it there with the rest."

He touched his hat to her and walked out the door. Just outside he stopped abruptly, his eyes narrowing as he watched the buckboard slowly pulling away from him down the street, the mules walking steadily forward with their ears twitching. Turning sharply he saw Joe and Beth a little way down the sidewalk speaking to Alice and Kathy Harper.

In that moment Adam forgot he was supposed to be a calm, reasonable man, forgot he was standing in front of Cass's General Store in the middle of Virginia City, forgot Mrs. Hammburg's warning about Clem and Clare.

"JOE!" Adam bellowed, in a voice that left no doubt that he was the son of Ben Cartwright. The sound turned heads all up and down the street. Joe and Beth spun around, and stared wide-eyed at him, and then their eyes opened wider as they looked past him. Seeing the look on their faces Adam turned. True to Widow Hammburg's word, Adam's bellow had sent the mules dashing down the street, scattering produce, milk, and roses as they went.

"Come on, Adam, we've got to catch them!" Joe yelled, snagging Adam's arm as he rushed past. Both men dashed after the runaway mules, which were now well on their way down Union Street. They made the turn onto G Street and Adam's face scrunched as the buckboard tilted onto two wheels and he waited for it to overturn. It didn't and the mules continued their wild careening down G Street. The speed of the mules had sent them far to the side of the street, and the buckboard slid into the boardwalk, sending barrels and crates soaring, increasing the chaos and destruction left in the wake of the flying mules.

Breathless Adam and Joe continued the chase, shouting and waving at those in the wagon's path. Praying that they moved in time. Adam knew if anyone was hurt from this disaster he would never forgive himself. Miraculously, the mules made it down G Street, leaving men and women, shaken but unscathed, behind them.

Adam hoped the mules tired soon. He wasn't sure how much longer he could keep up the chase. He could hear Joe wheezing beside him, as they both tried to squeeze a little more speed from already rubbery legs. He heard Sheriff Coffee yell as they sped past the jail, but couldn't make out what he said, and didn't really care at the moment.

Up ahead he saw the mules approaching the livery and the turn onto Washington. Adam slowed and closed his eyes as he anticipated the crash; he was sure the mules were going too fast to make the turn. But the crash didn't come as the mules suddenly made a mad dash left onto Washington. Adam stopped in relief, then he saw the buckboard tip onto two wheels once again, and he held his breath hoping. Only this time the speed was too great and he watched in horror as it swung wide and overturned. The momentum sent the whole mass—mules, buckboard and all—sliding with a crashing halt into the wide front windows of the Virginia City Bank.

To Adam's ears the silence following the crash was horribly loud. He stood mesmerized by the confused tangle of mules, buckboard and bank. He felt Joe beside him, shaking his head.

"Oh, boy... Oh, boy, Adam, are we in for it now," his voice quavered. "Pa's gonna have our hide for sure."

Adam couldn't respond. He turned and looked around at the destruction surrounding him. Men and women were picking themselves up from the dirt where they had leapt out of the mules' path. Boardwalks and hitching posts all along the street were shattered where the buckboard had crashed into them. Produce lay scattered among the remains of the crates and boxes the mules had sent flying. Cheese, butter, and milk mingled together in large smears among the broken jars and crocks they had been stored in. But most poignant of all, to Adam's way of thinking, were the roses; Widow Hammburg's gorgeous roses that were strewn over everything, their velvety colors mocking the desolation over which they lay.

JOE STOPPING IN front of him brought Adam back to the present. He raised his eyebrows at him and waited expectantly.

"Well?" Joe asked again impatiently. "What are we gonna tell Pa?"

"I don't know, Joe," Adam finally acknowledged, rubbing a hand across his face. The damages alone would set them back several thousand, not to mention the fines Sheriff Coffee was threatening them with. Thank goodness, the mules had been fine. A little scuffed up and a little jittery, but not seriously harmed.

"Yeah, well, we'd better come up with something, because Pa's gonna be madder than a polecat with his tail in a trap when he finds out!" Joe pointed out peevishly, his anxiety turning to frustration as his normally astute brother failed to come up with a way out of the mess.

"Don't you think I know that?!" Adam's own temper flared in the face of his brother's accusing tone. "It's not like it was entirely my fault you know! You were the one who suggested we help her!"

"Well, what was I supposed to do? Leave poor Widow Hammburg to take care of it all by herself?"

"Under the circumstances, that might have been best, yes! And if you did have to help, you should have left that niece of hers at home."

"Don't bring Beth into this, she had nothing to do with it!" Joe warned.

"You'd better believe she had something to do with it. If you hadn't been so moonstruck over her, none of this would have happened!" Adam retorted.

"Yeah, well, well..." Joe couldn't think of a response knowing that Adam was at least partially right.

The two brothers glared at each other for a moment. Then seeing the remorse in Joe's eyes, Adam sighed, and lowered his own. "Never mind, Joe. It was as much my fault as yours. I shouldn't have lost my temper."

Joe sat down next to his brother, and cupped his chin in his hands. "And I should have stayed with the wagon." They sat in silence a moment. "So what are we going to do?" he asked, his voice once again apprehensive.

Adam turned to him. "The only thing we can do. Tell Pa the truth, and hope we're still in one piece when he's through with us," he said resignedly.

"Somehow that doesn't sound like a very good plan, Adam." Joe protested, straightening.

"Well, if you've got a better idea, I wouldn't mind hearing it," Adam countered.

Joe sighed and shook his head. "No, you're right." He plopped his chin back onto his hands. The two men sat side by side, both in deep thought, both dreading the confrontation before them. Finally Joe spoke.

"Adam?"

"Hmm?"

"I'm really glad you're in this one with me this time."

Adam turned to his brother and gave him a lop-sided smile. "Uh, thanks, I think," he said amusedly.

"No, I mean it. Usually it's me and Hoss in hot water." Joe's voice was sincere. "I don't know, somehow, it just doesn't seem as bad knowing you're going to get it, too."

Adam looked into Joe's earnest green eyes and reached over

and ruffled his brother's hair fondly. "Well, I'm glad it helps." He smiled at him, and Joe grinned back.

The sound of the door opening caused them both to turn, and then stand quickly as their father walked in. Ben's face was stern as he laid his hat on the credenza to the left of the door.

"Boys, is there something you need to tell me?" he asked his voice deep and ominous.

Joe looked at Adam and gulped. Adam looked at Ben and tried to smile, but the look in his father's eyes killed it before it had a chance to begin. Pursing his lips together, he took a deep breath then let it out slowly. "Well, Pa, you see, it was like this..."

A Father's Prerogative

by Judy A. Lee

$\mathcal{H}$is shirt ringed with sweat, Little Joe took a long, satisfy-ing, drink from his canteen and then impulsively poured some water over his head to cool off. "Boy, will I be glad when this job's done," he exclaimed to his brothers.

Hoss nodded and took off his work gloves. "Yeah, me too," he said, wiping the sweat from his eyes. "I didn't figure on there bein' this much work."

Adam smiled ruefully. He was fairly certain Pa figured on it. Against his wishes, they'd taken a mid-week trip into town and thanks to Hoss's enjoyment of a good ruckus, had ended up in the midst of a barroom brawl. Consequently, he and his brothers had shown up at the breakfast table bruised and bleary-eyed; but instead of raising the roof with an ear-splitting lecture, Pa had merely suggested they load up the wagon and check out the fence line in the east pasture. "Yes, well, something tells me *Pa* knew the extent of it."

Joe gave him a curious look. "What do you mean by that, Adam?"

"Yeah," Hoss said, scrunching his face and wondering the same. As far as he knew, Pa had been in a pretty good mood this morning considering the little disagreement they'd had last night...and how late they'd gotten in...and how late they'd been to breakfast...and how banged up they were. Oh no! He gulped and waited to hear what Adam had to say with a sinking feeling.

Adam grinned at Hoss's pained expression. He could see his middle brother was having second thoughts about their supposed good fortune. "I mean our bruises didn't go unnoticed," he said, pulling his shirt from his pants and letting it hang loose, "and while Pa may not know the particulars, I'd bet my last dollar we're being treated to the proverbial slap on the wrist."

Hoss didn't know what proverbial meant, but he got the gist of it and nodded miserably. "Yeah, I reckon you're probably right. We told Pa we'd be fit for a full day's work and it'd be just like him to make us prove it. Dadburnit! No wonder he didn't yell."

Joe scowled, not wanting to believe it. "Aw, come on you two," he entreated. "He didn't yell because we're all adults, plain and simple. One thing's got nothing to do with the other. It just so happened the fence needed a lot of work...and it was just bad luck we had to chase down a few strays before we could get started...and that we had to use the team horses...all on an exceptionally hot day."

Adam and Hoss both gave him a humorous look, neither answering.

"What?" Joe exclaimed earnestly. "Is that so farfetched?"

Adam shook his head and smiled. When it came to matters of importance, he had no doubt Pa respected him as a man, but when it came to dumb trouble like this, he also knew the years had a way of disappearing and one way or another he'd be held accountable, especially if he'd thrown in with his younger brothers. With Joe being seventeen, there was no question about it. "Under the circumstances, I'd say he's letting us wallow in our own foolishness, little brother."

Joe heard the confidence in his voice and let out a defeated sigh. As much as he didn't want to admit it, his oldest brother was generally right when it came to second-guessing Pa. "Well, at least we didn't have to sit through a lecture."

"Oh, he'll get around to it," Adam replied. "He always does."

"Great," Joe muttered. "Something to look forward to."

Hoss chuckled and gave him a slap on the back. "Cheer up, little brother. Even if Pa does get to hollerin', ol Adam here is gonna get the worst of it." He smiled at Adam, his eyes twinkling. "As the oldest and self-proclaimed wisest, he should've set a better example."

Joe's eyes widened and a mischievous smile lit his face. "That's right," he said, nodding. "If older brother hadn't sent Jeff Bonner sailing over the bar with a round-house punch to the jaw, I never would've done the same to Rick's sorry hide."

Adam rolled his eyes. The truth was he *had* used bad judgment, not so much by fighting, but by siding with his brothers against Pa in the first place. There was no blaming them for that though; he'd had his own reasons for wanting to take an impromptu trip into town. But did his plans pan out? Did he get to track down the captivating woman he'd shared the stage with last week? No! Thanks to Hoss, he'd had to fatten a few lips, and he was just about to remind him of it when he spotted some riders closing in on them from across the meadow. His eyes narrowed. "Looks like we've got company," he announced as he kept an eye on the approaching men and retrieved a rifle.

Hoss and Joe followed his gaze and then hastily picked up their guns from the back of the wagon, feeling the same unease as their brother. "Who do you reckon it is?" Hoss asked.

Joe shook his head. "There's six of 'em, but I can't make anyone out. They're kickin' up too much dust."

Adam stared hard at the men and their mounts, looking for

something that might identify them. "They're coming in fast, all right."

Hoss took up a position behind the wagon and motioned for his brothers to do the same before they were all caught out in the open. "Too fast, if you ask me; maybe somebody's ridin' their tail."

"Or maybe they're *on* somebody's tail," Adam said, suddenly relaxing his stance and smiling. "That fella on the right is Roy."

Joe squinted. "Yeah, and the Zimmerman brothers are with him."

Hoss frowned. They might not be in any danger, but something bad had happened. "Must be a posse, then. Nothin' else would get Lane and Mark to shut down the smithy in the middle of the day."

Adam nodded and after trading a sober look with his brothers, he stepped around the wire and poles scattered on the ground and hailed the sheriff. Roy waved and rode up alongside him. Despite the serious nature of his business, he couldn't resist a little teasing. "Well now," he exclaimed, his mouth twitching into a little smile, "I'm kinda surprised to see you boys workin' so hard. I thought for sure you'd be nursing your bruises after that spectacle last night."

Fully aware Roy could have thrown them in jail, in addition to the heavy fine he'd levied against them, Adam held his tongue, but couldn't help the dry smile.

The men, as did Roy, let out a low chuckle. "Yeah," Lane said, ribbing him some more, "you fellas must've smashed every stick of furniture and every bottle in the place. I saw Cosmo this morning and he was still cussing you out. Says you're gonna end up owing him close to five hunnerd dollars."

Adam flushed, uncomfortable at having caused such damage and more than a little embarrassed that it seemed to be common knowledge. He glanced up at Roy, hoping to change the subject. "Surely, that's not what brought you out here, is it?"

The fun over, Roy sobered. "No, I'm sorry to say it's something a might more serious. Three men robbed the bank this morning and got away with close to fifty thousand dollars. Me and the boys tracked them to the mesa, but with it bein' so rocky around those parts, we lost their trail."

"Sounds like they know the territory," Joe commented.

Hoss's expression darkened. It was wrong any way you looked at it, but the idea of robbing from folks you knew was something that made his blood boil. "Anyone get hurt?"

Roy nodded. "They beat Mr. Weems pretty bad. Doc Martin's not sure if he'll make it."

Adam gave Roy a grim look. "You want us to scout around with you?"

Roy shook his head. "No, I just wanted to warn you," he said signaling to the men to head out again. "I rode by the house earlier, so your Pa knows to keep a lookout."

Adam nodded with a thoughtful expression and watched the posse ride off. It was likely Pa would worry, but if they got a move on they could finish the repairs and still get back to the ranch before it got to be too late. As it was, they'd be back after dark anyway. "All right, you two, let's get back to work, these post holes aren't gonna dig themselves."

BACK AT THE ranch, Ben sat at his desk, the ledgers open but ignored. It was well after sundown and his mind was on his sons. *Where are they? They should be home by now.* Standing up, he peered out the window, his thoughts worriedly drifting to the men who'd robbed the bank. Desperate men. Men who wouldn't hesitate to kill. Seeing no sign of the wagon, he sat down heavily in his chair.

Hop Sing came from the kitchen with a pot of coffee. "Don't worry," he said to Ben, smiling and pouring him a cup. "Boys be home soon, you'll see."

Ben gratefully took it. "Thank you, Hop Sing, but I'm not worried," he said, dismissing the idea as preposterous. "I'm just annoyed. They know what time we eat."

Hop Sing shook his head, not fooled by his boss's demeanor. "Why you look for trouble?" he asked. "Bad men probably long gone by now."

Startled by his directness, Ben eyed Hop Sing but didn't keep up the pretense. He admitted his worries with a brief nod. "I suppose you're right," he said, feeling a little foolish.

Hop Sing nodded and then headed back to the kitchen, knowing full well the worries of a father were not so easily alleviated. Mr. Cartwright wouldn't stop worrying until those boys showed up safe and sound, but it didn't hurt to try.

He's right, the boys are fine, Ben thought firmly. He'd sent them out to do a job and that's exactly what they were doing. He sipped his coffee and was still trying to convince himself when he heard the wagon pulling into the yard. He let out a relieved sigh and after a quick word of thanks, he went to the door. He found them on the porch, stomping their boots and knocking the dust off their clothes.

"Hi Pa," Adam said with an apologetic smile. "Sorry we're late, but we had an awful lot of work to do...as I'm sure you know."

A bit of humor sparked in Ben's eyes while his middle son went on to explain. "Yeah, a whole bunch of steers strayed through that break in the fence line. We had to round 'em all up before we could even get started."

"But don't you worry, Pa," Joe added with a smile, "we got 'em all back where they belong and finished sinkin' them new poles."

Ben nodded. It was just ordinary chatter, but it made his eyes shine. He was glad for the darkness lest his sons think him a silly old fool. "Good, good," he answered, "now go on, get inside, supper's almost ready."

Hoss sniffed the air appreciatively. "Hey Pa, is that roast pork I smell?"

Ben smiled. "Roast pork and sweet potatoes," he replied, giving Hoss an affectionate pat on the arm as he shooed him in the door. "Now go on, get washed up."

Turning to Little Joe, he gave him a gentle swat. "That goes for you too, young man. Hop Sing will have a fit if that meat dries up."

"Yes sir," Joe said with a grin as he hurried into the house, leaving Adam behind.

Adam eyed his father as they went through the door. The fact that he was awfully glad to see them hadn't escaped his notice. "Are you all right?"

Ben put his arm across Adam's shoulders. "Of course I am," he replied pleasantly. "Why do you ask?"

"Oh, I don't know," Adam said, drawing his words out. "I just thought you might've been worried. We saw Roy and he mentioned he'd come by the house."

"Now Adam, I know perfectly well you boys can take care of yourselves." It was a truthful albeit evasive answer and they both knew it.

A small smile played at the corners of Adam's mouth as he dared to press the issue. "Sure you do," he said, sounding unconvinced, "and I suppose that's why you seemed so happy to see us, right?"

Ben nodded slowly. No matter how old his sons were, he'd worry in times of trouble. It was a father's prerogative, just like it was a father's prerogative to sometimes set his wayward sons straight. "You're right, I *am* happy to see you boys," he said, his voice noticeably gruff now. "I believe you three have a lecture coming and I intend to deliver it just as soon as we're done with supper!"

The Grandest of Homecomings

by Camera_Chic

*H*oss slowly rolled over and then stretched his arms over his head. Taking a deep breath, he held it for a moment before letting it out with a contented sigh. The slamming of a door farther down the hall startled him out of his morning reverie, and he groaned and rolled onto his stomach. He heard his bedroom door crash open, and then his little brother yelled, "Adam's comin' home today! Hoss! Hoss, get up! Adam's comin' home today!" Hoss grunted as his breath was suddenly knocked out of him by the solid weight of Little Joe landing on his back. "Get up!" Joe yelled.

"Dadburnit," Hoss gasped. "He ain't comin' home 'til late tonight."

"But ain't you excited?" Joe asked.

Hoss pictured the nine-year-old's face, and had to sigh. He

rolled over, dumping Joe onto the floor. "Hey!" Joe yelped.

"Yeah, I'm excited. But it's also five-thirty in the morning, Joe."

"Yeah, but you normally get up now."

Hoss sighed again, and then smiled at Joe. "Why don't you go out and get started on the chores, since you're already up."

Joe thought for a moment, but obviously didn't realize the multiple purposes of that suggestion because he scrambled off the floor and said, "Okay. But hurry down, Hoss. We got a lot to plan today."

"We planned everythin' yesterday, Joe."

Joe didn't hear him, as he was already racing out of Hoss's room. He turned the corner, and plowed directly into Hop Sing. Much to Joe's relief, it was he, and not their cook, who ended up on his backside on the floor. "I'm sorry, Hop Sing!" he exclaimed as he stood up.

"Yell! Yell too much, early in morning!" Hop Sing admonished.

"I'm sorry, but Adam's comin' home today!" Joe grinned.

"Lucky father not here, not be happy with you yell. Brother not happy either." Hop Sing put his hand on Joe's shoulder and led him down the hall and downstairs. "You go; go get eight fresh eggs."

"What are you making, Hop Sing?"

"Flapjacks, eggs, ham."

Joe grinned. "Sounds great!" He turned and tore out the front door, yelling as he ran across the yard, "Adam's comin' home today! Adam's comin' home today!"

Hop Sing chuckled, and then turned back towards the kitchen. He set out some bowls, and then went to a counter near the door and picked up a sheet of paper and a pencil. He read it over, and then added two more things to the bottom, just in case the youngest Cartwright finished the other 27 chores before Adam and Ben arrived home.

HOSS TURNED FROM the window as he heard Hop Sing walk up behind him. He did his best to hide the disappointed look on his face. "I guess it took 'em longer than we thought."

Hop Sing nodded sympathetically. "Long ride from San Francisco. Be home tomorrow."

Hoss nodded, and then glanced back towards the window. "I guess I should make Joe come in now."

Hop Sing glanced out the window, where Joe paced back and forth along the porch step, occasionally glancing towards the trees bordering the darkening sky. "Let him wait few more minutes. I call him in."

"Thanks, Hop Sing. Good night," Hoss said, and then went upstairs, glancing once more towards the window and his brother.

Outside, Joe sank onto the step, and reached out, breaking a twig off of one of the bushes that grew near the house. He was tired and disappointed. He ground the twig between his fingers, before tossing it aside. The door opened behind him, and Joe glanced back to see Hop Sing coming outside. The man settled into a chair near Joe and looked out into the yard.

After a few minutes, Joe sighed. "They're not comin' tonight, are they?"

"Long journey," Hop Sing replied. "They arrive tomorrow."

"But Hoss and me worked so hard to get things ready today. We cleaned everything, and made decorations, and put up the sign..." Joe glanced up where the long strip of cloth still hung off the front of the house. Welcome home, Adam! it exclaimed. He and Hoss had worked on it for days.

"Tonight's disappointments be gone tomorrow. Go now, sleep. Father and brother be here tomorrow."

Joe sighed, and then stood up reluctantly. "Good night, Hop Sing," he said, and then went inside to his room to wash and change. Just as he was ready to climb into bed, he paused. He quickly left his room and then went to the next one. He knew Adam's room was spotless, even though it was too dark to see.

Hop Sing had cleaned it a week ago, and then Joe insisted on cleaning it again himself. And again. There wasn't one speck of dust anywhere. Joe closed the door behind him, and went to the bed, feeling around with his hand until he found the object he was looking for. He sat down, holding it. It was Adam's drawing set.

Before Adam left, their father had purchased him a special technical set to take east with him, and he had left this one behind. He had given it to Joe to take care of for him until he returned. Now, Joe knew what had had been doing; but as a child, it was quite an important responsibility, and he took it very seriously. He made sure the tools were clean, and he kept the box in a special place in his room. He had left it for Adam today, and a small part of him really hoped that Adam remembered giving him the responsibility, and would praise him for doing it well. The rest of him knew that it wasn't something that even needed to be done to begin with; yet, he still craved that praise.

Joe sighed and put the set down on the nightstand, and then sank back onto the bed with his eyes closed. What would Adam be like now?

A FEW HOURS later, Ben and his eldest son stumbled, exhausted, into the house. Neither of them had wanted to stop, being so close to home, so they had pushed on. Ben glanced at the clock. "It's almost one o'clock. You'd better go get some sleep. I'm sure Joe will be waking you bright and early tomorrow."

Adam chuckled, and Ben noted once again how much, and how little, his son had changed. "I'll welcome that greeting. I can hardly wait to see them both."

Ben smiled and patted Adam on the arm. "Good to have you home, son."

"I'm glad to be home. Goodnight, Pa," he said, and then went upstairs quietly, after grabbing a lamp. He reached his room, and then paused as he entered. With a smile, he closed the door behind him and then set the lamp down. For a few minutes, he just stood next to his bed, looking down at his youngest brother. He was all arms and legs now it seemed, and his hair was a mess of thick curls, unlike the baby-fine locks they had been. He had thick curly lashes, and a small defined nose, and those ears! Well, he hadn't quite grown into them yet. Even so, he was becoming quite a handsome young man, Adam had to admit.

Finally Adam shook his head, and moved to pick up his brother, but then paused. He didn't want to wake him. Carefully, Adam got changed, and then pulled a couple of blankets from the chest at the foot of his bed. He covered Joe up, and picked up the light and walked to the other side of the bed, where he got settled in. He looked once more to make sure Joe was still asleep, and then put out the lamp.

"ADAM! ADAM! ADAM! Adam, you're here! You're here, Adam! Adam!"

Finally Adam opened his eyes, to see his brother jumping excitedly up and down on the bed.

"You're home! You're home! You're home! Adam!"

Adam burst into laughter, and then swept Joe into his arms. "I missed you, buddy!" He felt his brother's arms wrap around tightly around him.

"I sure missed you," Joe whispered. After a few minutes he pulled away. "Wait til you see; we have so much to do today! We're going on a picnic at the lake, and we'll go see everything, we can go fishing, and tomorrow's your surprise party, and Hoss and I built a new corral in the back, and you have to see the horse I raised and she's a month away from having her foal, and...and..." Finally Joe ran out of air and words, and Adam grinned at him.

"Sounds like fun."

Joe grinned back, and then stood up on the bed. "Wahoo!" he shrieked, and then jumped off the bed and charged for the door. "Hoss! Hoss! He's here! He's here!"

Adam watched him leave, laughing, and then sighed and got out of bed. He wasn't likely to get a full night's rest for a couple of days, he was sure.

"Come on, come on, come on!" Adam heard Joe coaxing impatiently, and after a few seconds, Hoss half stumbled into the room with Joe right behind him.

"Adam!" grinned Hoss, and stepped forward and gave him big bear hug. "How was your trip?"

"It was fine. Glad to finally be home." Adam appraised his middle brother. He had grown too, since he left, and was now a bit taller than him, and definitely bigger.

Ben appeared in the doorway just then, rather ruffled, admonishing, "Boys."

Joe and Hoss turned to him. "Sorry, Pa," they said in unison.

Adam laughed. Things hadn't changed that much.

"WHAT WAS THE East like, Adam?" Joe asked.

Adam glanced over at Joe, and past him towards Hoss, who was looking interested as well. "Well," he started, settling back against the rock he was leaning on. "There were lots of people, and buildings. They have paved streets, not just dirt roads."

"What do paved streets look like?"

"It's like rock...laid down in a path between the buildings. And there are gas lamps along it to light the way at night."

"Wow..." breathed Joe. "How big are the buildings?"

"They are really big. So high, they have a lot of layers in them. Remember the drawings I was showing you, of some of the buildings I was reading about before I went?" Joe nodded. "Just like that."

"I can't imagine what they would look like in person," Joe said.

"They must be amazing."

"They certainly are. I'm sure soon you'll get to see some large buildings. More and more people are moving out this way, and pretty soon those people are going to want some of the things they were used to in the East."

"I got one!" Hoss yelled, pulling at his fishing line.

"Don't lose him! Don't lose him! Easy now!" Joe dropped his line, and leaned over Hoss, yelling encouragement in his ear.

"Joe, get off me, you're going to make me lose 'em!" Hoss yelped.

"Watch out! Watch out, he's gettin' away!" Joe yelled, and reached out and pulled at Hoss' line.

"Joe, I mean it!"

Joe yanked the line out of the water, flinging the fish into the air and his brother into the lake. "Ya got him, Hoss!" Joe yelled, oblivious to the fact that Hoss was now in the water under the branch he had been seated on. "Ya got him!" he shouted happily and put the fish on the line with the others they had caught, and then looked back, finally noticing the empty branch. He looked at Adam. "Where'd he go?"

Adam let out a guffaw at his obvious confusion. There was a splash, and then their wet and rather angry looking middle brother scrambled out of the water. He started towards Joe, who moved towards Adam. "Sorry Hoss!" Joe yelped, expecting Adam to protect him. Instead, he yelled in surprise as Adam caught his arms and held him in a bear hug.

"What do you want to do with this younger brother of ours?" Adam asked, trying to keep from laughing.

"Hey, this isn't right! Let go, Adam! I didn't mean it Hoss, honest!"

Hoss grinned. "I think he wants to go for a swim too, seein' as how much I enjoyed it."

"No! No!" screeched Joe, as his brothers grabbed his arms. "If I drown, Pa will tan ya both!" he yelled. They tossed him in, and then Adam laughed along with Hoss, waiting for Joe to come back up. After a few seconds, the water was still only rippling from the original splash.

"Hoss, he can swim, right?" Adam asked.

Hoss laughed. "Sure he can," he said, and then looked nervously into the water. "I mean, we were both swimmin' just fine last summer...he can swim..." he trailed off, all his confidence lost.

Adam quickly stripped off his shirt, and dove into the water, trying to look through the murky haze for his brother. The splash nearby told him that Hoss had joined him, and he swam, searching for a while before coming up for air. Hoss splashed to the surface just after him.

Adam was about to go down again when the sound of laughter stopped him. Turning towards the edge of the lake, he saw Joe doubled over on the ground. "Joseph!" he roared. "That wasn't funny!"

Joe stopped laughing for a full second, and then started giggling again, scrambling to his feet. "Sorry, older brother. Serves you right for throwing me in."

Adam shook his head. "Not the same at all. I wasn't intending to kill you."

"No, but I got you wet," Joe replied, before collapsing in a fit of laughter again. Adam splashed water at him, and Joe, instead of leaping out of the way, moved forward and extended his hand for his brother. Adam sighed and accepted it, and then they pulled Hoss out of the water.

"Let's go home and get dried off before someone gets sick," Adam said, putting an arm around Joe.

"Yeah, you wouldn't want to be sick for your surprise party," Joe said.

"Joe!" Hoss hissed, and Joe clamped a hand over his mouth.

Adam chuckled. "It's all right, Joe. I think you've mentioned it about three times so far."

"Joe, it was called 'surprise' for a reason!" Hoss admonished.

"I'm sorry, I didn't realize I was sayin' it!"

Adam shook his head. "It's all right, I'll just pretend I didn't hear it."

"Okay," Joe said, and happily wrapped his arm around Adam as they walked back towards their horses, lines and fish in tow.

JOE GLANCED AROUND carefully, tugging at the tie around his neck. Certain that no one was looking at him, he dipped the ladle into the punchbowl, and then poured the liquid into his glass. He dropped the ladle back into the bowl, and then turned quickly; right into Adam.

"Thank you, little brother," Adam said, taking the drink out of his hand. "Allow me return the favor by getting you a lemonade."

Joe rolled his eyes at him, and then took the glass he handed him with a sigh.

"I know you've already had at least one glass of punch tonight," Adam said. "And unless you want Pa to notice, this," he held up the glass he was holding, "Had better have been your last dip in the punchbowl for the evening."

"Yes, sir," Joe sighed.

Ben walked up to them just then, a young woman trailing him slightly. "Adam, Joe," Ben greeted. "Allow me to present Miss Abigail Jones. This is my eldest son, Adam, and Joseph you already know."

She giggled slightly as Adam took her hand, and Joe wrinkled his nose. "A pleasure to meet you," Adam said, bowing slightly.

"I am so happy to meet you. Your father tells me you just arrived home from the university. It's so wonderful to meet a cultured and educated gentleman in these parts."

Joe quickly stepped away. "Excuse me, please," he said, and when the adults nodded, he hurried away to find Hoss. Finally locating him in the kitchen where he was sampling some of the desserts Hop Sing had prepared, Joe sank into a chair with a frustrated sigh. "Can you believe her, Hoss? 'So happy to meet you...such a cultured gentleman...'" he mimicked Abigail. "It's sickening. I bet she conned Pa into introducing her to Adam just so she could talk to him about that stupid school idea."

"Oh, you're talking about Miss Jones," Hoss responded. "Pa doesn't think the school idea is stupid."

"But it is!" Joe protested. "I don't want to go to school!"

"Boys." Joe and Hoss turned to see Ben standing in the doorway. "Maybe you two should leave the kitchen and help entertain our guests."

"Yes sir," they replied together, and then followed their father back into the main room.

That evening, after the last guest had left, Joe finally cornered Adam as he was wiping down the dining room table. "I'm not going to school," he said. "I already know all I ever need to know to run the ranch. There's no need for me to learn any other nonsense about readin' and writin'. I'm good enough, and I'm not going." It was a carefully rehearsed speech, and he was a little taken back when his brother laughed.

"Joe, they don't even have a building yet, and already you refuse to go." Adam handed him two glasses.

Joe took them with a frown. "She wants to use the backroom in the mercantile until she builds a school."

"Well, she's not going to build it. The men in this growing community of families are going to build it."

"There aren't enough children to go."

"There's at least ten."

"Nine," Joe argued stubbornly.

Adam turned to him with an exasperated sigh. "Joe, do you think I'd travel for weeks, move all the way across the country, and live there away from my family for years if I didn't think that education was important to the growth of society?"

Joe thought for a moment. "I don't matter that much to society."

Adam snorted and turned away from him. "When you're helping run this ranch, you will."

"I already know everything."

"Joseph, why don't we save this argument until there's actually a school to fight about going to."

THE OPENING OF the school came very quickly. Ben was just as interested in starting the school as Adam, and with the two of them influencing the other leaders of the small but growing Carson City, plans for a schoolhouse were drawn up quickly. Books were ordered from San Francisco, and it was arranged to use a small room in back of the mercantile until the school building was constructed.

Joe observed all this with a sinking heart. He tried several different tactics to delay the inevitable, but with both his brother and father pushing for the new school, he knew it was a hopeless battle before he even started to fight.

The night before the first day of school, he lay awake in bed, trying to think of any other argument to get out of going. He'd already tried convincing them he was too old, that he was needed much more around the ranch, that it wasn't fair because Hoss didn't have to go, and that he already knew everything he needed too. He grumpily rolled over. It wasn't fair.

There was a gentle knock on the door, and then it was opened. "I know you're not asleep yet," Adam said. Joe rolled over and sighed. His brother walked across the room and sat down next to him. "Look, I got these for you."

Joe sat up, and looked at the objects Adam was holding. A slate and pencil, a paper tablet, three books, and a pen and ink bottle. "Adam..." he breathed. He leaned over and gave his brother a hug. "Thank you."

"I'll leave these here," Adam said, setting them on the table next to his bed. He turned back, and then smiled slightly at his brother. "I'm so proud of you, buddy. You know, you're getting something I always wanted growing up; the chance for a real education. I know you don't want to go, but you'll see...you'll really like it, I know you will."

Joe looked down at his hands. "But I really don't want to go. I don't want to leave the ranch, and Pa, and Hoss...or you."

Adam put his hand on the side of Joe's face. "Hey, I know. I didn't want to leave either. But at least you'll get to come home every day, and you'll still see all of us when you get here." Joe forced himself to smile at his brother, and then Adam smacked him gently and said, "Go on, get some rest. You don't want to fall asleep on the first day of school." He got up and left the room.

BEN LOOKED UP as Adam pulled the wagon to a stop in the yard. Adam set the brake, and then hopped down and started unhitching the team. Ben walked forward to help him. "How is our little scholar?" Ben asked.

Adam laughed. "You'd think he was being led to his death rather than a schoolroom."

"Were there many children?"

"About seven, I think. There weren't any older boys though."

Ben nodded. He and Adam had suspected that would happen, but didn't let on to Joe, knowing it would cause yet another argument. Most of the boys Joe's age were needed around their farms and ranches this time of year. Once most of the work was done they would be sent to school, but for now, Joe was likely to be the oldest boy there for a few months.

"What exactly did you tell Abigail Jones about me?"

"What do you mean, what did I tell her? I told her I had a son who valued education a great deal, and she seemed excited to present the school idea to you, to try to get it going. Why?"

"She seems to have some ideas, that's all."

"Abigail Jones?" Ben said in surprise. "I don't see why...she doesn't even know that much about you."

"Oh, yes she does," Adam said. "She knows where I went to

school, what I studied, how long I was there...and my favorite meals," he finished almost in a mumble.

Ben tried to keep from laughing. "How did that come up in conversation?"

"She invited me to her house, to have dinner with her and her mother and discuss the school."

"And what did you say?"

"Come on, Pa, it isn't funny. All she keeps talking about is how sophisticated I am, and how wonderful Boston must be...do you know she's never been there? She was born in Iowa. She said it was her lifelong dream to visit Boston some day. And New York, and Philadelphia." Adam sighed as he pulled one of the horses away from the wagon and tied the lead rope to a rail. "I just want to know who told her everything about me."

"I think that was Joe's doin'." Ben and Hoss looked towards Hoss, who had joined them. "He talked about you to anyone who would listen the last month or so. Miss Jones listened a lot."

"Wonderful," Adam muttered.

"I don't think he intended anything," Hoss said quickly. "He was just so excited that you were coming back home, well...I guess he said a lot. He made you out to be quite a hero."

Adam looked down intently at the buckle he was trying to undo as his anger quickly faded. He knew Joe had been excited to see him, but he hadn't realized just how much.

"Mr. Cartwright!" They all looked up to see one of their hands quickly riding towards them. He came to a stop. "We're gonna need some help...there's about six cattle and two little ones stuck in a mud patch. We can't get near 'em."

Ben, Adam, and Hoss quickly went into the barn, saddling their horses and grabbing ropes and axes, in case they needed to cut a few branches. Within a few minutes they were ready, and followed the man back to where the animals were trapped.

JOE SIGHED AND stood up. He'd been waiting almost a half hour for someone to come get him. All he had been looking forward to all day was seeing Adam outside, waiting with the wagon; but the street was still empty.

School had been long and difficult. They had done reading and writing in the morning, and then after lunch it was arithmetic, spelling, and history. All through the day, she had corrected them when they used improper language, made too much noise, or even spoke without raising a hand first. It was hard to remember all that, and then with the added difficulty of learning new things, and having no one his age to talk to...it had turned into a rough day.

"Joseph."

He turned and looked back as Miss Jones walked out of the mercantile.

"Where is your brother?"

He glanced back down the street. "I dunno, maybe somethin' held him up on the ranch, Ma'am."

"I see. Would you like me to wait with you?"

Joe shook his head, trying not to appear to be too against the idea. "No, ma'am, there's no need, really. He'll be here soon, I'm sure." Joe looked down the street again, and to his relief saw the familiar wagon coming closer. "There he is," he said, picking his books up and moving closer to the street.

As the wagon drew closer, Joe was slightly disappointed to see Hoss driving. "Sorry I'm late, Joe. Some critters got stuck in a mud hole, and me and Pa and Adam spent all day gettin' them out."

"It's all right, Hoss." Joe climbed onto the wagon next to his brother. "Goodbye, Miss Jones," he called.

As soon as they were away, Hoss let out a laugh he had obviously been holding back.

"What is it? What's so funny?" Joe asked.

"You and Miss Jones," Hoss chortled. "The two of you had practically the same face when you saw it was me drivin' and not

Adam." He started laughing again.

"It's not funny!" Joe snapped. "She had no right to be disappointed that he didn't come. I've been waitin' all day. Where is he, Hoss?"

"Back home, of course."

When Hoss didn't say anything else, Joe tried again. "Hoss...why didn't Adam come and get me? He said he would!"

"Joe...it was on account of Miss Jones...she said somethin' to him this mornin', I'm not sure what, but I know he didn't want to see her again today."

"What'd she say?"

"I already told you, I don't know. And he was mighty upset that she knew so much about him."

"What are you talkin' about?"

"All that talkin' you did with Miss Jones...tellin' her all about him. You better not do that anymore, Joe."

"Oh." Joe was quiet for a few moments. He hadn't realized the effects his talking had. "Well, at least there's nothin' left to tell her."

Hoss let out a guffaw, and urged the horses a little faster. They were almost home.

JOE DROPPED HIS head to the table with a sigh. They were just meaningless numbers staring at him. He knew how to add and subtract, but this whole multiplication thing was confusing. Miss Jones had explained it to the children a couple of different ways, and all of the others seemed to understand. That frustrated him the most. He picked his head back up, and then looked at the paper again. She had given them two assignments for arithmetic...to solve 20 problems and to write out the multiplication table three times.

"What are you working on?"

Joe looked up at Adam, glad for his company. "Multiplication," he replied. "Could you help me?"

"Certainly," Adam said as he pulled a chair next to him.

"I already wrote out the multiplication table, but it's not really helping."

"Hmm..." Adam looked at the paper with Joe's solutions written. "Yes, that certainly...isn't right." He glanced up. "Sorry," he said in response to the glare Joe gave him. "Well, it isn't that hard to figure it out. The difficult thing is remembering the rules...here..." Adam took his slate and pencil, and wrote down the problem. "Now, you just use the table to help solve it. You have 125 multiplied by 21...is she really starting you off with problems this hard?" Joe nodded. "Well, never mind, once you get the principle...here, you start on the right, and look at your table...what's one times five?"

"Five," Joe replied.

"Good, so you put five underneath the line I just drew, and now move onto the next number..." Adam finished the problem, talking it out as he went, and when he finished, Joe had a little more understanding of the process, even though he didn't quite understand the reason. Adam talked him through the next two, and then let him solve the remaining ones on his own, only speaking up when Joe got confused. "Very good...pretty soon you'll be on to division."

Joe sighed. "I don't want to be on to division."

Adam only smiled and clapped him warmly on the shoulder, and then glanced over at the clock. "Do you have anything else?"

"No. She only wanted us to work on the arithmetic and write out a paragraph from the Bible, which I already finished." Joe opened his paper tablet and showed him.

"Well done. Very neat writing," Adam praised. "Now you better get to bed. I'm taking you to school tomorrow."

Joe grinned, and then stood up and gathered his books. He was really happy to receive Adam's praise, and now he would get to spend time with him tomorrow morning as well. School might turn out better than he thought.

"ADAM, PLEASE PROMISE."

"Joe..."

"Please?"

"What if something comes up at the ranch?"

"Hoss and Pa can handle it. Someone has to come get me, why not you?"

Adam chuckled. "We could just leave you there. You could spend the time brushing up on your reading."

"That's not funny. My reading is really good. Miss Jones made us all read in class yesterday, and I did better than everyone except Jane Kelso, and Agnes and Martha Seton."

It must have been the way Joe said their names that prompted Adam to ask, "What's wrong with them?"

Joe sighed grumpily. "Jane and Martha are younger than me." Adam was about to answer, when Joe continued, "And they've been to school already where they lived before."

"Well, I was just about to say that they've been to school before. As long as you, Joseph Cartwright, are improving, that's all that really matters. If you compare yourself to everyone else, there will always be someone better."

"Sure, Adam. Are you coming to get me?"

Adam laughed and pulled the wagon to a stop.

"Oh, Mr. Cartwright!"

Joe hopped off the wagon as Abigail stepped outside the mercantile.

"Good morning to you, Miss Jones," Adam said.

"Now, I know you said you weren't available for dinner this evening, but I do have a surprise for you when you come back this afternoon!" Abigail twittered, all smiles.

Joe watched as his brother's face reddened. "Actually, um...ma'am, I won't be back to pick him up this afternoon. I'll be busy all afternoon and tonight. I am sorry," Adam said.

Joe stared at him, but Adam didn't look his way. Joe barely

heard the rest of the conversation, and then Adam pulled away from the building. He didn't look back. Joe turned, feeling his forehead tighten in anger. How could he? How could he let a silly woman come between them?

Joe sank onto the bench and stared at the floor. Miss Jones started the first lesson, and he didn't hear her when she called his name. He didn't even realize that she had spoken until she was standing directly in front of him. "Joseph."

Joe looked up at her. "Yes, ma'am...?"

"Are you paying attention? What did I just ask you?"

Joe glared at the girls on the other bench, who had started to giggle.

"Joseph!" Miss Jones said loudly, and Joe looked up at her.

"I'm sorry ma'am, I wasn't paying attention," Joe answered. He saw the disappointment come over her face, but he couldn't feel bad about it.

"Well, please try to pay attention for the rest of the day, Joseph. Now, I asked you about the history chapter we read yesterday. What was Columbus looking for when he first set sail?"

All Joe could think about was the unfairness of it. She was coming between him and his brother. Adam was his brother, and he had known him longer, and missed him longer than she had even known he existed.

"Joseph?"

"I don't know."

Miss Jones was silent for a few moments, and then she picked up a history text from her desk and opened it to the chapter they had read yesterday. "I want you to reread the chapter, and to write out the answers to the questions that are at the bottom of each page."

"Yes, ma'am," Joe answered quietly, and pulled out his paper tablet. He worked as slowly as he could, which wasn't that difficult; his hand was sore from writing so much yesterday. By the time they stopped for lunch, he was only halfway done with the chapter.

Joe picked up his lunch pail and went outside. He sat on the steps of the mercantile, well away from the girls who were talking and giggling. There were only two other boys, and they were brothers who were six and seven. They weren't in class today. Joe sighed as he slowly ate his sandwich. He should really be at home too. He used to be useful around the ranch. But now that Adam had come home, it was as though Pa didn't need him anymore.

The five girls stood up and stood in a circle, and then began to play a game. Joe had never seen it before, and it looked sort of silly. He stood up and walked down the street. He had a few minutes until lessons started again.

He wandered down the street, looking around at all the rudely fashioned tents and buildings. There was a spot near the end of the little cluster where the school was being built. Some men were working on it now. Joe knew that his father had supplied a lot of the wood for the building, and other men were doing their part by doing the labor. He stood and watched them work for a couple minutes. They were still working on the framework, but it looked like it was almost done and soon the walls and roof would go up.

Joe turned and continued down the street, and then when he passed the last house, he turned and walked back. When he reached the mercantile, his heart seemed to stop. The girls were gone, no longer playing in the clearing. "Oh no, I wasn't gone that long," he whispered, and then hurried towards the building, rushing inside and into the back room.

Miss Jones was standing at the front of the room, and when Joe came in she stopped writing on the board and looked at him. "Joseph, where were you?" she asked sternly.

"I'm sorry, ma'am, I went for a walk and I didn't realize I walked so long."

She didn't seem placated. "Take your seat and finish the history chapter," she said, and then waited until Joe was seated before continuing her lesson.

Joe stared at the page with his head down to hide the angry look on his face. This just wasn't fair...

"HOSS!" JOE EXCLAIMED as soon as he saw his brother in the store. He didn't realize his brother had been talking to someone until he got closer. Hoss reached out and put his hand on Joe's shoulder as he finished his conversation, and then when he was done looked down at his brother. "How was school?" he asked.

Joe didn't answer, but instead tried to tell the whole story with his expression. He knew his brother understood when Hoss nodded and sighed sympathetically. "Don't worry, little brother. Hop Sing's made a mighty fine dinner."

"Oh, Hoss, I wonder if you might do me a favor?" Abigail asked, walking out of the back room. "Could you please take this to Adam? I know he was too busy to come back and get Joseph this afternoon, but I wanted to make sure he got it."

"Yes ma'am," Hoss said, and took the plate from her, lifting the corner of the cloth that was over the top. "Well, dang but does that look like the best tastin' pie I ever did see."

"Why thank you, Hoss," Miss Jones said, smiling modestly. "Please let me know how he enjoys it." She smiled and walked away.

Hoss was shaking his head, and Joe grabbed his arm and tugged him towards the door. "Let's GO," he said, and Hoss laughed and followed him out. Joe jumped up on the wagon seat, and then frowned as Hoss got up next to him and handed him the pie. "I don't want to hold it, Hoss."

"Well, I gotta drive," he responded.

"Let me drive," Joe said, pushing the pie at his brother.

Hoss sighed and handed him the reins. "You know Pa don't want you to drive for a little while longer, Joe."

"You told me yourself, he let you drive when you were nine, and Adam too."

"I know, I know..." Hoss took the pie. "Don't tell him."

"I never do," Joe grinned at him, and then urged the horses on. After a few seconds, he said, "I bet it tastes awful."

"Well, it's Adam's pie; we'll have to see what he thinks about it."

Joe looked with curiosity at the grin on Hoss's face. "Hoss? What's so funny?"

Hoss laughed. "You'll see," he said.

"It's not funny!" Adam roared, but Hoss did nothing to contain his guffaws.

Joe was laughing too, but it was mostly at Hoss's reaction to Adam's outrage. He didn't understand just what his brother was so upset about.

"Now, Adam, Abigail Jones...is...well..." Ben trailed off.

"Is what Pa? Ridiculous? I don't know where she got all these crazy notions, but I'd just as soon she get them out of her head, even if I have to avoid going into town for a month!"

Joe stopped laughing. "Adam, no!" he protested, shocked and disappointed that his brother would even think such a thing.

"Maybe we even ought to take Joe out—never mind, I don't mean that." He turned to Joe, who had begun to have hope. "Education is more important than that. But I think Hoss might have to take you to school for awhile."

Joe angrily stood up. "Fine!" he snapped at Adam. "See if I care!" He turned and tore up the stairs, slamming his door but instantly regretting it. Ben was strict about things like that. Joe waited awhile, but there was no sound of anyone coming. After a few minutes he just got undressed and pulled on his nightshirt. He wasn't really hungry anyway, and right now he was too angry to face the rest of his family. Within a half hour, he was asleep.

In fact, he didn't even hear when Ben came into his room right before dinner, to talk to him and bring him down. His father just shook his head slightly and then tucked him in.

JOE SIGHED AND shifted his weight again. He heard the children behind him finishing their work, and because it was Friday, as soon as they were done she was letting them leave. Joe had informed Hoss of this policy when he dropped him off this morning, and so he was hoping his brother was here soon. He had been standing in the corner at the front of the room for most of the afternoon, after refusing to do his work. When he told her he didn't want to do the problems, she didn't really have anything to say, and then sent him to the front.

Joe sighed. It was worth it if it meant he would never have to come back. He was hoping she got frustrated enough that she'd either leave Adam alone, or ask that he stay out of school. Either one would be fine with him.

Joe listened as another child left.

"Joseph."

Joe turned back to the room. It was empty. He walked to the front of Miss Jones's desk. "I am very disappointed in you," she said. "You're older than most of the other children, you need to set an example for the younger ones. I know how much your father and brother wanted you to come, and now I have to ask, why are you doing this? Do you have anything at all to say for yourself?"

Joe shook his head. "No, ma'am," he said quietly.

"I'll need to speak to your father about this. I'm going to write a note, and I wish to see him by Monday. If he's not able to come into town, I'll even make a trip to the ranch."

Joe cringed as she started to write the note. Adam would certainly be angry with him if that happened.

"Joe?"

Joe froze at the sound of his father's voice, and then closed his eyes and dropped his head down.

"Mr. Cartwright," Abigail said, standing up. "I was just writing you a note..."

"Oh?"

Joe winced. It wasn't a good 'Oh'.

"I wonder, if you have some time now, I need to speak with you about Joseph."

"Certainly," Ben replied. "Joseph, go wait outside."

Joe picked up his books and turned and walked past his father. He couldn't bear to look up at him. Outside, he climbed onto the wagon, and then sank against the seat with a sigh. He was in trouble. This was going to have the opposite effect he intended, he was sure.

After about 15 minutes, Joe watched as his father walked out of the mercantile. He didn't look at all happy, and he said nothing as he climbed onto the wagon and unlocked the brake. "Hyaa," he urged the horses on, and Joe tried to distract himself from the feeling of doom by watching the landscape.

When they pulled into the yard, Joe got down and started to help unhitch the team. "Go to the barn, and check on your horse. She foaled today," Ben said. Joe stopped, staring at him, and then almost ran towards the barn.

Ben watched him go, and then turned to the wagon with a sigh. "Adam," he called.

"Yes, Pa?" Adam said and walked to him, where he started to help unhitch the team.

"Your brother refused to do his work in school today. Do you have any ideas why he might do that?"

Adam let out a sigh and thought for a moment. "Do you think he's trying to get kicked out of school?"

Ben nodded. "I think it's a good possibility. Can you think of any reason why?"

"He didn't want to go to begin with, even before this thing with Abigail Jones," Adam replied, rather defensively.

"Adam, he's in the middle of this. It's not fair to him."

"That's why I'm not taking him to school anymore."

"That's hardly the solution, Adam. I'm going to talk to him, and I'm going to tell him he'd better not get in trouble at school again. I'm also telling him that you're taking him to school tomorrow."

"Pa—" Adam protested.

"Adam, it's real important to Joe," Hoss spoke up, quietly.

Adam glanced down. "I'm sorry. I guess I didn't think about Joe."

"I know, Adam. And I know it's difficult. You've been on your own for the past few years, you've hardly had to think about anyone else. But Joe has grown up a lot, and you need to realize it," Ben said, and then went to talk to Joe.

"He missed you, Adam," Hoss said.

Adam couldn't reply. He knew all they had said was true.

BEN WALKED INTO the barn and towards the mare and her new colt. As he got closer, he saw a small figure huddled in the stall with her.

The boy had obviously been crying, and he had a scowl on his face. Ben sat down next to him, and Joe turned and leaned against his chest. Ben wrapped his arms around his son.

"I was supposed to be here," Joe said quietly. "How come no one came and got me from school when she started to deliver? She was mine, Pa. I wanted to do this, from start to finish. I...worked so hard. It's not fair."

Ben nodded. "I know, Joe. But she delivered quite quickly. By the time we could have gone out to get you and come back, the colt would have been born."

Joe sank against Ben. "I know," he whispered. "That's why I'm not going back. I miss out on too much here."

Ben waited a few seconds before asking, "You're not just talking about the colt, now, are you?"

Joe shook his head. He started to say something a couple

times, but then just sighed.

"You miss your brother a lot, I'm sure."

"He just got back, Pa! And now I never get to see him. He never even takes me to school anymore; not ever since Miss Jones started chasing him."

"Abigail Jones is not chasing your brother," Ben said firmly. "Who told you that?"

Joe shrugged. "I heard a couple of the women in the mercantile saying it. They didn't know I heard them, I think."

"I'm sure," Ben responded with a sigh. Joe probably didn't even know what it meant. "Joe," he said, changing the subject. "I certainly want you to go back to school. There is a lot to learn yet."

"But I don't need it."

"You certainly do. Suppose you took 450 head of cattle to sell, and you knew they went for, let's say, four dollars a head. Now suppose the man buying gave you one thousand four hundred dollars for them."

Joe let out a whistle. "That's a lot."

"Yes, but one thousand eight hundred dollars was what you were supposed to get."

Joe was quiet for a while. "Oh," he finally responded.

"Not to mention contracts. There are a lot more settlers moving this way, and buildings and mines being built. A contract protects you. You need to learn how to read well, and how to understand words you don't know. You never sign a contract without understanding everything in it, son, and the schooling will help you."

Finally Joe nodded. "Yes, Pa," he said.

"Now, I don't want to get any more notes or anything like that about you from Miss Jones. You're to behave well in school, just as though I was there. As for Adam, he's going to be taking you into school tomorrow. Why don't you go inside and start working on your schoolwork, and I want to check it before dinner."

Joe looked up at him. "Pa, please don't tell Adam about what happened."

"Why?"

Joe looked away, and then finally said, "I don't want him to be disappointed in me."

Ben smiled slightly. "He's not, son."

"HEY, JOE?" ADAM asked at breakfast.

"What is it, Adam?" Joe replied, but he knew what the question was going to be.

"Well, you know I'm going to meet with some mining companies today. I was wondering if it would be all right if Hoss takes you to school this morning, so I could get an early start for my trip. If it's not, that's okay, but I just thought I'd ask and see what you think."

Joe looked at Ben, who didn't give any indication of what he was thinking. He looked at Hoss, who gave him a slight wink and a nod. "Sure, Adam," he said, finally. "When will you be home?"

"I'll still be able to pick you up from school, but this way I'll have a little more time to discuss the contract."

Joe smiled. "Good," he said, and then dropped his fork next to his plate. "I'll go get the wagon ready, Hoss." He got up and ran out the door.

When he left, Adam glanced over at Ben, who caught his eye and nodded. He turned back to his breakfast. It wasn't that he needed permission from Ben for his request, but he just wanted to make sure he had approached it correctly and that Joe wasn't secretly upset with him.

"HOSS? WHAT DO you think we could do to get Miss Jones to leave Adam alone?"

"What do you mean, Joe?"

"You know what I mean. There's got to be something we can do."

"That's Adam's problem, and I'm gonna let him deal with it."

"Please Hoss?"

"Well..." As much as Hoss just wanted to stay out of it, he knew that Joe wasn't likely to give up anytime soon, nor would Adam stop dreading the daily rides into town. "Well, I do have an idea..."

JOE WAS WAITING when Adam pulled up outside the mercantile. "Hi, older brother!" he greeted him.

Adam laughed. "Well, hello, younger brother. How was school?"

"Good and bad. We have to memorize the times-table."

"I see...what was the bad part?"

"Adam!" Joe punched his arm as his brother started laughing.

"Oh Adam!"

Joe looked behind him with surprise at Miss Jones. He thought his and Hoss's plan had worked.

"Good afternoon, Miss Jones," Adam replied.

Her eyes were teary, and she held her hands clasped in front of her. "Oh, Adam, Joseph told me all about it. And I just wanted to say, an unrequited love is the heart's deepest sorrow. I was thinking perhaps you would care to join me on a picnic this Saturday? I would love to listen, if you'd like to talk about it."

Joe stared at her, his mouth slightly open. Adam had a similar expression. "I'll let you know," Adam choked, and then urged the horses quickly away from the store. As soon as they were away from the town, he pulled the wagon to a stop. "Joseph, what did you do?" he almost shouted.

Joe flinched. "It wasn't all me! Hoss came up with the story, and I just told it to her!"

"What story?"

"I didn't mean it, Adam! I thought it would help!"

"What story, Joseph?"

Joe was almost in tears. "We...Hoss and I thought if we told her that you were in love with someone else, she'd leave you alone."

"And? Is that all?"

"Well, I mean I told her that you had a girl you were courting in the East, but when you moved back she didn't want to come, and so you had to leave without her." Joe watched as Adam closed his eyes and leaned back in his seat. "What is it?"

"Joe..." Adam finally said, exasperated. "Don't you know anything about romance?"

"I'm nine," Joe replied, in a small voice. What had he done wrong?

Adam just shook his head, and then opened his eyes and urged the horses on. They got home, and Hoss was standing outside, smiling. "Hiya, Joe, Adam! How was school..." He trailed off, seeing the look on Adam's face.

Adam jumped off the wagon, and then pulled Joe down and took hold of his arm, marching him towards the house. "Hoss, inside," he barked as he strode past.

"Pa!" Adam shouted once he was inside, and then seeing Ben seated at his desk, dragged Joe with him to it. "Pa, do you know what your son did?"

Joe squirmed, trying to get out of Adam's hand. "You're hurting me, Adam..." His brother released him, and Joe rubbed his arm.

"What did he do?" Ben asked, looking from Joe to Adam, and then to Hoss.

Adam glared at Joe and Hoss, and then explained to his father what they had done. Ben managed to keep a straight face. "I see," he said. "What do you have to say for yourself, Joseph?"

"I'm sorry, I was only trying to help," Joe whispered. "I started it, by telling her all those stories about how wonderful Adam was, and I was just trying to get her to not like him as much."

Ben nodded and stood up. "Telling stories that are lies isn't going to help, son," he said walking around to the front of the desk where he leaned against the edge. "And Hoss, I'm surprised at you, putting these ideas in his head."

"I'm sorry, Pa," Hoss said quietly.

Ben sighed. He knew he could easily sit down with them individually, tell them what they did wrong and how to make it right, but they wouldn't learn how to get along that way. Hoss was fine; he had been older when Adam left for school, and they still had pretty much the same relationship. Joe had just been a child though. He hardly remembered his older brother as a person; the entire time he was gone, he did nothing but talk about how wonderful Adam was. He failed to see his failings and mistakes, shortcomings and stubbornness. Adam, too, seemed to not know what to make of his older younger brother. Just a few years makes a large difference in a child that young, how he reacts to the world around him, and what he thinks about his place in it.

"We'll not discuss it anymore today," Ben said.

"Pa!"

Ben gave him the best stern look he could muster. "That's enough, Adam. Your brother didn't intend to do anything wrong."

"Sure, he didn't mean to do anything wrong, but he hasn't done anything right!" Adam missed the intense hurt look that came over Joe's face as he turned to him. "You caused this whole mess. What do you suggest doing to get out of it?"

Joe thought for a moment, and then looked up at him. "I could tell her that you really are a horrible person, that I made up everything nice that I said about you, that...that..." Joe struggled to find the right words. "That you're a mean, stuck-up, and selfish...hussy, that you don't care about anyone else and you're so stupid you can't tell a skunk from a house cat!" Joe turned and started to run out of the room, but Adam grabbed him, stopping him.

"Where in the world did you get 'hussy'?" Adam asked.

Joe turned, puzzled, as Ben and Hoss burst into laughter. "Well, Hoss told me it meant someone who wasn't a nice person."

Ben reached forward and ruffled his son's hair. "It usually implies a woman, Joe, not a man. And it's not a word I want to hear you say."

"Yes, Pa."

Ben stood up, and Joe watched as he and Hoss left. He wondered where they were going, but then when Adam didn't let go of him, knew it was so the two of them could talk. Adam left his hand on Joe's shoulder, and led him behind the desk where he pushed him gently into Ben's chair. He knelt down in front of him, and Joe was glad. He felt really small with Adam standing over him.

"Joe..." Adam shook his head. "I don't even know what to say."

"I'm sorry, Adam, that I caused all this trouble for you," Joe said quietly.

"No, I'm sorry. I'm sorry that the only time we've spent together has been on the wagon on the way to school."

Joe looked down, and traced over the patch on his pants with his finger. "I just missed you, Adam." He looked up. "Can't you talk Pa into letting me stay out of school?"

Adam shook his head. "No, I'm not going to do that." He paused for a moment. "Joe...I know you missed me, and I missed you too. But...it can't ever go back to the way it was before I left. We've both changed. It will never be that way again." When Joe started to cry, Adam quickly swept him up. "No, no, no..." he said. "I didn't mean we wouldn't be close like we used to. I meant that things change. I've been gone for a few years, Joe. Things have changed during that time, but not the way I feel about you, buddy. That's always been the same."

Joe pulled away from him a little, so he could see his face. "Adam?"

Adam smiled slightly, and ran his hand over Joe's face, wiping the tears away. "I love you, little brother. That will never change."

Joe smiled and hugged him. "Love you too, Adam."

176

"Tell you what," Adam said as Joe pulled away. "Let's go shooting tomorrow, just you and me."

Joe grinned. "That would be great, Adam," he exclaimed. "And you know, I think I know what you can say to Miss Jones."

Adam stood up, putting Joe down. "I'm not sure if I want to hear this, but go ahead."

Joe smiled up at him, bright and helpful. "Why don't you just tell her she smells? That really works to keep girls away."

Adam managed a straight face for a few seconds, but then the image of him telling Miss Jones that she smelled became too much, and he burst into laughter. "How about you just let me worry about that, Joe?"

Joe smiled. "Okay."

For Love and Honor

by Mel Hughes

This story is based on the episode Death at Dawn written by
Laurence Mascott

"Walk faster, damn you!" Sam Bryant said under his breath, yanking the rope that bound Ben Cartwright's hands behind him.

"I'm not a calf to be branded," Ben replied quietly, making no attempt to pick up his pace. "And if you wanted me to be in better shape for my return, you shouldn't have had your thugs pound me so hard."

Bryant ignored him, intent on the crowd ahead, but Ben smiled, feeling sweat on the hand that held his arm as Bryant called out, "Listen to me—all of you! Look! I brought Ben Cartwright back! I didn't do nothin'! And...an' you done right, hangin' Farmer Perkins!" Hastily, he began to untie the knots, and Ben felt the man's fear in the way his hands fumbled uncertainly with the rope. Ben suppressed the smile he felt...everything would be all right now, of that he was sure. There was a crowd in front of the jail, but he had eyes only for three men—his sons.

Things happened fast then—dimly Ben recognized that wild-eyed kid McNeill, pushing through the crowd with a rifle, shouting something about how Bryant had let them all down, had let the Farmer down, and then the kid was shooting. It was more weakness and the suddenness of Bryant's letting go than Ben's own common sense, but whatever it was he found himself lying in the middle of the street with bullets whizzing over his head as McNeill took his indignation out on Bryant. Then there was a hail of gunfire in return, and he realized it was his three boys, all with deadly accuracy pouring lead into McNeill with such force that the kid was knocked from one part of the porch to another, landing on the ground already dead. Ben glanced back, the movement hurting his rope-burned neck and taxing his back where the men had kicked him, but he had to be sure. Sam Bryant would terrorize Virginia City no more; he was dead.

When Ben managed to turn his head back, all three of his sons were with him. Joe, murmuring, "Papa!" like a child, and Hoss, with tears in his eyes, were pulling him to his feet; Adam circled Hoss and came up from behind almost timidly, reaching his hand out—but drew back as if burned as soon as he touched his father's jacket.

Ben cast a brief, puzzled glance at Adam. He felt a little crazy and dizzy and elated all at the same time as Joe asked if he was all right. "Yeah, I'm all right," he said with a grin. "I'm fine...you know something?"

"What?" Hoss asked, and as he turned Ben vaguely noticed Adam's hand, still in mid-air, almost touching him but a world away.

"You boys look awful good to me," Ben said, his voice catching involuntarily.

"Dear God, let's get out of here—let's go home," Joe muttered fiercely.

They headed down the street together toward the stable to

pick up their wagon. Out of the blue, there was a dragging stumble and Adam disappeared. They stopped in surprise and turned to see him on his knees on the ground. Hoss reached over to help him up, but Adam avoided his touch. "I tripped," he muttered angrily, managing to get up alone, and he looked at them all as if defying anyone to disagree, even though there was nothing in the street for him to trip over.

"No lollygagging, son," Ben tried to joke. "We need to get home."

"No," Adam replied, his voice hoarse but still commanding. "Pa, you need to see Dr. Martin first."

"I don't, Adam," Ben replied. "I told you, I'm fine. And I really want to go home."

"You're not. There's dried blood on you and you have some bad rope burns on your wrists and..." his voice trailed off.

"Your neck," Hoss whispered. "Pa, he was really gonna do it, wasn't he?"

"No," Ben said evenly. "He was just trying to bully me. None of this matters. I can't wait to get home."

"He was braggin'," Joe said suddenly. "That kid was braggin' before about how they beat you when they caught you. You might have something busted inside, Pa. We need to go to the doctor's. Adam's right...again."

"He always is," Hoss agreed with a sad kind of smile, and he looked at Adam, but Adam refused to meet his eyes, and stepped away from them.

Ben had a strange feeling that there was more being said than what he was hearing, but he let it go and allowed them—Joe and Hoss—to tug him over to the doctor's office.

Adam went over to fetch the doc out of the crowd still gathered, all talking and whistling and making ooh's and ahh's over the shot group in McNeill's body; they set up a cheer as Adam approached. He ignored them and grabbed Paul Martin by the arm. "Can you examine my father; make sure it's all right for him to come home?"

"Of course," the doctor replied, and they crossed the street together. "You're a very popular man in town this morning, Adam—in fact I think the whole Cartwright family is pretty popular today."

"Sure—until next week. Then we'll be those damned high-falootin' Cartwrights again, the ones who 'own the town' and need a good butt whippin'," Adam replied bitterly. "Paul, take good care of him; I'm goin' over to the livery for the wagon and our horses. Back in a little while."

Funny; after the events just transpired, Paul Martin wouldn't have thought Adam would let his father out of his sight. But practicality was always good, he told himself as he mounted the steps to his examining room. By the time the wagon was brought around, he was done. Ben had some tender spots in the places Paul prodded, but with a little rest and lots of good nursing—never a shortage of good care when a Cartwright was injured—he'd be all right. Based on the assurances of all three that Ben would be quiet and careful, he'd given Ben a mostly clean bill of health. Of course, that had been a certainty from the time he saw Ben's face. There was a man who wanted to go home.

They all helped Ben back outside afterward, somehow managing to make it look as if they were not helping at all, and found the wagon, Sport and Cochise. Only 24 hours ago the four had come into town, Adam and Joe riding, Ben and Hoss in the wagon, ready to pick up supplies and quaff a few brews before heading home again. Funny, it seemed a lifetime ago.

Paul looked at Adam, who had just walked up from a nearby alley. "You need a lookover as well, son?" he asked kindly, and realized immediately that he'd made a mistake. It didn't take a doctor to recognize the white face and wet, red-rimmed eyes of a man who'd just puked his insides out, and now he'd drawn everyone's attention to it. Adam sent him a loaded glare and turned wordlessly to his horse.

It took two bounces before Adam managed to pull himself into the saddle. Ben and Hoss were already in the wagon; Joe swung easily aboard Cochise. Paul sighed as he watched them depart. Someday, he'd have to see if, among the updated medical classes being offered, there was anything for "being tactful."

It was a quiet ride. Weak and tired, Ben still tried to make conversation about how the spring runoff was affecting their low pasture, but all he got from Hoss was "Pa, you need to save your strength. You heard Doc Martin; you need to rest."

Joe and Adam were completely silent. A couple of times Adam muttered something about needing to check Sport's shoes, and pulled up, insisting that the others go ahead. Ben could only wonder what was going on, but Hoss quietly overrode his arguments about leaving Adam behind, murmuring that Sport was a fast horse and Adam would have no problem catching up. But as he said it, he looked over at Joe's grim face, and shook his head.

Only once before had they ever seen Adam look like this: right after the bullet he'd intended for a wolf had hit Little Joe instead. Oh, he'd stayed calm enough—except for threatening the life of that extortionist Dowd, perhaps, but that was understandable. A couple of days afterwards, though, when Joe was awake and moving about, when Pa was home to take over and things were looking up again, Adam had started disappearing for hours at a time, and when he was around he was white-faced and sick looking, not to mention bad-tempered and non-communicative. Then they'd found a note in shaky writing on the kitchen table, with some nonsense about fence repair. He'd been gone four days then, and Hoss had wondered if he was really heading back East to civilization. But on the fifth day Adam had returned, with not a word said to anyone of where he'd been, what he'd been doing, or why. Even Pa's taking him aside for a talk had not brought forth any information. Right now Pa was dizzy and sleepy, not noticing the signals, but Hoss and Joe could see them, and while Joe didn't know what they meant, Hoss was reading them as easily as Adam would read off a quote of Thoreau.

"Take Pa inside and put him to bed...get Hop Sing to give him some beef broth." Adam took the reins of the nearest horse on the buckboard, holding them up close to the bit. "I'll take care of the horses and supplies. Don't wait supper for me."

"I don't need beef broth; I'm no invalid," Ben protested. "And you need help with all that."

"Just once, Pa, will you not give me an argument when I'm trying to get things done?" Adam shouted, and all three Cartwrights looked at him as if he were a stranger.

And maybe I am, Adam thought. "Pa, please," he continued a little more softly before Ben could explode back at him, "I've got a little too much energy right now. I couldn't sit down if I tried. I just want to work it off—and you promised Paul you'd be quiet, remember?" The pleading worked where the explosion had not. Hoss and Pa disappeared inside. Joe appeared at Adam's side though, and holding his hat nervously in his hands, he said, "Adam, I'm not askin' for me. If you're mad at me I understand. But don't—"

Adam walked away, and began to unload the wagon. Joe tossed his hat to the ground and began, wordlessly, to help. When the wagon was empty and the horses unharnessed, Joe took them for water, and Adam began un-tacking the saddle horses. Joe came to his side as he led Cochise into his stall. "I'll take him. You always rub his hair the wrong direction. Kinda like me and you, Adam, we're always rubbin' each other the wrong way."

Adam turned away without replying and took Sport by the reins, only to find Joe by his side again. "Adam...look, I was wrong before. I swear to you, I just didn't—couldn't—understand the thinking you were doin'. And I still think you could've guessed wrong...and I don't know if I could've lived with that." With that, he returned to Cochise, never hearing Adam's whispered, "I know." Joe finished currying and feeding his horse, and finally, Adam was left alone.

It didn't take long to take care of Sport. But his saddle he had put to one side, and now he led out a black mare and replaced the saddle on her.

Hoss walked in while he was tightening the cinch. "Don't," he said quietly but urgently. "Please."

"I just need to think for a while, that's all," Adam replied. "Nothing to worry about."

"Easy for you to say," Hoss returned. "What are we gonna tell Pa? You know he'll want the whole story of what happened while he was gone. I'll face up to it, Adam; I know I was wrong. But you got no call to run away when he wants answers."

"No," Adam said, turning to look up at his brother. "He'll sleep for a long time, anyway. Besides, the beauty of Pa is that no matter what he's thinkin', he won't ask until he thinks we're ready to talk. I can't talk about this right now, Hoss. I don't know if I ever can. Feel like I got a grizzly bear on my chest...."

"Because me and Joe let you down? We tried to tell you—"

There was a world of hurt in those summer-sky blue eyes. Adam shook his head forlornly, wishing he could put a hand on his brother's shoulder, but right now it was hard enough just to saddle a horse. He was pretty sure he'd break in pieces if he tried to touch Hoss. "Can you really ask that? Do you think I blame you? No, Hoss. Never. I just...I just can't think straight right now. I have to get out of here."

"And do what? Where will you go? What'll you do that's gonna get all this out of your head? If you know, then please tell the rest of us, 'cause we'd like to go there too."

"I don't know. Maybe I'll go hunting. Or fishing. Or just ride till I run out of road. I don't know, dammit! I just...I can't stay here right now. How can I look him in the eye without seeing those burns on his neck and knowing I put them there?"

Without waiting for an answer he translated his raw nerves into action and jumped into the saddle. Surprised, and sensing his tension, the mare shook her head and plunged straight ahead.

"Adam!" Hoss cried, to no avail. Adam slapped the mare's flanks with the reins, and she tore off, leaving Hoss in the dusty barn trying to breathe...and formulate some believable excuse that would satisfy his father.

IT WAS A routine Thursday night at Bella's; the piano was tinkling tinnily in the background, and the specialty of the house— nothing more than rotgut with a fancy label on the bottle—was flowing freely despite the especially sparse population of the house on this night.

One of the main customers was a good-looking stranger who had grabbed a corner table early that day, anchoring himself there and slowly but steadily poisoning himself ever since. He had no interest in any of the card games, and less than no interest in any of the painted ladies roving the place and trying to catch his eye. His one true love seemed to be Bella—the name of the "specialty liquor" (as well as the name of the house).

Liz knew with her own special intuition that the stranger wasn't after a roll of dice or a turn of cards; probably nothing else either—one of the hermit types, she would have thought. But she couldn't help but wonder what he was doing there. This little one-horse town had grown up around a swing station for the stage line, but few people ever came in and stayed. Now and then a miner passed through, or a few cowboys looking for a fancy lady to spend some time with. But this fellow wasn't a stage passenger. He wasn't a miner, either, though he seemed richer than one. He was dressed like a cowboy or even a gunslinger, wearing black from head to foot and carrying a Colt low on his hip but covering it all with a yellow barn jacket that seemed to say "no, really, I'm harmless." He had ridden into town that morning slowly and deliberately; she'd gotten up to pull her shade down so she could sleep a couple more hours when she saw him. He'd headed right into Bella's, and one of the day girls told her he'd planted himself purposely in that dark corner and looked daggers at anyone who came near him without a refill for his glass.

It was 9 p.m. and while nobody minded the fellow drinking the night away there—he paid cash after all—there were better and more lucrative ways to pass the time, especially when the cowboy was halfway decent looking and free with his gold. Liz grabbed a full bottle of Bella's and ambled over to the stranger.

"Looks like your glass just plumb stays low," she said quietly. "It's cheaper by the bottle, and it'll do the job faster."

The cowboy looked at her through glassy hazel eyes. "Don' wanna get drunk," he slurred. "'s why I am slinking it drolly."

"You hold it very well," she said with a straight face. "I'm Liz. What's your name?"

That was funny, the way his face changed when she told him her name. She wondered if his wife's name was Liz, too. But there was another quick change when she asked for his. He thought sullenly for a minute, and finally mumbled, "Stoddard."

"That's different."

"Guess so." He refilled his glass and looked up, surprised to see her still there. Something like manners possessed him then, and he nodded toward the bottle. "You wanna drink?"

"Just happens I do," she smiled. "Even happen to have a glass with me." She sat down with him. "Gonna be in town long?"

No reply. She tried again. "Funny you picked this town to pass through. People like to say Bella's is right next door to nothing."

He snorted and looked around, seeming suddenly to realize where he was. He looked back at her, pushing his hat back to reveal a high forehead and black, wavy hair.

"Can we go somewhere 'n'...talk?" he asked.

She raised an eyebrow and smiled. *Even better than a card game.*

BEN HAD NODDED off over the beef broth they had tried to feed him, and had not awakened since. Although he was resting quietly enough now, eventually he'd wake up and then they would have to explain Adam's absence—whereupon both boys knew all hell would break loose.

"We gotta go after him," Joe announced.

Hoss had his forehead wrinkled in worry. "I know it. But there's no point in doin' it now. You saw him; he was ready to fall apart. I doubt he got ten miles before he made camp."

"Then we can catch him at his camp."

"And do what? Make him more outta sorts than he already is?" Hoss sighed explosively. "We'll wait'll morning. You know how things are, Joe; everything always looks better come morning. He may even come back on his own."

"You don't believe that any more'n I do," Little Joe retorted.

IT TOOK THE combined efforts of Liz and Annie, another saloon girl, to pull "Stoddard" up to number three. He managed to sway to the only chair in the room, and sighing, poured himself into it. Liz shut the door and went over to him, aiming to pull off his boots.

"Don't," he said quietly when she touched him.

"Look," she replied, "I know you cowboys always wanna die with your boots on, but—"

"No, you don' get it...I wanna tell you a story."

Oh dear Lord, she thought, not another "I wanna tell you a story." Those guys invariably spent half the time whining and crying and the other half puking.

"You ever been to Vir—Virzhin—Virgina Szitty?"

At Bella's, the rule of the house was that the customer was always right. This guy was paying for the booze, so she smoothly glossed over his pronunciation and said, "Once. Thought it would be a big fancy place like my home in San Francisco, but all it was, was overpriced."

"Yeah...you ever hear any news from there?"

"Not since Sam Bryant took over the town a couple months

back. He likes people to come into town but doesn't seem too keen on givin' em back. Are you one of his pals?"

"Not by a long shot. So you didn't hear about him dyin', or his shindy...cindy...sinnacut gettin' shut down."

"Lord, no, Mr. Stoddard!" Hey, she thought, maybe this would be a decent story after all.

"Ever hear of the Carrots...Carrits...Carrytes?"

It took a minute. "Oh, yes, the Cartwrights. Sure, who hasn't? They make up a lot of the entertainment we get out here, or at least they did until news stopped coming out of Virginia City. Ben Cartwright, owns half the country around Virginia City. Hacked it out of the wilderness. Adam, the oldest—the brains of the outfit, the one who holds everything together. Hoss—right up there with Goliath from the Bible, only nicer, and a little bit shy. Little Joe. The romantic one. Kisses every girl he sees and fights every man."

"They are friends of mine," Stoddard intoned gravely. "These are real people, lady, not legends, so get all that pigswill outta your head. Two of them walked in on one of Brant...Bryant's... men, killin' another fellow. Th' guy got arrested and sennanced—sentenced—to hangin'."

"Hah. Bryant wouldn't let that happen."

"Well, thass what I'm trine to tell you about. Lady, you talk too much."

Gee, Bella's rules made life difficult sometimes. "Sorry, Mr. Stoddard, I won't interrupt again."

"So the sherf..." he paused, went cross-eyed for a minute, and finally continued, "SHERIFF...deputized all four of the Carrots. Nobody else would help. They're all scared of Brant. But the Carrots did it. Only then Pa...uhm, Pa Carrot, thass what they call him, he...he went to walk the judge to the stage. An' he din't come back cuz Brant's men got 'im." He peered closely at her. "You keepin' up with me? You're not sayin' nothin'."

"I'm following your story, Mr. Stoddard. You mean Ben Cartwright, is that it?"

Stoddard gave an exaggerated nod. "Yeah. Him."

"Was he killed?"

"I'm comin' to that!" he replied sharply. "So Brant's—Bryant's—men got 'im and kicked the...shtuffing...outta him and took him and hid him somewhere. And my friends, they din't know whereta look. An' Bryant sent a note to the sherff that he had Ben Carrot and was gonna hang him if they hanged Parmer Ferkins..." He went cross-eyed again and squinted, finally shutting his eyes and trying again, very slowly. "Farmer...Perkins."

"Farmer Perkins?" she leaned forward, a gleam of genuine interest in her eye. "That sorry, no good—I'm sorry, Mr. Stoddard, but I know that man, he's been here before and he should be hanged ten times over. Did you see my roommate Annie, the one who helped bring you up here? What he did to her alone was worth a hanging. Shame your friends had to let him go."

"Who said they...lemgo?" Stoddard replied blearily, focusing on her again but with difficulty. "Anybody else would've let him go. Anybody normal. But not Ad'm Carrot."

"Adam...if he says he'll do something, you can bank on it. You know him very well?"

"I know him VERY well. Donchu listen to rumors. He's a mule-headed jackass."

The loathing in his voice made her sit up straight. "I thought the Cartwrights were friends of yours."

"Not that Carro-CARTwright," he said fuzzily. "Not him. You know what happened out there? He said he could read Sam Bra—Bryant's—mind. Said Bryant was only bluffin'. His own brothers told him he was crazy. But he was acting sherff—sheriff. He went out in public and told everybody that he was gonna hang Perkins, and if Bryant wanted to hang Old Man Cartwright, it was just fine with him. Only thing, he said—if you hang Ben Cartwright the next hangin' will be YOU, Mr. Bryant. Lord, can you imagine...if he and Bryant had both followed through, half of Virginia City would be strung up from the rafters by now."

"You lost me, Mr. Stoddard. Who didn't follow through? And what happened?"

"Cartwright's own brothers told him he was wrong," Stoddard repeated, his head in his hands. "They said he was power drunk on accoun' of the badge. Said he was gambling with their pa's life. He never even denied it. He just said this was how it was gonna be. And come the dawn, he marched Perkins out to the gallows and hung him like a slab of bacon in a smokehouse."

She knew she wasn't supposed to say anything, so she managed not to say "Good!" aloud. But the way he looked at her, he seemed to know she was thinking it.

"Sure, he d'served to die," he mumbled, wiping his eyes and nose on his sleeve before putting his head back in his hands. "But did Pa?—I mean, Ben?"

"Of course not, but—did he die? You said 'if they both followed through' as if they didn't. But Adam did. So did Bryant also follow through, or not?"

"It doesn't matter," he insisted with the absolute moral conviction always exhibited by the very intoxicated during an argument. "What kind of son—what kind of son puts his father's life up against anybody else's, much less a no-count like Perkins? Even if he didn't like the old man, shouldn' he have been a better son than that?"

"You're sayin' Adam didn't like his father?"

"No, dammit! I'm sayin' Adam Cartwright is a conceited, self-centered know-it-all. He's always so sure he's right. Gets a notion in his head and will risk anything rather than back down from it. Pa could've just as easily died right then and there. You should've seen the marks on him...you should've seen—a neckerchief can only hide so much." His voice faded to a whisper and he looked out the window with wet, sightless eyes. "It was my fault. He coulda died, and it was my fault."

"But Ben Cartwright didn't die," Liz said softly. "He didn't, did he? Bryant backed down, went to jail and was hanged himself. Right?"

"Wrong. Ben Cartwright didn't die, no thanks to his darlin' eldest boy. Bryant did back down, and one of his own men got mad about it and shot him down. So then Joe, Hoss and I shot him. Joe had killed one of them the night before, so that made four of the main members of the, um, synnacut—syndicate— down for good. The others started leaving town, and fast. And of course right now bein' a Cartwright in Virginia City is enough to buy your weight in steak 'n' beer...but that's only right now. Next week, there'll be another, more popular flavor again."

Liz sat very still, not too surprised about Sam Bryant, but the growing suspicion that she was talking to Adam Cartwright himself had crystallized. And, having talked his head off for the past two hours, he seemed to be starting to come out of his alcoholic stupor as well.

"So that's why you're not in Virginia City," she said. "Can't abide the honor. You don't feel worthy of it."

"Nor th' h'pocrisy," he replied evenly. "Sticks to your boots worse'n what you pick up in a pasture."

"But why are you so angry at yourself? It sounds to me like things worked out really well for all the decent people. Taking Bryant's power and hanging Perkins will make some of the best news ever to come out of Virginia City. And your father didn't die...I mean, your friend's father didn't die."

"Sheesh," he muttered. "You lie worse'n I do."

"All right—Mr. Cartwright. Back to the point here. Everybody else in Virginia City is celebrating. Why aren't you?"

"Because I gambled with my own father's life!" he shouted. "Isn't that obvious?"

"Not really, no. Even if your father had died, it would've been Bryant that did it, not you. And for what it's worth, I think you're probably right about Bryant. He was a bully, and if you'd given in to him he likely would have killed your pa anyway. But standing up to him and showing him he couldn't scare you, I think you saved your father's life."

He looked hard at her, and had opened his mouth to reply

when she reached up and put her finger to his lips. "I listened to you. Now you listen to me—gentlemen don't interrupt."

He raised an eyebrow and then bowed his head exaggeratedly, with a bit of a smirk.

"We're taught when we're little that we're supposed to lay down our lives for our friends. Isn't that so?"

"Yes," he replied grimly. "That is what we're taught—but that's not reality."

"Maybe, but it's a principle your father lives by, right?"

"So?"

"So, seems to me like he would've been glad to lay his life down for a whole town full of people, if it would actually stop the killings and all. Your father's that kind of man. Tell me, was he mad at you when it was over?"

"Don't know. Couldn't look at him without seein' those red marks on his neck. Ever look at somebody an' no matter how hard you try, you just can't look away from one part? I couldn't see my own Pa without seein' his neck instead of his face. An' I knew I was the reason he had those inzzurrs...INJURIES. It was easier...not to look at all. So...I left."

"Hmph." She thought a minute. "What about your brothers—are they still mad?"

"I...don't think so. But they don't know why they're not mad; they just know Pa's alive."

"Well, suppose things had played out different, Mr. Cartwright. Suppose you let Farmer Perkins go, and Bryant gave back your Pa. What would've happened then?"

The question brought about almost instant sobriety. "My father would never have spoken to me again, that's certain. I would've let him down, him and his cursed principles...."

"Forget him for a minute."

"As if I ever could," he said with a smile.

"What about Bryant and Perkins? What would they have done?"

Adam shrugged. "They would've gone on as before. Human life

in Virginia City would be worth less than dirt. When men like that are uncontrolled, they'll go as far as they think they can, and then further still."

"So you saved the town, didn't you?"

"I don't know. I suppose. Maybe."

"Then it sounds to me like your story had a happy ending, Mr. Cartwright, and I honestly don't know what you're bustin' a gut about now. If your father's safe, the guilty parties were taken care of, and nobody's mad at you, why on earth are you 40 miles from home, right next door to nothing, and sittin' up at midnight with a second-rate—"

"No." Adam Cartwright looked at the floor. "Liz, you've been a real first-rate lady about this whole thing. Thanks for listening— I just wanted someone to talk to. Someone who didn't know me. Who didn't already have expectations; who could help me get the grizzly bear off my chest. I wish you had been that person; I had no idea the stories came out this far."

"Mr. Cartwright, I came here from California. The Cartwrights are known even there. So I don't think you'll find somebody around here who's never heard of you."

"Well, since you seem...to know all about me, then you ought to know I can't live up to my own publicity. Nobody could. I can't talk to my brothers about it. They think I'm nothing but a walking abacus."

"I don't know what those things are, abacuses. They don't sound very good."

"Oh, they're great, if you want a job done. They're just functional summing machines, that's all. And that's all my brothers think I am. Now do you see why I can't talk to them? And Pa...oh, he'll say I did exactly what he would've done, but I know better. I just wanted someone who would listen—and be honest. And...I think you did listen, and you were honest, and I appreciate that. Thank you."

"And how'd you happen to pick me to talk to, and not Annie or Gemma or Florrie? Did you think I was the prettiest?"

He chuckled as a deep red blush suffused him, from the tips of his ears right down to his throat. "No. And don't get insulted...I picked you because you look a little bit like a picture of my mother—and you also have her name. She died when I was born, and I always used to pretend she was listening, whenever I needed someone to talk to. Only today, it wasn't working, so when I stopped in here, it didn't take long to figure I'd be bending your ear for a while, soon as I got up my nerve to do it."

"Well, I'm a bit disappointed I reckon," she shrugged, with a demure smile. "But only 'cause I think I'm lots prettier than Annie."

"You are," he said, with one eyebrow raised. He sighed and wiped a dirty hand across his face. "Boy, I could sure use a bath and a shave right now..." And with that, the last 48 hours caught up with him and he slowly slid down the chair to land on the floor. Liz quickly checked his pulse. Normal as anything. The guy was sound asleep.

Liz tried to drag him to her bed, but he was too heavy. Sighing, she called Annie, and with some difficulty they managed to remove his boots and get him on the bed.

"Now what do we do with him?"Annie asked.

"I dunno," Liz replied. "I guess he can stay here."

"Well, Liz, you may like him, but come daylight, it's my time and I want him gone. That's where we sleep, in case you forgot."

"True, but I thought you might make an exception this time." She pointed down. "You're lookin' at your redeemer, girl. That's the man who hung Farmer Perkins."

"WHAT!?!"

"I'm tellin' you, I got it right from his lips. He was actin' sheriff in Virginia City the last two days, and yesterday mornin' he hung Perkins by his very own self."

"My shoulder still pains me, and that scar on my stomach ain't ever gonna go away. Damn that Farmer, I hope Satan's roastin' him up to his neck in boiling oil this very minute." Annie looked appraisingly at the limp, dirty figure on the bed. "And this fella sent him to his reward, huh?"

"He did. Annie, that's Adam Cartwright."

"I don't care who he is, if he took the Farmer outta this world, he's a friend of mine."

Liz and Annie ended up taking the rest of the night off. They slept on the floor, but then since they had both slept in worse places, and under worse circumstances, it wasn't too bad.

"BLAST IT ALL, I don't want any more beef broth!" Ben Cartwright shouted. "I am fine, and I want bacon and eggs just like any normal person."

"Pa, you ain't even been home 24 hours," Hoss pleaded. "You're supposed to be resting."

"I've been saying ever since yesterday that I feel fine, and I do."

"You've been asleep most of the time, Pa," Joe said. "How do you even know how you feel? You ain't been awake long enough to know anything."

"You might as well ask how a horse knows how it feels." Against the appalled looks of his sons, Ben placed his feet tentatively on the floor and stood up. "There. I'm not dizzy, I'm not sick. All I've got is some bumps and bruises, and they'll heal on their own."

He put on his robe carefully. "Where's Adam? I'm surprised I haven't seen him fussing over me all night like you two, but thank goodness he at least seems to understand I mean what I say."

Neither son responded, looking rather pointedly in different directions but decidedly away from him.

"All right," Ben said, in dangerously quiet tones, "where is he?"

"There was a cow calvin'—"

"He had to fix a fence—"

Hoss and Joe stopped as their words overlapped, and looked at each other.

In town, it was said that Ben Cartwright's glare could set fire to a haystack at forty feet. It was that look that Hoss and Joe now faced. "Perhaps the two of you would like to hold a meeting first to come up with a SINGLE lie that doesn't contradict another one!"

"He left yesterday, Pa, right after we got home," Joe said. "He never even came in the house."

"Why?"

"We don't know, exactly," Hoss replied softly.

"He was mad at me." Joe shook his head. "I reckon I deserved it. I gave him a pretty hard time after Bryant grabbed you, Pa."

"No more'n I did," Hoss added. "But he said before he left that he wasn't mad at neither of us. Pa, he was mad at himself. I think it shook him up pretty bad, seein' what happened to you and thinkin' about what could've happened."

"Balderdash," Ben almost spat. "Has anybody even looked for him?" The words were spoken as he headed to his bureau for a shirt.

"I sent a hand into Virginia City and one to Carson City last night, but they didn't find anything," Hoss replied. "I didn't much expect 'em to."

"Well, there's only four directions to pick from," Joe retorted impatiently. "And I'm pretty sure he wouldn't go to either Virginia City or Carson. Too much...what's that word he uses, 'adulation.'"

"Yeah, but there's a real dearth of places besides them two."

"I know." Joe scratched his head.

"He mentioned hunting or fishing..." Hoss suggested.

"But we're pretty sure he didn't do that either," Joe stated. "So we were gonna go look for him as soon as we got you situated, Pa."

"Me, situated?" Ben bellowed. "Situate yourselves! I'm not going to be treated like a five-year-old here." By now he had his trousers and socks on as well, and had reached for his boots.

"Pa, please, we'll find him," Hoss promised. "Just let us go. We gotta settle things between us anyway."

Ben took a deep breath. "I don't know what happened among you three while I was gone, and I don't much care. What I care about is right now. Right now, Adam is gone, and you two look like you couldn't find an elephant in a bathtub if it was wearing a pink nightgown and a couple of cowbells! Get the horses saddled—that means Buck, too—and be ready to leave in five minutes. *We* are going to find *my son* and bring him home."

"He's our brother, too," Joe muttered, turning on his heel and stamping out. And Ben smiled.

"HE TOOK PEPPER Nell," Hoss announced as they headed to the barn. "She was the only second stringer put up when we came in."

"Well, at least she's got feet the size of buckets," Joe nodded. "Shouldn't be that hard to track."

"Wait a minute." A look of revelation came to Hoss. "He said maybe he'd ride till he ran out of road..."

"Bella's," they said in unison.

"He wouldn't dare," Ben retorted.

Hoss shook his head. "Everybody who wants to ride till they run out of road goes to Bella's."

"Yup," Joe seconded. "Pa, it's the place that's right next door to nothing."

ADAM CARTWRIGHT WOKE up just before noon, with a bit of a hangover, but still ravenously hungry and dying for a bath. There was no restaurant in this hole; Bella's place served as restaurant, hotel, and bath house, so he was on his own. But the ladies had a large tub in their room, and since they were already awake, he asked for some hot water and a razor while he got a change of clothes from his saddlebags. Annie, who had introduced herself quite warmly for reasons unknown to him, promised she would shave him herself. Liz, thankfully, ushered her downstairs to help get some breakfast together while he bathed. He didn't feel that all was right with the world just yet, but maybe it would come over time. Of course, he'd have to see Pa first, not something he was looking forward to. He should never have left without at least talking to him first; he knew that now. But they would have that talk, and however bad things were on this side of it, he was pretty sure things would—one way or another—be better after. And he'd never seen anything so bad that a little bit of singing wouldn't help....

And so it was that when Ben, Joe and Hoss Cartwright arrived at Bella's just a little after noon, they heard their brother's pleasant baritone from the upstairs window above the street, trumpeting "Farewell and adieu to you dear Spanish ladies...." Joe and Hoss exchanged a triumphant glance. For once, they had figured their brother out. Boy, would he get a shock. Although, as they sneaked a peek at their father's face, they reflected it was probably not as big as the shock he'd get on finding out who else had come along with them.

ADAM BARELY HAD time to get his pants and shirt on before the two girls had trooped in, one bearing a shaving cup and a straight razor with a pitcher of steaming water, and the other carrying a cup of coffee and a plate of eggs and ham. He smirked a little. "I'm good, but not that good. I can't eat and shave at the same time."

"Don't be silly," Annie said. "She'll feed you; I'll shave you. Plenty of time between bitin' and scrapin.'"

Dubiously, he nodded.

"YOU CAN'T GO up there," a man shouted when Ben, Joe and Hoss came through the door and headed toward the stairs. He was ignored until he tried to grab Ben by the arm, whereupon Hoss turned and slugged him.

"You should've let me do that," Ben grumbled, following Hoss.

"Faster my way," Hoss replied.

The slowdown was just enough that Little Joe arrived alone at the top of the staircase and opened the door to find Adam at a table, alternating between bites of breakfast being hand-fed to him by one girl, while another carefully scraped the third-day beard from his jaw.

"Adam?" Joe squeaked, and quickly slammed the door behind him, leaning back against it with all his weight. A second later he flew across the room when the door burst open on Hoss's second try, and it was Hoss and Ben whose jaws dropped.

"Um...morning, fellas," Adam said, manfully forbidding himself to blush while his brothers exchanged shocked glances, although he was fairly certain the blood had just drained out of his body and into the floor on his recognition of his father. *Toujours de l'audace*, he thought, and lifted his chin defiantly. "How are you, Pa? Anybody want breakfast?"

"Uh—no, thanks, Adam," Joe stammered. "We were just— just—um...."

"I couldn't eat a thing," Hoss lied sincerely. "Like Joe said, we just wanted to, um...."

"It's past noon," Ben said, very quietly.

"I just woke up," Adam replied. "Ladies, these are my brothers, Hoss and Joe," Adam gestured vaguely, seeing as how there was no way a sighted person could mistake the two. "And this gentleman here is the lord and master of the Ponderosa, Ben Cartwright. Hoss, Joe, Pa, this lady barber here is Annie, and my own personal chef is Liz."

"Morning, ladies," the two brothers mumbled, and Ben made no sound while Annie and Liz graciously nodded at him and then returned their attention to Adam. Courteously, he waved the girls back and rose from his chair. "Duty calls, ladies, but I do thank you for making me feel so welcome. Now, it would seem I have a legend to live up to. Again."

Somehow, Adam managed to smile at his two unexpected friends before turning and bolting down the stairs. Well, at least he'd gotten one laugh out of all this, as he was pretty certain there would be hell to pay now for the rest of the trip.

They all mounted up and turned their backs on Bella's; after a glare from Ben, Hoss and Joe moved up to take the lead and Ben reined in Buck, despite the horse's head-tossing protests. Adam likewise slowed down Pepper Nell, who danced a little before settling into a walk beside Buck.

"Care to explain anything to me?" Ben asked coolly.

"Not really, Pa," Adam replied honestly.

Ben slowed his horse still more. "All right," Ben ground out. "Just tell me this: was it worth it, waking up hung-over and reeking?"

"Oh, Pa, for the love of—" Thank heaven they had created such a distance between them and Hoss and Joe, or his near-wail would have reached their tender ears. "Pa, really, you're not that gullible, are you?"

"I'm not sure how gullible I am, at this point," Ben replied. "Adam, you're a grown man; you can do what you want. If it's your desire to spend all your nights at a place like Bella's, I can't and won't do anything about it. But it's not how you were raised."

"And if I spent every night doing what I did last night, I would be getting drunk and whining like a whipped puppy, no more and no less, Pa."

"Well," Ben said hesitantly, "in that case, may I ask what you were looking for?"

Adam shrugged. "Absolution. Forgiveness. Comfort. I don't know."

"Find it?"

An explosive sigh. "Nope."

"What did you find, then, if not what Little Joe thinks?"

"Understanding, I guess. That's all."

"Maybe you didn't need the forgiveness," Ben suggested. "And I'm sorry I went to sleep after we got home, but if you had stayed around long enough for me to wake up, you might have found your understanding and your comfort without having to go to *there* for it."

"I couldn't have asked, Pa. I couldn't even look at you. That's why I left."

"I'm not that blasted ugly. And running away is not the act of a grown man."

"I was a grown man long enough to do what needed to be done," Adam said through clenched teeth.

"And just what needed to be done?"

"Hanging Farmer Perkins. It needed to be done. I did it. Leave it there, Pa."

"Adam, I can't. I'm proud of you for that, at least. It's just what I would've done."

"That's a lotta bull, Pa!" Again Adam restrained his voice. "Tell me you would've done it if Bryant had Joe or Hoss, or even me, held hostage. Ben Cartwright would walk into hell barefoot and offer himself up to the devil on a spit just to keep any one of his boys alive for one extra hour. Tell me your principles mean more to you than your children. Tell me and convince me, because I know better!"

A very long, strained silence followed.

"You're right," Ben finally said, quietly and with some chagrin. "But if it matters, I told Bryant you were doing what I would've done. At least we presented a unified front."

"You know, don't you," Adam replied, "that if you had died there, I couldn't have lived with that. Hoss and Joe would have blamed me, but no more than I'd have blamed myself."

"Hoss and Joe would have realized the truth eventually, and I would have thought you'd know—that if I had died, it would have been Bryant's fault and Bryant's doing. Not yours. I know your brothers didn't understand your reasoning. And don't think they didn't get an earful from me, Adam. I spent the whole ride out here telling them how wrong they were."

"But Pa, don't you see, they weren't wrong! It doesn't matter if it was Bryant's doing or not. Principles don't mean anything without the people those principles are supposed to protect. All the principles in the world couldn't have comforted them—or me—if you died because I held the law dearer than you."

"Maybe not, at first. We both have reason to know that *nothing* is comforting in the first days after someone you love dies. But it would've dawned on you all, bit by bit. And son, I couldn't have lived with *myself* if you had let that murderous Perkins loose on Virginia City again."

"Adam, here's why I couldn't have done what you did. The situations don't even closely resemble each other. It's part of the settled order of things that a parent not outlive his children. You and Joe and Hoss would be sad if I died—but it would kill me if I lost one of you. It's a physical law, not just something we're used to. Out in the wild, the most timid deer on earth will fight a cougar to protect its fawn, and will gladly die to keep the fawn alive. A bird will feign a broken wing to lure the fox away from the nest full of chicks, and if it dies, it dies happy, knowing the young will survive. And that's the way it should be—the world itself would end otherwise." Ben looked over at Adam. "But that doesn't mean that what *you* did was wrong. It was as right as...well, Adam, you're the literary one. Don't make me quote Richard Lovelace to you."

Adam thought about that for a while as Pepper Nell and Buck plodded solemnly along. "Don't tell me you've read *Lucasta*. I don't think I've read it since college."

Ben shrugged. "I have been known to pick up an occasional book, you know. Even yours."

"Which poem are you talking about?"

"I don't know the name. Your mother was the Lovelace devotee, not me. But what he said about honor—I can't remember it all, just the last two lines. About love and honor, and not having one without the other. That's the thing I have loved most about you for years, son. I've never seen it so strong before in anyone, not even your brothers, and certainly not me."

"Who do you think I learned it from?" Adam said dryly.

Ben shook his head. "I've always wondered. Maybe it was from your mother. She had a fine sense of honor. I'm just a fellow who does what needs to be done...most of the time. But I couldn't have done what you did, and I'll thank God daily for the rest of my life that I wasn't put in that position, just as I'll also thank him daily that just as he promised, he put the right person in the right place at the right time. And that person was you, son."

"Oh, Pa..." Adam swallowed hard. "Pa, if you just knew..."

"I do. Leave it with the Lord, Adam. I told you, no forgiveness was ever necessary."

Adam sighed long and shakily.

"Reckon we better catch up with your brothers before they come back looking for us," Ben said, not unkindly.

The ride back probably didn't feel as long as it was, just because the 900-pound grizzly bear on Adam's chest had gone away. He was still very quiet on the way home, not joining in with his brothers' banter. They accepted this, figuring it was a result of whatever chastisement he'd gotten. And little more was said between him and his father, but then there was nothing else to say.

THEY REACHED HOME, and Ben dropped any pretense that he wasn't tired; he could barely stay awake long enough to make it to his room.

"That'll teach you to go leaving your sickbed to look for the wandering boy," Adam chided.

"That'll teach you to go running off, wandering boy," Ben replied sternly. Then he smiled, and Adam looked down at the floor, blushing, and smiled back. His father squeezed his shoulder briefly and then trudged slowly into his room.

Hoss and Joe, however, seemed determined not to leave Adam, even following him to his door.

"We just wanted to tell you again," Hoss began, but Adam shook his head. "Don't. I'm not mad at you; I never was. I'd just as soon not talk about it, ever again."

"Does that mean you're not gonna have any more hissy fits and *wun away fwom home*?" Joe put in, his eyes gleaming mischievously. "Or make us come and rescue you outta some saloon?"

"Yeah, that was sure not run-of-the-mill," Hoss added. "Joe's supposed to be the one havin' hissy fits, Adam, not you—and it's supposed to be you rescuin' us, not t'other way around."

"I never had a hissy fit in my life," Adam retorted in mock outrage. "And don't be too sure I appreciated that rescue. Besides, that wasn't just *any* saloon."

"Hey Adam—is it true they got paintings on the walls of Greek ladies wearin' sheets? We were in and out so fast I didn't get to look!"

"Sorry, Joe. You saw more of Adah Menken in *Mazeppa* than you would've seen in there. It's a pretty tame place, you know—after all, it's right next door to nothin'."

He went in his room and searched among the rows of books, and finally found it: *The Poems of Richard Lovelace*. Without hesitation he turned to the Lucasta poems and found "To Lucasta, Going to the Warres."

True: a new Mistresse now I chase
The first foe in the field;
And with a stronger faith imbrace
A sword, a horse, a shield.
Yet this inconstancy is such
As you too shall adore;
I could not love thee, deare, so much,
Lov'd I not Honour more.

Inner Strength

by pbeaking

ittle Joe Cartwright awoke with a start. He found himself
in his own bed with the noon day sun streaming in
through the window. He looked around the room and found that
he was alone. At first, he was bewildered.

"It must be Saturday," he mumbled.

Then his memory came rampantly flowing back. The 7-year-
old shot out of bed and instantly collapsed on the floor in pain.
His ankle was heavily bandaged and his right arm was in a sling.
He managed to use his bed to regain his footage and hobbled out
the door into the hallway. Tears started to well in his eyes as he
recalled the events of the last few days. He had to see his Pa and
headed straight for his room. As he approached, he noticed his
oldest brother, Adam, sitting in a chair reading outside the door.

Joe reached for the knob, but Adam gently placed his hand on
his and said, "Joe, not now...Pa needs his rest."

Joe looked up at his 19-year-old brother with pleading eyes.

"Please, Adam, I have to see him," he begged.

Adam scooped his younger brother into his arms and placed him on his knee.

"Joe, you will...in time. Pa needs to rest and recover from his injuries. The doctor said that he shouldn't have visitors right now so try to understand, okay? And what are you doing out of bed yourself young man?"

Joe did not answer. He leaned into his brother, placing his head on Adam's shoulder. Adam squeezed Joe close. His face deepened in concern as he reflected back over the events of the last few days. He'd never forget the sight of his father and brother staggering into the yard, bloodied, bruised, and bedraggled. The two had left that day for town aboard Buck, Ben's trusty buckskin horse. All Adam knew was that his father and brother had never reached town and neither of them had been in a condition since then to even begin to explain what had happened.

The two brothers sat silently for quite some time, each comforting the other. It was Joe who broke the silence and interrupted Adam's thoughts.

"Adam, I'm sorry," he said softly. "This is all my fault."

Little Joe's eyes filled with tears. Adam could see the boy was distraught, but as much as he wanted to know what happened he wasn't sure if this was the time or place.

"Joe, I'm sure whatever happened was an accident. You and I both know you wouldn't deliberately hurt Pa. The important thing is you two are all right. Once Pa is better we can talk about what happened, okay?"

Adam began to rise. "Now let's get you back into bed where..."

"No, Adam," Joe interrupted. "I want to tell you what happened. It's my fault because...I didn't do as Pa said."

The tears flowed down his cheeks.

Adam intervened. "Joe, are you sure you're feeling up to this? Maybe you should rest for a..."

"I want to...I have to...please," Joe said in frustration.

Adam wiped the tears from his little brother's eyes. He could tell that the boy was carrying a burden that he could no longer bear on his own.

"Okay, Joe. I'll listen," he said.

Joe heaved a huge sigh and then began.

IT WAS A beautiful morning as Pa and Joe meandered down the road toward town. It wasn't very often that Pa and Joe did things alone, and both father and son were enjoying their time together. About half way to town, there was a watering hole. Joe loved stopping there because Pa gave him time to run around and stretch his legs while Buck filled up and rested. The two dismounted near the water's edge, and the buckskin horse gratefully lowered his head to the water. Ben grabbed the canteen from the saddle and took a big swig, then handed it to his son.

"Joseph, I think I'll rest underneath that tree for a while. Buck looks a little tired after the long day he put in yesterday."

Joe finished his drink with a loud swallow.

"Is it okay if I go explore a little, Pa? I won't go far. I promise."

Ben sized up his son for a moment. He knew all too well that when his seven year old wanted "to explore" he needed to set strict guidelines.

"Alright, son, but you may *not* go beyond that tall pine over there *nor* that big rock over yonder, understand?"

Joe nodded and responded with a "Yes, Pa," before running off.

Ben smiled as he watched his son instantly run toward the big pine tree. *Leave it to him to explore the outermost border first*, he thought, shaking his head. He then squatted down and propped himself up against the trunk of a nearby tree. He folded his arms and pulled his hat over his eyes.

It didn't take long for Joe to find the confinements of his father's "laid out fence" boring. Nothing spectacular caught his eye by the big pine, so he walked over towards the large rock and climbed atop for a better look. His eyes peered off into the horizon to the unknown land he so desperately wanted to explore. Suddenly, something caught his eye not too far off in the distance. Joe squinted and realized it was a sign of some sort, but he couldn't read it. *I wonder what it says*, he thought. Joe glanced over his shoulder at his father, who was still snoozing in the shade. Buck was grazing on a clump of grass that he had found near the watering hole.

It's not that far...I could go and see and be back and Pa wouldn't even know. He stood contemplating for a few moments before jumping down and venturing out beyond.

When Joe reached the sign, it said "DANGER." Just to the right of the sign were some wooden planks lying on top of the ground. They were sporadically strewn across one another, and Joe could tell there was a hole beneath them. He tested the first plank. It seemed sturdy enough to hold his weight, so he ventured out to the middle and peered down into the darkness.

Joe did not notice his father quickly approaching from be-hind. In the short distance it took Ben to get to his son, his anger had grown to a boiling point. He reached out and grabbed his son's arm and spun him around to face him. "What do you think you are doing, young man," he bellowed. Joe looked up in shock. He had never seen his Pa so angry. Just then there was a loud crack, and the boards began to give away. Ben shoved Joe to ground just before he himself plummeted through the rotten planks into the darkness.

For a moment, Joe lay on the ground, wincing in pain. His father had thrown him down with such force that he had landed directly on his wrist. The boy felt the bone snap and the pain shoot up his arm. Joe had also hit his head on a rock during the fall and a thin stream of blood began to slowly trickle down the side of his face. Despite his injuries, it didn't take long for the boy to realize about his Pa and what had happened to him. He scrambled over to the opening in the ground and began shouting, "Pa...Pa...are you okay?"

Nothing but the boy's own echo answered.

"Pa...Pa...answer me, please. I'm sorry...Please, Pa."

This time Joe heard some soft groans.

"Pa...please...answer me...can you hear me?"

Joe buried his head in the dirt and began to cry. What had he done? There was silence for a few more minutes; then Joe heard a feeble cry from the depths of the darkness.

"Joe?...Joe?...I'm here, son." Ben uttered weakly.

"Pa!... What have I done?" Joe shouted out in dismay.

Ben had fallen into an old mine shaft. He could tell both legs had been broken in the fall, and his right arm had been punctured by one of the sharp wooden planks as they gave way beneath him. The impact with the ground had left him momentarily disoriented.

With all his injuries and pain, his mind was on one thing...his youngest son. He tried to steady his voice and sound reassuring as he spoke once again.

"Joe. I want you to go get Buck and bring him here. Everything will be fine if you do as I say."

His father's words fell on deaf ears. The pangs of guilt erupted and Joe could only utter, "I'm sorry, Pa," over and over and over.

Ben felt himself wavering on the verge of unconsciousness. He had to make the boy hear him, so he took in a deep breath and spoke with all his energy.

"Joseph! That's enough, young man. I don't need your apologies right now. I need you to do as I say. Now stop this foolishness and get Buck."

Then there was silence.

"Pa?" Joseph apprehensively asked, but Ben deliberately did not answer the boy.

This silence snapped Joe to attention. He arose, wincing in pain. Holding his wrist, he stumbled towards his father's horse and led him back to the opening.

Ben felt the blood oozing from his arm and knew he needed

to stop the bleeding. He tore the sleeve off and wrapped it tightly around the wound. The pain in his legs was beyond excruciating, and his head was pounding from lack of air in the shaft.

Soon he heard his son's apprehensive voice. "Pa...I have Buck."

"Good boy, Joseph. Now tie the rope to the saddle like I've shown you and toss the other end down the hole."

Ben did not know how far he had fallen, but he could only hope the rope would be long enough to reach him.

Joseph walked over to Buck and looped the rope around the saddle horn. He couldn't use his other arm to help replicate the knot his father had practiced with him time and time again. He did the best he could and hoped the makeshift knot would hold strong. He then threw the rope down the hole.

Ben was snapped back into consciousness when the rope hit him in the face. He propped himself up into a sitting position and wound the rope around his chest. He, too, had difficulty tying a knot with only one good arm, but made do with what he could.

Again his boy's quavering voice reached him. "Pa, are you okay?"

Ben felt weak and, although he could not answer strongly, he managed to direct his son once more.

"Joseph, I want you to lead Buck away from the hole. Do not stop or look back, regardless what you hear from me. Do you understand?"

Joe replied, "Yes, Pa. But what if..." He could not finish.

"Joseph, do as I say and everything will be fine."

Joe grabbed Buck's reins and started leading him away. Ben felt the tug and muffled his cries as he waited for the broken limbs to bear weight. A moment later, the pain was unbearable. Ben yelled out a blood-curdling scream before surrendering to the unconscious.

Joe had never heard his father yell like that, and it tore into his heart. He momentarily wavered, but reliving his father's words, he found the inner strength to push forward. A few moments later, Ben lay aside the hole face down. Joe ran to his father, reaching his good arm around his shoulders. He laid down beside him and this comforted the boy. There the two remained for quite some time.

Joe was startled awake by his father's groans and raised his head. He began scanning his father's body. He stared at the blood stained arm and grimaced at the mangled legs of his Pa. The gruesome image brought tears once more.

Ben drifted back into consciousness and was becoming aware of his surroundings.

"Joseph," he said. "Are you alright, son?"

"Yes, Pa," was all the boy could say through his sobs.

"Listen to me, Joseph. I need you to take Buck and go get help. Buck knows the way home, and he'll get you there."

"No, Pa, I won't leave you!" Joe shouted.

"Joseph, you must do as I say. I need..." Ben gasped and was unconscious once more.

By now Joe was emotionally and physically exhausted. His arm was aching, and he no longer had his father's guidance to help him. He had to act quickly, but what should he do? He was afraid to leave his Pa to the wilds, yet his Pa had told him to go get help.

Suddenly he remembered Adam telling him once about making a makeshift gurney out of pine tree branches.

"Maybe I could do that and tow Pa home." And so, Joe began his task.

He found some branches on the ground and used part of the rope to tie them together. When he compared it to his Pa's body frame, however, it was too small. The sun was starting to set, and it soon would be dark. Joe knew no one would come looking for them until morning. Fear was starting to control his thinking.

He raced through the woods looking for more branches. As he rounded a bend, he saw the opening to the mine that his father had fallen into. It was boarded up with wooden planks. Joe raced down the hill toward his newly found treasure. Just before he reached the base, he stepped into a hole and tumbled, twisting his ankle in the incident. This was the breaking point for the youngster. He laid his head down and sobbed, not from the pain, but from defeat. He was past the point of exhaustion and fell asleep with tears streaming down his face.

Ben Cartwright awoke with a start in the twilight. He looked around to find himself alone.

"Joe!...Son?!" Ben attempted to call, but the words were barely audible.

Had his son gone for help like he asked? Just then he heard Buck snort. The horse was still with him. That meant the boy was somewhere nearby. He called out for Joe once again with all the voice he had left. Joe was startled awake by his father's call and just hearing his voice from the darkness brought strength to his son once more. He hobbled over to the opening of the mine and managed to pull off three planks. He painstakingly carried each board back to his father's side. Without a word, he managed to tie the boards to the branches he had already rigged up behind Buck. Darkness had settled in by the time he had finished his task. Joe backed the horse up to position the gurney next to his father. He leaned down really close to his father's face and began talking to him.

"Pa, I need your help. I can't move you by myself. Can you roll over on your back?"

Ben was not fully alert, but he understood what his son wanted. He muttered a weak, "I'll try, son."

Joe then positioned himself along side his father, grabbing hold of his vest.

"One...Two...Three," he shouted, and both father and son reached deep within their inner souls to muster enough strength to complete the task.

"...AND THEN I towed Pa home," Joe softly concluded his story.

The story had taken over an hour to tell, and Adam listened

silently, offering his brother a shoulder to cry on as needed. Adam, too, found himself fighting back tears. Inside his heart was breaking. He sympathized with his brother, knowing of the ordeal he had just gone through. He also knew all too well that his brother's stubbornness would make it difficult for him to let go of the guilt, and that it would be some time before his father was well enough to even discuss what had happened with the boy.

Adam realized that he had to make Joe understand that even though he had done wrong, he had saved his father's life. When it really mattered, he had pulled through and did what he had to do. But what could he say that would help ease the pain?

After a moment, he spoke. "Joe, thank you."

The boy looked at his older brother and gave him a puzzled glance. It wasn't the words he expected to hear.

Why was he thanking me? Joe wondered.

Adam continued. "I'm proud of you, Joe. It's because of your fast thinking that we still have Pa here with us right now. If you would have left him out there, he may not have been so lucky."

Joe pondered his brother's words, but remained silent. After a moment, however, Adam could see an ever so brief grin break through the sullen tear-stained face. Well, it didn't cure everything, but it was a start in the right direction.

Adam gave Joe a big hug and then said, "Let's get you back into bed where you belong."

Joe hesitated. He just had to see his Pa.

"Adam, please let me see Pa. I just have to..." Again the tears began to fall.

Adam studied his brother for a long moment. He knew the boy had been through an ordeal and needed reassurance that everything was going to be fine. He also did not feel like dealing with Joe's stubbornness and forcing the boy to bed.

"Joe, if I let you see him, you have to promise me you will then go to bed."

Joe hastily nodded his head up and down. Adam lowered his

brother to the floor and took him by the hand. The two then entered Ben's room.

Ben Cartwright was propped up in bed with his arm in a sling and his legs tightly bound and immobile. He was sleeping soundly. Joe walked up alongside the bed. He studied his father's face for a few moments before carefully climbing up next to him and laying his head down on his chest. He could hear his father's heartbeat and steady breathing. It was soothing.

The boy's presence awakened Ben, and he opened his eyes slowly, gazing down at his youngest son. He weakly took his hand and began caressing the boy's back. Tears welled in his eyes as he reflected back on what they both had been through.

To Joe, his father's touch meant so much. It told him that he was no longer angry with him, that he was proud of him, and that he still loved him.

Adam watched in silence as the two fell fast asleep. It put his mind at ease to see that they were both on their way to recovery. It would take some time, but eventually everything would return to normal. He knew all too well that Joe and his father would be having a long discussion about this little incident in the future, but for now they had found peace with each other, both relying on their inner strength to pull them through.

Ride the Flume

by Lyn Robinson

$\mathscr{J}$oe struggled ineffectively against the cold waters. He knew that a person's life was supposed to pass before them as they died, but it was only the last four days that came to mind, along with the thought that his father would never forgive him for drowning. If only he had done as his Pa said or even as Adam had said...

It had all started when Joe rode into the house mid-afternoon four days earlier. Ben and Hoss had headed down to a small ranch south of Carson City the previous day with some breeding stock they were selling and wouldn't be back for two days. At the same time, Adam had headed into town on business while Joe went to check the herd in the south pasture. But there were few problems there, and Joe finished soon after lunch on the second day and headed home, wondering if his older brother would be there. He hoped Adam would be busy somewhere else and not at home to find him another job to do.

As he rode in, Joe found he was out of luck—Adam was busy cutting wood out back. Joe hesitated and, as he watched, Adam took a piece of wood he'd cut, went over to a shape traced on the ground and fitted the wood in, before he carefully measured another piece and started to cut it. Adam was so absorbed in what he was doing that he was totally oblivious to his brother's presence and, for a minute, Joe was tempted to sneak away and have a lazy couple of hours down by the creek. But his curiosity got the better of him.

Joe moved forward. "What are you up to, Adam?" he asked.

Adam finished the cut and took the piece of timber over to its place and then grabbed his shirt from over the hitching rail and slipped it on, the sun making his body gleam with a sheen of sweat. He didn't bother doing the shirt up but headed into the house, ready for a break. "Come on, Joe, let's go raid some cookies and get some coffee, and I'll explain," Adam offered.

"Where's Hop Sing?"

"He went into town. I think it was his number five cousin who's sick this time, but no matter, he's left us stew and pie for supper."

Joe followed his brother, but he couldn't help looking back. "Just what is that, Adam?"

"It's going to be a boat," Adam replied.

"Mighty funny shape for a boat, isn't it?" Joe observed. "It's sorta skinny looking! Anyway, why are you building a boat?"

Adam ignored his brother and went to get coffee and a plate of doughnuts, before settling by the fireplace. Joe joined him and impatiently asked, "What are you up to?"

Adam didn't bother answering until he had finished his first doughnut, but then he leaned back in the chair sipping his coffee, and Joe could see the glint of pure mischief in his brother's eyes. It wasn't that common a sight, and Joe couldn't help a broad grin. It soon faded, though, as Adam began talking.

"I was in town yesterday, and Flood and O'Brien were there from Frisco. They wanted to discuss some business, so I joined the four Irishmen for dinner."

Joe asked cynically, "And did you have a hangover this morning?"

"Well, you know what those four are like when they get together; it got quite convivial. We sorted out the business problems before dinner and, afterwards, Dan de Quille joined us, and we chatted a while."

"What does that have to do with building a boat?" Joe demanded.

"Patience, little brother. I'm getting there." Adam grinned broadly, but he wasn't deliberately trying to tease his brother. "The discussion turned to lumber, and James Flood asked how we got the lumber to the mines. He was intrigued by the idea of the flume, and he suggested a man could go down it just as well as a tree trunk. John Mackay and O'Brien both disagreed but, rather to my surprise, Jim Fair supported Flood."

"Well, I think John and O'Brien are right; you'd lose all your hide going down that flume. It'd be a mite rough."

Adam laughed. "They weren't suggesting going down unprotected, Joe, that's why we need a boat."

The light dawned and Joe said, "So that's why the boat is so skinny—it's to fit in the flume!"

"You got it, little brother. The argument went round some, and then Jim Fair remembered that I'd designed the flume, and he asked my opinion. I reckoned it would be safe enough, provided the boat was made securely and you held on tight. It became a bet, and I landed the job of designing and building the boat."

"So when are you going?" Joe asked.

"On Saturday, provided the boat is ready on time, the five of us."

Joe sighed heavily; he would love to have joined his brother. "So John Mackay and O'Brien gave in," he commented.

"Oh no, nothing was going to get them into the boat! I'm not certain if Fair and Flood will be so sure this morning, but they were adamant about going last night, and even our esteemed reporter Dan de Quille is going along. He says he trusts me if I say it's safe, particularly as I'm risking my own skin going along."

"That's only four," Joe noted.

"Well, there was some hefty bidding in the Washoe Club for the fifth place and even more betting on how many of us would reach the end of the flume intact. Shortest odds were on none, not even the boat."

"So who else is going?" Joe prodded.

"Well, I said that I would need some help to complete the boat on time and my assistant in building it ought to have first chance at the spare place. Fancy a wild ride, Joe?"

Joe stuttered, "You mean I—could I—can I—?"

Adam chuckled, and he reached out and gripped Joe's arm. "Yes, brother, if you want to join me, the place is yours."

"Wow! How fast do you reckon it will go? You once said those logs did a mile in a minute, didn't you?" Joe asked eagerly.

"They do or maybe a little more. The boat won't go quite as fast—there'll be more friction—but fast enough to be exciting."

"How far you planning on going?"

"The fifteen miles from the mid-terminus. We'll need to stop the lumber going down for a while and get the bottom pool cleared, so we don't crash into logs there, but otherwise it should be safe enough."

Joe frowned suddenly with a thought. "What's Pa going to say?"

Adam grinned. "I'd guess he'll say that there is no way we are going, but as he won't be home until Friday, the boat will be finished and it will be too late to back out."

"Do you think Pa will see it that way?" Joe said dubiously.

Adam knew exactly what Joe meant but he replied, with rather more confidence than he felt, that he would deal with their father. For now they had a boat to build, and the brothers went outside to work in complete amity for once.

Two days later the boat was completed and double roped, and Adam was fixing strong ropes round the inside in short loops. That puzzled Joe, but Adam explained, "I told you that we need to hang on tight, particularly when the boat leaves the flume. Those are to hang onto."

"How are we going to get the boat into the flume? It's heavy," Joe wondered. Adam had used complete trunks for his boat, each about six inches in diameter, and Joe was right; the boat was very heavy, but Adam wasn't worried.

"Hoss is due back tomorrow; between the three of us we can cope," he responded.

Well-pleased by their handiwork, the brothers went in to eat and then settled for a game of chess and a peaceful evening.

The boat was the first thing Ben saw when he rode in just before lunch the next day, and, surmising that it meant no good, he bellowed for his sons. Joe came out of the barn, attempting to look innocent but failing abysmally. Adam sauntered out from the house where he had been updating the ledgers, and Joe took refuge behind his eldest brother. "Good to see you back, Pa. Successful trip, I hope?" Adam asked.

Ben growled, "Yes it was, but what tomfoolery have you two been up to while my back was turned? What is that object?"

"It's a boat, Pa. A bit crude, I admit, but I would have hoped it was recognisable," Adam deadpanned.

Joe flinched at his eldest brother's foolhardiness in fanning the fires of an obviously already irate father. But much to the younger son's surprise, their father visibly relaxed. Ben could see the pure mischief in his eldest son's eyes—something he hadn't seen for far too long—and, although he was sure Adam was up to something that he wouldn't really approve of, it couldn't be very serious if Adam looked like that. Ben grunted and went in for some coffee. He would extricate more details out of his sons later.

In fact, it wasn't until they had all four finished dinner and, full of crisp roast pork and all the trimmings, were sitting over coffee that Ben referred to the strange boat. Adam made an entertaining story of his evening in the Washoe Club, and it took a while for Ben to realise that both his eldest and youngest sons were intending to ride the flume the following day. Hoss had gotten the full story out of Joe earlier in the afternoon when he'd arrived home and, a bit worried, he had sought out his eldest brother with one question: was it safe? Adam had looked at him, slightly annoyed, and replied, "Do you really think I would let Joe come if it wasn't?"

"Nope, I know you wouldn't. Sorry, Adam, I didn't need to ask. Sounds a mite scary, even so."

"Let's say it should be an exciting ride, but with Jim Fair going, there is no way I'm not," Adam said.

"Reckon I'll be down at the end to meet you both."

"That would be helpful," Adam said gratefully. "There's no way we can wear either our gun belts or our hats, so if you would take them down to the end and meet us there with them, I'd appreciate it. I'd feel about half-dressed in Virginia City without either of them."

Hoss nodded and then, trusting in his big brother, he gave up worrying. He now sat back only half-listening to the story Adam was telling their father, but he couldn't miss the loud thump as Ben banged his hand down hard on the table and laid down the law that neither of his sons was going in this untried boat. Adam sat calmly looking at his father as Hoss and Joe decided to go and check the horses again for the night. Ben was about to stop them, but then he looked at his eldest son and knew that was where the real fight lay.

Ben went and poured himself a brandy, determined to calm down and make his logical son understand that he could not entrust his own life and, perhaps more easily, his younger brother's life, in an untried boat just for a meaningless bet. He took a couple of minutes and then marshalled his arguments, but his control wasn't helped by the tinge of distinct amusement with which Adam considered him.

Adam made no real attempt to answer his father point-by-point; he just waited patiently for Ben to run out of steam. Then he got to his feet, and, leaving his coffee cup on top of the newel post, he turned. "Trust me, Pa, I am a good engineer. The boat and the trip are safe. I wouldn't take Joe with me if I wasn't completely confident, and you can't expect me to let others try out my design without me. Don't worry—it'll just be an exciting ride."

Ben opened his mouth to continue arguing, but under Adam's steady gaze, he closed it again. He could only do as Adam asked and trust his eldest son as he had done for so many years. His son smiled tautly and then went upstairs with his usual grace.

Hoss and Joe kept out of the way for the rest of the evening, and with no one to take his worry out on, Ben headed for bed. He was in no better mood the following morning at breakfast, and for once the meal was virtually silent as all three brothers avoided provoking their father. Adam had been up very early, and all the chores were complete so Ben had no excuse to stop them; but that didn't improve his temper. Logically, he knew his sons were grown men, and he had no right to tell them how to use their leisure time, but when they were putting themselves at risk logic didn't help.

Ben was determined not to have anything to do with this insane boat ride, and he ignored his sons as they laid their plans out on the porch. Adam had arranged to meet the other three participants up at the mid-terminus about nine-thirty. He was going to launch his boat on the ride down the flume exactly at ten and was reckoning on it taking around twenty minutes to cover the fifteen miles to the terminus near town. From what he had heard the other night, about half of Virginia City was proposing to be there to greet them, if only to settle the multitude of bets. One of the bets was on the amount of time the ride would take, which meant they had to launch exactly on time. Hoss was of two minds: he wanted to see his brothers off, but he also wanted to see them arrive. The distance involved precluded him doing both, so he settled for helping them to get the boat into position and then he would ride into town to greet them, taking their gun belts and hats with him.

Adam wasn't sure how long it would take to get the boat into position, and so the brothers started edging it up a ramp onto one of the wagons soon after breakfast. Ben heard them but made a determined effort to work on the ledgers. After a few minutes, he had to admit he was making so many mistakes that he was wasting his time, and, almost begrudgingly, he got his coat and went out to saddle up Buck. Just in case Adam was wrong and either of his sons was hurt, or God forbid even worse, he couldn't let them go on such a sour note, Ben thought as he rode out for the mid-terminus.

Adam was very glad of Hoss' great strength, as the brothers fought to position the unwieldy boat correctly over the flume. Adam had set up block and tackle to suspend the boat a few inches over the flume until they were ready to go, and he had already stopped more logs from going down. He had arranged with an old friend, Jake Donavan, to check the arrival area and ensure that it was clear, otherwise he feared a collision with one of the large logs at the bottom. Eventually everything was ready to Adam's satisfaction, and the brothers passed their gun belts and hats to Hoss, promising to see him later, and Adam promised to buy the beer in thanks for his help. Hoss grinned broadly, but he couldn't help himself and told them both to be real careful. Adam gripped Hoss' shoulder momentarily. "Don't worry, we'll be fine. See you in town."

Hoss was just riding out when he saw his father ride in, but since Ben didn't seem to want to talk to him Hoss headed on for town; there wasn't too much time if he was to beat his brothers there. Ben went over to his other sons and considered the boat now in position over the flume. He could see now why Adam had designed it the way he had and, knowing the flume and how exactly it had been designed and built, his worst fears were eased. There was no way the boat could capsize on the way down—it was too good a fit in the flume. It still seemed foolhardy in the extreme, but there was no point in saying anything more, and he just gripped Joe's shoulder and took his oldest son's hand. "Just you two be real careful. We have too much work to do for you to be injured," Ben cautioned. "I'm going to join Hoss in town and see just how much fuss you have really caused with all this."

Adam smiled broadly, his eyes alight, glad that his father had come out, but he didn't say anything and it was left to Joe to remark, "Thanks for coming out, Pa, see you in town."

Ben couldn't help adding, "Just promise me you'll be careful."

"Sure, Pa," Joe said.

Later, when he would be struggling to breathe and trying to find out which way the surface of the water lay, Joe would remember that promise and swear at himself for not keeping it. But now...

The other three participants rode in just as Ben left, and although Dan looked as though he regretted his alcoholic bravado, the two Irishmen seemed relaxed. All three regarded the boat that Adam had built with considerable interest. Dan turned to Little Joe. "So, you are joining us on this mad escapade?" he asked.

"Sure am," Joe replied. "After all the hard work I've done over the last couple of days getting this boat ready, I wouldn't miss it for the world."

Jim considered the boat and then turned to Adam. "Which part of the boat did Joe build?" he asked mischievously. "I'd like to sit somewhere else."

Joe just grinned at the teasing, but Adam replied seriously, "It was a joint effort and needed two pairs of hands." He motioned to the boat. "I suggest we sit like this," he said, indicating where he wanted each man positioned, his younger brother immediately behind him and Dan at the back. Adam was proposing to take the front position himself and had equipped himself with a stout short stick to fend off the side of the flume if necessary—just in case there were still any logs in the way at the end of their ride. Half a dozen hands were on site, and Adam had told them exactly what to do on his order to launch the boat.

As ten o'clock approached, Adam had everyone take their positions, and he reached up to remove Dan's hat. Dan objected to its removal, but Adam promised him he would get it back if he relinquished it now; otherwise, he was be bound to lose it on the journey and might never see it again.

Adam had made sure that his watch agreed with Quincy's, the bartender in the Washoe Club, who was holding the bets on the time of the race. So at the moment his watch indicated ten, he signalled his men to cut the supporting ropes, and the five men were launched on the ride of their lives.

Adam had made a superb job designing the boat so that it fitted smoothly on the flume, and the rushing water, combined with gravity, accelerated them quickly to a speed none of them had ever known outside of a railway carriage. Adam had warned each man individually to keep their hands inside the boat and to hang onto the ropes he had positioned for that purpose at all times. He had tried to explain that if they didn't, they might travel straight forward while the boat went round a corner, the different directions causing definite risks to life and limb. At first his warnings seemed hardly necessary as all five men held on like grim death, with the sides of the flume and the rock face whipping past their faces. However, as they found the boat successfully negotiating the corners, the sheer adrenaline rush was enough to make them shout and start to wave their hands and punch the air. Three times Adam had to shout a warning to hold on—twice at his little brother and once at James Flood.

As the boat rocketed down the flume, they seemed to surge forward at every new turn, and the countryside became a kaleidoscope of colour as it rushed past. Their little boat buffeted from one side of the flume to the other and then slid down the centre for a while before the pattern repeated all over again.

Once or twice it seemed to threaten to leave the flume altogether and fly off into the woods, and all five were left with no breath for talk—although more than one yell was heard, surprised out of them as the boat turned a new curve in the flume.

None of them had any idea how long they had been travelling; it seemed to go past in a flash, and yet in a strange way they had always been flying through space in their small boat. Eventually, Adam could see the final terminus and the crowd of people waiting. He managed the breath to call, "We're there!" before the boat took off from the protective custody of the flume and was launched into the water.

It was at that point that Joe forgot everything he had been told and everything he had promised his father and elder brother, and with a shout of sheer exultation and pure adrenaline, he punched the air with both fists.

As he let go with both hands, Joe's body carried forward just as the boat hit the water and was slowed by the friction of impact. Adam was horrified as Joe went flying past him into the water. Adam had one hand gripping the rope to keep himself safe and the other holding the stave in case he needed to push the boat away from anything in the water, and there was no way he could grab his brother.

On the shoreline, Ben had joined his middle son amongst the hordes of bystanders, and they could only watch in horror as Joe went into the water. Most of the others were too busy working out the effect the time of arrival and the number still in the boat had on their bets to worry, but for the Cartwrights time seemed to hang still.

Joe couldn't believe he had been so stupid as to let go with both hands after all big brother had said, but he had. He couldn't breathe, and he couldn't find the surface of the water, and maybe he wouldn't have to face the wrath of his father and brothers because he would be dead, but...

Suddenly Joe felt a tight grip on his arm; somehow he knew whose grip it was, and he knew he was safe. He had known that grip all his life, pulling him back from danger or preventing his escape when he had been up to mischief. Then he was being pulled up to face an exceedingly angry elder brother. Adam had dropped the stave and, seeing Joe in the water, he had leaned over dangerously, with Flood holding onto his legs, and managed to get a grip on his brother just as Joe seemed to be sinking again. With the help of the two Irishmen, he had pulled Joe up until at least his arms were over the side of the boat. Adam's face said exactly what he would have liked to tell his little brother, but as Joe coughed and spluttered trying to get his breath, Adam had the sense to leave his recriminations until later.

Once Joe had managed to get his breath, they helped him to climb back into the boat, and then the five men paddled the awkward craft closer to the shore where Hoss waded out to pull them in.

Ben was standing waiting with his arms folded, and he glared at both his sons. Once he had seen his eldest son pull Joe up, he had begun breathing again himself. Now looking at his youngest son's very sheepish expression, he could see that Joe wasn't hurt, just embarrassed.

Adam sighed, "Pa, I told him to hold on."

Joe tried to get his brother out of trouble. "He really did, Pa, at least a hundred times, and I meant to, but..."

Ben raised an eyebrow. "But, what?"

Joe's eyes danced with excitement. "Pa, you have to try it! I've never felt anything like it, so fast, it was like flying and I just... well I guess I just..."

Ben looked questioningly at Joe, but Joe couldn't meet his gaze. "I'm sorry, Pa. I forgot," he apologized.

Ben looked round at his eldest son, who shrugged. "He never changes, Pa. Just a magnet for trouble. But he's right—it was one heck of a ride."

With both sons safely back on dry land, Ben could only shake his head. Dan came over, and for once the tall reporter found himself lost for words. After his initial terror, he had thoroughly enjoyed himself, but just how he was going to write up the experience, Dan didn't know. For now he wanted a drink to celebrate his survival, and the five men, all wet and bedraggled but delighted with life, led a triumphant procession back to the Palace for a drink. Now that the town had seen the party's safe arrival, half of them wanted to ride the flume themselves, and Adam was fending off ever more extravagant offers for his boat. Eventually, the others drifted away, and the brothers found themselves alone for a minute as Ben mediated between the Irishmen, crowing over their successful ride.

Hoss glared at his little brother. "You sure know how to get us all in trouble."

Joe grinned. "I knew big brother was there to rescue me."

Adam shook his head. "If only you had listened in the first place!"

Joe clapped an arm around Adam's broad shoulders. "I will next time, honest, I will."

Adam and Hoss met each other's gaze and slowly shook their heads. They knew their little brother too well, but then Adam laughed, "Come on, I promised to buy the beer. I should have known better than to involve you, Joe. It was asking for trouble!"

"Oh, I'm very glad you did, big brother—it was one hell of a ride!"

Based on a true story. Documented by an old Virginia City photograph, two of the Silver Kings, James Flood and Jim Fair, did introduce the idea of riding the flume when they went down one with reporter Dan de Quille and two other men.

He Was Laughing

by Calim11

Hoss

He was laughin'.

I ain't heard it in so long I was surprised when those deep tones sorta carried over everyone else's. It made me smile. My brother Adam was laughin'.

Ya see it was a mite shockin' in that...well, my brother ain't had it so good lately. A woman he was gonna marry run off with our cousin without even lookin' back, and afore that he done hurt hisself real bad fallin' offa ladder and couldn't walk for a spell. Then ta top it all off, once he got back onta his feet he lost two valuable timber contracts which hurt him somethin' fierce.

Now Pa...Pa don't exactly keep his thoughts ta hisself mosta the time, and this weren't no different. When Adam come home without them contracts he started blamin' that woman and then

Adam for not payin' attention. They got inta an awful fight and I thought Adam was gonna leave for good this time—and I couldn't say as I blamed 'im.

That boy puts in an awful lotta work 'round the ranch and sometimes I think Pa forgets that. They's been together so long, seem ta know what the other's thinkin' way afore I do, that I think Pa takes 'im for granted, doesn't tell 'im often enough how glad he is that he's here and how much he loves 'im. And now that he was feelin' especially low what with losin' out on a family and then not bein' able ta help us with the round-up on account o' his back, Pa jest started yellin'. I could tell by the look on older brother's face it weren't goin' down well and, if it hadn't a been Pa standin' there, he woulda decked 'im. Instead he jest up and walked right outta the house, got back on his horse and lit out.

Well, I couldn't jest let 'im go, not like that anyway, so's I gave Pa a hard look and took after my brother. Ya see I've always known Adam would up and leave one day. It's not that he don't love the Ponderosa like Joe or me or Pa, he does it's jest that he's got a yearnin' in his belly ta see other things. I'm thinkin' that's 'cause he was always movin' as a young 'un. Never stayed in one place long enough ta feel settled 'til he come here. And that's fine if'n he wants ta see the world, but he should leave when he wants not 'cause he's mad or don't think Pa respects 'im no more. That ain't a good reason ta walk away from nothin'.

A course he walked away from Laura but, and I havta say it, that was a wise choice. That woman was jest a whiner, and then ta two-time 'im like that...well, that wasn't right. Now I ain't got nothin' against Will feelin' what he did. Sometimes ya cain't help where yer heart takes ya but that woman...The only good thing about her was Peggy and Adam loved ol' Peggy a lot more than Laura so's it's a good thing Will took her offa his hands. But it still rips at yer heart, ya know, thinkin' ya ain't never gonna find a woman ta share yer life with.

Well I finally caught up ta Adam and we had us a long talk. He and I've always been able ta talk about everythin' and he jest poured out his heart ta me. The last time I heard 'im talk like that was when he hadta shoot Ross Marquette. That nearly done 'im in but I managed ta git 'im talkin' then and it seemed ta settle 'im some. It was the same here. Older brother jest needed someone ta talk to without bein' judged and we both knew Pa and Joe woulda worried 'im ta death about Laura lyin' ta 'im. I ain't like that. I've had my share o' problems with women and my luck's run about the same as Adam's, but I know that callin' 'em names and tossin' in yer face that ya picked another loser ain't gonna do ya no good when yer in pain, when yer thinkin' this is it.

When I was sure he weren't gonna leave on the mornin' stage, I left 'im out there in the dark ta gather hisself while I went on home and gave a piece o' my mind ta Pa. Now, I don't normally do such things but I was riled and Pa knew it jest from the look on my face. Joe always said I look like a mama bear tryin' ta protect her cubs when I get like that and I'm thinkin' he might be onta somethin' 'cause Pa took a step back from me when I came ramblin' inta the house and slammed the door behind me. I waved my finger and poked 'im—yeah, I poked 'im—and wanted ta know where he got off accusin' Adam o' doin' anythin' but his best for the ranch and the family. Didn't he remember that jest a bit ago it didn't look like Adam was gonna walk again and that hasta prey on a man that if'n he's stuck in a chair for the rest o' his life how's he gonna prove hisself? How's he gonna be a man that a woman wants around?

I also wanted ta know why he hadta keep throwin' Laura up in his face when we all know he felt somethin' for her even if'n it weren't true love; and how could he chastise 'im for losin' them contracts after all he's been through and the fact that he feels as low as a snake's belly already without 'im harpin' on 'im.

I stopped then, waitin' for an answer as I stared at Pa noticin' for the first time I was towerin' over 'im. I ain't never thought o' that afore. Pa's Pa, a towerin' man by hisself but this time I felt like a giant protectin' my brother. I backed away then 'cause it weren't my place ta scare the man. I was jest so God-awful mad at it all! I jest wanted ta take the world and shake it, hopin' some happiness would fall Adam's way.

Pa had that look, a stunned look I'd guess ya'd call it, and jest stared at me and I turned away, stuffin' my hands in my pockets. I apologized for speakin' ta 'im that way but then I turned and told 'im that I love Adam for all he's ever done for me. He held me close when Mama was killed; he looked after me and taught me when we was on the wagon train and then helped me with my learnin' when everyone else was makin' fun. He and I share a link that's different than the one I share with Joe and even with Pa. It runs much deeper. We don't havta worry about how we're gonna react or what we're gonna say and we always know that the other will be there when needed. And even though we've come ta blows a time or two we always made up, always understood that the love we share runs deep and even death wouldn't split us apart. Pa had ta know that if'n he didn't already.

He looked unsteady and sat down in his big chair. Carefully I rested a hand on his shoulder tellin' 'im that we all look out for each other and we all look up ta Adam for pavin' the way for us. But that don't mean ol' Adam don't need help once in awhile hisself and surely don't need his Pa mouthin' off at 'im like that especially after what he'd been through.

I left it at that and went ta bed. I don't think Pa ever said nothin' about what happened but I could tell Adam knew jest by the way he smiled at me the next day and laid a hand across my back. We jest stood there and looked at the lake and I was happy I could be there for 'im like he'd been there for me so many times afore.

He's my brother and I love 'im and I don't take kindly ta folks, Pa or not, treatin' 'im like dirt.

So, after all this time, it was nice ta hear 'im laughin'.

Joe

THAT WAS ADAM...I'm sure of it.

That deep laugh he gives out when he finds something truly funny. I'm just surprised is all. I haven't heard him laugh like that since, well since that woman started messing with him...that Laura.

I never liked her. She was just way too much work and belly-ached over everything! The only good thing about her was her daughter, Peggy, whom I know Adam adored. In fact, I believe he was just marrying Laura to have Peggy as a daughter. Not a very good reason to get married but, for Adam, it was an interesting reason because I never thought he'd do something like that. I always thought he'd marry for love just like the rest of us.

Oh, I don't know. Maybe he thought he loved her. I thought I was in love with my fair share of women. I just never thought it would happen to him.

Of course he was spending a bit too much time on their new house and leaving her to fend for herself. That's when Will stepped in. I wanted to just punch him down to the ground when I found out what happened but Adam told me it was all right. I didn't believe him, of course, but I still left it alone 'cause he was hurting so from his back and I didn't want to add to it with all my questions. I'm always full of them, always have been and I annoy the hell out of everyone until I get answers. But this time, this time I backed away. Adam would talk when he wanted although I was pretty sure he'd only talk to Pa or Hoss. He and I don't have that type of relationship, never have. Oh, when I was younger maybe but when he came back from college it all changed. I wanted to be a man and he wanted to be my Pa, always telling me what to do...well, that's not true. He just wanted what was best for me. He always has. I just took it wrong most of the time.

But whether or not he truly loved Laura, its still gotta hurt—being rejected, I mean. You wouldn't think that would happen to him. He's good looking, tall, strong and smart. He knows poetry and Shakespeare and how to build almost anything and yet all those accomplishments haven't gotten a wedding ring on his finger. I wonder if it ever will.

I got a true appreciation of what my brother was feeling when I tagged along with him to Stockton to finalize those damnable contracts, the cause of all our current turmoil. Pa couldn't go 'cause he'd tripped over one of Hop Sing's chickens and wrenched his knee and the only person who knew the contracts beside him was Adam. Now older brother had just gotten to the point where he didn't collapse at the end of each day in terrible pain from his back but accepted that he was the only one to go. I went along as kind of a nursemaid even though I didn't tell him that but he's smart enough to figure it out 'cause there wouldn't be any other reason for me to go with him—I don't know anything about the contracts and don't want to.

Well, we took the stage which was a huge mistake since it irritated Adam's back to the point that we had to get off about twenty miles from Stockton and buy some horses or else he wouldn't have made it in one piece. Then we got there and the meetings and bidding times had changed to where they overlapped each other by an hour. We couldn't miss these or we'd miss out on the contracts, so I had to head to the second one to represent us until Adam could show up.

When he did I knew the first meeting hadn't gone well by the dark look on his face. But, once again, I kept my questions to myself and let him take over, while I slipped out the back to try to make sure we got a room for the evening, but that didn't happen either. I hated to tell Adam that we were destined to sleep on the hard ground again but figured once he'd won this contract he wouldn't care.

I met him outside the meeting hall with a smile, only to have it wiped clean by the searing look in his eyes.

"Let's go," was all he said as he limped past me toward the hotel.

"Adam!" I called running after him. "I couldn't get a room.

They were all booked up. All the hotels. Something about a rodeo in town and people comin' from all over."

I hated to tell him that watching him stop in the middle of the street, letting his shoulders slump as he rubbed the bridge of his nose. Giving a heavy sigh, he turned toward the livery. I trailed after and we got our horses and, without a word, rode out of town heading for home.

It wasn't until much later, after I'd given up tryin' to get him to talk as we sat across from each other 'round the campfire that he finally spoke up.

"I lost both contracts," he said in a dejected voice as he stared into the flames, pulling the collar up on his jacket.

He'd said "I" not "we". I couldn't think on how to answer that so just went with the old standby. "I'm sorry, Adam."

"Me, too." He sighed then, a heavy, desperate sigh. It was like all the problems he'd been facing of late had finally piled up to the top and were about to collapse in on themselves.

"We'll get 'em next time," I tried with a grin, hoping to give him some sort of support. He just harrumphed and painfully eased himself onto his back.

"I'm going to sleep. I think I can still do that right."

My heart cringed at those words as I watched him try to find a comfortable position then finally settle. I laid back myself and lost myself in the stars.

I can't say as I've ever felt sorry for my brother. He always seems to have it all. But then I started thinking on his early life on the wagon train with Pa then Hoss, never having many friends as a child, losing his Ma and Inger and then Marie. Then having to shoot his best friend and facing that devil in the desert. For someone who seemed to have everything, he'd lost a lot and never was able to hold onto love for very long.

Well, the next day we rode on, mostly in silence, and made it home late. I offered to put up his horse for him since I could see he was having trouble with his back. He quietly thanked me, then headed on in. It took me a minute to figure out where all the noise was coming from and I stuck my head outta the barn when I heard the front door slam and saw Adam barrel his way toward me.

Ripping the reins from my hand, he mounted and headed out at a fast clip. I called after him but I got no response so headed toward the house only to see Hoss come out next and I could tell he was fuming mad. I called after him too and got nothing back so instead went into the house to find Pa pacing back and forth, stopping every once in awhile to hold his knee. When I mentioned that he should sit down before he fell down I got such a tongue lashing it nearly took my head off about the reason he'd sent me with Adam in the first place was to keep him focused, take his mind off that woman and his back and what did I do? Well, according to Pa, nothin' much since we lost both contracts. When I tried to fight back he just glared at me, told me to get outta his sight and stalked into the kitchen.

Now I was mad so I headed back to the barn to talk with Hoss. It seemed the safest place at the moment. But then Hoss came rocketing outta the barn on Chubb and disappeared into the night leaving me to call after him as well.

Now I was left, hands on hips, with my brothers ridin' off into the night and me left behind without so much as a how-do-you-do. So I decided the best thing for me right then was to go to bed and stomped my way across the yard, through the front door and up the stairs, mumbling to myself about fathers and brothers and contracts.

It wasn't until later, much later, I was awakened by Hoss's deep voice talking real loud downstairs, talking to Pa like I'd never heard him, and I wondered how long he'd still be living with us. It was only then I figured out what was going on and got mad all over again but this time I was mad at Pa. And that was a new feeling.

I know Pa loves us, not one more than the other, but he often excludes Adam. While he heaps praise on me he won't on Adam; he always assumes Adam will be the responsible one; he expects him to do things right and never make mistakes and that's just impossible even for big brother. I know losing those contracts was a big blow to Adam; I saw it in his eyes when he walked into the room and his comment of maybe sleep was something he could still do just plagued me. Adam's not your vulnerable type, never doubts himself—or if he does nobody sees it—so it's hard to think that he feels that way sometimes. He's doing the best he can and Pa should know that. He always does the best he can and just because it usually turns out right doesn't mean he can't fail.

But he's my brother and I love him and would do anything for him. And if it meant standing up to Pa to make him see what he was throwing away, then I would.

Oh, there it is again, that laugh. It reminds me of the good times.

Ben

IT MADE ME turn, that sound. It's music to my ears—my eldest son's laughter. I've missed it so. He's had such a trying time of late what with that woman falling for his cousin, his accident and then...me.

I preach to my boys about not jumping to conclusions, about hearing all the facts, and what do I do? I jump to conclusions and when I do hear them I dismiss them. Whatever has happened to my patience? I fear it's gone the way of my dark hair.

Oh, I've tried to apologize and he tells me it's fine, but I know it isn't. I think he believes I've lost my trust in him, which is far from the truth. He may not be able to make up his mind when it comes to women, but business...in business he's rock-solid— which is why I was floored we lost both contracts.

There was no reason, at least as far as I could tell, to come home empty-handed. That was right after he'd gotten back on his feet and wasn't able to do ranch work, so he took on both contracts like he always does. I blamed him for not paying attention;

for letting this thing with Laura and Will distract him. How could I do that? My Lord, my son was going to be married; was building a house to start a new life then it all came crashing down upon him as he fell from that ladder. And what did I do? I accused him of not paying attention. Well of course he wasn't paying attention! I wouldn't've paid much attention either, given the circumstances.

I remember it as if it was yesterday, hearing those words come out my mouth and not being able to stop them; seeing the crushed look on his face at their meaning; watching him storm out into the night with Hoss trailing after him. How could I?! He was obviously in pain; he wanted to complete those contracts to prove to me that he was still worth something to all of us, and I accused him of not caring.

"What do you mean you lost the contracts?" I asked, stunned at the loss.

"Just that, Pa," he answered in a tired voice that I chose to ignore.

"Well, what happened?" I cringe now at the memory of those words.

"We were outbid on the first contract. There was no way we could go lower, Pa, without losing money."

"And the second?"

He looked at me, then lowered his eyes and I had to strain to hear. "I made a mistake in the figuring. I'm sorry, Pa."

Fury filled me. I'd been depending on those contracts to support the purchase of four new bulls to further improve our breed and now that was gone.

"You're sorry?" I asked as I pushed myself to my feet, wincing at the twinge in my knee. He just nodded. "That's all you have to say?" He looked at me then.

"What do you want me to say, Pa? I made a mistake. I'm sorry."

"You're not sorry," I said. "You were never in favor of buying those bulls."

I watched his dark eyes narrow and his jaw set. "Are you suggesting that I intentionally lost those contracts?"

gesting that I intentionally lost those contracts?"

"If that woman..."

"That woman has a name, Pa. Laura. And she has nothing to do with this. Why don't you just come out and say what you mean?"

"All right," I said placing hands on my hips. "I don't think you care about the ranch anymore, Adam, not since that wo...not since Laura. You've been depressed and a bear to live with, and if you don't like it here maybe you should leave and go live in that house you were building for her!"

I saw it then but didn't recognize it—the shock that crossed his face soon to be replaced with a crushed look as he stepped back. Fury came next as he spun, grabbed his hat and stormed out, slamming the door behind him. It was then that I saw Hoss standing near the kitchen, glaring at me with such anger that I could reach out and touch it. He dropped his sandwich onto the table and took off out the door. I heard a horse leave the yard just as Joe rocketed through the front door.

"What's going on?" he asked, seeing me pacing back and forth and stopping every so many paces to hold my knee. "Maybe you should sit down, Pa?" he said to me and I nearly took his head off.

"Why'd I send you with Adam, Joe? To keep him focused. What were you doing? Sitting in a saloon charming all the ladies?"

"Now just a minute, Pa, we..."

"I don't want to hear your excuses! Get out of my sight!" I yelled, stomping off into the kitchen. I vaguely heard the door slamming shut as I forced myself to sit at the kitchen table. It was then I heard another horse leave the yard and dropped my head into my hands.

Maybe it was the fact that I was brooding in the dark kitchen by myself when I heard Joe stomp up the stairs, or possibly that as I paced in front of the fire until the early hours of the morning that I began to understand exactly what I'd done. Oh, I wanted to blame it on the pain in my knee or my sons deserting me when I needed them, but eventually I came to understand that I was being a pig-headed numbskull who was putting the benefits of the ranch before the welfare of my sons...one son in particular.

Adam is my rock and always has been. He knows the workings of this ranch better than I do and to accuse him like that of not caring...well, I would've decked the man that said that to me. And now I might never see him again all because I'm an idiot. I doubt that he would forgive me this time.

My attention moved quickly to the door when I heard a horse enter the yard, hoping it was Adam but knowing it wasn't, and as Hoss barreled into the room, I tensed at the determination written across his face. He came at me, and I stepped back—then he poked me and reminded me that maybe Adam wasn't in love with Laura so much as the idea of marriage, but it hurt still the same when he realized his own cousin was moving in on his territory.

"How dare ya accuse 'im o' not carin,'" Hoss said to me his blue eyes flashing their anger. "He'd lay his life down for any of us; he'd sell everythin' he had ta save the ranch and ya accuse 'im? I cain't believe that ya don't know yer own son. I cain't believe that yer so selfish ta think that he'd do anythin' on purpose jest ta make ya mad. What's the matter with ya, Pa? That boy lives and dies for us and ya jest tore his heart outta his chest and stomped on it."

I couldn't find the words and just swallowed, waiting for him to continue.

"I believe I stopped 'im from leavin' but I wouldn't blame 'im for cuttin' out, goin' someplace where he won't be judged so harshly without benefit of an explanation. I bet ya ain't even asked Joe what happened. I bet ya accused 'im o' not doin' his job of babysittin'."

Yes I had. I never let him explain.

"What's happened ta ya, Pa? Ya used ta care about people's feelin's. Is that only when it benefits you? We don't need them bulls now; they can wait 'til the next contract or the next one after that. Why don't ya put what ya want aside and ask yerself what Adam needs right now—he needs understandin' and love. Think ya can give a little o' yerself ta 'im right now 'cause if'n ya cain't well I can. And if talkin' ta ya like this gets me thrown out well maybe I'll jest move in with Adam at the house he was buildin' for that woman!"

He headed straight for the stairs and slammed shut his bedroom door and I stood there stunned. What had I done? My God, I'd dismissed Adam as if he didn't matter, not taking into consideration that he was still hurting over the loss of Laura and Peggy to another man; that his inability to work properly at his job was making him uneasy and vulnerable, making him question himself and then the contracts...

All because I wanted some new bulls.

I waited up for him to come home, waited to apologize and make Adam understand that I valued him just as much now as I ever did and that I was proud of him in so many ways. But he didn't come home that night and I was left with a guilty conscience that was well deserved.

I didn't know where he was for a week; couldn't find him or anyone who'd seen him and I was sure that Hoss had been wrong—that Adam had left without a word. It wasn't until Brent Hopkins showed up with two bulls in tow that it occurred to me where Adam had gone.

"They're already paid for, Ben," Brent informed me, handing over the bill of sale with Adam's name scrawled across the bottom. "Told me that he'd come up with the money for the other two by the end of the month. You can pick them up then." He handed me their tethers, tipped his hat and headed out and I could've just cried. This was not the action of a son who didn't care, and I knew he probably had to cash in some of his own stock to pay for these.

I had to find him. I had to apologize. I had to ask forgiveness.

Tossing the bull's tethers off to a hand, I grabbed Buck and headed out, my intuition taking me to the one place I hadn't looked—the house he'd been building for Laura, the house that had caused so many problems. And that's where I found him.

I looked down on him, seeing him sitting quietly against a rock, just staring at the half finished house. I eased Buck down the trail to leave him next to his horse and slowly walked toward Adam. He never moved, never looked at me.

"Adam," I said as I neared getting no response. I eyed him then sat down next to him watching him fold arms across his chest. "Are you sure sitting against that rock is good for your back?" I asked, hoping to get some response.

"It tells me when it isn't," came the short answer.

I followed his gaze to the struts and braces before us and my heart was crushed a bit more at the loss of so many things.

"Adam, I..."

"What do you want, Pa?"

I shouldn't have been taken aback by the tone, the non-emotional tone that cut so severely through me, but I deserved it and he had to know that.

"I've come to apologize for what I said the other night. It was mean and nasty and completely undeserved. I put my wants above everything else and that was wrong." He didn't say anything but just kept staring straight ahead. "Brent Hopkins delivered two bulls to me today and told me that the other two could be picked up at the end of the month. Interesting since I haven't actually paid for them."

"Don't worry about it, Pa. Your uncaring son bought them for you," came the tart response, those dark eyes finally meeting mine. "Now, if you don't mind, you're trespassing." He pushed himself up then and swayed a little. I reached out but he moved out of my grasp and walked stiffly away.

"Adam!" I called, scrambling to my feet, feeling that each step he took from me was one that I wouldn't get back. "Please. What can I do to make this up to you? I'll do anything."

He stopped then. "Anything?" he asked without turning and I

nodded like a child wanting another piece of candy. "Just leave me be," came his quiet answer.

He started off again to disappear around the back of the house and I could've died right then.

I had no choice but to leave. He'd thrown me off his land and I hadn't come out here to make him uncomfortable, so I mounted Buck and headed out—soon to meet Hoss coming toward me in a buckboard. He said nothing to me as he passed and I pulled up to watch him as he came to a stop, Adam coming forward to greet him. They traded smiles then went to work. And what were they doing? They were dismantling the house and stacking the wood into neat stacks soon to transfer them to the buckboard. He was taking down his dream, his own Ponderosa; removing from his sight everything that reminded him of his loss. And that's all I'd been doing—reminding him of it.

That had been four weeks ago and now I was hearing him laugh. I smiled at the sound, remembering all the other times I'd heard it over the years. Then I turned and headed toward the door. No reason he should see me. If he was laughing I didn't want to ruin his evening. Besides it was getting hot in here and a breath of fresh air would do me good.

Adam

I SAW HIM walk out the door and excused myself from the conversation I'd been having with Harvey Phelps and the antics of his one-year-old to weave my way through the crowd. The night was chilly, and the stars shone brightly. and it was nice to take notice of them again after these long couple of months of depression I'd been living since...well, since Laura left me.

I can't say as I wasn't surprised, not much really. I knew it wasn't going to work but I'd asked her and she'd agreed and it just didn't seem right to back out. That's not what I do. I make a promise and I have to stick to it no matter what. Well, I finally realized that I should thank cousin Will from the bottom of my heart for taking her off my hands because it would've been torturous.

Ever since she left, I've often thought on what it is that keeps a woman from loving me enough to marry me. Everyone tells me I would be a good catch for any woman. So where is this 'any woman'? I've tried tough girls, small girls, large girls, frilly girls...blonds, brunettes, redheads...blue eyes, brown eyes, green eyes...and nothing! Of course my brothers aren't doing much better so I guess it's just a curse. The Cartwright Curse, as we call it, in full bloom. Just my luck I'll find someone on my death bed and then she won't marry me because I'm gonna die.

I shouldn't worry so except I'd really like to have children, to give Pa a grandchild, give my brothers nieces and nephews, and I can't do that unless some poor unsuspecting woman decides to take a chance. But getting married just to get married...well, that's just plain stupid as Hoss would say.

Hoss. I love that big galoot. I wish I could be as open as he is when it comes to expressing my emotions; it would probably keep me out of a lot of trouble if I could just say I love you or I hate you or I know I made a promise and now I'll have to break it. But I don't see that coming anytime soon.

Ah, the night's chillier than I thought, and I'm putting off the idea that my father is standing about ten paces to my left and I should just go over and stop all this thinking. Thinking always seems to get me into trouble. Well, that and my good old Cartwright stubbornness that I get from both my mother and father. Well, here goes.

"Getting colder," I began. "Bet the first snow is early this year."

He stiffened and slowly turned, those dark eyes filled with trepidation as they swung my way. I looked away before he could catch me and watched the stars. He cleared his throat.

"Ol' Paddy Oxford says it'll be two weeks from now to be exact."

"Well, I've never known him to be wrong," I answered, forcing myself to look at him. I opened my mouth but...

"We got the other two bulls," he quickly said. "They're perfect. Should improve our stock for next year."

I nodded. "Good."

"I've got the money ready to deposit back into your account," he gave me and I narrowed my eyes.

"They were a gift, Pa," I answered feeling the hackles rising on my neck. Calm yourself. "I had to do something to make up for..."

"To make up for nothing," he interrupted holding my gaze. "You didn't do anything wrong."

"I don't want the money, Pa."

I glared at him until he nodded then turned and stared out into the night again and I followed suit, wondering if this awkwardness between us would ever end.

He cleared his throat. "It has come to my attention that I've been...that I've been a bastard to you of late and I want to apologize."

"Pa..."

"It's true. Please don't deny it," he said with a slight frown. "I didn't handle things very well with you after Laura left and I'm sorry. I was worried about you and I let that feed into my anger toward Laura and Will. Let me finish," he said as I started to object. He sat down on the bench.

"I've always wondered why my boys can't seem to find a woman to settle down with, and then you found Laura. I must say I was surprised. She just didn't seem like the right girl for you—she had no passion, no fire in her eyes when she looked at you—and I was worried that you were making a mistake. But how do I gently tell my son that the woman he thinks he loves doesn't love him?"

"You tried, Pa," I answered sitting down next to him.

"I did. But it wasn't my place. I was just afraid that you were walking into a mess and knowing you you'd just plow right on ahead because you'd given your word...a worthy virtue, by the way." I gave him a slight smile. "But one that can dig you in deep.

Despite you telling everyone that you were fine, I knew you weren't—because this time you really came close, and that's just gotta pull at a man. Of course I didn't help by constantly bringing her up every time you held your back or winced or couldn't get out of a chair without help. That was mean and nasty and something a father shouldn't do to his son.

"And then to accuse you of not caring..." He broke off then and shook his head, rubbing a hand across his face. "Hoss blasted me on that and I deserved it." He looked at me then and laid a hand on my leg. "You are my most trusted companion, Adam. With you I feel that I don't need to say the same things I need to say to Joe. With us it is understood that we love each other and trust each other. But in all that I lost sight of the fact that you are my boy, my son, and I should be open enough to tell you that I value your opinion; I know that I don't have to look over your shoulder and that you'll take care of your brothers and me even at the cost of your life. And you do it out of love not just responsibility. I knew all of that and yet I committed a most serious crime—I forgot for a time. In my haste to pull you from your depression I trampled on your feelings over and over again, and for that I am ashamed. Can you ever forgive me, Adam?"

I looked at him, really looked at him and could see the guilt pouring out of him. I admit my feelings had been hurt...and yes I do have feelings. I just don't spread them out for the world to see like Joe. And he had hurt me, made me question my worth to the family. Did they only look upon me as a worker and not a brother or son? Was I only as good as my brain? Should I move on and try to see if my name was all I was or was there truly more to Adam Cartwright then being Ben Cartwright's son?

But now with my father giving me that look...you know, the one where all he'd really like to do is turn back time and start over. How could I not forgive him and move on? Nursing bad feelings only lets them grow into seething anger that has a tendency to take over a person, leaving them with nothing but an empty life.

I gave him a half-smile and covered his hand with mine. "I can't say as I appreciate how you did it, Pa," I began. "But I do appreciate that you cared enough to say it in the first place. Laura wasn't the one and I would've ruined three lives instead of just mine. Peggy would've been pulled in two trying to figure out which one of us to side with, and that's a decision I would never want her to have to think on at such a young age. I truly loved her and never wanted to hurt her."

He gave me a little smile in return and a nod then pulled his hand from mine and embraced me. I returned it, feeling whole again for the first time since Laura left.

"What say we go back inside," I said, "and dance a few dances, drink a few cups of punch, then head on home."

"I'd like that," he answered and started forward—only to stop as I waggled a finger at him.

"Just don't try to set me up or I'll turn tail and run," I said with a grin.

"You've gotta deal. Let's go."

He patted me on the back and the two of us stepped back inside, our laughs mingling with the fiddle music going on inside, both about to be accosted by Clovis Strikhem and Bertha Mae Trindel, the town spinsters.

It took both Pa and me half a second to turn tail and run, both of us laughing as we reached the safety of our horses and ran all the way home.

It was nice to hear him laughing.

It was nice to laugh again.

This story was based on the episode "Triangle," written by Frank Cleaver.

Our Mother's Keeper
by JeanieC

*A*dam Cartwright didn't feel the knife's blade go in: He watched it slide in almost as if it were happening to someone else.

Later he would think how slowly it all seemed to come about though, in fact, it was over in seconds. He saw the flash of the flat of the blade and, before he had time to react defensively, that blade slid easily right through his black shirt and into his belly.

He watched the blade disappear into his belly and felt, not pain really, but more a kind of sad disappointment: He knew their pleasant ride home had just taken a dicey turn. The blade wasn't long by hunting knife standards—only about four inches—but Adam guessed it would do what the bastard intended, sure enough.

Adam looked down to see his attacker's fist still holding the knife's handle, the hilt pushing in on his shirt hard enough to make an indentation. Already, Adam could see his black shirt darkening with his blood; he noted the stain forming a teardrop shape as it traveled down toward his belt. He reached down a hand and closed his fingers over the drifter's wrist.

Adam looked up then into the filthy, bearded face of the drifter. The drifter looked back at Adam, his eyes wide, perhaps not believing he'd done what he'd done.

It seemed like they stood there for some time, faces close in their violent intimacy, but Adam, in going over it again later with the sheriff and for the trial, figured it couldn't have been more than five or ten seconds. At any rate, the drifter finally came back to himself and pulled his hand away, bringing the knife—and Adam's hand—with it.

And that, Adam felt. It was like the blade was carrying his insides along with it as it slid back out the way it had gone in. He let out a low grunt of pain, and it turned into a cough that hurt like hell.

The drifter roughly jerked his hand free of Adam's weakening grip and took two steps back, fascinated at the sight of the wound he'd caused. Adam's hand remained aloft after being torn from its grip on the other man's wrist, and it hung there between them.

"Whuh?" The sound from Adam's mouth—not a real word at all—seemed to shake his attacker free of his shock, and he turned and ran.

Adam looked down at his belly again, and the deep sadness at what he saw almost overwhelmed him. The dark stain was getting bigger—alarmingly so—and his thoughts went immediately to his father. If only he were here now...

Adam instinctively pressed his right hand over the wound and then watched the blood, bright red now, leak out from between his fingers. Maybe it was better when all he could see was that dark spot spreading on his shirt and down below his belt. It was starting to make him feel a little funny, watching the blood trickle along his knuckles, down to his fingertips, form drops of scarlet brilliance and fall one after the other onto his denim-covered thigh.

Adam dropped to his knees then. He vaguely noted a stab of pain in his left knee—*must be on a rock or something* is what he thought—but mostly he was just caught off guard when his legs wouldn't support him anymore. He couldn't see Hoss anywhere, but he knew he couldn't be far. He called to his brother, not with a shout, but barely a whisper: "Hoss."

HOSS CARTWRIGHT HAD been fighting a battle of his own but was lucky that none of his three opponents had pulled out a knife. He was keeping busy with one man on his back, his arms wrapped around Hoss' thick neck. Another had hold of Hoss' right bicep while the third was jabbing punches at his chin, dodging wild swings from Hoss' left fist.

Then from over to their left and behind them came the fourth drifter's low call, "C'mon—let's get outta here."

The three who were tussling with Hoss looked over. "What you done there, Micah?" one asked.

"I stuck him," Micah hissed. "Now let's git."

The other three didn't wait for more explanation. They released their various holds on Hoss and ran for their horses. Hoss put his hands on his knees and bent over at the waist, breathing noisily, while Micah stooped to pick up the fat wallet that had dropped to the ground and stuffed it into his shirt.

He glanced back once at Adam, who was still on his knees and preoccupied with the blood oozing through his fingers. Then Micah grabbed the reins from the hands of one of his already-mounted companions and, after mounting up, wheeled around and led the way back from where they'd come.

Hoss heard, rather than saw, them leave. As the hoof beats grew fainter, he blew out a great huff of relief and, still leaning over at the waist, tried to catch his breath.

"Dang it, Adam," he said, still panting heavily between words. "Pa ain't gonna be happy we lost that money. Reckon we should get after 'em right away?"

Hoss took one more big breath and felt like his heart finally was slowing down in his chest. "Not exactly even odds at three to one, brother. How'd you get so lucky to only draw one a' those drifters?"

When still there was no answering retort from Adam, Hoss straightened up and turned to look behind him. Adam was kneeling on the ground looking right back at him. That was strange.

"Adam, whatchya doin'? Sayin' a..." Hoss stopped speaking and the big grin, which he had just noticed was making his split bottom lip pull painfully, disappeared. He'd been about to ask Adam if he was saying a prayer those drifters' horses all threw a shoe.

But Hoss saw something about his brother's posture that did not look right—he had his right hand pressed to his belly. Adam kept his eyes fixed on Hoss and finally said his brother's name aloud. That's when Hoss knew for sure things weren't as they should be. Adam looked shadowy kneeling there and kind of afraid. But it was his voice that told Hoss for sure something wasn't right.

"Hoss...I'm in trouble." Just those four words—spoken not in Adam's usual strong baritone, but in a weaker, higher-pitched voice that didn't belong to his brother—set Hoss' heart pounding once more.

Adam looked down again at the bright blood making red tracks across the back of his hand and that's when Hoss finally followed his brother's gaze.

"Lordy, Adam! What's happened to ya?" Hoss was at his brother's side in about eight long strides.

"I'm in trouble, Hoss," Adam repeated in that same strange voice. He looked down at his belly yet again as Hoss got down on one knee by his side. He reached out and put one arm around

Adam's shoulders and another under his left forearm. Adam still gripped his belly with his right hand. "He had a knife. I'm bleedin'...pretty bad, I think." Adam's voice had a tone of despair.

"Adam—now listen to me," Hoss said loudly and urgently. "I want you to come over by our bedrolls and set down."

Adam thought there was no chance he was going to be able to rise from his knees, much less walk the ten yards or so over to his bedroll. He gave Hoss a look of exhaustion and pain and fear.

"I don't know. I feel...strange—I'm not sure I can make it." He paused and took a couple of shallow breaths, keeping his eyes locked on Hoss'.

"Just try to stand up. I'll help ya—now, c'mon." Hoss put both his arms under Adam's arms and lifted. Adam let out another grunt of pain as he got to his feet once more.

"Ah god, Hoss, it hurts," Adam said with a moan, his jaw clenched tightly against the intense pain in his gut. He finally released his hold on the wound in his belly and, turning into Hoss, grabbed at his brother's white shirt with his bloody hand. He stood, his legs trembling, his hand gripping a fistful of Hoss' shirt front and pulling two buttons off in the process.

"I'm in trouble," Adam said a third time, wearily resting his forehead against his brother's shoulder, and Hoss knew that was true for both of them.

"I'm gonna help ya—we'll be just fine," Hoss said and absolutely meant it. Hoss saw their situation as serious: They were out on the trail, one of them wounded and bleeding, miles from home or help. But he was good at putting first things first and not getting too far ahead of himself, so he put those worries out of his mind just for now.

Hoss tilted his head down toward his brother's, which still rested on his shoulder, and said, "Hold onto me now and I'll get ya over to your bedroll." Adam obediently tightened his already firm grip on the shirt at Hoss' chest as Hoss reached down behind his brother's knees and swung him up into his arms.

Again, Adam let out an involuntary gasp, which he cut off by clenching his teeth with jaws already taut in pain.

"Sorry, Adam." Hoss looked down at his brother's belly—the dark stain on his shirt looked huge now—and walked the dozen or so paces to where their bedrolls and saddles were laid out a couple of feet from each other. He slowly crouched with his burden, put one knee down and, leaning forward, placed his brother carefully onto the blanket. Adam still had a tight hold on Hoss' shirt and Hoss reached up to gently pry his fingers apart. He held Adam's shoulders off the ground and placed his hand down by his side. He looked first at that huge, soaking dark stain on his brother's shirt and then at his own shirt front, hanging loosely and open at his chest now and stained with his brother's blood. His brother's blood! So much of it, standing out shockingly against his own white shirt.

He looked into Adam's pale face. His brow was furrowed and his mouth drawn down as he fought against the intense burning in his gut. His eyes were shut tightly but popped open immediately when Hoss softly spoke his name.

"I'm gonna get your extra shirt to make a bandage, OK?" Adam nodded and his eyes slid shut again. "You gonna be OK for a minute?" Hoss asked. Adam nodded again without opening his eyes. His breath came quickly and shallowly and seemed to stop just short of a whimper.

Hoss lay Adam gently back so his shoulders were resting on his saddle and reached over to Adam's saddlebags. Rummaging through first one and then the other, he finally pulled out a cream-colored shirt and turned back toward Adam. His face still was drawn as he fought the pain.

"Sorry 'bout makin' a mess of your bags over there, Adam," Hoss said apologetically as he reached into his pants pocket and found his pocket knife. He opened the blade and cut a slit at the tail of the shirt then began to tear a three-inch strip off the bottom.

"And sorry about having to tear your shirt," Hoss added.

At that, Adam let out a short laugh that ended with a groan.

"We got ourselves bigger things to worry about than my shirt," Adam said, pausing to catch his breath and to concentrate. Even so, a smile briefly replaced the drawn look of pain on Adam's face.

"I know we do...but I still hated to do it." Hoss pursed his lips as he folded the strip over and over to make a thick bandage. "OK, Adam, you ready?"

Without opening his eyes to look at Hoss, Adam nodded, his saddle rocking slightly with the movement.

Hoss reached down and began unbuttoning Adam's shirt, wincing a little and drawing in a quick, hissing breath when he reached the fourth button where the material was saturated with his brother's blood.

"How bad is it?" Adam asked without opening his eyes. He knew it had to be pretty bad, just judging from the way he felt generally and the sharp pain in his gut that surged with each shallow breath he took. But still he hoped, irrationally he knew, to hear Hoss say, "It don't look so bad."

"Just a minute...I'm havin' trouble with this last button." Hoss' large fingers were now slippery with his brother's blood and trying to slide the small button through a buttonhole when the cloth was so sodden was a real chore. He briefly considered just ripping it but was afraid being too rough might cause his brother even more pain.

Finally, Hoss pushed the button through the hole and began pulling Adam's shirt away from the wound. He had to tug a little where the knife's blade had driven some of the cloth into the wound. When Adam winced and gave a shudder, Hoss was quick to glance up at his face and say, "Sorry." He tugged the sodden shirttail out of Adam's pants and dropped the whole left side of the shirt onto the bedroll.

Now he could see the hole in his brother's belly and his first thought was, "That doesn't look like much." It was a narrow slit and only about two inches long. But Hoss knew the wound had to be much deeper than it was wide. It wasn't pumping blood like

Hoss had seen the day Charlie Tanner had split his leg open with an ax. But the blood was oozing steadily out of the wound, matting the dark, curling hair that covered Adam's belly, and Hoss knew he had to stop it somehow.

"Adam, I'm gonna hafta press down hard with this bandage, all right?" Hoss hoped his brother was ready. He almost wished Adam would lose consciousness, to spare them both the pain of what he was about to do, but then realized he'd really be all alone in this. Though he knew it was up to him if his brother's life was to be saved, he knew he'd feel much more alone if he didn't have Adam to talk to through it all.

"Yeah...go ahead," Adam said, his words punctuated by the short breaths he was taking to lessen the pain.

Hoss picked up the thick pad of cloth he'd made and pressed it down firmly over the wound. Adam immediately let out another grunt of pain that turned into a long, low moan. It ended with him nearly crying his brother's name in a low growl, hissing out the final S in his name.

"Sorry, Adam...sorry," Hoss said anxiously, sounding in nearly as much pain as his brother. Though he knew he was doing what had to be done, it was hard to be the one inflicting this hurt on his brother. He kept pressing firmly as Adam settled back into short breaths alternating with quiet moans as he blew the breaths out.

Hoss was worried: He had only one more idea to try if this pressure didn't stop the bleeding. It wasn't something he relished having to do, but he knew Adam couldn't stand to lose too much more blood, and he'd have to decide quickly if this didn't work.

His wrist was starting to ache. He looked at Adam who kept his eyes tightly closed as if to shut out the pain.

"Ya doin' OK, brother?" Hoss asked, unable to keep the worry from coming out in his words.

"I'm OK. It just hurts a bit...I'll be fine. Can we get outta here?" Adam finally opened his eyes and found his brother's face close to his own as Hoss leaned over him, one hand still applying pressure to Adam's belly. Hoss was staring back at him, his forehead furrowed with concern. Both were consumed with the fix they were in.

"Just a bit? Sounds to me like it hurts more than a 'bit'." Hoss shook his head at Adam's stoicism. "It's OK to tell me the truth."

"If I was to tell you, I might believe it myself," Adam said with a faint grin.

"Well, if I can get this bleedin' stopped, I think there's a good chance we can leave." He nodded in the direction of the picket line where their two horses still were tied. "Those varmints didn't take our horses, so we're in luck there."

"That's good." Adam paused and then almost whispered, "Has it stopped yet?" His weak voice made Hoss look quickly back to his brother's face.

"I dunno...I'll check." Hoss carefully lifted his hand holding the bandage away from the wound. He knew without looking the bleeding hadn't stopped; he had felt it soak through onto his hand. His certainty was confirmed by the huge blossom of red on the bandage when he moved his hand and the continued seepage of blood from Adam's wound. Hoss held the bloodied bandage up for Adam to see.

Adam's disappointment was evident and another emotion now edged onto his face: fear. If the bleeding didn't stop, he knew he was a dead man.

"Adam, now don't you worry. I got me another trick up my sleeve." Hoss put the bandage back over the wound and picked up his brother's hand. He gave it a quick squeeze—both of their hands bloody—and placed it palm down over the wound.

"Now just hold that tight and wait for me." Hoss turned to leave his brother's side.

"Hoss! Whattya mean? What other trick? Where are you goin'?" Adam's voice was frantic as he weakly grabbed at his brother's sleeve, and one thought repeatedly ran through his head: *Don't leave me!*

Hoss turned back and saw the look of panic on Adam's face

and felt his hand clutching at his arm. He grabbed and held Adam's hand as he sought to comfort him but also tried to remain completely honest with his brother about what was to come.

"Do ya remember what Pa did two springs ago when that roan got a deep cut on her chest after runnin' into that broken fence rail? How did he fix it and stop the bleedin'?"

Adam blinked once, then twice, as he tried to focus on what Hoss was saying and recall the incident. A roan two years ago? Why, Pa had heated an iron in the fire and...

"Oh, Hoss..." Adam looked up at his brother then with a variety of emotions quickly taking turns in his wide eyes: first realization, then fear and finally resignation.

Hoss watched it happen and saw that Adam knew what was in store for him then. "I know, Adam, and I'm sorry. If there was another way you know I'd try it first. I jus' can't wait no longer." Hoss thought he might dread what he had to do more than his brother. For a wound that large, the heat would have to be applied for a long time.

Bigger than either his older or his younger brothers, Hoss had often served as their protector. Though the three Cartwright boys occasionally scrapped amongst themselves, sometimes seriously, when someone from outside the family threatened one of them, the other two were right there to back him up. And as often as not, Hoss was called upon to take on the largest—or if the odds were not even, the most—of their attackers. How many times had Adam been getting the worst of things during a tussle and waved his younger but larger brother into the fray because he knew Hoss could get the job done where he couldn't?

But it had never been true that Hoss would set out to deliberately seriously hurt one of them. Certainly it had happened once or twice that he HAD hurt one of them, but it had never started out being his intention. Even Joe, who delighted, it seemed, in teasing and tormenting his older brother, never came in for the abuse that Hoss could have inflicted if he'd been a revenge-minded man.

So faced now with the prospect of surely causing his brother agonizing pain, Hoss thought he'd rather inflict it upon himself if only that would help the situation. The last thing he wanted to do now was cause Adam more pain than he already was in and that thought made Hoss feel sick. The only thing that frightened him more, in fact, was the thought of his brother bleeding to death while he watched.

"I know, Hoss," Adam said after having let the reality of their only option penetrate his foggy mind. "It's the only thing you CAN do. You have to..." His voice trailed off a little. "I sure wish you didn't, though," he said wistfully.

"I don't want to neither. But it's gotta be done and the sooner the better." Hoss looked over to where their morning fire still burned and noted the hot, glowing coals at its center. "Now you just keep your hand there..." Hoss paused and placed his hand over his brother's on the knife wound. "And I'll be back in just a little while."

Adam looked into his brother's eyes and nodded. Hoss saw the fear but also saw trust in Adam's eyes and that trust gave him confidence in his decision.

Releasing his hand from Adam's with one final pat, Hoss pushed himself up from his kneeling position and went over to inspect the fire more closely and think his plan through a little. They didn't have an iron with them this trip, so he'd have to make do with the best substitute he could find. He turned and started walking.

HOSS THRUST THE thick, peeled stick of hardwood he'd cut not far from their camp into the coals and then took it out. Though he felt some urgency at what he had to do, he also wanted to make sure he prepared his tools—and his patient—correctly. He continued putting the stick into the coals and pulling it out after a few minutes, trying to get the right balance of heat and hardness without burning away his stick.

When Hoss thought it was nearly ready, heated blazing hot, he placed it carefully on the hot rocks of their fire ring. He stood and walked the five paces over to where his brother lay on his back, shirt opened wide, his hand still clutching the saturated bandage. Adam's pants also were dark with his blood now, the stain reaching about two inches below his belt and then falling back around his left side toward the ground. Hoss noted Adam's whole right hip looked soaked, but that couldn't be, could it? How could he lose that much blood and still be conscious?

Hoss got down on one knee at his brother's side and again put his right hand over Adam's. Adam's eyes opened quickly as he started and then groaned.

"Didn't mean to startle ya," Hoss said.

"It's OK. I was just thinkin' and didn't hear you coming," Adam said, his breathing sounding easier now.

"Does it still hurt as much?" Hoss asked, looking doubtfully at all the blood once more.

"Doesn't seem to. Maybe I'm just getting used to it," Adam replied.

Hoss chuckled a little at that and held up the canteen he carried. "You'll be needin' something to drink, Adam." He uncorked it and handed it to his brother. Adam tipped the canteen to his lips and drank, some of the water running out the sides of his mouth and trickling down his chin to join the sweat pooling at the base of his neck. He handed the canteen back to Hoss and wiped at his lips with the back of his hand.

"That hurt like hell, but it tasted so good."

Hoss chuckled again and said, "I wanna clean things up a little for ya. Give me your hand?"

"My hand?" Adam held his right hand up in front of his face to inspect it and seemed surprised at all the dried blood he saw there. "Is that all mine?"

"It sure is. I had a good amount of it on me too, but I already washed up. I aim to do the same for you." Hoss held up another portion torn from Adam's shirt and soaked with water. Adam held his hand out to his brother who gently scrubbed the dried blood off, turning the cream color of the cloth a dirty pink.

"There...that looks a little better," Hoss said, satisfied with his work. Then he asked, "What were ya thinkin' about when I came back?"

"Huh?" Adam squinted, trying to remember. "Oh...just how careless I was to let them get the drop on us," he said regretfully.

"Aw, Adam, that weren't your fault OR mine," Hoss said, shaking his head. "They'd likely been following us since San Francisco. They knew you was carrying all the money from the sale so they'd probably seen us at the stockyards."

Now it was Adam's turn to shake his head. "I still should have been more alert on the trail."

"What's done is done," Hoss said firmly. "Right now we have to think about getting you home." He ducked his head for a minute and then looked back at his brother. "There's only one way we can do that, ya know."

"I know, Hoss. I know." Adam looked resigned to the pain that was to come.

"OK, I'll make it quick." Hoss sought to reassure his brother, but he also wanted to tell him exactly what he was planning. "I'm gonna lay the whole length along the cut, OK? I wanna make sure I cover the whole thing," Hoss told him.

"I'm as ready as I can be." Adam looked up at his brother. "Steady hand, OK?" He reached out with his now clean right hand and grabbed onto Hoss' thick forearm. "Steady?" His eyes were asking for reassurance; Hoss hoped he could give him what he needed.

"I'll be careful. I promise." Hoss placed his hand over his brother's which still held tight to his arm.

"I know you will." Adam released his hold on Hoss' arm. He trusted his younger brother with his life. "I think it's worse when you know it's coming." He closed his eyes again.

Hoss didn't have any words of comfort to offer; what Adam said was true. He stood again and went back to the fire. He picked up the stick and thrust it once more into the coals until the embers on it began to glow orange. Then he pulled it out and returned to Adam.

"Want somethin' to bite on?" Hoss asked.

Adam shook his head, apprehension showing plainly on his face now.

"OK, here we go. Take my hand." Hoss reached down with his left hand to grab Adam's left hand. He held it firmly, not in a normal handshake, but in an arm-wrestling grip.

Hoss carefully but quickly placed the red-hot stick lengthwise along the wound in Adam's belly, and the agony began for both of them.

HOSS WOULD NEVER forget the smell of burning flesh and hair or Adam's hoarse cries of shock and pain as the fire worked its magic in cauterizing the wound.

Adam knew nothing for several minutes but overwhelming pain: It didn't come in waves, but one steady blast searing into the flesh on his belly, making the pain of his stab wound seem no worse than a sliver.

Hoss had been prepared for Adam instinctively to move away from the source of the pain but while seemingly every muscle in his body went rigid when the burning stick touched him, Adam forced himself to stay put and let the fire do its work.

Neither would ever forget how tightly Adam's hand clamped down on his brother's hand or how firm and strong Hoss' grip was in return. The brothers' bond was forged through an Indian's arrow, years spent growing up together in wagons on the trail and the building of their ranch. This would only serve to make that bond even stronger.

And when he took the stick away from the wound and Adam

was left sweating and gasping for breath, Hoss could see that his idea had worked. The blistered and red flesh was seared closed around the cut, and it was bleeding no more.

"It worked, Adam! The bleedin' stopped." Hoss was relieved until he looked from his brother's belly to his face and saw Adam's pale skin, his profuse sweating and the grimace that seemed like it might become permanent on his face. His eyes were shut tightly, and his breaths were again quick and shallow. The paleness of Adam's skin beneath his day's growth of beard looked bad enough, but the skin on his forehead looked almost waxy and was covered in droplets of sweat.

"Adam!" Hoss said, a little louder now. "Didja hear me?"

"Huh?" Adam spoke dully and didn't open his eyes—Hoss thought maybe he was concentrating on beating back the pain.

"It worked...we can get going home now," Hoss said, thinking ahead to how he might get Adam on his horse.

"Mm-hmm," came the mumbled reply.

"Lordy, Adam, I'm sorry," Hoss said, instantly chagrined at being happy at his success while his brother was left fighting waves of agony.

There was no answer to this and as Hoss watched, Adam moved his right hand to again try to cover his wound, perhaps to try to relieve his pain?

"No, don't touch it. Leave it be...we don't want to break it open again." He took the wrist he'd grabbed and placed it at Adam's side. "Didya hear me?" he said.

Satisfied with the nod he got in reply, Hoss said, "OK...I'll get us packed."

"ADAM!" HOSS PUNCTUATED his call with a little shake of his brother's arm not more than ten minutes later and was relieved when Adam opened his eyes and really seemed to see him.

Seemed like all he'd done so far today was call his brother's name.

"Yeah?" Adam replied weakly.

"We're all packed up and ready to go. How do you feel about getting on a horse?" Hoss asked.

Adam knew he had no real choice but he would much rather lie right here and wait for Hoss to go for help. The thought of moving, much less getting up on a horse, made him feel sick when what he most wanted to do was sleep. But he'd been doing some figuring and he thought they were at least one more day from the Ponderosa and much further away from help if they were to turn back. He knew without asking that Hoss would refuse to leave him here alone for two days, so he'd have to climb up onto that damn horse.

"If that's what I gotta do, let's get to it," Adam said gamely, trying to take a deep breath without prompting that tearing sensation in his belly. "Any ideas on how I'm gonna get on said horse?"

"Yeah, I done thought about that and I got just the thing if we can get you over to that fallen tree yonder," Hoss said pointing. "See how tall that butt-end is? Stand on that and I think we can manage."

Adam looked from the tree Hoss pointed out, back to his brother and said, "Hoss, I'm impressed with your resourceful-ness."

"My what?" Hoss asked.

Adam quickly said, "That's a great idea." Hoss' face went from screwed up in confusion to wearing an easy grin, marred by the split lip and massive bruising around one eye. Adam noticed this bruising for the first time. He must have looked into Hoss' face a dozen times in the last two hours—how could he not have taken note of such damage?

"What happened to you?" Adam asked, concern in his weak voice.

"To me? Where?" Hoss replied, puzzled.

"Your face."

"Ohhhhh…" Hoss reached up a hand, touched his eye and winced, pulling his hand away. "I reckon those other fellas don't look so good neither, but it WAS three on one, remember."

Adam smiled and asked, "Does it hurt much?"

"Only when I touch it, so I'm not gonna do THAT no more. Now let's see about gettin' you ready. I'm gonna need that saddle and your bedroll now." Hoss squatted down by his brother's side again. "If you can stand, I'll get you ready to go in a few minutes."

"I'm ready." Adam felt about as far from ready as he ever had, but the longer he lay here, the less he'd feel like moving. And he knew they had to get going. He held out a hand to his brother who grabbed it and also put an arm around Adam's back and lifted.

Adam came to his feet with a guttural moan and stood swaying slightly and gripping Hoss's arm tightly. The world felt strange and looked stranger: tilted and kind of fuzzy. Adam closed his eyes and concentrated on keeping his balance. If the buzzing in his head would just quiet down a little, he was sure he could think of what he was supposed to do next.

"You OK?"

To Adam's ears, Hoss' voice sounded distant. Adam said, "Yeah, but I can't stand here long. I'm gonna have to sit down."

"Let's get you over to that tree, then." With Hoss supporting a heavily dependent and groggy Adam, the two slowly shuffled over to the log. Hoss sat him down near the small end of the log, then returned to saddle Adam's horse and pack up the final bits of their camp before helping Adam mount up.

SEVERAL HOURS INTO their ride, Hoss looked back at his brother for what was probably the twentieth time since they'd had to slow to a walk. He was growing increasingly concerned about Adam's ability to sit a horse. The blood loss appeared to be taking its toll on his brother as he swayed and nodded in the saddle, often unable to hold his head up. It was a good thing his horse followed Hoss obediently because Adam wasn't doing anything more with the reins than hold them loosely in the same hand that also gripped the saddle horn. The other hand, his right, wrapped around his side with his arm tucked into his belly. His shirt still hung open, stiff with dried blood.

Everything about his posture shouted pain and exhaustion and Hoss knew that, while Adam would not say anything about wanting to stop, he had to if he didn't want to kill his brother. He pulled his horse up and dismounted. Adam's horse stopped when Hoss did and stood quietly.

"Adam, c'mon...let's get you down offa there," Hoss called up to his brother. He got no response. Adam just sat slumped in the same position, his hat hiding his downcast face. Hoss gently shook his brother's thigh.

"Hmmm?" Adam sounded groggy; Hoss couldn't see if his eyes were open but he was relieved to get some response.

"Let's get down and take a break."

"Gotta keep goin', Hoss," Adam said, quietly but fairly distinctly. "Shouldn't waste time."

"I think your ridin' time is over. I can't have you fallin' off your horse and bustin' open that cut or your head."

"I can ride," Adam protested weakly. "We gotta keep goin'."

"Adam, you CAN'T ride. You can barely sit. Stop arguin' and put your arm over my shoulders." Hoss spoke sternly, hoping Adam would just do as he asked. Adam sighed and leaned down to let Hoss pull him off the saddle.

"That's it...I'm gonna fix you up a nice place to set a spell."

When Hoss had settled Adam once more onto his bedroll under a massive pine, he checked the stab wound again. The cut edges were still fused shut so there was no bleeding but the burns had begun to look nasty. The whole left side of Adam's belly was angry red with big blisters all along where the hot stick had been placed. The very inside edges were puckered and black.

Hoss curled his lips back from his teeth in distaste and gave a sharp intake of air. Was the cure worse than the problem?

No, he decided. The burning had been necessary to stop the bleeding and now Hoss had to get Adam home so a doc could look at his burns. But he felt pretty certain he had to get Adam home quickly, by tonight. He needed lots of water, good food and a way to keep the wound clean away from the dust of the trail.

He looked down at his brother again. While Hoss watched, Adam turned onto his right side, facing Hoss, and drew his knees up toward his belly. He wrapped both arms tightly around himself and moaned quietly with each short breath he let out. Hoss put out his hand and rubbed Adam's nearest shoulder gently.

"Sorry Hoss...guess you're right...I'm about done," Adam said between breaths. It sounded to Hoss like he was talking through a clenched jaw and Hoss continued to rub his shoulder in hopes of helping him relax a little.

"Don't worry 'bout a thing. Ol' Hoss is gonna take care a' things, big brother." He noted a trace of a smile curving Adam's lips.

"Thanks 'big' brother," Adam said. He unwrapped one of his arms to put a hand atop the one Hoss had on his shoulder. "What's your plan?"

"We're about an hour's ride from the Marcus place. I'll ride there and get Foster to loan us a wagon to get you back to the Ponderosa in fine style. We should be there before midnight, if all goes well."

The faint smile returned once more to Adam's face. "Well, considering how well this day's gone so far, I hope we're in for some better luck." He was silent for a few seconds, then he asked, "I don't suppose I can talk you into just ridin' for home and bringing Pa back, can I?"

"For home?" Hoss looked horrified at the thought. "Adam...that's hours away. I can't leave you alone that long. It don't make no sense."

But it made perfect sense to Adam by this point. The constant pain that gnawed in his belly brought his focus very narrow: All his thoughts were on home and his father. Home was his safe haven and his father was the beacon that drew him there. If he couldn't get home, why not have his father come to him? For now, plainly put, he wanted his pa.

"I'm a real mess, huh?" Adam tried to make light of what he'd suggested, now that he realized by Hoss' reaction that apparently it was absurd. "I'll be fine here waiting for you to get back from the Marcus place."

"Are you sure? You gonna be OK here by yourself for a few hours?" Moments ago, Hoss had been sure he'd struck on the perfect plan to get his brother safely back to the Ponderosa since having to abort his first plan of the two of them making it on horseback. But now...what if Adam forgot he was supposed to wait for him and tried to get back on his horse to ride for home?

"I'll be fine." Adam dropped his hand off Hoss' to grab a handful of the blanket he lay on. He twisted it in his fist: Concentrating on that rather than the pain in his belly helped a little. "Just ride fast, OK?"

"Are you sure? You'll stay put?" Hoss still wasn't convinced.

"I'm sure." Adam wished Hoss would just go if he was going. He was feeling stranger by the minute and he felt certain if Hoss knew how bad he was feeling, he wouldn't leave him at all and then where would they be? "I'll be right here when you get back. Right here...I promise." The words were harder to put together now and Adam wasn't certain they had come out right.

Hoss looked doubtfully at his brother's closed eyes, his fist clutching a corner of the blanket and his curly hair soaked with sweat. But really, what choice was there? "All right, Adam, I'm leavin'. I'll ride fast." And with one final squeeze of his brother's shoulder, Hoss stood and headed for his horse. Hoss couldn't know that final squeeze didn't even register in Adam's fevered mind. He was heading off somewhere else for the duration of Hoss' ride.

HOSS KNEW WHERE he was going and he didn't have to think too much about the route, so his thoughts were dominated by worry over his older brother's welfare. He hated to leave him alone but he knew it was their only option if Adam were to survive.

Hoss also thought he had the better of the deal since he got to be doing something for the next several hours instead of just waiting. Hoss could be a patient man when necessary, like when he was waiting for a bite at one of his favorite trout streams. But when one of his family members was in trouble, Hoss was a man of action. Give him something to do or he'd go crazy. It was good he was making this ride for help; he just wished he hadn't had to leave Adam alone to do it.

Hoss didn't do a lot of down-on-his-knees, hands-folded formal praying but he often said them in his thoughts when his father was off on a trip or if Joe was breaking a particularly green horse. Now that Adam was in such trouble, Hoss found himself saying a simple prayer in his head: "Keep him safe." Soon the phrase got caught up in the rhythm of his horse's hoof beats and he found it changing to a litany of sorts, running over and over through his mind, in time with his horse's hooves: "Keep him safe, keep him safe, keep him safe." He rode like that—those three words repeating in his head—for miles.

ADAM CLUTCHED TO his chest the canteen Hoss had left with him. He still lay on his side, waiting for his brother's return. It was hard for him to tell how much time had passed since Hoss had left him behind to go for help. He could take out his watch and check the time, but reaching into his pocket was a lot more effort than he felt like mustering.

In fact, Adam was being very careful not to move at all now. The one time he'd pulled the cork from the canteen to take a drink, that little bit of movement had made him so dizzy, it had taken many minutes before he'd felt the earth stop its rapid spinning. So he'd wait for another drink until his brother came back for him, thank you very much.

The thought that Hoss perhaps would not make it back to him did not even enter Adam's mind.

HOSS RODE BACK into the clearing where he'd left his injured brother nearly three hours before, hoping and praying he'd find Adam as before. Foster Marcus drove his team right behind him. Foster had been more than willing to come along when Hoss asked him for help and together they'd covered the wagon bottom with straw and some extra blankets from the Marcus bunkhouse.

As they drew near enough to make out the still form under the tree, Hoss let out the breath he hadn't realized he was holding. He had hoped he would return to find things as they had been, but until he actually saw for himself.... Hoss dismounted near where Adam lay and Foster pulled the wagon a few feet from Hoss' horse and called out, "Let me know what you need me to do, Hoss."

Hoss waved to him in acknowledgement and went over to check on Adam. The sooner they could get him out of here, the better. He knelt again at Adam's side, put a hand on his right shoulder and said, "Adam?" He got no response so tried again, this time a little louder and accompanied it with a gentle shake of Adam's shoulder.

"Mmmmmm..." was all the reply he got.

"C'mon, Adam...ya gotta wake up for me." That wasn't really the truth. Hoss could just as easily pick his brother up again and tote him over to the wagon. But Hoss wanted Adam to wake up and talk to him, to reassure him that he was still with him.

This time, Hoss was rewarded with two words: "Back already?"

Adam's voice was weaker still and hardly more than a whisper but Hoss was glad to hear it, nonetheless.

"Yep, we're back and ol' Foster's got his wagon all fixed up for ya. What say I help ya get into it?" Hoss grinned down at his brother.

"Sounds fine," Adam whispered through lips that hardly moved, rolling slowly over onto his back, letting out a guttural groan as he did. Hoss lifted the shirt aside, stiff as an old piece of burlap, and looked at the wound. It didn't seem too much different from the last time he'd checked it.

Hoss reached out and placed his hand, not on the wound, but on the skin next to it. Adam's torso jerked as he flinched away from Hoss' gentle touch, and he sucked in air quickly through his teeth as he turned his face away.

"Easy, Adam," Hoss said as he put his other hand on his brother's shoulder. Hoss left a hand on Adam's belly for a moment: The skin felt hot. Hoss put his hand over on the other side of Adam's abdomen, and it felt warm as well. He reached up to put a palm over Adam's forehead and the skin there also felt warm. Seemed like his brother was starting up a fever.

"Doggone, Adam...you ain't all here with me, are ya?" Hoss left his hand on Adam's forehead and Adam rolled his head back toward Hoss. His eyes opened but they looked bright and glassy, a change from hours earlier when Hoss had left him to go for help.

"C'mon...take some more water. Where's your canteen?" Adam looked down at the canteen he still held in his arms and Hoss followed his glance. "Lemme have that and I'll help..." Hoss paused as he shook the water container. "Hell, Adam! This thing is just about full. Didn't you drink none while I was gone?" Hoss looked at his brother, worried.

"I couldn't...too dizzy," Adam managed in a weak voice.

With that Hoss turned around and motioned to Foster to come over to them. When he had pulled the wagon over next to them, Hoss said, "Hold those horses steady while I get him into the back, Foster. We need to get going outta here and on to home. We can't waste any more time here."

HOSS FELT LIKE he could allow himself the luxury of relaxing just a little. Foster said he felt in fine shape to drive on to the Ponderosa.

"Just don't you worry about me, Hoss. You set back there with your brother and make sure he's OK," Foster had said to Hoss when they'd started off. And with Adam securely pillowed on the straw and covered with blankets, Hoss took Foster at his word.

After staring for awhile at his and Adam's horses following along behind the wagon they were tied to, he closed his eyes and began to doze.

ADAM KNEW HE was on the move somewhere but strangely, he didn't care where. He could feel the jostle and jog of the wagon beneath him which caused his head to roll slightly back and forth, and he was hot, so damn hot. He felt the sweat beading on his face and trickling down his temples, but felt too wretched to reach up and wipe it off. He had suffered high fevers before and vaguely recognized the ache that covered seemingly every inch of his body and the malaise that sapped his energy and made him unable to do anything more than lay there under the moonlit sky.

Adam's mind began to wander away from this wagon and back to another wagon and another fever. He'd been 5 years old and his Pa and Ma hadn't been married long when he'd come down with a fever. He had felt miserable and while his Pa had driven their wagon, his Ma had sat in the back with him, bathing his forehead with cool water and singing softly to comfort him. They had stopped just before crossing a creek and Ma had gotten out of the wagon to get some fresh water, assuring her little boy she'd be back soon. And she had been, just as she'd said.

Adam reached out from under the blankets and felt for his mother's soft hand, but instead found a thick, muscular forearm, covered with coarse hair: his brother, Hoss. He briefly smiled but then felt more muddled than ever: If his mother were here then Hoss couldn't be more than an infant; yet here he was, all grown up and next to him in the wagon.

Adam's forehead wrinkled and he gripped his brother's arm tightly in his confusion. That steady presence gave Adam something to hold onto; whatever was happening to him and wherever they were going, he wasn't alone. His brother was with him and would watch out for him. Adam's forehead smoothed as he drifted away again.

HOSS HADN'T BEEN sleeping for long and his mind started waking up before his body did. There was something wrong, but he couldn't quite remember what it was. There was something he had to do, someone he had a grave responsibility to but it wasn't quite with him yet. Then he felt a hand grabbing at his arm. He opened his eyes to the cool blue light of the moon and his brother's hand clenching the muscle of Hoss' forearm. He sought Adam's face to see if there was anything newly wrong with him.

Adam looked to be sleeping but fitfully. He had reached out to clutch at Hoss in a dream, perhaps. "Adam, you're OK. Adam?" Hoss reached for his canteen again and leaned down to lift Adam's head slightly so he could have a drink. He didn't really wake up, but still managed a few swallows and that's what was most important to Hoss. He gently let his brother's head back down to rest on the straw and then poured a little of the water onto his fingers and smoothed it over Adam's hot forehead and temples.

"Hey Foster?" Hoss called up to the wagon seat.

"Yeah...you awake already?" came the reply.

"You sure you can see where we're goin' with it gettin' dark like this?" Hoss yawned immediately after saying this last.

"Why, Hoss, it's a full moon tonight. There ain't gonna be a problem driving this team with a route this good. Can't you see the road just 'bout as plain as day?" Foster called back, half turning.

"I guess I can, at that. How much longer, you figure?"

"Prob'ly about four more hours at this rate. The horses are fit and fine and the weather's good so ... yeah, four more hours. OK?"

"That sounds fine, Foster. I sure 'nuff appreciate all you're doin' for us." Hoss removed his hat and scratched his head before replacing it. He yawned again.

"Don't give it a thought, ya hear? It's what friends do." Foster turned around in the seat to again face fully forward and concentrate on the road ahead.

"Hoss? Ma's gonna be right back, OK?"

Hoss whipped his head around so fast to look at Adam, the source of the question, that later he'd think he surely must have looked mighty comical. Adam had spoken the words clear as day, but still, Hoss thought he MUST have heard them wrong. Adam's eyes were closed and he wasn't saying anything now.

"Adam? Did you say somethin'?" Hoss peered at his brother. It was harder to see him now in the gathering gloom of evening. "Adam!" Hoss spoke sharply that time, more sharply than he had intended, but the words his brother had spoken had unnerved him.

ADAM DIDN'T SPEAK often of their mother, the one they had shared for too short a time out on the trail West.

Joe's mother, Marie, had been a good mother to them all, but Hoss and Adam shared a bond over their mother, Inger, that only the two of them could understand. Hoss hungered like a starving man for anything anyone could tell him about his mother. When his Uncle Gunnar had briefly visited the Ponderosa, Hoss had been disappointed that he couldn't tell his nephew more about her. And then with his death went any chance of a long discussion about Inger.

His pa? Well, Pa could only talk about Hoss' mother from the viewpoint of a husband. Sure, he could tell Hoss what a wonderful mother Inger had been but she was Ben's wife, first and foremost, and that's really how he saw her. As badly as he felt for his boys when she died, at the moment when Inger's life was steadily draining away, he could think of nothing but his loss. When he realized he held his dead wife in his arms and the tears came as he buried his face in her hair, it was himself and HIS loss—the loss of his wife—that was at the top of his mind.

No, it was Adam Hoss most relied on in recent years to keep the memory of their mother alive for him. And that had not come about easily, but only because Hoss had finally grown desperate enough to ask his reticent brother.

Hoss had gone to Adam's bedroom late one evening about three months after Uncle Gunnar's death. He had been unable to shake the feeling of despair that he had lost the last person who could talk to him about his mother besides his father. And he had screwed up his courage to bring the subject up with his brother.

Adam was in bed but was awake and reading by the yellow light of an oil lamp. He looked up as he heard a light tap at his door and then watched it open and saw Hoss' head poking through. "What's on your mind, Hoss?" Adam was surprised to see his brother up this late: Usually Hoss was in bed and snoring before Adam ever put out his reading lamp. What's more, once he opened the door all the way and wordlessly entered the room, Adam saw Hoss was still fully dressed, right down to his boots.

"You haven't even been to bed yet?" Adam asked him, a quizzical look on his face. Hoss shook his head and stood silently at the side of Adam's bed, looking a little hangdog with his hands thrust deep into his front pants pockets. "Sit down, why dontcha? You have something on your mind?" Adam knew that was a silly question: Of course he had something on his mind. But he had to go about this the right way or risk making his brother go silent on him.

"Well...I been thinkin', Adam." Hoss raked one hand through his mussed brown hair, putting it into even more of a state of disarray. Adam waited patiently. When Hoss wanted to talk, he often took his time going about it. Adam had been holding his place in his book with an index finger, but now reached over to the bedside table for the playing card he was using as a marker and closed the book around that instead. He set it on the table and looked at Hoss again.

"What's on your mind, Hoss?" Adam gently asked again.

"You knew our ma, Adam...like a son knows a ma, didn't you?" Hoss now had his thumbs hooked into his pants pockets, trying to look casual, like that sentence hadn't been difficult for him to say to his brother. But the way Hoss was looking directly into Adam's eyes told him there was nothing casual about the question.

The question took Adam by surprise. The three half-brothers didn't speak much to each other about their respective mothers. Their father often talked to them about the three women he had married and buried but his boys didn't speak at length about their mothers to each other. It was as if they each wanted to save the one thing that was theirs, and only theirs, for themselves.

Joe was still too young to fully realize how Marie had been a mother to Adam and Hoss as well. He thought of Marie as his alone, and that was fine with his brothers. Someday perhaps he'd question them about their memories to add to those he had stored away or that his father had shared with him.

Adam had no one to question about his mother other than his father. He long ago had exhausted his father's cache of stories about his mother and Ben could tell Adam no stories about her as his mother, since she had died so soon after giving birth to him. Adam certainly had no personal memories of her, though his father had tried mightily to create some for him when Adam was a child.

As far back as Adam could remember, Ben would put his only son to bed each night and tell him about his mother, Elizabeth, who lived in heaven but who looked down on him and watched over him every day. Ben told Adam how much she had loved him and how happy she'd been to have had a son.

Though Adam felt a great loss at the void his mother's absence created, for all Ben's efforts, Elizabeth Cartwright was mainly a picture on his father's desk and a music box on Adam's bureau.

Hoss' question marked the first time he'd come to Adam, alone, to ask him about Inger. And Adam smiled as he remembered the tall, smiling, Swedish beauty who had come into their lives during their trek across the country: These were his real memories, flesh and blood memories, not just stories.

"Yeah, that's how I knew her, Hoss. She was my ma...the only one I'd had, really." He looked up with a grin into his brother's face from where he sat up in his bed. "Would you sit down? If we're gonna have this talk, I can't be lookin' up at you the whole time...I'll get a pain in my neck!"

Hoss ducked his head in embarrassment and perched on the edge of Adam's bed. He faced Adam and finally said straight out, "What can you tell me? It ain't the same hearing it from Pa. He can't tell me what she was really like as a ma."

Adam crossed his arms behind his head and leaned back against his headboard. The smile stayed on his face as he allowed his mind to go back to a time when he first felt like he had a real family at last.

For as long as Adam could remember, they had been journeying West, just he and his father. He had always been envious of the families he saw that had both a father AND a mother, who cooked and mended and patched up small hurts, and sometimes included even a younger brother or sister. So when his father had met Inger, Adam had taken to her immediately. If he could have chosen his ma, she's exactly who he would have picked. And that's just what he told Hoss.

"Really? You liked her right off, huh?" Hoss couldn't keep a big grin off his face. How it pleased him to hear such a thing.

"Oh yeah. She was so...so good, Hoss." Adam got a pensive look on his face as his eyes went from Hoss to his bedroom window. "I didn't think back on it until I got a lot older, but it's really something for a man or woman to take on someone else's child in a ready-made family. But that's just what our ma did. Thinkin' about it now, remembering how happy she made me feel ..." Adam stopped, still looking out the window. Hoss saw his eyes were a little bright, but said nothing. He quietly waited for Adam to go on.

"She just made me feel like we had a real family for once. A complete family, you know? I'd never had that before. It had just been me and Pa since...well, since forever." Adam looked at Hoss then, seeking confirmation of his feelings. Surely Hoss had felt the same thing when Marie had come into his life.

"Yeah, I do know. I know just how you felt." Hoss nodded. And Adam knew that he did.

He continued, "She didn't have to be that way, though. She probably could have won Pa over and treated me just well enough to get by. But she loved me, Hoss. She did," Adam said almost defensively. "I could feel it and she told me so. She told me every night before I went to sleep. Every night ..." His voice trailed off again, remembering a small boy nestled into his blankets, his mother leaning over him, quietly completing their bedtime ritual.

This is what Hoss had been looking for: his brother's feelings about their ma, because then those feelings could be HIS feelings. "So then what happened?" he asked.

Adam lost the pensive look he'd worn and grinned at his brother. "You mean, hurry up and get to when you're born, right?" He laughed out loud at his brother's transparency.

"Well, sure, Adam. That's why I come in here." But Hoss

laughed too, his throaty chuckle that sounded like it came straight from his belly.

"One day the wagon got stuck climbing a hill," Adam continued, "and Pa got out to push at the front wheel. Ma sent me away from the wagon and she was supposed to go too, but she said she wanted to help. Pa told her to get away but she stayed to push anyway because, well...the women had to pitch in just like the men on that trip. They did things women in Boston or Philadelphia would never have dreamed of doing."

"She got knocked down when the wagon moved suddenly and rolled down the hill a ways. Pa ran over to her and that's when we found out she was carrying you. She felt bad she hadn't told Pa yet, but she had wanted to wait and now she was scared she'd lost you in the fall. Pa was worried too, sure enough."

"They was worried about me, 'fore I was even born?" Hoss marveled at the thought of his pa, who worried enough about his sons as grown men, fretting about his unborn child.

"Well, sure. Sometimes a fall can cause real problems for women who are in a family way. And it caused problems on the wagon train because Pa wouldn't budge and we had a deadline to meet and other folks on the train were put out that we were stayin' in one place." Adam paused, remembering the angry exchanges between the men and his father.

"But then it was OK. Ma called out that she was fine and we should be on our way. Pa was so happy when Ma told him she'd felt you movin'."

"Movin'. I was movin' around." Hoss was nearly speechless at this story he'd never heard before this moment.

"So then everything was fine and we got on the trail again and Ma and Pa were so happy, Hoss. They were just so happy and so was I. It was the best time of my life." Adam smiled, remembering long days helping his father drive their team and nights sleeping snugly tucked into the back of their wagon. Strange how just the addition of Inger, only one person, had made his family seem so much larger.

"So what happened when I was born?" Hoss asked, getting impatient for his physical appearance in this story.

"Well, Pa wasn't even there when you were born. Did you know that?"

"Sure...Pa's told me that much. He said he came back to the train, and there I was, bigger 'n life." Hoss grinned at Adam and waited for the obligatory crack about his size.

"You're making it way too easy, 'big' brother." Adam grinned back at him. "Anyway, I WAS there, except I had to wait outside the wagon. One of the women, Mrs. Cooper, was in there with Ma and she told me everything was going to be fine and I just had to wait awhile and I could meet my new brother or sister."

"Which did ya want, Adam?"

"A brother, of course." Adam's grin grew bigger. "That's what Pa wanted, too. So I waited and pretty soon I heard you squawlin' ..."—Hoss leaned forward and jabbed him in the shoulder with his fist—"and Mrs. Cooper stuck her head out of the back of the wagon and said my ma wanted me to come meet my new baby brother."

"And didja?" Hoss asked.

"Well sure. Ma was sitting up in the back and she looked real tired, and her hair was a little mussed..." Adam leaned back again and closed his eyes, remembering. "She looked so proud and so happy but she didn't forget about me, just because she had you now. She couldn't wait to show you off to me.

"She had you all wrapped up in a blanket with just your head poking out. I couldn't believe how big you were! I'd seen one or two other brand-new babies who'd been born on the trail and they weren't half your size." Adam opened his eyes and looked at his brother again. "I thought we were really something, having the biggest baby on the train."

Hoss' look turned to one of embarrassment as the color in his face got a little deeper but Adam told him sincerely, "No really...I was proud of that. Still am proud of your size, Hoss. You've used it to get me out of a jam more than once."

"So when did Pa get back?" Hoss asked, wanting to move the conversation back to something that didn't make him feel so funny inside. His older brother was proud of him?

"He got back later that night. The minute he rode up, he said the men were telling him Ma's time had come. The birth of a baby on the train was mighty big news, let me tell ya. He said he climbed into the back of the wagon so fast, he about gave Ma a fit. She didn't know who was busting in on us. We were in there talking and suddenly there was Pa."

Adam took a deep breath in and blew it back out in a heavy sigh. His voice took on a dreamy quality. "Hoss, I wish you could have seen the look on his face when he first looked at you. It was really something. I've only seen it one other time and that's when Joe was born."

Hoss shook his head slightly. "Ya know, Adam, I'll bet Pa had that look three times."

"Hmmm? What do you mean?"

"Well, I bet he had that same look when you was born, too."

"Oh...that's right." Adam laughed at how he'd forgotten about his own birth. "Well, that's something we'll never know." Hoss realized Adam was right: There was no one left alive who could describe for him the look on his father's face the first time he saw his oldest son. Hoss felt sorry for Adam then, that he didn't have an older brother to share memories of his ma with him, like Adam was sharing with Hoss.

"Anyway, I wanted to name you. I asked Pa if I could but he looked at Ma and asked her, which I guess was only right." Adam looked a little chagrined at his memory of the boldness of his 6-year-old self.

"Before you were born, Pa had been telling folks on the train that you were either going to be named after his father or Ma's father: Joseph or Eric. He even said if you were Eric then his next son would be Joseph. Leave it to Pa to get his way after all, huh?" Hoss snorted laughter at that one and Adam joined him laughing at the joke. Ben Cartwright was well known around the

Ponderosa, and even Virginia City, for having things his way and, in this case, their brother Joe was the proof.

"So Ma said she wanted to name you Eric, after her father, and Pa looked like he thought that was a good idea, and that was when I made my move."

"Your move?" Hoss knew they'd decided to call him Hoss because of a suggestion by his Uncle Gunnar but he couldn't imagine Adam's part in the whole thing.

"I reminded them about Uncle Gunnar telling us he hoped we'd call you Hoss. I guess they'd both just forgotten and when I reminded them, Ma's eyes lit up and she looked up at Pa, saying she remembered now. So Pa said we'd use both names and see which one stuck, but I knew which one it was going to be." Adam smiled in satisfaction and Hoss said, "Looks like someone inherited a little bit of that 'gettin' your own way stuff' from Pa."

"Well, don't you think Hoss is a much better fit than Eric?" Adam looked at his brother and Hoss smiled back at him, trying to imagine it. "I just can't see calling you Eric. I just can't. I never have, either, not since the day you were born. Pa tried it a few times, but he knew." Adam grinned smugly.

"He still does try it every now and then," Hoss said, "mostly when he's introducing us to folks. What about Ma? Did she ever?"

"Sure, she tried it on you a few times, too. But it just didn't fit with your nature, Hoss. You were so big and so happy and..." Adam's face turned serious all of a sudden. "We were all four happy then. So happy..." His voice trailed off and stopped and Hoss knew the story Adam was remembering now.

Hoss knew the details, but there was no way he could know that story as intimately as Adam did. He knew Indians had attacked them and they had crouched in the corner of a way station while Pa and the other men fired out the windows. And when one of the men had gotten shot, Ma had placed her new son carefully into Adam's arms and then, taking up the discarded rifle, began shooting out the window with the men. And then an arrow had ended their happiness, too quickly after it had begun.

Adam was remembering as well, in a way that Hoss never could. He saw their ma fall with the arrow in her back and cried out to their pa. He wanted to jump up and run over to her and hug her and beg her to be OK. But he knew he had to keep his baby brother safe in his arms and out of harm's way. Ma had given him to Adam to protect and that was his job and he couldn't do anything else. So he kept his arms wrapped around Hoss and watched Pa hold Ma until she breathed her last, watched him cry over her, and he looked down at his baby brother who didn't know anything about the tragedy that had befallen their little family. As he looked into the chubby face of the brother who already had stolen all their hearts, Adam had thought, "Now we're alone again."

And suddenly three seemed many times fewer than four.

"Adam?" Hoss put a hand on his brother's blanket-covered leg.

"Hmmmm?" Adam said, shaking off his somber thoughts. "Sorry ...just thinkin'." He was silent for a few seconds and then looked into his brother's ice-blue eyes and said earnestly, "She seems more my mother than my real mother does, Hoss, and that feels wrong but it feels right, too. I feel guilty as hell about it, like I'm disloyal to my own mother, but I didn't know her at all. She's just a pretty lady in a picture to me."

He gave a humorless laugh and said, "I used to look in Pa's shaving mirror and then look at her picture, trying to see if there was some way we looked alike. I never could see it, though. And I don't remember a thing about her...there's no way I could, though heaven knows, I tried to imagine I did before Inger came along." He laughed briefly at his childish folly of making up memories of his mother.

"But I DID know your mother and I loved her so much and I know she loved me...loved us." Adam's voice broke a little at the end, but his eyes remained dry and locked on his brother's.

"Our ma, Adam. She was OUR ma," Hoss gently corrected his brother.

"OK, our ma, then," Adam took another deep breath and sighed. "Our ma. Sure you don't mind sharing?"

"Nahhhhh. Seems like she had enough love for both of us." Now it was Hoss' turn to look a little dreamy. "Adam? I...I..." He stopped. He wasn't sure what he wanted to say. Adam sat waiting.

"Thank you, brother. I just wanna say thank you. I feel like I know our ma a lot better tonight, is all." Hoss looked away now toward the window. "Can we talk about her again sometime?"

"Sure Hoss...anytime. Come and ask me anything and I'll tell you what I can. It was a long time ago, but those memories, the good ones and a few of the bad ones, seem like they'll never fade." Adam reached out and clasped the hand that still rested on the blanket covering his leg. "Now maybe we'd better think about gettin' some sleep. I think Pa has a whole list of chores waiting for us in the morning."

"That's the truth, for sure." Hoss stood and walked to the door and then looked back. "G'nite, Adam."

"'Night, Hoss."

"ADAM!" HOSS REPEATED sharply once more, and that time the word had its intended effect.

Adam's eyes opened and he looked around him as if wondering where he was. "What's wrong?" he said, a little fuzzily.

"Oh, only about everythin' but we're just a few hours from home now, so they'll be fine soon enough," Hoss said, trying to sound confident. He put his hand on his brother's forehead again and felt the slick sweat come away on his palm. Adam had grown hotter while he slept and the only thing Hoss knew to do was give him water. "C'mon, Adam, raise up a little so you can have a drink."

"I don't want one." Adam sounded a little petulant, but didn't protest when his brother simply scooped his shoulders up and put the canteen to his lips. He took two swallows and then turned his face away causing the water to spill over his cheek, before Hoss had a chance to pull the canteen back. Hoss let Adam lay back on the straw once more, his eyes closed. Hoss could make out his features pretty well now that the moon was high above them and he watched Adam stir restlessly, perhaps trying to find a position on his makeshift bed where he didn't feel the pain so much. His hand went again and again to his side where his stab wound was covered with his bloodstained shirt and a layer of blankets only to flutter away once more, restlessly moving above his head, to his chin, onto his chest, into his hair.

"Ma, my stomach hurts," Adam said, sounding exhausted by the relentlessness of the pain.

Hoss started again and spoke his brother's name once more: "Adam?" His eyes obligingly opened, though Hoss wasn't sure who Adam saw sitting next to him.

"Ma ain't here, Adam," Hoss said gently.

"She isn't?" Adam peered up at his brother and reached out his hand toward him. "Hoss? I thought...I musta been dreamin', I guess."

Hoss put his hand out to hold his brother's still restless hand and said, "Was it a nice dream...the one about Ma?"

"Well...she was here. Don't remember..." Adam's voice trailed off as if he had simply forgotten to finish the sentence he had started and then closed his eyes once more.

Hoss kept watch over his older brother then, in the back of the wagon, while Foster Marcus drove them on toward home. The horses' hooves beat a rhythm onto the dirt road that once again reminded Hoss of his prayer: "Keep him safe, keep him safe, keep him safe."

HOSS THOUGHT HE had never been so relieved to see his home as he was when Foster drove the wagon around the barn and into the yard of the Ponderosa ranch house. He got up on one knee and looked past Foster's back to see lamps burning inside as the front door opened and, blessed be, his father coming through it onto the porch.

"Foster?" Ben called to his old friend as he held a lamp higher, confirming his identification. "What in tarnation are you doing here this time 'a night?" He'd been expecting his sons to arrive home, in fact had been waiting up for them.

"Ben, there's been trouble," Foster shouted from the wagon seat as he reined the team in.

"Trouble?" Ben's dark eyebrows nearly met in the middle as his friendly smile turned to a scowl. "What kind of trouble?"

Foster set the brake and looped the reins several times around its handle. "Trouble with your boys, Ben." He hooked a thumb toward the back of the wagon before beginning to climb down.

The moment Foster had spoken the words "trouble" and "boys," Ben had paid him no more attention and turned toward the back of the wagon. He saw Hoss leaning over something in the straw and then he straightened up and said, "Hey Pa."

"Hoss! What's happened to you?" Ben was alarmed at the disheveled state of his middle son, including the cut lip and bruised face, but once his eyes caught sight of Hoss' shirt, wrinkled, smeared with rust-colored stains and open nearly to the waist, he knew there had been more than trouble out on the trail. "Are you all right?"

"Yeah Pa, I'm fine. It's ..." Hoss began, but Ben would not let him finish.

"Where's Adam?" The words were no sooner spoken than Ben reached the back of the wagon and saw his oldest son nestled into the straw and covered in blankets. In the light from his lamp, Ben saw Adam's dark hair stuck to his head in curly, sweaty clumps. "What happened to you, boy?" he asked in dismay.

"I was gonna tell ya," Hoss said impatiently and shoved an arm under Adam's shoulder, another under his knees, and hoisted his brother into his arms. Adam's limbs dangled loosely as Hoss leaned over the end of the wagon with his blanket-wrapped brother and said, "Here, Pa. Can you take 'im?"

"Of course," Ben said, handing the lantern off to Foster and reaching up as Hoss leaned down to deposit Adam carefully into his father's arms.

Ben braced himself to accept his son, not a small burden, and, once he was holding him securely, looked down at Adam's hectic color and face shiny with perspiration and knew, at the least, he was very ill.

As if to confirm Ben's sense that it was more than just illness, Hoss said, "Pa, he's been stabbed. It happened early this morning, just after sunrise." Now that his responsibility for Adam's life had been passed along to his father, both literally and figuratively, Hoss allowed himself to finally feel his fatigue.

"Thieves...after the money from the cattle sale. Four of 'em came up on us in our camp and one of 'em pulled a knife on Adam. He stabbed 'im right in the belly, I guess, and then they rode off with all our money." Hoss panted a little after unburdening himself to his father and added, looking worried, "I got the bleedin' stopped but he's gotten some worse since this afternoon."

"We have to get him upstairs," Ben said and turned toward the door.

"Pa, maybe we should send Joe for the doc right away," Hoss said, jumping down from the wagon and taking the lantern from Foster.

"We can't," Ben said, stopping. "Joe's already in Virginia City. He was playing cards and said he'd stay in town tonight. That's where I left him."

"I'll go for the doc," Foster said, "if you can loan me a horse."

"Take one from the barn," Ben directed. "And Foster—find Joe in town, will you? Tell him he has to come home right away. Tell him what happened."

"I sure will, Ben. Don't you worry; the doc'll be back here soon." Foster strode off toward the closed barn door.

Ben turned back toward the house and carried his son up to his room.

"HOSS, CAN YOU help me with him?" Ben held a clean cloth up as he looked around at his middle son. He hated to ask him because he so obviously was worn out, but they had to try to bring Adam's fever down. That much he knew even without the doctor's expertise.

"Yeah, Pa. I'm fine...really." He sat on the opposite side of Adam's bed from his father and reached for a cloth to dunk into the cold water. He squeezed the excess water out and began to mop the perspiration off Adam's chest and shoulder. Ben was doing the same to Adam's face and neck.

For his part, Adam hadn't had much to say since they brought him upstairs, just a few mumbles and a loud moan when Ben had caught his foot on the door as he carried him through the doorway. Ben had placed him on his bed and Hoss had held Adam in a sitting position, arms draped over Hoss' shoulder, while his father had finally relieved his son of that blood-stiffened shirt. Ben looked at it in disgust before dropping it to the floor behind him.

As he worked on his brother, Hoss wondered if Adam was going to ask about their ma again and, sure enough, almost the minute Hoss had gotten the thought in his head, Adam piped up, his voice suddenly clear as a bell, if a little bit whiny: "Ma, I'm hot...get these blankets off, can't ya?" Now it was Ben's turn to look startled.

"Did he say 'ma'?" Ben asked Hoss, a surprised look on his face. Hoss nodded but stayed silent and Ben turned back to Adam and said, "Your mother's not here, son." Then he looked at Hoss once more.

"Hoss? Would you go downstairs to my desk and get Elizabeth's picture? Maybe it will comfort Adam a little if he has it here beside his bed when he wakes." Ben turned back to his task once more; Hoss just bit his lip and remained where he was.

"Well, son...what are you waiting for?" Ben looked up at Hoss, surprised that he hadn't gotten moving.

"Pa?...I don't..." Hoss paused. This was a hard thing to say, because he knew his Pa had loved his first wife intensely. She had been his first love, after all, and bore him his first son. But he knew it had to be said, so he let it out in a rush: "It ain't Elizabeth he's talkin' to. It's our ma...it's Inger."

"Inger?" Ben looked back at Adam who was saying nothing more but had gone back to the same restless hand movements as in the wagon. "Inger...my love," Ben thought and was, as usual, hit with emotions churned up by the mention of the name. But usually he thought of Inger when Hoss was in trouble or hurt. When Adam was in trouble, it was always Elizabeth's face he conjured up and Elizabeth he talked to during any bedside vigils. Adam was Elizabeth's son, not Inger's.

As if to contradict that very thought, Hoss said, "He told me once that his ma—Elizabeth—was just a face in a picture to him. He felt bad thinkin' it, and...and disloyal, but he said it was the truth. He said my ma—our ma—was the first mother he'd ever known and she was who he thought of as his ma."

Ben looked at Hoss's earnest face and knew it must hurt him to be saying this right now. It hurt Ben even more, though. Had he not done a good job keeping Elizabeth's memory alive for his oldest son? He had tried, but...Adam, without any memories of his own of his mother, must have felt like she was just a ghost. And Inger, with her sunny smile and disposition so like her son's, had embraced Adam as if he were her own. For that Ben had been so grateful. His young son had been grateful as well, Ben knew; the positive change in Adam when Inger came into their lives had been evident.

"Why didn't I know that?" Ben asked, looking stricken.

Hoss shook his head at his father. "Aw, Pa, Adam didn't wanna tell ya somethin' like that. It would only make you...well, make you feel like ya do right now, I guess. And I tol' ya, Adam felt mighty 'shamed about feelin' that way anyway. He didn't feel like it was right that he should love my ma more than his own." Hoss didn't add how grateful he was that Adam HAD felt that way because if he hadn't, Hoss wouldn't have been able to share those long talks with Adam about their mother. He didn't need to take things that far with his father right now.

"Ma, please take 'em off me," Adam begged as he pushed fruitlessly at the bedclothes, and their attention turned back toward him. "I can't stand it bein' so hot."

"Ma's not here right now, Adam," Hoss said soothingly and at that, his brother opened his eyes. "Hoss? Where is she? Hoss?" His color was high now and his eyes, while open, didn't seem to be able to focus on much of anything.

It hurt him to say it, but Ben asked Hoss once more: "Go downstairs and get your mother's picture off my desk and bring it up. Maybe that will help him." And Hoss got up then and started down the stairs. Ben turned back to the bed and said, "Adam?"

Adam turned his head toward the sound of his father's voice and said, "Pa? I'm glad you're here, Pa. Hoss said Ma's not here right now."

Ben swallowed hard at that and said, "No, she's not, son. Why don't you close your eyes and get some sleep." And Adam did.

HOSS STOOD BY his father's desk, looking at the framed portrait of his mother, Inger. He carried it over to the mirror on the wall and stood looking, first at his face and then at the picture. The sound of hoof beats broke into his thoughts and he went to open the front door. Racing up to the rail was a buggy carrying Dr. Martin and Joe. Joe was driving, and the doctor sat next to him clutching his bag.

"Boy, I'm sure glad to see you fellas, and I know Pa will be too!" Hoss said loudly as he came through the door onto the porch.

"I'm just glad to have made it here in one piece," the doctor said, having climbed out of the buggy as soon as it had stopped. He glared back at Joe and then walked onto the porch. "Where is he?"

"Up in his room, Doc." Hoss pointed back through the front door and the doctor went through it. Hoss looked back at Joe as he was tying the horse to the rail. "Why was you drivin' the doc's buggy?"

Joe joined Hoss on the porch. "Foster found me before he did the doc, so I went with him and told the doc I could drive here faster knowin' the road like I do and it bein' nighttime and all." Joe shrugged. "Foster said Adam was hurt bad, and I didn't wanna waste any time getting the doc here. Foster's bringin' my horse back."

He stopped then and looked up at Hoss with a grave expression. "How bad is he, Hoss? I gotta know before I go up there."

"I don't know for sure. He was awake and talkin' most of the day but this evenin' he took a turn. He's got a bad fever now and..." Hoss shrugged; he didn't know exactly what to say to Joe. He guessed he would just leave things in the doc's hands now. He'd gotten his brother this far—alive—by his sheer determination that he would not see him die. Now the exhausted man was relieved to turn the responsibility for Adam's care over to someone else.

Joe stared at him for a moment longer, briefly put a hand on Hoss' shoulder and then headed for the door. Hoss turned to follow his brother, the framed picture still in his hand.

BEN USED ONE of the damp cloths to wipe the sweat from his own forehead. He hadn't realized he was perspiring so until Dr. Martin was done cleaning and treating Adam's stab wound and

burns. He'd been as gentle as possible with the painful proce-
dure, but Adam, in his delirium, had fought him, and in the end
it took both Hoss and Ben to hold Adam down while the doctor
worked on him.

It had been awful to witness his son struggling to break free
from their grasp, shouting and cursing them for what they were
doing to him. He was totally out of his head now, which was
disconcerting for Ben. It was his eldest—his Adam—who lay
there, but he didn't know his father or his brothers. He only
knew someone was causing him great pain and Ben hoped that
same strength he had used to fight his "tormenters" could be
used by Adam to fight his fever.

Dr. Martin stood at the bedside table repacking his bag, and
then placed several packets by the basin. "I'm leaving you some
more sedative powders, Ben. He should sleep for awhile yet and
I'm hoping the fever will break by dawn."

The doctor continued, "It's a miracle, or something like it, that
the blade didn't hit any organs or cause any bleeding inside.
Hoss, did Adam ever have any blood in his mouth?"

"Nosir, he didn't. The only blood was from his belly wound."
Hoss thought that had been plenty, thank you.

"Well, I think our biggest worry right now is the fever, then,
and we'll just have to wait and see on that."

"Thank you, doctor. I sure appreciate you coming out here in
the middle of the night," Ben said.

"It's a good thing I did, Ben. It's safest to get a wound like that
looked at as soon as possible." The doctor turned to Hoss. "I
know it looks bad, Hoss, and that wound cleaning wasn't the
nicest thing to watch Adam go through, but I want you to know
you saved his life today."

Hoss slowly shook his head and said, "Aw, Doc, I was just
takin' care of my brother."

The doctor shook his own head and said, "No, if you hadn't
been there and thought quickly enough to cauterize that wound,
Adam would have bled to death on the trail, plain and simple."

Hoss shrugged then. It hadn't been a conscious decision on his part; there really had been no decision to make. He could not have let Adam die.

Ben clapped a hand to his son's shoulder. "We're sure glad he was there, Doc. And sure glad he had the presence of mind to do what he did." Ben squeezed Hoss' shoulder and looked into his son's eyes. "I know that must have been a difficult thing to have to do to your brother, even though you knew it was the only thing that could save his life."

"It was awful, Pa. Plain awful...but Adam sure was strong," Hoss said, and then swallowed hard, remembering Adam's hoarse cries, the powerful grip of his hand, the smells and...He shook his head and added, "It worked and that's all that matters now."

"That's right, Hoss." Ben nodded. "He's going to be fine." Ben was determined to see that it was so.

The doctor had finished packing up his things and grabbed his hat. "Well, gentlemen, I'm going to take my leave. Please, Little Joe..." He held up his hand, palm out, as the youngest Cartwright stood up from the chair he'd been sitting in by the window. He grinned at the doctor who said, "Really...I can drive my OWN buggy back to town just fine, thank you."

He walked over to the door and then stopped to look back at the father and sons. He said, shaking his head, "Heaven help anyone who gets in the way of a Cartwright trying to go to the aid of another Cartwright." With a wry grin, he jammed his hat onto his head and was gone.

"Joseph, I hope I don't have to send you for the doctor again anytime soon," Ben said to his youngest with a stern look. "Aw, Pa, there was no way I was going to let the doc drive...he'd have had that pony going at a trot the whole way," Joe said.

"Well, he may have felt that getting here at a little slower pace was better than not getting here at all!" Ben began, his voice rising, and Joe, sensing his father working up to a thundering lecture, quickly pointed over to his sick brother on the bed. "Pa, did Adam say something? I thought I heard him call your name."

Ben immediately turned back toward the bed and went to sit next to his eldest, his just-begun lecture on his youngest forgotten, just as Joe had hoped.

"Boy, you sure know how to make things happen," Hoss said to Joe, an admiring tone in his voice and immediately was seized with a tremendous yawn.

"Well, thanks for the compliment, but don't you think you oughtta get a little rest? Why don't you go lay down for awhile?" Joe said. "Pa and I can take care of the compresses for his fever. Doc said he's gonna sleep awhile anyway."

"I think I might nap a bit, Joe, for sure. But I'm gonna do that right here in this room. I'll take your chair and you take mine." And with that, Hoss went over to sit in the chair by the window that Joe had vacated when the doctor left.

Joe grinned, took Hoss' place by Adam's side and reached for the wet cloth in the basin of water. He looked down at Adam's belly, now covered with the doctor's fresh white bandage and his young face grew sober. "That was somethin', huh, Pa?"

"Hmmmm? What's that, Joe?" Ben looked over to his son but kept dabbing the cool cloth on Adam's face.

"Oh, just when the doc was scrubbing at those burns and..." Joe gave a little shudder at the memory of Hoss and his father using what seemed like all their strength to hold his oldest brother down on the bed so the doctor could do his work.

"Oh." Ben doused the cloth in the cool water again and squeezed out the excess. "Well, I know that wasn't very nice to watch, Joe, but Adam was out of his mind. He isn't all there right now...It hurt him something fierce, but he likely won't remember." Ben paused in his work and looked over at Joe's somber face. "Besides, what's that Adam used to say years ago when he'd get tossed off a horse or when you boys would get into a scrap? 'The only way to hurt me is to kill me.' Isn't that what he said?"

"Yeah, that was it." Joe smiled at some of his memories.

"Well, we're not going to let it go that far." Ben smiled back at his son.

Adam slowly turned his head to one side on the pillow and then back again, blew out a chuff of air and raised his hand once more to his head and then down to his bandaged abdomen.

Ben reached out and grabbed Adam's hand away from his wound and held it in his own. "Adam? Can you hear me son?"

"Mmmmm...hurts..." Adam's words ended in a breathy groan.

Ben picked up one of the envelopes of sedative powder the doctor had left, tapped the contents into a glass and then poured it half full of water. He said, "Lift him up, will you, Joe?" and when Joe had gotten his arms under his brother's shoulders and raised him slightly, Ben put the glass to Adam's lips. "C'mon son...drink this down for me." Adam slowly but steadily drank until the glass was empty and when Joe had settled him back against the pillow, he opened his eyes.

"Joe?"

"Yeah, Adam, it's me. Didn't wanna miss your homecomin'." Joe smiled down at his brother.

"Hey, Joe..." Adam said in a tired greeting and then his eyes went back to his father. "Pa? Where's Ma? Is she back yet?"

Ben grinned a little at his son's confusion, but he guessed that's the sort of chaos a fever created in the mind. Ben reached over to the night table to get the photo Hoss had brought upstairs with him. "She's not, son, but here's her picture. Would you like to look at it for awhile?" He put the framed photo into the hand he still held in his own and then brought it up in front of Adam's eyes.

Adam stared at the photo for several seconds and a smile broke onto his wan, sweating face. His eyes closed then and Ben let the hand that held the photo down gently onto Adam's chest.

Joe had watched all this wondering just what was going on. The picture his father had given Adam was Hoss' mother, not Adam's. He looked up at Ben and said as much.

"I know, son, and I'm not sure we'll ever be able to talk to Adam about it. But this is what Hoss told me." And Ben told Joe the story of Adam and Hoss' bond with their mother, Inger.

DAWN'S PALE LIGHT was coming through Adam's bedroom window when Hoss was shaken awake by his father. "Son," Ben said in a low whisper, "I'm going downstairs and get some coffee for us all."

"OK Pa..." Hoss rubbed a hand over his face, first up and then back down. "How's Adam doin'?"

"He's better. I think his fever is down and he's sleeping more comfortably." Ben looked back at the still form on the bed remembering the bone-jarring chills that had wracked Adam's body between bouts of sweats during the early morning hours of this day. "I'm hoping later he'll be more himself."

Hoss stood to take his father's place at Adam's side as Ben went downstairs. As Hoss sat, he observed Joe who had leaned forward in his chair and slept with his head cradled on his arms on the edge of Adam's bed. Adam's left arm lay by his side, the back of his hand brushing up against Joe's curly brown hair. His right hand lay on his chest, still holding Inger's framed portrait.

"Hoss." The whisper brought Hoss' attention to Adam's face and he quickly put one of his hands on Adam's forehead. "I feel better."

"You do feel better...your fever ain't gone, but it's sure a lot lower." Hoss reached down for the portrait and said, "Whatcha got here?" He held it up for Adam to see.

"It's our mother," Adam said, a smile transforming his face. "Where'd that come from?"

"I brought it up from downstairs. Pa asked me to...thought you might like to have it last night." Hoss kept a careful eye on his brother, watching for a reaction, and he got it.

"Pa did?" Adam looked first alarmed and then guilty: His secret was out? Surely Pa would have told Hoss to bring him a picture of Adam's own mother, Elizabeth.

"You was talkin' to her, Adam, and he told me to go bring you the picture of your mother. I didn't hafta tell him, but I wanted to. I'm proud you think of my ma as yours. I thought it was about time Pa knew that." Hoss' look was one of defiance and his frown line creased the space between his eyebrows.

"So...what did he say?" Adam asked, not sure if he wanted to hear the answer.

Hoss replied, "He was surprised more'n anything. I guess he hadn't thought about how it might be for you. But he wasn't mad, and he's the one who told me to go ahead and get the picture of my mother 'stead a yours."

Adam thought that one over for several seconds. He wasn't sure if he'd ever bring this topic up with his father and he hoped his father wouldn't bring it up with him. But he was relieved he no longer carried the burden of keeping his real feelings from him. It wasn't that he didn't love and respect his mother—he did. It was just that he didn't know her.

Now he glanced down at his sleeping youngest brother and back up to his middle brother. "You remember yesterday when I wanted you to ride for Pa and bring him back? That's just about the last thing I remember 'til right now. You remember?"

"I sure do. You had me plum worried. That was the craziest thing I ever heard you say...up to that point, anyway." Hoss grinned at Adam. He had a few things to tell him about some of the choice phrases that he had let loose with during his delirium.

But Adam wasn't in the mood for joking; he had something serious to say and it had to be said between just he and Hoss. He reached out for Hoss' forearm and, grabbing hold of it tightly, looked straight into his brother's blue eyes. "I just want you to know, Hoss, it was you I needed all along. You were the one. You ARE the one."

Hoss covered Adam's hand with his own and ducked his head, turning it sideways to look back at Adam. He raised an eyebrow, smiled and said, "Gol' darn, Adam. You'da done the same for me. I don't even hafta ask if that's true because I know it is. What'd I say to our ma the next time I see her if I had let ya down?"

Adam relaxed his grip on his brother's arm and said, "I just needed to tell you...in words. I don't say it enough."

"Well, you said it just fine and I heard you." Hoss set the picture down on the bedside table then reached over for the water pitcher and poured another half glass. "Here now, why don't you have another drink and get some more rest?" He helped Adam raise up a little and he managed a few swallows.

"Thanks...I guess I am still feelin' not quite...right." Adam's eyes slipped closed and Hoss put his hand back to his brother's forehead. Still a touch warm but not nearly the blazing heat of those few hours after midnight, so Hoss was hopeful all that was needed to heal Adam now would be a lot of rest and time.

Steps in the hall brought his eyes to the doorway in time to see his father enter carrying a tray laden with a coffee pot and several china cups and saucers. At this, Joe raised his head off his arms and, after raking a hand through his hair and stretching, sniffed the air. "That fresh coffee, Pa? Sure smells good."

Hoss said, "Pa, Adam woke while you were gone and he IS better. His fever seems a lot lower and I think he's going to mend. He talked to me and he was makin' sense so..."

"That's wonderful," Ben interrupted as he set the tray down on the bureau. "Such good news for such a beautiful morning!"

Hoss grinned at his father's noticeable relief and finished his thought. "So I gave him some more water and he dropped back off to sleep."

Ben smiled back and said, "Come and help yourself, boys." Both Hoss and Joe got up to pour themselves cups of hot coffee and take them back to their chairs. Ben stood at the end of the bed, sipping from his own cup and looking at the sleeping face of his oldest son.

As he replaced the cup on the saucer, his eye went to Inger's portrait on Adam's bedside table. It stood alongside Elizabeth's music box. He thought, "Liz, Hoss said he didn't mind sharing his mother and I sure hope you don't mind sharing your son."

Looking up at his father, Hoss followed his gaze to the portrait of his mother. He looked back at his father and said, "That's what we talked about, Pa. Adam knows you know an' he's relieved you're not mad." Hoss paused here, frowned and, tucking one hand into his front pants pocket, he looked back at his sleeping brother. "I think it was a real burden for him to keep his true feelings from you all these years."

Joe followed Hoss' words intently but didn't interrupt. Hoss continued in his role of go-between for his father and his brother. "He does love his mother. It's just that...that our ma is the one he knows best," Hoss finished, hoping he was saying it right, hoping he could make his father understand.

"I know, son, I know. I'm just so sorry that Elizabeth never got the chance to raise her son." Ben turned and put his cup back down, then walked over to pick up Adam's music box. "She would have been a wonderful mother; Adam missed out on so much not having her in his life."

Ben didn't open the music box but just held it in his hand and let his mind travel back to a day many years before when he had given it to Liz upon returning from a sea voyage. His whole life had been before him then, his dreams not yet even fully formed in his mind much less realized. Look at how much he had accomplished and gained between that day and this: His ranch, his fortune...and the three wives who had given him his three wonderful sons. He just hoped he hadn't let any of them down.

He had always thought of them distinctly as being from their mothers alone, not considering the hand that Inger had had in molding Adam or even what effects Marie had had on Hoss. He had only considered that they had him, their father, in common. It had taken Hoss, his middle son and peacemaker, to make him see there was much more to his oldest son than just the woman who had given birth to him.

"Pa, do ya think my ma and Adam's ma...well..." Hoss scowled and cut his eyes over to Joe, looking for the first signs of his younger brother's laughter. But Joe maintained a somber look on his face realizing that a discussion such as this was no time for jokes.

"What, son?" Ben looked curiously at Hoss.

"Do ya think they've talked to each other...ya know, up in heaven?" Hoss looked at Joe again, but if he had the urge to giggle, Joe was doing a good job at stifling it.

"They have, Hoss..." came Adam's weak voice from where he lay in bed. "I'm sure of it." Ben looked over at his oldest. Adam was struggling to keep his eyes open and his face still wore the sheen of perspiration but he looked—and sounded—more alert and himself on this new day. Surely he was on the mend now.

"I'm sure of it too, Hoss," Ben said. "And I have a feeling Elizabeth is more than grateful to Inger for the way she embraced Adam as her own." Ben reached down, took Adam's hand in his own and said, "I know I am."

Where Angels Fear To Tread

by Kathleen T. Berney

Hopelessness was briefly replaced with a feeling of panic and, as he struggled to fill his lungs, he knew this breath would be his last.

The great, yawning expanse between his feet—the frail strand of solidity upon which both had been tenuously planted—and terra firma had reduced his fellow passengers to tiny black dots. From this great height they looked more like fleas or specks of dirt, with nothing at all to distinguish them as human beings. Worse still, their conveyance seemed no more than a child's toy, poorly constructed and extremely fragile, ready to fall apart at the slightest provocation.

"Stupid," he gasped. "Stupid, stupid, stupid!" By nature, he was impulsive, foolhardy, and reckless, oft times charging headlong into places where angels feared to tread.

"He's an adventurous lad, so full of life, he's just bursting at the seams," his father had remarked on countless occasions. *"A joy to behold, even if he IS responsible for my having all these white hairs...."*

With an anguished cry, he squeezed his eyelids shut as tight as he possibly could, in a desperate bid to obliterate that dreadful panorama spread out below him. His stomach lurched and, although his eyes remained shut tight, he could still feel the world about him spinning faster and faster, like the top his father had given him a long time ago on the occasion of his fifth birthday. He felt himself teetering as the muscles in his hands and fingers began to relax.

A collective gasp rose from the people gathering below, drawn to the scene of danger, and its potential for unspeakable tragedy, like bees to a saucer full of sugar water. His body lurched, prompting his hands and fingers to tighten their grip on the narrow handholds.

"H-How?" he whimpered softly, his words nearly lost in the thunder of his racing heart, and the blood pounding in his head and ears. "H-How in the world c-could I b-be so...so damned stupid?"

You don't stop and think, son.

He could hear his father now, speaking just as clear as if he were standing right here beside him.

That's your trouble. You're always rushing headlong into places angels fear to tread. You've got to learn to stop and THINK first, BEFORE you rush in....

For what seemed to him a terrible eternity, he clung white-knuckled for dear life, two thirds of the way upward toward his goal, his body completely paralyzed, his mind numb.

The high, thin wail of a young child, coming from a place high above him, rudely jolted him back to his senses. He slowly raised his head and forced himself to open his eyes. The sight above froze the very marrow in his bones. The child he had so boldly...so foolishly and recklessly set out to rescue, had crawled out to the edge and now leaned dangerously far forward. He focused his gaze on the young boy, silently willing him with all the strength he had within him, to move back, well away from the edge. Instead, the child leaned over farther.

With heart in mouth, he immediately resumed his climb, barely aware of the movement within his limbs, propelling him steadily upward. He had to reach that child before the unthinkable happened. That thought, that goal, dominated and consumed his mind and his thoughts to the exclusion of all else. The feather-light touch of his fingertips against the very top triggered an explosive burst of adrenalin that sent him flying up what little remained of the climb, and over the top.

For a moment, he remained on his hands and knees, gasping for breath, his sweat-soaked body trembling like a leaf.

"M-M-Mister?"

He slowly raised his head and found himself staring into the pale, tear-stained face of a boy, no more than three or four years old.

"I...I w-want my m-mama," the boy whispered, his eyes filled with terror and despair.

Pull yourself together, Cartwright, he silently, sternly admonished himself. He then took a deep, ragged breath and asked in as calm and steady a voice as he could muster, "What's your name, boy?"

"P-Patrick," the child replied warily.

He smiled. "Patrick, do you ever play horsey with your papa?"

Patrick returned his smile with a shy, tremulous one of his own. "Y-Yeah," he replied, nodding his head. "Papa and me play horsey lots 'n lots."

"Good," he murmured softly. "That's very good, because you and I are going to play horsey now."

Patrick favored him with a dubious glare. "We are?!"

"Yes...we are," he affirmed, "and if you do exactly as I say, we're going to find your mama waiting at the end of the ride. Would you like that?"

The boy solemnly nodded.

"What you're going to do is get up on my back, put your arms around my neck, and hold on real tight, until I tell ya to let go," he said. "Think you can do that?"

"Yes, Sir," Patrick replied with confidence. "I *know* I can, 'cause I'm a real good horsey rider."

"I kinda thought so," he said. "You have the look of a real good horsey rider."

Patrick beamed. "I do? Really?!"

"Yes, you do. Really," he replied. "You ready?"

"I'm ready," the boy replied.

He hoisted the child up onto his back and with one last exhortation to 'hold on tight,' he slowly lowered himself down onto his hands and knees, and began to ease his way back over the edge.

It took nearly every ounce of the iron will and stubborn determination he possessed to relax his arms just enough to allow him to begin his descent. He tentatively extended one leg downward, his booted foot desperately seeking a secure hold. After a dreadful eternity of groping about in mid-air, his foot finally touched upon a secure place. He jammed his foot into the opening and, with heart in mouth, he tested it to determine whether or not it would bear his full weight and that of the frightened child clinging to his back for dear life. Relief, deep and profound, surged throughout the entire length, width, and breadth of his body, leaving him weak-kneed, and perilously dizzy.

Get hold of yourself, Cartwright, he angrily castigated himself once again. Gritting his teeth, he forced himself to ease downward, moving one hand down to the next hold, then the other.

"M-Mister?" the boy queried, his voice shaking. "My arms hurt."

"I need ya to hold on just a little bit longer," he exhorted the boy. "Can you do that?"

"I...I think so," the boy replied, his voice filled with uncertainty and doubt.

"You can do it, Patrick," he declared stoutly, as he began to extend the other leg downward. "I *know* you can, because you're a good horsey rider. A *real* good horsey rider."

"M-My arms hurt awful bad," Patrick moaned softly.

"Another minute, Patrick...that's all," he continued to exhort and encourage, his voice filled with a calm, reassuring confidence he was very far from feeling. "Another minute. All ya have to do is hang on for just another minute. You can do it," he murmured softly. "Just one more minute, Patrick...you can do it." He repeated those words over and over and over, until they became as a kind of mantra, drawing his thoughts away from his trembling legs and the cramping muscles in his hands, fingers, and forearms...focusing them entirely on the boy.

A woman's anguished cry assailed his ears the instant he stepped down once more on terra firma. He had a vague awareness of a young woman, with flaming red hair, her face white as a sheet, snatching young Patrick from his arms...of a man not much older than the woman, his face pale, his eyes round and staring, seizing his hand, and vigorously pumping his arm up and down, words of gratitude tumbling out of his mouth one after the other, after the other...of a crowd of people...men, women, and children...pressing close, thumping him on the back, shaking his hand....

Without warning, the faces began to blur and melt into a single fleshy mass. His knees buckled, and he felt himself falling. The last thing he remembered, before the blackness overcame him, was the voice of a man, a powerful man, one well used to issuing orders and having them obeyed, shouting for someone to "...grab the boy and follow me!"

BEFORE OPENING HIS eyes, he felt the softness of the down stuffed mattress beneath him. It had been a long time since he last slept in a real bed. For a moment, he was certain that he was dreaming....

Suddenly, his eyes snapped wide open.

"Welcome back to the land of the living, lad...."

He gasped and, upon turning his head, he found himself staring up into the stern visage of Captain Abel Stoddard.

"You gave us all quite a turn this afternoon," the captain observed, not unkindly. "For a moment there, I thought sure I was going to have to send a man up to rescue you and the boy. You alright?"

He nodded, thoroughly chagrined as he felt the needle prickly rush of blood to his face. "I...I'm sorry, sir," he murmured, his voice filled with remorse. "It was a stupid, foolish thing I did this afternoon...."

"Aye," the captain replied, "that it was...and I hope you'll never forget that. But it was also a brave and courageous thing you did today, too, boy. Never forget that, either."

For a moment all he could do was stare up into the captain's face, open-mouthed with shock, too stunned to speak. "C-Courageous?" he murmured, when at last he found his voice. "No, sir. I...I wasn't brave or courageous, I...I was afraid. The whole time, I...I was so afraid— "

"What's your name, lad?"

"Cartwright, sir. Benjamin Cartwright."

"Well, Mister Benjamin Cartwright, I want you to pay very close attention to what I have to say," the captain said in his most stern, most authoritative tone of voice. "Bravery and courage haven't a thing to do with *not* being afraid."

"They...they don't?" Ben queried with a bewildered frown.

"Of course not, lad. True courage is the strength and the will to act, when you *are* afraid," the captain continued. "That's what you did this afternoon."

Ben exhaled a soft, melancholy sigh, and shook his head. "It wasn't *me*, sir," he said. "It was the boy. When I looked up and saw him under the rail around the crow's nest, leaning so far over the edge—"

"Don't sell yourself short. The boy inspired you, perhaps, but even so, you *still* had to reach inside and draw upon the strength here..." the captain touched the place over his heart, "...to make yourself move. No one can do that for you."

"Y-Yes, sir," Ben murmured, not knowing what else to say.

"You're a good lad, young Benjamin," the captain said, with a bare hint of a smile tugging hard at the corner of his mouth, "and if you keep on doing what I tell ya, you're going to make a very fine sailor. A very fine sailor indeed!" Assuming, of course, that the boy's foolhardy recklessness didn't land him in an early grave....

"In the mean time, I'd suggest you g'won down to your bunk and grab yourself some shut-eye. I've been told that you're scheduled to stand the morning watch, beginning at one bell."

"Yes, sir," Ben replied with an eager smile. "I'll be ready."

Abel Stoddard grinned. "I know you will be, lad. In the mean-time...be off with ya." He watched as the boy made his way across the short span of deck between the captain's bed and the door to his cabin. "Yes, sir," he silently mused, "Young Benjamin is a fine young man...and a fine *looking* one, too. Give him another year, maybe two, to fill out properly, that boy's going to be a real heartbreaker."

In another year or so—less actually, given that girls seemed to come to an awareness of such things as boys, falling in love, and all the folderol that goes along with the aforesaid—his young daughter Elizabeth would, no doubt, come to agree with his assessment of one Benjamin Cartwright. For a minute, he seriously considered locking her up in her room when he came home from the sea, especially if young Cartwright happened to be on the same ship.

Finally, he smiled first, then began to chuckle softly. *Abel Stoddard, you're getting daft in your old age,* he chided himself, while still laughing. *Even if Liz WAS of a mind to fall in love with a sailor...which she ISN'T...she'd NEVER fall in love with young Benjamin....*

He just plain ain't her cup of tea!

The Shadow of Thy Wings

by Delores J. Barnosky

Adam Cartwright was terrified. The bile in his stomach kept surfacing and he washed it down with another cup of strong stand alone black coffee. He had not eaten in over twenty-four hours knowing his body would reject nourishment of any kind. Everyone expected him to be the calm brother, the calm son, the calm Cartwright, slow to anger, never impulsive, the thinking brother who never acted without sizing up all the logic of a situation. Now he wished he could be like his youngest brother, Little Joe, throw himself down somewhere, beat his fists on the ground and cry. He wished he could be like the middle brother in the family, Hoss, who would pick someone up and throw them through the window of the saloon and send everyone floundering to get out...but, Adam Cartwright had to remain calm...there was so much at stake.

Adam had just humiliated himself in front of a lot of men in the saloon and the pounding in his chest and the burning skin on his shoulders, neck and ears had not yet stilled. He had shown them his calm exterior and wondered if anyone knew what was really going through his body...could they hear his heart pounding...see the redness of his face...feel his tangible anxiety? He had to be strong as there was so much at stake.

When he was alone, he paced, put his jacket on and took it off, sat at a desk, then stood and paced again, looked out the windows countless times, rubbed his face with his hands and sighed very deeply...then someone would come back and he assumed his calm exterior. Was it for their benefit or his? There was so much at stake.

Adam Cartwright always had to be right. For some reason, it was bred into him to be right and not accept failure. He had that kind of reputation. Whatever was wrong, he would make it right even if it took his own personal sacrifice...but, this sacrifice was too costly. If he failed this time, his life would cease forever to be as charmed as everyone thought it was...yes, even his own thoughts about his life, the wonder of it, the wealth of it, the wisdom of it...over in a single heart beat. How he wished it was his very own beating heart that was at stake as he would consent immediately to the sacrifice had fate allowed him to do so. There was so much at stake; only a willing sacrifice could be expended.

He and his brothers, Hoss and Little Joe, had argued intensely a very short time ago...harsh words and accusations were thrown about the streets of Virginia City. With so much at stake right now, the only common thread among the three men was their intense love for their father.

There was such a disagreement transcending the previous premise that Adam had delivered the solution to the dire problem hanging over their heads...they were now separated in the plans, words and actions taking place. The three men parted...going in three different directions. Adam returned to his pacing and worrying place. He couldn't get comfortable...he could not recapture his previous resoluteness...he was fearful that he could be wrong and his stubbornness was pushing him into making the most dangerous decision ever in his life. His stomach cramped violently and his head throbbed.

Adam stopped thinking long enough to sit at the desk and rest his forehead on his upturned hands...a terrifying sight came to his closed eyes...a large piece of granite by the edge of the lake, with exquisitely carved words extolling the greatest man he ever knew, "Here Lies Benjamin Cartwright, Beloved Father, a Man of Vision." Adam jumped back to alertness. What if he was wrong? How could he live with such a terrible mistake? Would his family ever forgive him? No, he decided, they would not...life as he knew it would vanish forever and he would leave the only home he ever knew. He stood up to leave, intending to send someone to find his brothers...maybe it was not too late...there was so much at stake.

Adam donned his jacket and hat and adjusted his gun belt. Stepping out onto the boardwalk, he noticed the streets were completely deserted. The only noise he heard was the raucous laughter and tinny piano sounds from the saloon down the street. He leaned against the post under the sheltering roof overhang...still thinking and wondering...presently he heard footsteps on the walk coming from his right side. He recognized the hired man from the livery and cautiously stopped him when he was close enough to speak, and lightly put his hand on the man's shoulder.

Adam asked the man if he had seen his two brothers any-where. The man scoffed at Adam, brushed the unwanted hand from his shoulder and proceeded to insult Adam verbally, telling him how ignorant he was to take such a chance, that all his high and mighty education didn't mean he knew right from wrong, in fact, he was sure the proud Adam Cartwright was a fool and was about to make the biggest mistake of his life...he didn't know anything and his heart was cursed!

Adam backed away and looked at the man's surly countenance. His father's face came into his vision, and he suddenly remembered words spoken by his father to his youngest brother at a troubling time in the young man's life... "Son, when a man knows something deep down in his heart, when he really knows, he doesn't have to argue about it, he doesn't have to prove it, just knowing it is enough." As Adam turned to walk away, the man asked loudly and rudely what did he want him to tell his brothers if he saw them. Adam looked hard at the man and told him to tell his brothers he would see them at sunup.

It took forever for sunup to arrive. Adam remembered his father telling him that waiting was always the hardest part of any decision, waiting for the outcome. He knew he was right but that did not take the terror from his being. A nagging doubt kept creeping into his head and he could not help but think about his father, his nobleness, his truthful approach to every aspect of his life, and his love for his sons...what was that quote his father had always impressed upon him when having to make a hard decision? "How excellent is thy loving kindness, O God! therefore the children of men put their trust under the shadow of thy wings, They shall be abundantly satisfied...for with thee is the fountain of life: in thy light shall we see light."*

Adam Cartwright had been in the shadow of his father's wings all his life, now they both were under the shadow of the wings of God...it was the only way to see light...and there was light...it was sunup...the time had come.

Adam stepped out into the dim light of day just as the sun was peeking through the dirty buildings across the street. Even though the morning air was chilled, his shirt was soaked with the sweat of anxiety and was sticking to his skin. He rested his right hand on the handle of his pistol as his stomach churned, *"Oh, God...Oh, Pa,"* he thought, *"forgive me if I'm wrong."* He heard the ominous sound of the gallows door dropping. Adam had heard it before in his life and it had never been a pleasant experience. He quickly looked away and felt fearful that he would have to vomit in front of everyone watching. He heard the dull twanging of a taut rope and looked back to see two dusty boots swinging close to his face. The Farmer was dead.

Psalms 36:7&9

This story was based on the episode "Death at Dawn" written by Laurence Mascott

Kiss and Tell

by D. J. Kouba

It was a just a single kiss. Admittedly, it had been a long, slow, thorough, and certainly not chaste kiss but still a single kiss nonetheless. Unfortunately, it had not gone unseen. No, the moonlight that had made Cindy Anne shimmer and glow had also allowed her three older brothers and a rather large cousin to witness that kiss, which was why Little Joe Cartwright found himself held by Beau Crawford on one side and Travis Crawford on the other. Little Joe's stance was defiant, but his breaths came too quickly, and his eyes were fixed on the horse-whip in Axton Crawford's hand. The fact that there had been two other witnesses to the kiss was the reason that Axton's whip had not already bitten into Little Joe's flesh.

"He's dishonored our sister, and, by heaven, he will get what he deserves!" Axton's deep bass growled the words.

Adam Cartwright's voice remained calm as he said, "While there might be some points we agree on, Axton, what he deserves is probably not one of them."

"No matter what you agree on, we'll be having the skin off his back for what he's done!" The large cousin whose name escaped Adam at that moment was only a half an inch shorter than Hoss Cartwright and about ten pounds heavier. He took two steps forward. Hoss matched those steps but then stopped at a single gesture from his older brother.

Adam kept his eyes fixed on Axton Crawford; Axton would be the Crawford deciding for the clan. "The boy kissed your sister, yes, but dishonored her? Certainly that is overstating things."

"What would you call it, Cartwright?"

"Foolish. Impulsive." The words slipped smoothly from Adam's tongue. "Also inappropriate. Little Joe knows that." Adam allowed his eyes to leave Axton Crawford's face just long enough to send a chiding glare in Little Joe's direction. "Still, he obviously wasn't forcing himself on her, and it went no further than a moonlight kiss."

"A girl ain't got nothing more than her reputation and..."

"Cindy Anne's reputation will remain totally intact if you and your kin do not start a brawl that draws an audience. If the seven of us set to fighting, there's no way the town won't end up knowing the reason why. That is the only way that Cindy Anne will be truly hurt by this whole incident."

"Joe's a talker," Beau Crawford observed, giving the arm in his hands a jerk.

After considering several possible replies, Adam said, "True, but he is not a total fool, and he is entirely capable of holding his tongue when necessary. I'm sure that Little Joe has no delusions about what we would be unable to prevent happening if Cindy Anne became the subject of gossip due to this indiscretion."

"I wouldn't say anything about it anyway!" It was the first time that Joe had spoken since being grabbed by the Crawford brothers. Every eye there turned toward him. "Cindy Anne's a nice girl." He raised his chin. "It's only you thinking bad of her!" The words had been tossed directly at Axton, and they stung.

"Shut his mouth," he hissed. Beau and Travis both moved, but stopped at the sound of a single word.

"Joe!" Adam's voice held a tone of command that drew all attention back to him. "You will not speak again until asked." Adam drew in a deep breath and let it out slowly. "Axton, both of these children have misbehaved, on that we agree. That the matter must be dealt with is a given but take a moment to consider how to best deal with it. The Cartwrights prefer to keep discipline a family matter."

"He's not a little boy! We ain't talking about pecking her cheek behind the schoolhouse." Travis Crawford was sixteen, exactly six months older than Joe Cartwright.

Adam took a step toward Axton, "No, if we were, I'd be paddling his behind already." He flicked his eyes toward Travis and lowered his voice as if speaking only to the eldest Crawford, "You wouldn't call him a man though, would you?"

Throughout the conversation Hoss had kept his focus on his younger brother. He knew Adam needed to make Axton Crawford think of Joe as a child and not a young buck on the loose; he also knew Joe would take each reference to his youth as an insult. With Adam's last statement, he saw Joe's eyes spark and his body jerk; Hoss stepped directly into Joe's line of vision and gave a sharp, quick shake of his head.

Axton turned to look at his sister. Cindy Anne had been standing in the dark sobbing into her hands since her brothers had appeared. Adam stepped to his side; he spoke in a voice that reached only Axton's ears. "He's no more a man than she is a woman."

"He has to be punished."

"He broke the rules that our pa has set for his behavior, and I assure you Ben Cartwright never suffers disobedience lightly."

Axton turned and looked directly into Adam's eyes. Adam

barely more than mouthed the words, "He's my baby brother." The message that he would never allow a whip to touch Joe was clear.

Axton turned and stared at the boy in his brothers' grasp. "You've done wrong."

Adam and Hoss both forgot to breathe until Little Joe's chin dropped, and he said simply, "I'm sorry; we shouldn't have left the dance. My pa taught me better."

"Just like your pa taught you boys," Hoss's voice slipped in behind his brother's, "Still, I expect there ain't one of us here ain't kissed a pretty gal at a dance or such." His tone was light and cajoling and bespoke gentle memories.

Axton turned back to Adam. "He will be held to account?"

"You've my word."

"He's not to speak to her."

"He won't unless your family gives permission."

"Boys, let him go." Axton gave the order in a clear, flat tone.

"You sure, Axton?" Their cousin voiced the question, but Beau and Travis kept their hold on Joe until Axton replied.

"Let him go. We're taking Cindy Anne home."

Little Joe's knees almost buckled as he was released, but he stayed upright as the Crawfords gathered around Cindy Anne and led her away.

Hoss reached Joe seconds before Adam and shook his head sadly as he stared down at the boy. Little Joe swallowed trying to dislodge the lump in his throat.

"Adam," he croaked. Adam raised his hand and shook a pointed finger in Joe's face.

"Don't! Don't say a word, not now and not on the way home. Get on Cochise..."

"But Cindy Anne..."

Hoss watched Adam's jaw clench. "It's a bit late, boy, to start thinking about the consequences for that little gal if her pa finds out. Just ya go get on your horse like Adam said and leave things be until we're home," he chided while steering his younger brother away from his older. When Joe was out of ear shot, Hoss said, "He'll mind now."

"Oh, yes, he'll mind now." The comment ended with grinding teeth.

"You gonna tell Pa?'

Adam brought his hand to his nose and rubbed the bridge. "Don't tell me not to, Hoss. If Alistair Crawford finds out, this might not be over."

"I don't think them boys will be telling Mr. Crawford. Cindy Anne's the baby and a gal. They want Joe punished, not Cindy Anne."

"Still, they're bringing home a girl whose eyes are swollen from weeping; they may not be able to avoid telling their folks."

"True. Still..."

"I think it's necessary, and you heard me give my word."

"Yeah, ya promised he'd be held to account, but ya didn't say who would be doing the accounting."

"Do you really think it should be me?" Adam's tone was sharp and bitter.

"I know ya hate it, but..."

"It's not just that, Hoss. I do think Pa needs to know; that he needs to be aware; that he's the one to handle it."

"I expect you're right; it's just that Joe's not likely to see it that way." Hoss shifted nervously and looked in the direction that Little Joe had gone.

"No, Little Joe will see it as his older brother tattling to his pa, so he will be in trouble for something that he's sure that brother has done himself." Adam's curse was barely audible.

Hoss placed his hand on his brother's shoulder and squeezed. "Part of him knows it ain't like that." Adam made no reply. Hoss sighed and offered, "Maybe, well, this time I could..."

Adam shook his head and smiled slowly, "You'd never get the words out. No, I'll see to it. Go ahead with Joe, but keep him in the barn until I get there."

"Sure. He ain't gonna be in no hurry to run into Pa no how."

"No, I don't suppose so." Adam's voice was hard-edged. "I'll see to our leave-taking. We don't want people wondering where all the Crawfords and Cartwrights disappeared to all of a sudden."

"Right." Hoss took a few steps and then said, "Adam…"

"Don't, Hoss, just get the boy home." Adam strode back toward the dance while Hoss headed toward the horses.

HOSS CHEWED HIS lip and studied his younger brother's back as he followed him home. He did not even attempt a conversation but waited for Little Joe to speak first as they unsaddled their horses.

"Adam's gonna tell Pa, ain't he?"

Wondering just how many times Little Joe had asked him that exact question, Hoss sighed before answering, "He thinks it's necessary."

Joe snorted. "I just bet he does!"

"Now don't you go getting in a temper! It was you that…"

"Messed up, and now Adam's gonna see that Pa knows all about it."

"It ain't that way, Joe." Hoss's tone was chiding.

"All I did was kiss a girl." Little Joe's voice had developed a whine. "Is that so bad? You were the one that said all you had done the same. I bet even Pa kissed girls before he was married."

"I wouldn't go trying that argument with Pa; he's done blistered all our behinds for things he did and got blistered for when he was growing. It ain't so much that ya kissed her anyways; ya broke the rules, Pa's rules. The fact that ya didn't deserve that horsewhip don't mean ya don't deserve no consequences. Pa has reasons for his rules. You should be able to figure out some of the reasons he set those ya broke tonight."

"Adam…"

"Saved your hide, boy!" Hoss declared as his eyes sparked. "If he hadn't noticed ya gone and come after, well, you'd have a lot more powerful hurt than anything Pa would ever do to ya."

"I could have..."

Hoss snorted. "Only a foolish little boy could make himself believe you could have taken on all four of them Crawfords. Lord, Joe, it wouldn't have been no sure thing if the three of us would have had to fight them."

Little Joe let his temper surge, "I'm not a little boy! First Adam and now you..."

Hoss grabbed his brother by the shirt, gave him a shake, and then shook his head knowing Little Joe always picked being mad over being scared. "Adam did the best job of settling things he could. Even if we'd fought them boys off tonight, you would have had to worry about that whip when you went out alone later. Unless Mr. Crawford stirs things up again, which I don't think will happen, well, things will get settled tonight." Hoss watched the anger drain from Joe's face and released his hold.

Joe's chin dropped, and he dug the toe of his boot into the dirt floor. "Pa's gonna be so mad. Maybe... I heard Adam give his word, but maybe..."

"You're gonna have to answer for what ya done."

"I know, but..."

"You'd rather answer to Adam than Pa?"

"He's already mad; Pa ain't yet."

Shaking his head yet again, Hoss just said, "Finish up with Cochise."

Adam had not yet arrived when Hoss and Joe had both finished with their horses. Hoss walked over to the open barn door and leaned his back against the jam. He gazed out at the night sky as he spoke to his brother, "Joe, I've got it in my mind to tell ya what I think ya should do, so here it is. You need to go in there and tell Pa before Adam does."

"Tell Pa? But Adam might decide..."

"That's just it. Adam shouldn't have to decide. He shouldn't have to decide, and he shouldn't have to be the one to walk up to Pa and hear him roar and have him glaring at him. He shouldn't have to feel guilty because the look on Pa's face says he didn't keep a good enough eye on ya."

"What? Feel guilty? Pa don't blame…"

"He does some. Oh, not after he simmers down, but them first few seconds after Adam tells him, sometimes he does, and Adam sees it."

"Hoss, I…I never…"

"No, ya ain't never and neither have I 'cause Adam's always been the one. Well, he's elder brother and that's the way of things, but if you're so dang set on not being a kid, ya should go on up to the house and tell Pa, so Adam don't have to."

"Hoss?"

"I've had my say. I'm gonna stay here and wait for Adam. You go on. If ya tell Pa or not, well, that's up to you."

Joe trudged silently past his brother to the house.

ADAM LED SPORT into the barn and looked around. Seeing only Hoss, he asked, "Where's Joe?"

Hoss stood and shifted from one foot to another before he said, "Joe's up to the house."

"What? I told you to keep him in the barn until I got here."

"I know ya did, but, well, I sent him up to the house."

Adam's brow furrowed, and his hands moved to his hips. "You sent him up to the house? Hoss…"

"I sent him to tell Pa about what happened tonight."

"You sent Joe to tell Pa!" Surprise put an edge on Adam's exclamation.

"Yes, I did. I don't know if he will, but we're gonna wait here and give him a chance."

Adam rolled his eyes. "Our little brother isn't much for confession even when he knows he is well and truly caught."

"No, he ain't, and, like I said, I don't know that he will tell Pa, but I told him he should."

"You told him he should." Adam repeated and rolled his eyes again.

"Yeah, and I told him why, and I think maybe he's grown enough to do it."

This time Adam snorted. "I suppose you told him I was sure to tell Pa and he could make a better tale of it."

"No, that ain't what I told him." Hoss moved closer to his brother. "It's no matter what I told him. We're gonna give him time to tell Pa on his own and Pa time to deal with him if he does."

Adam tilted his head to look directly into his younger brother's eyes as his arms slowly moved across his chest.

"I've settled my mind on it, Adam," Hoss stated as he returned his brother's stare.

Adam's hands tucked themselves into his armpits. "I see. Well, then, I'll just give Sport the grooming he deserves." Adam turned toward his horse and muttered, "Missouri mule!"

Hoss moved to Sport's opposite side. "I'll give ya a hand then."

Adam looked across the horse's back. He knew that his brother had heard his last comment. "You are, you know, but then you're my favorite Missouri mule."

Hoss's smile showed the gap in his teeth. "Never hurts to be somebody's favorite." Together they gave Sport a thorough rub-down.

HAVING ACCOMPLISHED EVERYTHING feasible in the barn, Adam and Hoss walked to the open door. There was now a light in Little Joe's room, and the door to the house stood open. Silhouetted against the door was a man they both knew must be their father. The two brothers looked at each other, and Adam gave Hoss a backhanded pat to his stomach. Then the two of them walked across the yard. Stepping up onto the porch, both Adam and Hoss surveyed Ben Cartwright. Each of them noted that the belt

Ben had been wearing earlier was no longer threaded through his belt loops.

"He told you then?" Adam kept the volume of his inquiry low.

"Yes, he told me." Ben's voice still held an edge.

"Pa..." Hoss began, but Adam's voice overrode his.

"I'm sorry, Pa. I should have kept a better eye on him."

"You've nothing to apologize for, Adam. According to Joe, you prevented a bad situation from becoming much worse."

"Those Crawford boys, well, Pa, they're way too hot-tempered and, well, they was making a mountain out of a molehill. Adam handled it though." Hoss used his most cajoling tone.

"Joseph said that he left the dance with the girl, took her out in the moonlight, and kissed her. Is there something more that I should know about his behavior?"

"That about sums it up, Pa. Like Hoss said, Cindy Anne's brothers were, well, being overprotective," Adam answered smoothly. Then his brow furrowed, and he added, "She appeared quite willing, Pa; Joe didn't..."

"I should hope not! Still, he's barely sixteen; she's younger, if I'm not mistaken. Is she even fifteen yet?"

"I think she's only a few months younger than Joe, Pa; in fact I'm pretty sure," Hoss rushed to interject.

"They're both young, and I really don't think that... well, I think that kiss was all either of them expected of that walk in the moonlight." Adam's hand went to his left ear as he spoke and then tugged it several times. When his pa made no comment, he said softly, "Pa, Joe had a real scare out there tonight, much as he tried to act otherwise. I really don't think he'll be too quick to try it again with any girl."

Ben's hand moved from his hip to his face, and he rubbed his chin. "Well, I hope your younger brother has learned several lessons tonight." He dropped his hand and asked, "Do I need to speak with Alistair Crawford?"

Adam cleared his throat and then answered, "I don't think... well, Hoss and I both think that Cindy Anne's brothers will probably not say anything to their father, so, well, unless someone else wakes those sleeping dogs, I'd just let them lie, Pa. If Alistair Crawford, well, I'm sure he'll come to you if he, well, if the two of you need to talk." Adam and Hoss both held their breath until their father answered.

"I suppose you're right. I've dealt with Joe, so..." Ben moved so that he suddenly caught sight of his sons' faces in the light from the door. Shaking his head, he reached out and patted Hoss on the back and then placed his hand on Adam's shoulder. "What's done is done, and I've forgiven Joe, so you two needn't look like you'll be attending his funeral tomorrow. There's only one more thing I want to say before we put the matter behind us."

"What is that, Pa?"

"I want to thank the two of you for looking out for your brother."

"Aw, Pa!" Hoss smiled and ducked his head.

"No thanks needed," Adam said with a smile of his own.

ADAM HEARD HIS door creak followed by his name. He looked up from his seat on the edge of the bed and saw his younger brother in the slit created by the partially opened door. Setting down the boot he had just removed, he asked, "Is there something you need, Joe?"

Little Joe slipped into the room before he answered, "I, uh, I, uh...are you mad?" He had stopped just inside the door and shifted nervously from one foot to another.

"No, I'm not mad," Adam answered matter-of-factly and reached down to tug off his other boot.

His brother edged a foot closer and then stopped again. "You sure? Umm, 'cause you've got cause to be."

Adam set down the second boot next to the first. "I know I do, but I'm not, not now anyway." He gave his brother a long, contemplative stare as the boy once again shifted from bare foot to bare foot and rubbed his hand down the side of his nightshirt.

Swallowing convulsively, Little Joe managed to utter, "I'm sorry for messing up your night, Adam. I've done already talked to Hoss, and things are right with us."

"That's good."

"I told him that he could...if he was mad he could...he didn't, but, well you know Hoss. If you..."

"Have I ever when Pa already has?"

"No, but..."

"I accept your apology, little brother; things are right with us too."

"Thanks, Adam, and thanks for saving my hide from them Crawfords." Little Joe made no move to leave, and Adam motioned toward the bed. Joe slowly made his way toward his brother, but when he reached the bed he did not sit down, only stared at the floor.

"I'd never let anyone do that to you, Joe. You know that, don't you?"

"Even if I deserved it?"

"You deserved what Pa gave you, Joe, no more, and no, I would never think you deserved that."

"The Crawfords..." Little Joe's words sputtered to a halt.

"Cindy Anne's brothers overreacted, but then...Joe, I think maybe they were so angry because they were mostly scared for a little girl they love."

"I wouldn't ever do anything to hurt a girl!" Little Joe's voice was filled with indignation, and he looked directly at Adam for the first time since he had entered the room.

"No, you wouldn't; I know you wouldn't, and the Crawfords probably don't really believe you would either, but, Joe, there are men that would, and if you could lead Cindy Anne away from what she's been told, what she's been taught, well, then..." Adam watched Little Joe's eyes drop once again to the floor. "And there's the fact that they were right about a girl's reputation. Joe, a reputation is a fragile thing, easily broken and very hard to repair. In this sort of thing, well, for a girl...folks can be really hard on the girl, Joseph."

Little Joe bit his lip. "Yeah."

"And some fathers are not as quick to forgive as Pa is."

"Mr. Crawford?"

"I don't know him well enough to say, but, like Hoss said, I don't think Cindy Anne's brothers will say anything to their father."

"I hope not." The tremble in Joe's voice caused Adam to reach out and pull Joe toward him. "I didn't, I mean, I didn't think..."

Adam allowed a small smile to flit across his lips. "Joe, you might have noticed this is one time I haven't asked you what in tarnation you were thinking." He squeezed his brother's arm. "That's because I know just what you were thinking."

Little Joe blushed. "Adam!" Then the indignation left his voice. "I just wanted to be with her, and maybe, well, I just wanted to kiss her."

Adam's hand squeezed gently as he said, "I know, but there are some steep inclines where if you drop a ball it just rolls right away from you. That's why Pa sets rules, Joe, so things don't roll away from you and right over a cliff. " Adam watched Joe's fingers pluck nervously at the bedclothes. "Joe, kissing Cindy Anne wasn't what was bad; your disobeying, your getting her to disobey and not thinking about the consequences for her, that's what Pa punished you for. The kiss, well, you and she, especially Cindy Ann, are just too young is all." Adam heard his brother's sigh. Smiling he patted Joe's back, "Now, when you're grown..."

"Pa will still have rules."

"Well, yeah, but..." Adam's grin flashed a message to his brother, and the shadows left Joe's eyes.

Adam's own eyes grew serious again. "Joe, you know you can't speak to Cindy Anne or send her a note or anything like that, don't you?"

"I heard you tell Axton."

Adam recognized the lack of agreement in his brother's voice.

He took Joe's chin in his hand and stared directly into his eyes. "You will not, little brother, is that clear?"

"Yes, Adam, I just..."

"I know, and when the dust settles I intend to speak to Axton."

"Will you ask him to tell Cindy Anne I'm sorry I got her in trouble and, well, I didn't...I just..."

"I'll ask him to let Cindy Anne know that you did not mean to hurt her and did nothing out of a lack of respect for her, also that your not speaking to her will be only out of respect for her family's wishes. Will that do?"

"Yeah." Little Joe turned and gazed at the door. "Adam, have you kissed lots of girls?"

"Now, that would depend on what you consider lots, wouldn't it?"

Joe turned and looked down at Adam. "You're not going to tell me, are you?"

"No, but then neither am I going to ask you about your other kisses," Adam retorted smoothly.

"My other, but—"

"Joe, Hoss and I saw that kiss clearly enough to see that it was most definitely not your first." Adam's grin was wicked. Little Joe sputtered but failed to form a bona fide word. "Actually, I'm gratified that you've managed to follow one rule."

Joe's brow furrowed. "What rule?"

"That a gentleman doesn't kiss and tell." Adam swung his hand slowly enough for his fingertips to swat only cloth as Little Joe dodged away. He leaned back on his elbows and smiled at his little brother. Joe caught the smile and returned one of his own. Then he turned and walked toward his own room. As Joe closed the door of Adam's bedroom behind him, the smiles on both brothers' lips shifted slightly as each remembered something he would not tell.

Premonition

by EPM

$\mathcal{S}$urprise was the first thing he felt after the bullet plowed into his chest. To die here in some dirty, dusty cow town, killed by a lucky shot. He wanted to laugh but the blood that filled his lungs wouldn't allow it. His only consolation was watching the crimson stain that spread across the shirt of his adversary. A faint smile twisted his lips as he fell forward onto the muddy street.

Adam Cartwright stood in the middle of Virginia City's main roadway, his gun hanging loosely at his side. The skirt of his black broadcloth coat was pulled open by the wind. He looked up at the ominous sky. Lightening streaked and what had been a low rumble of thunder now became louder as the rain fell harder. He looked at John Hatcher's still body and knew that he was dead.

Adam let out a deep breath that became a shudder as he thought of his part in the death of another human being. Suddenly, a sharp pain caught in his chest and caused his breath to shorten. He looked down to see the bright red stain that marred the front of his pristine white shirt. Letting his gun drop, he raised his hand to touch it. He watched as the rain and blood mixed on his hand then fell in droplets to the thirsty ground below.

A shout caught Adam's attention and he looked to see his two brothers and his father running toward him. With legs that would no longer hold him, he fell to his knees. All thoughts were crowded out of his mind now but one. He wanted, needed to tell his family that he loved them. Hoss and Joe knelt at his side, one to the left, one to the right. His father was on his knees in front of him. He turned to each of his brothers and smiled. Knowing he had little strength left, he saved his words for his beloved father. Looking into the deep brown eyes, he mustered a crooked grin and said, "Thanks Pa, for everything. I—" The grin faded and he fell forward into the waiting arms.

A crack of thunder shook the house and lightening illuminated the night sky. But Adam Cartwright was already awake. He sat bolt upright in bed, sweat running in paths down naked flesh. The dream had come again.

JULY HAD DRESSED the Ponderosa in the deep greens of midsummer. There had been plenty of rain that spring so any signs of drought were hidden behind rushing streams and tall, lush grass. Adam Cartwright was a man with a mission. A mission to ride into town and tend to ranch errands and to find himself the tallest, coolest beer money could buy. As he rode, he let Sport have his head. He remembered with a smile the faces of his younger brothers when his father had asked him to go. Joe was on the verge of saying something to his father when he was silenced with a look.

Adam argued with himself as he rode down Virginia City's main street. Should he do those errands first or satisfy his craving for that cool beer? Normally, there would be no contest. Adam rarely let what he wanted interfere with what was needed. But today pleasure won out and he tied Sport in the shade of the porch overhang of the Silver Dollar. He mounted the steps two at a time and walked through the half-doors. "Make it tall and cool, Sam," he said. Sam O'Brian was the owner and bartender of the Silver Dollar and a friend to each of the Cartwright brothers.

"Adam, it's nice to see you. Where have the three Cartwrights been hiding?" Sam asked.

"Not hiding, Sam, just buried in a ton of work. I'll tell Joe and Hoss that you miss them though." The honey-colored liquid arrived and Adam lost no time raising the beer to his lips. As he did, he looked in the mirror in front of him. There, in the reflection, sat Danny Flynn. He was in a poker game with three other men. Adam recognized two of them as down on their luck farmers but the third man was Jake Maguire, a professional gambler and gunman.

He knew Danny Flynn as an arrogant and self-absorbed young man who had gone to school with Joe. As Adam recalled, both boys got into more than their share of trouble. The difference was that Joe had grown up but Danny remained the spoiled son of Caleb Flynn, indulged by his father and three older brothers. Adam let out a small sigh then went back to his beer.

"You cheated. I saw you take that last card off the bottom." Danny Flynn directed his anger toward Jake Maguire and got to his feet. Both of the hapless farmers moved quickly to the other side of the room. "Get up, Maguire, or I'll shoot you where you sit." The gambler didn't move.

Adam put his beer down and turned to watch the unfolding events. Before anything else could happen, Sam put a shotgun between the two men. "There'll be none of that in here. Pick up your winnings Danny and go home, otherwise I'll call the sheriff."

After a moment's hesitation, the young man started to pick up the pile of money before him. Adam relaxed and took the last swallow of his beer. "Thanks, Sam," he called out. "I'll tell Hoss and Joe you said hello." He walked out into the bright sunlight and untied Sport. Scratching the horse's chin, he said, "You need a long, cool drink too old boy? Well, no beer for you, someone needs to get us home."

The sound of the gunshot made Adam jump forward, hitting his hip on the railing. He turned and ran back into the saloon. It took a moment for his eyes to adjust after being in the bright light. When they did, he was greeted with the sight of Danny Flynn lying on the floor. A pool of blood crept from beneath his body and started to run across the floorboards. Adam didn't need to look for any signs of life. He knew there couldn't be any with that much blood. He knelt beside the body of not Danny Flynn the troubled youth but Danny Flynn the boy who spent his school days with his younger brother. He had held the same promise as any other young man. But now the youth and the promise were gone. Adam reached over and Danny Flynn's eyes were closed for the last time.

Adam stood up. The angles of his face hardened into sharp edges. He stared at Jake Maguire and said, "Why, why would you kill a boy?"

Before Maguire could answer, Sam said, "He didn't have a choice, Adam. The boy turned and drew on him." Adam changed his stare to Sam. "That's the honest truth. I got no reason to lie."

SHERIFF COFFEE TALKED to all the witnesses in his office. Adam sat quietly in a corner, only adding to the conversation when asked a direct question. "All right," Roy said, "I guess there ain't much else to say. You can all go now."

Adam got up but Roy put a restraining hand on his arm. "Would you wait just a minute, Adam?"

After everyone had left, Roy said, "You blamin' yerself? You couldn't have known Danny would make a fool play like that."

"If I'd just stayed a little longer, maybe I could have done something. The kid would be safely on his way home, instead of dead." Adam walked toward the door.

"I'm goin' out to tell Caleb now. You go on home." Roy put on his hat and followed Adam to the door.

"I'll go with you. I'd like to—" Adam started to say.

Roy interrupted. "You go on home like I told ya. It'll be hard enough telling yer own family."

Adam gave Roy a sad half smile and walked through the door.

BEN WATCHED HIS eldest son ride toward him and wondered why Adam had chosen to meet him. Even as he came closer, nothing gave him any indication that something might be wrong. He smiled and said, "Thought your old man couldn't find his way home?" When Adam didn't react to Ben's kidding, he knew there was something on his son's mind.

"No, I came to tell you there's been a shooting. Danny Flynn is dead." Ben thought he could detect a tremor in his son's voice.

"Danny? What happened?" Ben was astonished at Adam's news. He knew that Caleb Flynn loved his boys as much as he loved his. He also knew that Caleb let young Danny do just about anything he wanted, regardless of the consequences.

Adam took a deep breath then relayed what had happened in the Silver Dollar. When he finished telling his father, he added, "I'll never know—if I had just stayed until the boy was on his way home."

"Adam, don't do this to yourself. You're not responsible for what happened in that saloon. How were you to know he would try to draw on Maguire?" Ben could see the toll Danny's death was taking on his eldest.

"What am I suppose to tell Joe? How do I explain it to him?"

Adam reined Sport toward home.

Adam had gone to his room as soon as he and Ben reached home and put away their horses. Ben sat waiting for dinner and for both of his younger sons to return. He picked up his pipe and let out a small sigh. He hoped a little time would allow Adam to see things more clearly. His thoughts were interrupted by the sound of footfalls on the porch.

Hoss and Joe tried to squeeze through the door at the same time but Hoss' sheer bulk sent Joe flying forward. Joe's laughter filled the room. He came to rest in front of his father's chair. Ben stood up.

The laughter faded when Joe saw his father's face. "What is it Pa?" Hoss joined them.

Before Ben could answer, Adam's deep voice floated down from the stairs. He stood on the landing and said, "Danny Flynn was killed today in a gunfight."

"What—Danny? But Danny was my age. We went to school together. How could he be dead?" Joe moved to the cold hearth and sat down. His face betrayed his shock.

Adam came down the stairs and stood before his youngest brother. He told Joe what happened in as few words as he could then waited for his reaction. "I don't know what to say. Maybe if you'd stayed until Danny left but—"

Before Joe could finish, Adam said, "I'm going for a walk. I won't be late." Ben started to say something but thought better of it. The door closed quietly.

Joe continued to sit in confused silence while Ben's gaze stayed on the newly closed door. Hoss stepped forward and said, "Don't worry Pa. You know how Adam has to study things over every which way before he can understand them." Ben smiled at Hoss' observation of his older brother. "He'll come around. It'll just take him a little time to chew over what's happened."

"I don't want him to think it's his fault," Joe added. "He shouldn't be blaming himself."

"Just tell him that when he comes home, son. That would be

the best thing he could hear right now." Ben placed a hand on each son's shoulder and said, "Let's go eat. Adam will come back soon."

But Adam didn't come back right away. It was dark and it appeared as if everyone had gone to sleep when he opened the front door. He knew Hop Sing would have left him a plate in the warmer. Summer or winter, between cooking and baking, the stove was always warm. A lamp had been left burning in the living room, no doubt by his father. He picked it up and walked through to the kitchen. Between the lamp and the bright moon, the small room was bathed in light. He pumped up a glass of fresh, cold water and took the still warm food off the stove. A smile came to his face when he sat at the small table. There had been more than one night when he and Hoss had been banished from the dining room to the kitchen. Their father had told them if they insisted on acting as children then they could just eat at the children's table.

Just as he started his meal, he heard footsteps. Adam looked up to see his younger brother standing in the doorway. "Want some company?" Joe asked.

Adam pushed out the opposite chair with his foot and said, "Be my guest, that is, if you don't mind sitting at the children's table." A sly smile slid onto his face.

"I remember crying and having a fit because you and Hoss were in here and I wanted to be with you two. Poor Pa didn't know what to do." They both chuckled.

"Adam, I wanted you to know that I don't blame you for what happened to Danny. Yeah, I admit I was shocked there for a minute, but you couldn't have known." Joe waited.

Adam put down his fork. "Thanks, Joe. I appreciate that. He was just so young. Maybe he could have turned himself around, in time." He took a minute to gather his thoughts. "But now there is no more time."

"Danny seemed headed for trouble since we were kids," Joe replied. "I know I got into some too but Danny never seemed to learn from the trouble he got into. Maybe that's because his father and brothers were too busy trying to cover things up or making excuses for him." Joe serious face turned into a grin. "I don't remember Pa ever making excuses for us!" Adam just shook his head.

"Well, we need to get to bed. There's still plenty to do," Adam remarked. "And I'm bone tired."

"Do you think the funeral will be day after tomorrow?" Joe asked.

"Yeah, I imagine so. I'm not quite sure what to say to Caleb Flynn," Adam answered.

A little surprised by Adam's reply, Joe said, "Are you going?"

"Of course! Why wouldn't I go? They've been neighbors for years." Adam felt himself getting angry and he didn't really know why.

"Ok, I just thought that maybe under the circumstances, you would—" Adam interrupted him.

"I'll be there, Joe. Now let's get to bed." Adam picked up the lamp and ushered his brother into the living room and toward the stairs. "Joe, wait," he called and lifted the lamp between them. The light brought their faces out of the shadows. "Thanks." Both brothers smiled in understanding.

THE BEAUTY OF high summer was beginning to disappear behind the oppressive heat. Far off in the mountains, thunder rumbled, keeping alive the hope of a cooling rain. The Cartwright buggy stopped in front of the Flynn ranch house. They could see family and friends gathered at the top of a grassy knoll beside a mound of freshly dug earth.

The four men got out and started up the gentle incline. They were met halfway by Caleb Flynn and his three sons. "Ben, you and your boys are not welcome here as long as you have that coward with you." Flynn's gaze seemed to burn through the air as he stared at Adam.

"Now look here, Caleb—" Ben started to say, but Adam stepped forward and held up a silencing hand to his father.

"Mr. Flynn, I can only tell you how—" Adam felt himself knocked backward by a sharp blow to his mouth. He staggered but remained on his feet. Joe and Hoss moved to his side and the three Flynn boys stepped closer to their father.

The muscles around Ben's mouth tightened and his voice was harsh with self-restraint. "Caleb, my heart cries for you at the death of your son but blaming mine won't bring Danny back. Adam was not responsible for the decisions your son made."

"My boy died alone on a dirty barroom floor. Your son was there, Ben. He could have stopped it but he didn't. He walked out and left a kid to die." Flynn turned his attention to Adam. "You mark my words, Adam Cartwright. Before this summer ends, you'll be fodder for the undertaker." Before anymore could be said, Flynn and his sons turned and started walking back up the hill.

The Cartwright men returned home.

JULY SLID INTO August and Caleb Flynn's threat seemed to be just that. Adam refused his father's plea to stay close to the ranch. Time had helped him come to terms with Danny Flynn's death. And although he would always wonder if the outcome would have been different had he not left, he realized that the young man had made his own choices and had, unfortunately, paid a steep price for them.

The heat seemed endless and the air hung heavy with unfallen moisture. Adam had left the house early to check on the herds pastured on the western part of the ranch. Joe and Hoss planned on coming with him, but when he awoke everyone was still asleep and he didn't have the heart to wake them. Sleep had become a rare commodity in the dog days of summer, so he let them be. Adam smiled. He'd get his "digs" in when they showed up.

Fortunately, the grass was still plentiful despite the excessive warmth. Adam rode between bunches of cows noting that this year's crop of calves looked well fed and healthy. He saw dust rising from the trail. He had been waiting for his brothers to show up. Now his thoughts turned to how best to tease them about sleeping in.

Adam continued riding. Suddenly he heard the sound of a rope cut through the still summer air and felt it tighten around his body, pinning his arms to his sides. The rope became taunt and he was pulled backward off his horse. Momentarily stunned, he lay on the ground looking at the legs of several horses. It tightened again and he felt himself being dragged across the pasture. He stopped abruptly and was yanked to his feet. Adam closed his eyes for a moment, waiting for his head to clear. When he opened them, he was looking into the face of Caleb Flynn.

"Think I'd forgotten about you, boy?" Flynn asked. His fist snapped Adam's head to the side. Still bound by the rope and held by Flynn's sons, he was unable to defend himself. He could feel the line of blood as it slid slowly from his lip to his jaw.

"You really think you'll get away with this?" Adam asked as he stared back at his attacker.

Flynn looked around at his boys and laughed. "Why, we don't have to do nothing, Cartwright. You ever heard of a gunman named Hatcher?" Adam didn't answer but, like everyone else in the territory, he knew Hatcher's reputation as a fast gun. "No? Well don't worry. He's heard of you. I hear tell he can be bought to kill any man, for enough money."

"And what makes you think I'll go willingly to the slaughter or that I won't involve the law?" Adam said.

"Your kid brother and my Danny use to run together in school as I remember. It'd be a shame if something happened to him, being so young and all." Flynn's sons joined him in laughing at Adam's response.

"Leave Joe out of this!" Adam shouted. He struggled until the rope bit through the material of his shirt and imbedded itself into the flesh of his arms. "He had nothing to do with your son's death."

Flynn grabbed Adam's shirt and dragged him closer. "We'll leave him alone just as long as you keep your appointment with Mr. Hatcher." Flynn gave him a twisted sneer. "And keep the law out of this!" He signaled for his sons to tie Adam to a lone cottonwood. "Why don't you give the coward a taste of what will happen to his brother if he doesn't do what we ask?"

Helpless to do anything against the blows that punished his body, Adam concentrated on not giving them the satisfaction of hearing him cry out. Finally, the beating stopped and he heard the sound of retreating hoof beats. He leaned forward into the rope's embrace and let his head hang down. It occurred to him that Joe and Hoss would soon be there. He couldn't tell them the truth. What would he say—? He let himself drift into the void.

"WHY DO YOU suppose Adam let us sleep in this morning?" Hoss asked as he wiped a handkerchief across his sweat-streaked face.

Joe looked up into the sky, hoping to see some sign of relief. "Got me, but I got a feeling we haven't heard the last on the subject."

They rode on, finally reaching the western section of the Ponderosa range. Joe saw Sport in the distance, loose and grazing contentedly among the cattle. "Now that's odd. Look at Sport. Adam wouldn't just let him go that way, especially still bitted like that."

"Yeah, it is kinda strange at that. Adam!" Hoss shouted. "Hey Adam, where are ya?"

They both remained silent to listen but heard no returning call. "Let's have a look around," Joe said. The brothers went in different directions.

Joe was the one who saw him first. The picture of his brother tied to a tree, head hanging down, stopped Joe in his tracks. Recovering, he ran forward, calling for Hoss as he did. Gently, he lifted Adam's head in his hands. Speaking softly, he hoped for some kind of response. "Adam, it's Joe. Adam—can you hear me?"

Slowly, Adam's eyes opened. He lifted his head and tried to smile when he saw his younger brother's face. "You two finally make it outta bed?" His eyes closed and he dropped his head into Joe's hands once more.

Hoss pulled his knife and cut the ropes. "Oh Lordy, Adam. Who did this to you?" They eased him to the ground and Hoss held him while Joe ran for a canteen. Adam began to come around and both of his brothers breathed a sigh of relief.

"What happened?" Joe asked again.

Adam hesitated only a moment. "Rustlers—caught them trying to move the herd." He put a hand to his damaged face. "They decided to have a little fun before they left." He tried to push away from Hoss but the pain made him stop. He gasped and blinked hard. "They must have heard you coming and decided not to take a chance."

Looking at his battered brother, Joe's green eyes turned dark with anger. "They couldn't have gotten far." He rose. "Trailing them should be easy."

Adam struggled to get up. "No," he shouted. "You're not going anywhere." The effort left him breathing hard and sweat broke out on his face.

"Adam's right, Joe! What you gonna do when you catch up with them?" He started to help his older brother to his feet, keeping a steadying hand on his arm. "Besides, I need ya to help me get him into town."

Adam jerked his head up. "Town—why would I be going to town?"

"Cause you need ta see a doctor, that's why," Hoss answered.

Adam pulled away from his brother's hand and straightened

up as much as his body would allow. "I don't need to see a doctor. I'll be just fine at home."

"Now most of the time I'd agree with ya but this time you can't see what you look like. You really want Pa to see you like this? He'll have a fit." Hoss waited for his brother's logical mind to mull over what he said.

"We can't just let them get away with beating Adam and trying to take the herd," Joe said.

"We ain't. We'll talk to Roy when we get Adam into town. Now come on you two. I ain't arguing all day." Hoss enjoyed his moment of authority and neither brother disagreed.

ADAM SAT SLUMPED forward with his legs dangling off the side of Paul Martin's examination table. His whole body ached but he knew there was no serious or permanent damage. "Where's my shirt?" he asked no one in particular.

"I'd like you to stay overnight," Paul said as he went to retrieve Adam's tattered shirt.

"You were roughed up pretty badly and I'd feel better if I could keep an eye on you."

"Thanks, Paul, but I'll feel much better at home. And you know Pa, he's not about to let me too far out of his sight." Adam reached for the torn and blood splotched shirt.

"Joe, why don't you go over to the mercantile and get Adam a new shirt?" Hoss said.

Joe watched as Adam was about to protest his going and said, "What's the matter with you? First you don't want me to trail those rustlers, now you don't want me going across the street?" He was having a hard time holding on to his temper and trying to understand his brother's behavior.

"It's not that," Adam snapped back, "It's just—oh hell, go. And don't be all damned day about it either!" He wrapped his arms around his aching ribs and fought through the pain.

Hoss and the doctor gave each other a questioning look. "He'll be a few minutes. Why don't you lie down and rest until he comes back?" Paul offered. Adam didn't fight the idea or the helping hands.

When Joe returned, he helped his brother to sit up. "See, I'm back and all in one piece. Think of that," Joe said. His smile was bright again as he couldn't resist teasing his older brother.

Adam sat up and smiled back. "Don't take advantage, kid. I won't be down all that long." He slowly slipped into the shirt and began buttoning it.

"Sorry, they only had black," Joe said.

"That's ok, it matches my mood. Hoss back yet?" Adam asked.

"Not yet," Paul said as he took his patient's pulse once more. "Sure you won't—?

Joe interrupted. "Where'd Hoss go?" he asked.

Adam slid off the table and leaned back until he was steadier. He stiffened at Joe's question. "He went to tell Roy what's going on. Come on—let's go home." He picked up his gun belt and hat. "Thanks, Doc."

"Remember Adam—" It was Adam's turn to interrupt. He gave the doctor a warm smile. "I promise Paul."

"Can I help an old man to the door?" Joe's eyes sparkled as he asked.

"I'll let you know if I need you, boy," Adam said as he passed his brother.

BY THE TIME they got home it was getting dark and Ben came out on the porch to meet them. The shadows hid the worst of Adam's injures but they could not hide the grunt of pain when he dismounted nor the guarded posture when he walked.

"What is it son? What happened?" Ben asked.

Afraid that if he stopped, his abused body would give in, Adam kept walking. "I'll tell you inside Pa. I'm afraid I'm about done in for one day." His foot hit the porch and he staggered. Ben reached out and placed an arm around his son's waist. He guided him through the door and to the settee.

Adam lay down and closed his eyes. He decided even his eyelids ached and the last thing he wanted was to try and find the strength to lie to his father. Instead he kept quiet and let Hoss and Joe relay what had happened. The three voices seemed to swirl about him then fade as he began to feel detached from what was going on. His mind drifted back to Flynn's face. Adam had no doubt that the man would carry out his threat just as he had no doubt that he'd do anything to protect Joe.

The voices became louder again. Beyond exhaustion, Adam struggled to sit up. "I'm tired. Can we continue this in the morning?"

Ben looked guilty for a moment then replied, "Of course son. I'll help you upstairs. "

Adam rose and leaned against his father as they walked up the stairway and into his room. Seeing his bed, he felt as if it had never looked better. He sat down on the edge and started to reach for a boot.

"Let me help you, son," Ben said as he bent and quickly removed both of Adam's boots.

"Thanks Pa, I can take it from here." He unbuttoned his shirt and winced as he took it off.

Ben drew in a quick breath when he saw the purple and deep blue bruising that crisscrossed his boy's body. He drew himself up and said, "We'll get them, Adam. I promise."

Adam held his father's eyes. He wanted desperately to blurt out the truth. But instead he turned his head and said, "Goodnight, Pa. I promise I'll call you if I need anything."

Ben stepped forward, wanting to touch his son but he knew the gesture would only make Adam uncomfortable. Instead, he stayed his hand then said, "All right, son. I'm here if you need me." He closed the door quietly when he left.

It was that night, amidst the distant thunder and lightening, when the dream came for the first time. He remembered feeling as if he was being pulled by something from the edge of an abyss and found himself sitting upright in his own bed. The dream didn't fade with his waking.

ADAM HEARD THE argument before he saw the opponents. He was just coming down the stairs when Joe's higher-pitched voice rose over the lower rumble of his father's. "If we don't go soon we won't have a chance to catch whoever it was that hurt Adam and tried to steal the herd. Just what are we waiting for?" Joe's frustration mixed freely with his anger and fear.

Ben's eyes narrowed as he stared at his youngest son. In a quiet, barely controlled voice he said, "Young man, you'd better rein in that temper. We will go as soon as Hoss and I are ready. If you are in such a hurry then make sure the men are ready to ride while I check on Adam." Joe turned away than headed toward the door. He stopped when he heard his father's voice again. "And Joseph, I suggest you think about how you address me in the future. Is that clear?"

"Yes, sir," he said, mustering a contrite reply. "I'll go see to the men."

"No, Joe, don't go." Adam proceeded down the stairs as Ben, Hoss and Joe all looked at him, waiting for more.

He stood in front of his family and confessed his lie. "It wasn't rustlers—it was Caleb Flynn."

Stunned, the three men stood speechless. Finally, Ben spoke up. "But why—why tell us it was cattle thieves?"

Adam moved away and stood in front of the hearth. After a moment, he turned and faced them. "Because if I don't do what they ask, they'll hurt Joe." He took a breath. "I thought it would be easier if I just did what they said without anyone knowing the truth. I was wrong." He sat down heavily on the cold stone.

"Hurt me, why would they—?" Joe stopped when his father

held up a hand.

"What is it they want you to do, son?" Ben asked.

Hoss moved closer to his older brother. Adam looked up and gave him a faint smile then answered his father's question. "They want me to meet John Hatcher in Virginia City." The words came out flat—no anger, no fear.

It was Hoss who spoke first. "John Hatcher has killed every man he's ever faced. Has Caleb Flynn lost his mind?" His voice held anger and disbelief.

Adam's response was calm and measured. "No, I don't think so. He's a man who's lost a son and he blames me for his death. He thinks it only fair that I die too."

"Hoss, Joe—please go outside and tell the men we won't be riding out." Ben didn't take his eyes off his eldest.

"I'm not afraid of Caleb Flynn or his boys," Joe announced.

Hoss put a hand on Joe's shoulder. "We know you're not. Come on now and let's do as Pa asked." He guided his younger brother to the door.

When they had gone, Ben asked, "Oh Adam, do you think so little of your family that you'd prefer to face something like this alone?"

Adam heard the hurt in his father's voice. "It's not that, Pa— it's Joe's life we're talking about. I can't take that kind of chance."

"And I won't let you take that kind of chance with your life! John Hatcher is a killer. And as fast as you are, you're not a professional gunman. You don't kill men for money." Ben stopped for a moment. "Your principles would get in the way of your gun." Adam didn't have an answer.

Hoping he'd gotten through to his son, Ben said, "Come on now, let's go see if Joe's calmed down yet." Father and son walked outside and found Hoss and Joe at the corral fence.

"We sent most of the men out to the hay fields," Hoss said.

"And I'd like you to join them, Joseph, while I go into town." Ben waited to see if his youngest would object.

Joe glanced at his brothers then looked back at his father.

"Alright, Pa, but like I said, I'm not afraid."

Ben put his hand on Joe's shoulder and said, "I know son but I am. Please be careful." Joe mounted and rode out toward the east meadow.

"I'm going in to see the sheriff. I'll be home before supper." Ben started for the barn to saddle Buck.

"Maybe I should go with you." Adam stepped in beside his father. "Roy will want to talk to me."

"You know you shouldn't be riding that far. I'll take care of this." Ben was adamant.

Adam knew he should argue the point with his father but he didn't have the strength, especially since he knew he would lose this battle. He let his father continue to the barn by himself.

It was quiet now, since everyone had left. Adam and Hoss kept a companionable silence as they did the morning chores. Finally, Adam sat down to rest, unconsciously rubbing his aching ribs. He looked up at his brother and asked quietly, "Do you think I'd have a chance against Hatcher?"

Hoss stopped working and leaned on his pitchfork. There was no hesitation before his answer. "No Adam, I don't think you would."

Adam just gave him a half smile and nodded his head in agreement. "Come on, let's go see if baby brother is working or just playing boss."

"I DON'T CARE Roy. I want the man arrested!" Ben Cartwright was shouting loud enough to be heard outside the sheriff's office and a small crowd stopped to listen.

"Now Ben, I said I'd go and see Flynn, but you know as well as me that he'll have an alibi and it'll be his word against Adam's." Roy Coffee was trying to keep his temper. He understood Ben's anger, knowing that two of his sons had been threatened.

Ben paced the office in front of the sheriff's desk. "Talk to him—that's not good enough! I want him locked away!" Ben stopped moving. "And Hatcher—what about him?" The crowd outside inched closer when they heard the gunfighter's name. They knew he was in Virginia City for a reason, they just didn't know why.

"I've had a conversation with Mr. Hatcher already. He denies being in town for any particular reason. I can't arrest a man with no paper out on him or who hasn't caused any trouble. All I could do was warn him." Roy's own frustration was beginning to show. "Now that I know about Flynn's threat against Adam, I'll go talk to him again."

"Talk? My son's life is at risk! I'll not see Adam shot down and bleeding to death in the middle of Virginia City's main street!" He stopped walking and moved closer to the sheriff. His voice dropped to a harsh whisper. "If I have to, I'll kill him myself. No matter how I have to do it, I'll kill him." Ben moved away and started for the door.

"I'm telling you now, Ben—stay away from Caleb Flynn and John Hatcher. Let me do my job." Roy Coffee watched as his oldest friend continued out the door.

The crowd scattered as Ben stepped onto the porch of the jailhouse. Without speaking, he mounted Buck and reined him in the direction of Caleb Flynn's ranch.

IT HAD TAKEN some hard riding and deep breaths before Ben could calm the thudding heartbeat that exploded in his chest. He reined Buck in and found that they were standing on the hillside where Danny Flynn was buried. The grass was trying to cover the newly turned dirt but the recent lack of rain left only sparse patches. He looked down the hill at the Flynn ranch house. Glancing once more at the grave, he set his shoulders and moved Buck forward.

"Flynn—Caleb Flynn!" Ben shouted. He didn't bother to dismount. "Come out, Flynn, or are you afraid to face a man without his arms pinned by a rope?"

The door opened slowly and a smiling Caleb Flynn walked onto the porch surrounded by his three sons. "What can I do for you, Cartwright?" he asked.

"Let's not play games, Flynn. You've beaten one of my sons and threatened another." Ben was trying to contain his rising anger, but the memory of the bruises and cuts that covered his oldest son's body fueled his rage. "Now you've hired some cheap gunfighter to goad Adam into a fight. Well, it won't work, Flynn. Stay away from my family or I swear, you and yours will be decorating that hillside before it's all over." Caleb Flynn's laughter followed him as he rode away.

Ben had taken his time riding home. The confrontations with Roy then Flynn had left him exhausted and depressed. The heat, without rain, only added to the charged atmosphere that seemed to surround his family. He stopped by the lake. This had all started because a hot-headed young man had gotten himself into a situation that was beyond him. To be honest, all of his sons had tested their limits at one time or another while growing up but they had been lucky enough or smart enough to escape any severe consequences. Danny Flynn had not. He swung Buck around toward home.

IT WAS SEVERAL days later and Ben had begun to relax a little. He rode into the yard and stopped to watch as his three sons worked to unload a wagon of hay into the mow. They had stripped to the waist and donned heavy gloves. Their work-hardened muscles glistened with sweat and hay chaff stuck to the moisture that rolled off them. He was sure the trio would visit the lake before the day was over. Their good-natured teasing rang in the air and he was glad to see they had forgotten Flynn's threats, at least for the moment.

"Well, it's nice to see you boys working so hard," Ben said as he pulled Buck up next to the wagon.

"Ah, come on now Pa, we always work hard—well at least I do," Joe answered. His broad smile lit his eyes.

Adam just shook his head but Hoss said, "Yeah Pa, Joe has worked real hard today. That's because Adam and me have been right next to him all day long. He couldn't have sneaked outta work even if he'd tried." Hoss laughed.

"I don't try to sneak outta nothing, ya big ox," Joe shot back. With that, a lively back and forth ensued between the two youngest. Adam pulled a handkerchief out of his pocket and wiped it across his sweaty face. He sat down on the side of the wagon emitting an involuntary grunt of pain. His father's head instantly swung toward the sound.

Ben's voice stopped the bickering. "Adam, you really shouldn't be doing hay! Paul told you to take it easy."

Adam held out his hand to his father. "And he was probably right. How about helping me down?"

Ben's mumbling could barely be heard by his sons. "You'd think he'd be old enough by now to know how to take care of himself. Do I have to be here every minute?"

Adam smiled at his father. "What was that you said, Pa?"

"Never mind. Get down here and get cleaned up. You should be resting." Adam let Ben fuss knowing any protestation would just make the situation worse. He looked back at his brothers as he walked into the house and winked. His brothers grinned back at him.

After a cooling bath, Adam realized just how tired he really was. The dream had been coming every night and sleep began to be elusive. Dressed only in jeans, he slipped into the living room and lay down on the settee. Just for a few minutes, he thought to himself. I'll just close my eyes for a few minutes.

When he opened his eyes, Adam knew that more than just a few minutes had passed. He could see the lengthening shadow of Marie's grandfather clock stretch across the floor. And he could hear Hop Sing as he deposited the plates and glasses on the table for dinner.

He glanced around and saw his father sitting in his favorite chair, reading the latest edition of the Enterprise. A faint smile crossed Adam's face. His father—the one and only constant in his life. It didn't seem to matter what situation, what trouble; his father was there for him. And he, in turn, felt the same toward his brothers. He would do anything, sacrifice anything, for their well-being. He only hoped he wouldn't have to.

Ben put down his paper and Adam sat up as they heard the sound of horses in the yard. They waited for the brothers to come through the door but instead were greeted by Hoss' yell for help. Both men rushed outside. Joe was leaning heavily on his older brother. His left thigh was tied with a crude bandage. Blood seeped through the layers and dripped slowly downward.

Adam quickly supported Joe from the other side while Ben led the way into the house. Hop Sing met them at the door. "Have one of the hands ride for Doctor Martin," Ben said. They proceeded up the stairs toward Joe's room.

Beads of sweat formed on the young man's face, joining and running down pale cheeks. They helped him undress and get into bed. "It's not that bad, Pa," Joe said through gritted teeth. "I think the bullet just took off a little hide."

Ben placed the back of his hand on Joe's face and gave him a faint, reassuring smile. "Paul will be here soon, son. I know it hurts, but try not to move around too much."

Hop Sing entered with hot water and bandages. Adam and Hoss left while he and Ben tended to the youngest Cartwright. The door had barely closed when Adam asked, "What happened?" He didn't try to control his anger.

"I don't really know! Joe and I had just gotten outta the water and gotten dressed when there was a shot and he went down. I looked around but I didn't see nobody. I needed to get him home before he lost anymore blood." Hoss took a breath. "There was only one shot."

Adam's eyes darkened and the muscles around his mouth twitched. "Well I know!" He turned and started down the stairs. He felt Hoss' hand holding on to his shoulder.

"Now you just hold on there. I'm as mad as you are but we don't have no proof of who it was." Hoss held tight to Adam's shoulder. "You ain't gonna do yer self or nobody else any good if you go ridin over to Flynn's."

Adam shrugged off the hand that held him and started down once more. Hoss' words stopped him. "Don't do it Adam. You'll get yourself killed and that's just what they want." He moved forward and placed his hand lightly on the same shoulder. He felt the muscles underneath stiffen. "Don't give 'em the satisfaction." Hoss heard Adam push out a long, deep breath and felt the muscles under his hand relax.

Adam turned and looked up. His voice faltered as he said, "You could've just as likely brought him home over his saddle. I can't let that happen. You know that, don't you?"

"Yeah, I know that but not tonight. Tonight Joe needs you and Pa don't need to worry about you doin' something stupid. Come on now and pour me some of that brandy you and Pa are so fond of." They walked down the stairs to wait for the doctor.

Later that night Adam awoke, drenched in sweat from the heat and the same dream. He sat with his eyes closed for a moment, reliving the terror the vision had brought. Finally, he got up and walked to the open window, naked flesh hoping for the relief of a breeze. Flashes of lightening lit the distant hills and were answered by bursts of thunder. He grabbed his pants off the back of the chair and pulled them on.

The light coming from Joe's room led him down the hall. He watched as his kid brother slept peacefully, only occasionally wincing in his sleep. Doctor Martin assured them that Joe would be just fine after a few days rest. He looked over and saw his father in the rocker. His face was relaxed and the ravages of time and trials were hidden beneath the mask of sleep. How many times had the man sat next to one of his sons, wondering if they'd see the morning? They had been lucky this time but what about the next time? He knew he couldn't let there be a next time. He walked to Joe's side and placed a hand on his brother's arm. "No one will hurt you again—I promise," he whispered. He looked over at his father once more then walked out the door and down the stairs.

THE SUN WAS a fiery orange ball just lifting itself over the horizon when Adam opened the barn doors. Determined that Joe's life would no longer be in danger, he'd go to Flynn and tell him that he'd meet Hatcher. He knew they wouldn't hurt him. No, they had waited too long for their scheme to take root. They weren't about to ruin things now.

Adam smoothed the saddle blanket on Sport's back, careful not to leave any wrinkles. He stroked the long silken neck and felt some of the tension leave him. Just as he reached for his saddle, he heard the doors open once again. Ben Cartwright stood framed by the first beams of sunlight. As he walked further into the shadows of the barn, Adam could see the look of concern that marked his face. Trying to pretend that he was up early to start the day's work would be useless, so he made no excuses.

"Is Joe—?" Adam asked.

"Joe's just fine. He slept all night," his father replied. Changing the subject, Ben said, "It's a little early, even for you. Why the rush?"

"Let's not play this game Pa. You know where I'm going. I just hoped I could leave before anyone was up."

Ben stepped closer to his son. "You go up against Flynn and his boys and you'll be killed."

"Caleb Flynn is not interested in killing me himself, just seeing me dead." Adam pulled the cinch tight and looped it into a saddle knot.

"So you're going to tell him that you'll meet Hatcher. Is that your plan?" The angrier Ben got the quieter Adam became.

"What would you have me do, Pa? Wait til they kill Joe or maybe just cripple him for life?" Adam led Sport out of his stall and past his father.

"I'm his father! I can protect him." Ben's voice shattered the early morning stillness and seemed to keep ringing in the air even after he finished speaking.

Adam turned to his father and said, "What are you gonna do, Pa, tie the kid to the house forever? They won't give up. And they don't want you, they want me."

Ben's shoulders sagged and the fight seemed to pour out of him. Desperation crept into his voice. "Adam please—don't do this."

Knowing there was nothing more he could say, Adam led Sport out through the doors. His attention was drawn to the house as he saw Hoss walk through the front door. He cursed himself for not rising earlier.

Ben followed his son outside and was about to try reasoning with him once more, when he saw Hoss walking toward them. He gave a small sigh of relief. Of all of them, Hoss was most often the one who could reason with his oldest brother. Hard times had made fast friends.

The sound of riders coming in halted any further conversation. Adam was the only one who was armed. His hand brushed the top of his gun, removing the leather loop that held it in place. As the riders rounded the barn, he relaxed at the sight of Roy Coffee and his deputy. The three stood together, knowing the sheriff wouldn't be coming out this early with any good news.

Roy dismounted and greeted the three Cartwright men. "Ben, boys," he nodded at them.

Hoss answered, "Yer up pretty early this morning Roy. Anything wrong?"

"I came out fer two reasons. One ta see if you can tell me anymore about Joe bein' shot and—" He turned and faced Adam. "Ta tell you we found Jake Maguire this morning in the alley behind the Silver Dollar. He'd been shot in the back."

Without Ben knowing it, Caleb Flynn's name came out on a whisper. He looked at the sheriff and said, "You know it's him, Roy."

"I know there are plenty of men who would be glad to see Maguire dead and Caleb Flynn would be just one among 'em. We're on our way over there right now but I wanted to let you know about the murder first," Roy answered.

"I'll ride with you," Adam said, speaking to the sheriff but facing his father.

"No," his father corrected, looking back at his son. "We'll ride with you."

THE SUN WAS still rising when the small group approached the Flynn ranch. The Cartwright men agreed to Roy's demand that if they came, they were to ride behind him.

Caleb Flynn sat on his front porch, feet elevated on a post. He didn't bother getting up. As the riders stopped in front of him, he said, "What brings this distinguished group to my door so early in the morning?"

Roy spoke up. "Where were you last night, Flynn?"

"Why, I was right here sheriff. Is there a problem?" He couldn't quite carry off the look of innocence that he had pasted on his face.

"I suppose you got witnesses that'll swear to that?" Roy replied. The Cartwrights remained silent as Roy had requested.

"My boys'll tell ya. "Jack, Tom, Fred—where are ya?" Two of the Flynn boys walked out of the barn, pushing their guns back into their holsters. The third moved around the side of the house. All three stood next to their father.

They reminded Adam of a bunch of curs that slunk into a pack for protection. He knew their answer before they spoke. "Pa was here with us, all night and all day, for that matter," Jack Flynn said. "You got a problem with that?"

Roy's temper boiled over. "I got a problem with anything that ain't the truth. But I got no proof you weren't here neither."

"What's this all about sheriff?" the elder Flynn asked.

"We found Jake Maguire this morning behind the Silver Dollar. He'd been shot in the back." Roy waited for a reaction. "He's dead."

"Ya see boys—if ya wait long enough, God punishes those who kill innocent young boys." Flynn's eyes fixed themselves on Adam. "And those who leave the helpless to the wolf."

Ben could no longer contain himself. "I doubt very much if God was in that alley last night Caleb. But someone took a shot at my son Joseph and I tell you now, if he had been killed, even God couldn't protect you." He reined his horse toward home. Adam and Hoss fell in behind him.

It was during the darkest hours of night that Adam arrived in Virginia City. The pitch-black sky was split open by jagged bursts of lightening. The streets were all but abandoned. He stopped in front of the livery stable. Adam knew the owner would be home with his family so he bedded down Sport himself. The cracks of thunder left his mount dancing with nervous energy. He took his time caring for the fractious animal.

Satisfied that Sport had calmed down, he stepped out into the night, carrying his saddlebags over his shoulder.

Adam knew his father would come looking for him as soon as he realized his son was not at home. It had been a week since Joe was shot and Adam had hoped his father believed he was waiting for the law to handle the situation. And he hoped he'd have enough time to do what he had to without his family's interference.

He woke the sleeping hotel clerk as he entered the International House. For enough money the man would swear he hadn't seen Adam in a month. He asked for a room that overlooked the street. Tired as he was, if he lay down, he knew sleep wouldn't come. He took off his gun belt and sat at the small writing desk. A smile played across his face as he started to write but disappeared into a frown of concentration as he continued. When he had finally finished, Adam neatly folded the document and sealed it in an envelope. His bold hand wrote his father's name across the front.

Getting up, he walked to the window. Distant flashes of light lit the night sky. He gave a snort of laughter as he thought that these might be the last hours of Adam Cartwright, holed up in a hotel room, waiting to face a man who was undoubtedly faster than he. It had always been in his nature to analyze and question but he had neither the strength nor the inclination to review his life. What he wanted more than anything else was not to think about anything. He turned away from the window and picked up his gun belt, pulling the straps tight then pushing the belt down so that it rode lower on his right hip. He finished by tying the leather thong snugly around his thigh. Picking up the envelope, Adam tucked it safely in his shirt pocket.

THE RAIN THEY had been waiting for was just beginning to fall. Ben walked outside and stood on the porch, watching the large drops disappear into the thick dust. Joe and Hoss were already on the veranda drinking their morning coffee. It was good to have Joe up and around again, Ben thought. He glanced over at his youngest. A brief catch pulled at his heart, making him hold his breath. What would they have done if they'd lost him? It was more than his mind could grasp.

"What ya thinking about, Pa?" Joe asked.

"Nothing special, just enjoying the rain," Ben said, his somber look quickly covered by a smile. Joe wasn't fooled by his father's feeble attempt at hiding his thoughts.

Hoss interrupted. "Hey, it ain't like Adam to sleep late like this. Wonder what's keeping him in bed?"

Ben turned once more to watch the rain. "Your older brother hasn't been sleeping too well for some time now. It's probably just caught up with him."

Hoss could hear the worry in his father's voice. "Yeah Pa, I'll bet you're right. Them dreams have been comin every night."

"Dreams—what dreams?" Ben's fixed Hoss with narrowed eyes.

"Ahh—I thought he told ya about the dream he keeps havin'," Hoss stammered. He suddenly felt as if he had somehow betrayed his brother's trust. Adam had confided in him one day after a particularly bad night and he had just assumed that his father knew as well.

"No, why don't you tell me," Ben asked.

Joe saw his opportunity to leave. "Think I'll go see if Adam's awake." A slight limp was the only telltale sign of his injury as Joe hurried to the door.

Ben raised an eyebrow and crossed his arms over his chest. "I'm waiting," he said. Hoss knew at that moment just where his older brother had gotten that trait.

"Well now Pa, I think it's up to Adam to tell ya. I thought that he had or I never would've said nothing." The big man shifted from foot to foot.

Before Ben could answer, Joe pulled the front door open and said, "He's not there. Adam's not in his bed."

Without another word, Ben walked out into the rain, headed for the barn. He'd soon know if Adam had left. He unlatched the door and was greeted by Sport's empty stall.

He squeezed his eyes shut hoping when he opened them that the rangy chestnut would be standing in front of him. The rain started to drum a pattern on the barn roof.

Hoss and Joe stood behind their father exchanging a concerned glance. Joe spoke up. "He might have gone out early to check on the timber cutting."

"Yeah Pa, or he might've gone out to see if there's enough water for the cattle in the East Meadow," Hoss offered.

Ben deep, soft voice offered his opinion. "Or he may have gone to meet John Hatcher." He squeezed his eyes shut once more.

"I'M TELLING YA, Pa. I seen him myself. Came in long after dark and went right to the International House." Jack Flynn reported Adam's arrival in Virginia City to his father.

Caleb Flynn let a slow smile of satisfaction spread across his face. "Ya done good, boy." He sipped his morning coffee. "So the coward's finally walked into the trap, has he? Get the horses ready. I want to be there when Hatcher takes him down. I want to stand by and do nothing, just like he did when Danny was cut down." He got up and buckled on his gun belt. Looking up, he raised his fist in the air. "I swear Danny, before this day ends, Adam Cartwright will be judged by his maker."

PAUL MARTIN HAD been up most of the night. His thoughts turned to the young mother whom he had just helped deliver a beautiful baby boy. He let out a long sigh and thought how fortunate it was that he wasn't a drinking man or this would have been one of the times he'd definitely partake before noon. It was her first child and a big child at that. Before he could get there, the baby had started his way down the birth canal. The doctor had done everything he could to save both of them but in the end, the child had suffocated and he was unable to do anything about it. The mother was torn and bled badly. He only hoped she wouldn't suffer the same fate as her child. Paul knew medicine would advance someday and was sorry he wouldn't be around to see it. Enough of this, he told himself. I need my bed and some uninterrupted sleep.

Just as he started to climb the stairs to his bedroom, a brisk knock stopped him. It wouldn't do any good to pretend he wasn't in. His horse and buggy would give him away. Resigned, he turned and walked downstairs again. He was surprised to see the eldest Cartwright son at his door. "Adam—come in. Is everyone ok at the ranch?"

"Everyone's fine but you look like you've had a long night," Adam said. He waited to see if Paul wanted to talk.

"Just part of being a doctor—the very worst part. But enough— can I offer you some coffee?" Paul asked. "Won't take me a minute to make it."

"No thanks, I'll only take a moment of your time." Adam waited then reached for the paper he had put in his shirt pocket the night before. "I need a favor, Paul. Would you hold on to this for me?"

"Sure Adam, but I can see it's addressed to your father," Paul replied.

Not wanting to explain, Adam responded, "Yes, it is for my father but I want you to hold on to it in case—in case something should happen to me. If it does, then give it to him."

Paul took the envelope. "And if not?"

Adam smiled. "You may burn it with my compliments."

"I don't like this, Adam, not at all. I know—I've heard what's going on with Caleb Flynn and his hired gun. Don't be a fool! The man's a killer." Frustration spilled over in Paul's voice. "Just how much do you expect out of a country doctor?"

Adam knew there was more behind the doctor's words then a warning. He reached out and put a hand on Paul's arm. Smiling, he said, "And a damned fine country doctor." He put his hat on and said, "Thanks, Paul," and walked out.

THE RAIN STARTED coming down harder now. John Hatcher looked over the bat-winged doors of the Bucket of Blood. A kindly saloon girl had identified Adam Cartwright for him. Flynn had described him well but he needed to make sure. After all, he was only being paid to kill one man and it was a waste of time, effort and money to kill the wrong one. A shame really—killing this Cartwright fellow. He had heard what happened to the Flynn boy and it seemed he'd gotten what he'd asked for. Idiot kid! But Hatcher had little time for sentiment and killing Adam put money in his pocket. He watched his adversary leave the small house at the edge of town and return to the hotel. He looked once again at the cryptic note in his hand—30 minutes, in the street. He walked back inside, sliding his gun in and out of his holster.

ADAM HAD CHANGED into black dress pants and a white shirt. He topped it off with a long black coat and a thin black ribbon at his throat. It occurred to him that at least he could look the part even if he didn't have quite the skills to go with the look. He checked his gun once more and slid it into the holster. He put on his hat and left the room. He hoped that by calling Hatcher out early, Roy Coffee wouldn't be out yet. He saw no reason for the lawman's life to be endangered because of him.

With the storm's growing intensity, the sky became an eerie yellowish-green highlighted against the thick, black clouds. Adam walked into the street, the sound of rain drumming in his ears. It hadn't escaped him that this was exactly as it happened in his dream but he made himself concentrate on the present. He had to give himself whatever advantages he could and fearing a vision, no matter how real it seemed, diverted his attention. The cold sweat of apprehension gathered and began to soak through his shirt along with the warm rain. His hands hung loosely at his sides. Hatcher slid quietly into the street. They looked at each other for a moment then both men walked forward.

The Cartwrights and the Flynn's arrived at opposite ends of

town within minutes of each other. Caleb Flynn and his sons stood in front of the Bucket of Blood watching and waiting for their final revenge. Ben, Hoss and Joe were just turning the corner when a clap of thunder rattled the glass in the window-panes and the two shots could barely be heard above the noise. Both families froze.

The gunman knew immediately that he had been hit. He struggled to speak but the bullet had destroyed his lungs and they filled with blood at every heartbeat. Even as his vision narrowed, he could see the crimson stain that marked the shirt of his opponent. His mouth twisted into a smile as he died, lying face down in the mud of Virginia City's main street.

Adam dropped his gun and raised his hand to his chest. Blood and water mixed, thinning the color to a soft red. He lifted his head to the sound of someone shouting his name. His legs betrayed him and he found himself on his knees in the mud. He watched as his family appeared before him. Suddenly glad he wasn't alone, Adam smiled at his brothers and tried to say something to his father. But the words became lost and he only remembered the warmth of his father's body before there was no more.

Ben held his son close, rocking him in his strong arms. He kept chanting his name over and over: "Adam, Adam." Joe was about to run for Doctor Martin when a cry of nooooo exploded in the air. Caleb Flynn rushed into the street, gun drawn. His sons followed and the four men bore down on the Cartwrights. Caleb intended to make sure that the promise he had made to his son would be kept. Ben instinctively held Adam closer and covered his boy's body with his own.

Hoss and Joe closed in around the helpless pair. A bullet hit the ground between them. They returned fire and two of the Flynn boys dropped to the ground. A sudden groan came from Hoss as a shot tore through the muscle of his upper arm. Joe's quick reactions brought Jack Flynn to his knees. The oldest Flynn son dropped his gun and soon followed it.

In the confusion of the fight, both Hoss and Joe had lost sight of Caleb Flynn. When they looked around, they saw that he had circled to the left and was moving toward their father and brother. Ben saw him too and clutched Adam's still body closer to his own, bringing a soft moan from the injured man. Joe was about to fire when a warning shout stopped him.

"Stop right where you are, Flynn." Roy Coffee's voice rang above the sounds of the storm. He walked toward the man, gun ready to fire. Flynn stopped and looked at the sheriff. Without a word, he turned back and kept moving toward the two helpless figures in the street. A single gunshot caused Flynn's body to buck but he kept moving forward. Flynn aimed his gun for the last time but before he could fire, the sheriff ended his life.

All movement seemed to cease. The only sounds were those of the elements that churned about them. Finally, Joe pulled himself off the ground and knelt beside Hoss. "You alright?" he asked.

"Yeah, I'm fine." Joe helped Hoss struggle to his feet. "But Pa and Adam—?"

Joe saw the raw pain in Hoss' eyes and he took a deep breath, trying to control his own emotions. "Come on."

Roy was already at Ben's side. "You alright Ben? You been hit?"

Ben stared back with unseeing eyes, as if unable to comprehend his friend's question. He looked away from Roy then turned to Hoss and Joe. They were met with the same look of confusion in the deep brown eyes.

A crowd started to gather around the little group kneeling in the mud. "Come on Pa, let's get Adam outta the street," Hoss offered.

Ben loosened his grip and Adam's head fell away from his father's chest. Ben raised a hand and tried to push the wet curls back into place. "Yes, yes—Paul will help him." Roy got up and signaled for some men to pick Adam up and take him to the doctor's house. Ben relinquished his hold and stood up. Joe and Hoss walked on either side of their father as the small procession moved to the little house at the edge of town.

Adam was placed on the doctor's table. The men who had carried him in tipped their hats and mumbled words of regret to the Cartwright family. Ben stood at Adam's side trying not to see the blood as it turned his son's shirt more red than white. Joe brought him a chair. "Why don't you sit down, Pa?"

Paul Martin bustled into the room, his hair uncombed and shirt half tucked in. Roy had gotten him out of bed. He ignored the Cartwrights. With eyes only for his patient, he muttered, "Young fool! I told him! Why wouldn't he listen?" He held the stethoscope to Adam's chest and closed his eyes in concentration. Placing the instrument aside, he ripped the red and white shirt open. Without looking up, he said, "Please leave. I'll come to you when I can." Ben started to protest but Paul ignored him.

Hoss stepped forward. "Come on, Pa—come wait with us."

Ben noticed the blood stained handkerchief that circled Hoss' arm. "Hoss, your arm—"

"It's ok, Pa. Nothin to worry about. We need to leave and let the doctor take care of Adam." Hoss took his father's arm and started to guide him from the room.

Paul looked up from his instruments. "Is the bullet still in Hoss?"

"No doc, it went right on through. I can wait. Just take care of my brother, please." He continued to usher Ben from the room, trying to control the tears that swam before his eyes. Roy followed them out.

Paul called Joe. "Take some clean bandages and wash Hoss' arm then bind it up. I'll see to him later." Joe did as he was told but hesitated before he left. His pleading eyes met the doctor's.

"I don't know, Joe." Paul's frustration was now sadness. "I just don't know."

IT SEEMED LIKE hours since Joe had shut the door to the Doctor's surgery. Roy had left early on to take care of the grim task of seeing to the bodies that littered Virginia City's main street. Ben and Joe had done what they could for Hoss' arm. But Hoss refused anything for pain saying he needed to be ready in case Adam needed him.

Ben broke the silence, his worry becoming anger. "All this death—an entire family wiped out. And for what—revenge?" Ben got up and started to pace. "What a waste! What a senseless, useless, damnable waste!" He looked at his two younger sons. "And your brother was caught up in Caleb Flynn's madness." Ben raised his fist and pounded the wall. "I want my son to live!" he shouted.

Joe stood in front of his father and placed both hands on his shoulders. "Come on Pa," he said, his voice a soft whisper. "Come sit down."

Once Ben was seated again, Joe said, "Adam's in there because of me. I know he called Hatcher out because he was afraid Flynn would hurt me." Joe's face mirrored his devastation. "I could've taken care of myself. Why did he do it?"

It was Hoss who answered. "I know you didn't ask him to Joe— you didn't have to. Adam can't help who he is and part of him will always take care of us, whether we like it or not. He just can't help himself."

The three men became silent, each lost in his own thoughts.

PAUL MARTIN SAT at Adam's side. Every little while he would reach up to feel the young man's pulse. The surgery had been long and arduous. The single bullet had splintered on impact. From what the doctor could tell, Adam must have stepped sideways at the last moment. The fragments bounced along his ribs, some penetrating deeply, some not. The greatest damage from the injury was blood loss and it would be awhile before his patient stabilized. Adam came round after the surgery fairly quickly. Paul encouraged small sips of salted water followed by plain water but not too much. Experience had taught him that pushing fluids at this point would only result in them coming back up.

He knew Ben and the boys were suffering, not knowing about Adam's condition but he felt it more merciful to say something other than "I'm not sure", "I don't know yet" or "we'll have to wait". His thoughts were interrupted by a prolonged groan followed by a weak cough. "Pa," was pushed out on a thin breath.

"It's me, Adam—Paul. I'll get your family in a few minutes." The doctor once more reached for his patient's wrist.

"How bad?" Adam asked.

"Some damage, Adam, but not too much. You've lost a lot of blood." Paul answered.

"I didn't know in the dream." Adam stopped and closed his eyes against the pain and exhaustion. "I didn't know if I lived or not."

"Dream—what dream?" Paul asked but his patient had slipped into sleep once more.

Paul rolled down his sleeves and walked to the door. The three men came to their feet but before anyone could ask, Paul said, "Between the injury and the surgery, he's lost a lot of blood. It'll take his body some time to replenish it. I want to keep him here so I can watch him."

"Then he'll be alright?" Ben asked.

"I think so Ben. He's sleeping and that's what his body needs most. You and the boys can go on in." Paul led the way into the surgery. "Come and sit down Hoss. Let me look at that arm." Paul cleaned and re-bandaged Hoss' arm. "That's gonna hurt some. Joe, you make sure he takes something for pain so he can sleep. The doctor handed Joe a small envelope.

"I'll sit with Adam," Ben said as he took Paul's chair at the side of the table. "Why don't you boys go get a room? That way, you can rest for awhile."

Joe knew if he stayed there would be no way he'd get Hoss to leave. "Come on Hoss, let's do like Pa says. We can come back in a little while." Hoss frowned at him then looked back at his older brother.

Paul smiled at Hoss and said, "I really think he'll be ok. I promise to get you if anything changes."

Hoss walked to Adam's side "You just be here when I get back," he whispered than turned toward the door.

Joe felt his throat close as he tried to say something. Instead he squeezed his oldest brother's hand than followed Hoss.

THE RAIN'S INTENSITY had dwindled to a light drizzle. The sun had already gone down and the night sounds from town were muffled by the distance of the doctor's house from Virginia City's main street. Ben continued to sit at his son's side, offering liquids each time he awoke. Adam's pulse slowed and became stronger. Finally, Paul felt safe in going upstairs to rest with a promise that Ben would wake him with any concerns.

Adam's eyes opened and he found the familiar eyes of his father looking back at him. His normally rich, strong voice was weak and thin as he said, "I'm sorry, Pa."

"Sorry—what have you got to be sorry for, son?" Ben leaned closer to hear Adam's response.

"I know you don't agree—" Adam stopped to catch his breath. "The fight with Hatcher..."

"I'd be lying if I said I approved of your being in a gunfight but I know why you did it." Ben shifted in his chair. "Caleb must have been mad at the end. He didn't care if he died as long as he took you with him. And I have no doubt that he would have gone after Joseph again if you hadn't intervened."

"Did any of them—?" Adam wanted to know if any of the Flynns had survived.

Ben hesitated to tell his son the truth but he knew he had to. "No, they're all gone."

Adam squeezed his eyes shut and turned his face away from his father. Besides exhausted and weak, he suddenly felt empty. What trick of fate had led to an entire family being wiped out? And what part had he played in the tragedy?

Ben thought his son had drifted off to sleep again so he was surprised when he heard Adam say, "Pa, do you believe in premonitions?"

"Premonitions?" Ben repeated. "Well, I never gave it much thought son. Is this about your dream?" Adam gave him a quizzical look.

"Don't blame your brother. He assumed you'd told me." Ben thought for a moment. "It must have seemed as if you had lived it over and over again and then it came true."

'Yes, but I never knew how it ended, not really. I just assumed—well it doesn't matter now." Adam was sure he'd been witnessing his own death but he wouldn't voice that to his father. The man had been through enough. Besides, what did it matter now? "Tired—think I'll just sleep."

Ben kept a vigil over his firstborn, giving thanks that some higher power had intervened on his boy's behalf. The shadow of death had disappeared with the light of faith.

IT HAD BEEN about a week since the storm had bled the moisture out of the heavy air. Paul Martin was glad to see the grass turning back into the deep greens of late summer again. He watched as the wagon carrying Adam home faded into the distance. The doctor was confident that all his patient needed now was the healing touch of time.

Paul let the curtain fall and walked into the small kitchen. The cook stove burned low but enough to ignite the envelope that he dropped into the burner. He watched as the flames curled around the Last Will and Testament of Adam Cartwright then turned it into ashes.

My Journal Age 12 by Joe Cartwright

by Kaci

Dear Journal,

I'm in love with the prettiest girl in the world. She has blonde hair and blue eyes and she sways when she walks. *I could look at her all day.* Today in school I helped her pick up her books when she dropped them and then she smiled at me and I felt all strange inside. I want to ask her to the picnic on Founder's Day but I haven't told Pa yet. Oh...I know I smile and Pa will melt but sometimes Adam sticks his nose into my business. It sure would be easier if'n it was just Hoss and Pa.

Dear Journal,

It was the best day of my life! I took Annie to the picnic and we walked around *(that was kind of boring)* but then she started telling me about her father and how he was a gambler and he made lots of money and how her father will teach me how to play poker! I can't wait to go to her house, of course, I'm not telling Pa about the poker lessons.

Dear Journal,

Wow! Her father was great, he played for hours with me and even Annie played. I had the best time of my life! He talked about riverboats and casinos and something called "dens."

Anyway, we laughed and had the best time in the world! I'm going to teach Hoss, he knows how to play but Mr. Andrews taught me a few neat tricks with the cards, he said it was called palming.

Dear Journal,

Today, I showed Hoss how to play better and he got real huffy with me. I just don't understand Hoss sometimes, he's my best friend but sometimes he acts like Adam. He said I shouldn't be playing cards at my age and that Pa would tan my hide if'n he found out about it. I tried to explain that Annie's father taught me, but he wouldn't listen to me, but he gave me a hug and told me to be good.

Dear Journal,

Annie ignored me today and left with Seth Pruitt to walk home. She's been real testy lately. I don't understand girls. I want her to like me, but she says that I'm just not old enough for her, but we're the same age! I felt as if my heart was going to break when she smiled at Seth like that. I thought that was my special smile...

why is she doing that? I don't understand women...that's what Adam always says after he breaks up with someone, who knew that Adam and I would have the same woman problems?

Dear Journal,

It's been over a month since I wrote in you and I have a tale to tell you! Well, there was a big dust up with Annie and Seth. We had a big fight in the schoolyard and Seth being a year older and thirty pounds heavier won that fight. Now I don't hold it against him but I wish he hadn't given me a black eye because Pa wasn't best pleased about it. Hoss asked me what happened and I had to shade the truth the little, but he said he understood about women troubles and I was starting on the long road to perdition. *What is perdition?* I'm going to ask Adam, because if'n anyone would know, it would be him.

After the fight, Annie ran over to Seth and gave him a kiss on the cheek and I just stood there like an idiot and tried not to cry. Oh...I wasn't hurt that bad, just a few good bruises but inside I hurt like the dickens. She kissed him and held his hand and gazed at him like he was a god or something. I want her so bad to smile at me. I stomped off and got my horse and rode home, thinking up ways to get even with old Seth. I'm not saying revenge is sweet, but I was going to teach him a lesson in manners, a lesson not to take another fellow's girl.

So, it was a few days later and I set up Seth to take the fall. I feel real bad now that I did that but I just wasn't thinking straight then, I guess. I pretended to Seth's Pa that I was hurt real bad in the fight and I was going to tell my Pa and he was going to get Sheriff Coffee for Seth beating me up. Well, Seth's Pa lit into him good. I shouldn't have done that, but his Pa has forbidden Seth to the leave his yard for a month. I knew I could get Annie to like me again in a month.

Sure enough, as soon as Seth stopped coming around, Annie was hugging and kissing me again. I sure do like that. We have been getting a little...well...but I'm sure Adam did that too. He told me once that his first love was his best love. So, I'm not going to stop kissing her but sometimes she scares me. I know that sounds funny, but she is so....hot. I don't mean hot in heat...wait...yes I do. Sometimes I feel like I'm burning up...and then she puts her hands all over me and I think I'm going to burst into flames. That scares me plenty. I tried to talk to Hoss but he didn't understand what I was talking about, so I decided to talk to Adam instead, he must know what is happening to me.

I worked up the courage and approached Adam carefully. You have to sneak up on him, he's tricky like. Finally, Pa and Hoss went to bed and so I knocked softly on Adam's door. He told me to come in but looked surprised to see me at that time of night.

"Little Joe, what's the matter? Are you sick?" Well, he was bound to ask me that cause I never go to Adam for anything if I can help it...but this is an emergency. *I'm kinda of afraid of burning up.*

"No, I'm not sick. I...I want to ask you a question." At the look on his face I added, "I mean it's just between you an me." Now old Adam is quicker on the uptake than Hoss and Pa, so I could see he was thinking real hard.

"You want to ask me a question?" At my nod, he motioned me to the chair in his room. "Okay, ask the question then you get to bed."

Nothing makes a guy feel worse that sitting on a hard chair asking questions. So, I stood up and walked around his room looking at his things. I sneaked a peak at him but then I dropped my eyes because Adam' can stare at you like a hawk or something.

"Joe, ask me the question or go to bed." Well, that is Adam in a nutshell...he has no finer feelings for his brother's problems.

Standing still and wringing my hands I finally got the question out. "Adam, I'm in love...but I think something is wrong with me, can you help me?"

Adam sat there like a lump on a log and I was beginning to

worry I had gone to the wrong Cartwright, when he says, "You're in love?"

I shook my head yes.

"Hmm...well, Little Joe...I guess that you're about the right age to fall in love." Adam stuck right there and I could see the hesitation on his face. "It's completely normal to fall for a nice little girl at school."

Why...why did I come in to Adam? He just don't get it and I didn't want to say it out loud.

At my silence he frowned then held the bridge of his nose...I usually want to laugh when he does that cause you can just see old Adam's thoughts turning around in that brain of his, but this time I was hoping that he realized my problem.

"Look, Joe, every boy at sometime falls for the opposite sex." When my eyes grew large at the term sex...he restated the sentence. "I mean every boy falls for girls. That is completely normal. You must know this!" Adam was now sounding a little unsure of himself which didn't help me at all.

All right, I guess Adam ain't as smart as I thought. I was going to have to say it. "Adam...that's not my problem. I mean it is but it ain't."

"Isn't Joe, say isn't."

Sighing, I turned to go back to my room, when I felt his hand on my shoulder, he led me to sit down on the bed. "You're cold." He covered me up then said softly. "Just tell me Little Joe, I'm not a mind reader."

"I...I get hot," I whispered quietly.

"You're hot?" Adam started to pull the covers off me but my hands were clenched on them. "Not hot with covers."

Adam looked deep into my eyes and then I saw he finally got it! *Whew, it took long enough.*

"You mean you and a girl are..." Adam stopped, looking afraid to say it. "Joe, you're not doing anything bad are you?"

At my nod of yes...I thought for sure Adam was going to faint. But, we Cartwright's are made of sterner stuff than that and old

Adam' says, "You mean you're making love to a girl?"

I again nodded yes, and Adam's eyes grew three sizes, I tell you true, Journal. He looked like that time that Hoss had pole axed him with a right hook.

"I can't help it Adam, she is all over me, and I can't think when I'm with her." I spilled my guts without stopping, it finally came tumbling out. "I don't like this feeling...it's like I'm going to burst into flames!" I started to cry and he gathered me into his arms.

"Shh...Little Joe." Patting me on the back he finally laid me down on the bed. "You mean you're...you're hot from her kissing you?"

"Yeah...what did you think I meant?" I looked at Adam trying to read his thoughts, but he looked like his face got all red.

"Nothing...nothing." Wiping is forehead he forged ahead. "Joe, has Pa talked to you about the facts of life?"

"Yep, he says that the facts of life are day to day living and we must all try our best to get through the days of our lives." I repeated my Pa's exact words.

Sighing, Adam hid his face, then started to talk to me about his facts of life. I turned as red as Adam had...and I couldn't look at his face when he was through. I'm not sure he was telling me the truth...but Adam hardly ever lies except when he has to because of Pa.

"So, when you feel all hot like that, it's a warning to slow down, and get a grip on your feelings. At your age you shouldn't even be having feelings like that." At my scared look, he tried again. "I mean I know you are...but you're just a little boy, Joe. Give yourself time to grow up and leave Annie alone. I'm sure you don't want to have this talk with Pa."

Just the thought of this conversation with Pa broke me out in a sweat. "No, Adam I don't want that!" Adam reached for his handkerchief and wiped my eyes and told me to blow my nose. "Now, you go on to bed, Joe. Everything will be fine...but you must stop kissing Annie, you understand me?"

At my nod he pulled the covers off me and swatted my bottom, (*why do grown ups do that?*) and sent me to bed with a few deep thoughts. I never realized all that went on between men and women, and I was going to keep an eye out for such behavior.

Well, Journal...I guess that's all I have to say right now, but I'll keep you informed about my love life...because I know Adam said to stop kissing Annie...but I don't think I will. I will stop before getting real hot though, because Adam says it's is like bursting into flames when men do that...hmm...*it must not be that bad though,* or men would quit having children. I'm going to ask Seth, after all he must be over his mad by now...and he might not know these things, and I have to tell Mitch and...

Joe Cartwright
Age 12
1854

Invincible

by southplains

He battled back to consciousness, struggling against the pounding pain ebbing against him, and Adam's voice, low and rough, was the first thing he heard. Joe felt the soft brush of Adam's lips as his brother's harsh whisper sounded against his ear. The length of Adam's body lay against his, rigid and tense. Beyond that, all Joe knew was that something was ripping, tearing at his side, and he tossed his head in a strained attempt to escape it.

"Stay still! Damn it, Joe, stop fighting me..."

Joe's eyes were shut, but he could hear the desperation in Adam's voice.

"They're right on top of us, boy. For God's sake, don't move, and don't make a sound."

The anxiety in his brother's voice broke through enough for Joe to do as he was asked; he stopped struggling and lay still. He tried to open his eyes, but the effort to do so remained beyond him; he concentrated instead on trying to gather his wits enough to figure out what was going on.

"Don't move," Adam repeated, and this time his voice was so hushed that Joe wouldn't have heard it at all if his brother's mouth hadn't been pressed against his ear.

Adam was frightened; the sound of his fear washed over Joe, chilling him. The very thought that Adam was scared was enough to scare him, too, and it made him try harder to concentrate on what Adam was telling him. But the fire in his side made it hard to listen and hard to think. The pain of that fire was coming in waves, stronger and stronger now that he was awake, drowning out his thoughts, drowning out Adam's urgent whispers. A soft moan moved up in his throat and he tried to swallow it but it came out anyway, and as it did he felt Adam's fingers pressing hard over his mouth.

Somewhere in the back of his mind Joe wondered why his brother's fingers were so cold.

The need for air gradually took precedence over the pain in Joe's side, and he strained to open his eyes. When he did, Adam's eyes were not more than a hand's breadth away, their normal color of moss-laced whiskey now darkened with fear, and they were pinned on Joe's. Seeing that fear drew Joe's mind away from his own pain enough to jerk himself into further awareness of his surroundings.

They're right on top of us.

Danger was all around them. Joe no longer needed Adam to tell him so. He could smell it; he could taste it. He fought to remember what had happened even as he began to struggle out from under Adam's hand. Adam saw the lucidity come back into him, and slowly eased his hand away from Joe's mouth and raised one finger to his own lips in a hushing gesture.

Joe gave a tight nod, and when he did his cheek rubbed against cold, damp earth; the cold dampness enveloped him and pressed tight against his back. A slab of rock hovered inches above his head. Confusion fluttered at the edges of his brain; from what he could tell, which wasn't much, he was crammed into some sort of hole in the ground alongside his brother. He looked past Adam's shoulder and saw a thick wall of weeds and rushes, and through the weeds he could see the sparkle of sunlight on water.

The lake. The two of them were shoved up under a shallow undercut in the rock at the lake's edge, but for the life of him he couldn't remember how they'd gotten here. He turned his gaze back upon Adam; his brother was listening, listening hard, his eyes lifted upwards as though straining to see through the rock which lay so close over their faces. Adam's eyes flickered back to Joe, and the fact that fear still claimed them made Joe's stomach coil in upon itself.

The clawing at Joe's right side grew more insistent, and he carefully pressed his hand against the searing ache. His fingers met with warm wetness, and something else—an arrow shaft, broken off and protruding through his skin.

A fresh wave of pain moved through him, and with it, remembrance.

They'd been driving a freight wagon down through one of the most remote parts of the northwest section of the ranch, he and Adam, on their way back from a high outpost that was being set up as a new logging camp. The camp was due to begin operation early next week, and Pa had given them orders to haul in a load of supplies so that all would be in readiness by the time the logging crew arrived.

They'd arrived at the camp without mishap, unloaded the wagon and headed for home in good time.

"We'll be there before the sun sets," Adam had predicted, and Joe had been glad of it. The chill in the air would only increase once the sun set.

Not that the ride home wouldn't still be chilly, sun or no sun, and it had nothing to do with the coolness of the autumn breeze. The words Adam spoke about getting home were the first either of them had spoken since they'd left home that morning. They'd been at odds with each other all week, ever since they'd gone out to Ted Hannigan's place to have a look at a chestnut stud Ted had for sale. Joe was determined to have the horse, Adam had been against it, and the disagreement had escalated until they were both angry and frustrated with each other.

They'd argued all the way home from Hannigan's ranch that day, and it hadn't helped Joe's temper when Ben had sided with Adam that night at the supper table.

"Perhaps it's best that we rely on Adam's instincts on this, Joe," Pa had said gently. "Surely you don't deny that your brother has a lot of experience when it comes to dealing with horseflesh?"

Joe looked across the table at Adam, who let one dark brow rise as though only mildly curious as to what his younger brother's response would be. Joe couldn't help rolling his eyes as he looked back at Ben. "Well, no, Pa, of course I don't deny it. I know Adam knows a good horse when he sees one; that's why I can't believe he's being such a hard-head about this one. You should see the chest on this stud, Pa. He's—"

"Ted is selling him for a reason, Joe," Adam broke in. "He's wild and unmanageable—a rogue animal that probably should've been gelded long ago." Adam gave a pointed look to Pa. "After the horse broke Ted's foreman's leg last week, Ted decided to get rid of him before somebody got killed."

Ben's gaze sharpened. "Oh?"

The tone of that single syllable didn't bode well for Joe's argument, and he knew it. He looked to Hoss for support, but Hoss offered only a tiny, sympathetic smile and went on chewing his steak.

Joe sighed. He turned back to Pa, trying to keep the desperation out of his voice. "So he's high spirited. I'll give you that. But it doesn't change the fact that his conformation is what we need to match up with our mares. I admit he needs some work—"

"Work?" Adam spat. "I've told you before, Joe, no amount of work is going to turn that horse around. For Pete's sake, he's not even halter broke; that's what the foreman was trying to accomplish when he got his leg stomped."

"Why don't you let me worry about that?" Joe shot back. "You may be a decent judge of horseflesh, but I can ride anything you can't—"

"This isn't about your riding abilities!" Adam roared. "It's about the best way to improve our herd and you're not—"

Joe's voice rose to match his brother's. "He's going to be used for breeding, anyway. We don't need to be able to ride him."

"Breeder or not, you know every animal on this ranch has to pull its own weight. We have no need for a horse that can't work, regardless of its bloodlines."

"You know what? I'm sick of always having to bow down to your opinion," Joe shouted. "You decided against that animal the instant I said we needed it."

"I decided against that animal the instant I found out what he's capable of!" Adam bellowed.

They continued to try to out shout each other until Pa banged his fist down on the table and thundered, "Enough!"

Silence reigned as they both shut their mouths but continued to glare at each other. Pa took a deep breath to get his own temper under control and gave a hard look to both his sons.

"Now. This conversation will be conducted in a civil tone or not at all," he warned.

"That won't be difficult," Adam said, and wiped his mouth with his napkin. "As far as I'm concerned, the conversation is over. If you'll excuse me, Pa, I think I'll turn in early."

Ben drew his mouth into a thin line, then nodded and murmured an assent. As Adam climbed the stairs, Joe's cheeks flushed with furious heat; he felt his father's eyes on him, but he turned his attention to his plate and proceeded to push his potatoes around with his fork.

"Joe."

Reluctantly, Joe raised his eyes. Pa rested his chin on steepled fingers and sighed. "Joe, this horse—"

But like Adam, Joe found he had no taste for further talk that night. Why bother? The decision had been made. "I know, Pa. Adam knows horses. You told me." Abruptly he dropped his fork with a clatter onto his plate and shoved his chair back. "Excuse me. I've got some work to finish in the barn," he muttered and rose and headed for the door, slamming it behind him and leaving Hoss and Ben staring soberly over the table at each other.

Despite Adam's claim to the contrary, the conversation was far from over. The remainder of the week was spent with Joe and Adam throwing dark looks and even an occasional veiled insult at each other whenever Pa wasn't near enough to hear. Meals were spent either in sullen silence or tense arguments, and those arguments always circled back to Hannigan's stud.

"Ain't no horse worth all this belly-achin'," Hoss had finally grumbled one evening after supper, and had stomped up the stairs to bed, leaving the two of them shamefaced but each still unwilling to give in.

Pa, too, had finally had enough. He'd decided that the two of them would make the supply run up to the new logging camp, and Joe wondered if he did it as much to get a day's peace as he did out of hopes that his oldest and youngest sons would come to terms with each other.

Joe didn't care what his father's reasons were for sending them off together; it wasn't going to change how he felt. Adam was wrong about Hannigan's big chestnut horse. It was as simple as that. Joe knew it, and nothing would change his mind, even if— or maybe even especially if—Pa was inclined to lean toward Adam's decision on the matter.

So the horse was a little bad-tempered. Joe was convinced he could gradually work it out of the animal if given half a chance, but both his brother and his father refused to believe in him enough to let him even try. That fact rubbed against him like an ill-fitting saddle, and he found himself as angry at Pa as he was at Adam.

Being sent off in exile with Adam was like rubbing salt in the wound.

If Pa had hoped that they'd talk things over on the long drive to the camp and back, he'd been sorely mistaken. All day long they'd both taken considerable pains to keep from acknowledging one another, and while unloading the wagon, Adam had tossed a sack of oats at Joe with what could easily be construed as unnecessary force. Joe had retaliated by "accidentally" dropping an armload of shovels across the toe of his brother's boot.

Despite themselves, they'd eventually gotten the job done. They were both so worn out that when it came time to share a wagon seat for the ride home they didn't even mind overly much. They still weren't speaking, however, and Adam's comment about making it home before the sun set was more a thought spoken aloud than it was any attempt at making conversation with his brother.

As it turned out, Adam's prediction about making it home had been incorrect, and if circumstances had been different Joe would have gleefully taken the opportunity to tell him so.

This was one time, though, when Joe regretted the fact that his brother had been mistaken. They hadn't made it home at all; in fact, they had still been many long miles from home when a screaming band of Paiutes had come from out of nowhere, painted for war and bearing down on them with astonishing abruptness. The Indians had quickly cut off the wagon trail in front and behind, and when they'd opened fire Joe and Adam had been forced to abandon the team and dash for cover into the thick forest growth surrounding them.

They'd run for what seemed like miles with the warriors crashing through the trees behind them. At one point they'd managed to lose their pursuers by doubling back on their own trail, but the ruse hadn't worked for long. They'd heard the change in tone in the whoops ringing up through the trees and knew they'd been discovered once more, and they'd turned to run westward toward the lake, firing behind them as they ran.

Joe had been firing over his shoulder when he saw one of the braves draw back on his bow. He turned and wrenched his body to the side, hoping to avoid the arrow, and for a moment he thought he'd succeeded. But the next thing he knew he was lying on his back with an arrow sticking out of him, able to do little more than gasp for air. The Indians' cries grew closer, and he knew he was about to die.

Then Adam was there, firing back at the nearest braves and cutting them down one by one. He moved more quickly than Joe, by now only half-conscious, could follow with his eyes, quickly snapping the arrow shaft off and lifting Joe to his feet. He half-supported, half-dragged his brother through pines and brush and rocks; it was all Joe could do to stay on his feet.

That was all. The sound of Adam's whispers in his ear was the next thing Joe had been aware of. And now here they were, huddled under the earth together like a couple of scared rabbits.

He followed Adam's gaze back up toward the rock. The guttural sounds of the Indians' conversation drifted down to them. A scattering of dirt rained down behind the opening at Adam's back; Adam moved nothing but his eyes, catching and holding Joe's as they both held their breath.

They waited. The cold from the wet earth was seeping through Joe's clothes, and he started to shiver. Carefully, Adam passed his arm around him and pulled him closer. The warmth of his brother's body helped somewhat, even though Adam was shivering, too.

There was another rain of pebbles over the ledge above their heads. Over Adam's shoulder, Joe watched a moccasined foot step down into the mud. Another moccasin joined the first, then another, then three more. A quick glance at Adam's face told Joe that his brother knew they were there, even though Adam was faced away from them and couldn't see them. Joe again turned his gaze past his brother...no more than a couple of feet away the moccasins were milling through the mud, turning around, facing them...

If they were discovered now, there would be no escape. They'd be cut down like rats in a hole. *Don't move*, Adam's eyes warned, his throat working, but their bodies refused to acknowledge the need for absolute motionlessness and continued to tremble.

The warriors were talking in low, grunting voices, occasionally calling back to the Indians still further up the slope. They moved closer, the toe of one's foot mere inches from Adam. Joe let his eyes fall shut; if the sharp bite of a tomahawk was about to enter his brother's back, he didn't want to see it.

They waited, and waited some more, and the pain in Joe's side increased steadily, growing stronger and stronger in great rushing waves until finally it overrode even his fear. He could feel the thump of Adam's heart beating against his chest, and his own heartbeat joined into perfect unison with it. He felt himself begin to lose his grip on consciousness, and as he began to slide back into darkness, the irony of it struck him; after a lifetime of fighting his oldest brother's lead, even his body knew enough to fall into step with him as they both got ready to die.

"JOE, COME ON. Open your eyes."

Joe groaned. A bitingly cold autumn morning, the kind of day when all he wanted was to lie in bed a little longer, and here was Adam making a perfect pest of himself. Joe turned his face away from the sound of his brother's voice. It was too cold to get up yet, anyway—and where had his blankets gone? He was shaking from the cold.

"Joe. I need you to wake up." Adam again, his voice sharper and more demanding. Joe sighed, recognizing the determination in that voice. Adam wouldn't leave until Joe did as he was asked. He tried to open his eyes, but the lids felt weighted. He didn't feel so good, either.

Just a few more minutes of shut-eye, Adam. Then I promise I'll get up.

But it was no good. Adam grasped Joe's chin with his fingers, shaking his head back and forth, and called his name again. Joe tested the weight of his eyelids again and decided he could ignore his brother's calls whether he was yanking his chin around or not; he began to slip back underneath the comforting blanket of sleep.

Adam slapped his cheek, and the shock of it was finally enough to rouse Joe. He forced his eyes open, already halfway angry. Adam's face was hovering over him, looking absurdly relieved, and Joe's anger seeped away with the last vestiges of sleep.

Then the pain hit him again, and with it came the full-blown knowledge that it wasn't morning, and he definitely wasn't in bed in his room. No, he was lying on his back in the mud beside the chilly November waters of the lake. The sun, shining with empty promise, was rapidly moving toward its downhill slide into the mountains, and Joe was miserable, cold and hurting.

"Joe, do you think you can walk? We've got to go. They haven't given up; they'll be back," Adam was saying, his teeth chattering together, and Joe noticed for the first time that his brother was smeared with mud. He wondered if he looked as bad, and decided he probably did.

Could he walk? He wasn't sure. He tried to sit up, jerking in a breath at the pain in his side. He looked down and pulled his jacket back; along with the mud, his side was smeared with blood, both dry and crusted and wet and warm, but the arrow shaft was gone. Beneath his shirt his neckerchief lay padded against the wound, already so soaked that it was no longer absorbing any blood.

"I went after the arrowhead while you were still out," Adam explained. He held up an apologetic hand. "Lousy conditions, but I wasn't sure when we'd get another chance, and you couldn't go on with it still in there."

Joe sighed and nodded. It didn't feel any less painful, but at least he knew the arrowhead wasn't still inside causing more damage.

He felt for his gun; it wasn't there. Adam saw the movement.

"Your gun's back on the trail with mine. Decided we didn't need the extra weight since we didn't have any more ammunition. I shot up what we had."

Dismay settled in the pit of Joe's stomach, but he simply nodded and took Adam's outstretched hand, biting back a curse as his brother helped him to his feet. He leaned heavily on Adam, and was caught by surprise when his brother staggered beneath his weight.

"Adam?" Joe took in Adam's pale face and for a moment he was afraid his brother would fall. "Adam, what's wrong?"

"Nothing's wrong. I'm just skittish after almost having my scalp lifted. Let's go."

Joe dug in his heels to keep Adam from moving him along. "You don't look so good."

Adam's laugh was short and sharp. "There's a true case of the pot calling the kettle black. I'm fine. Now let's go!" He rolled his eyes in irritation when Joe stuck his chin out in stubborn determination and eyed him suspiciously.

"Something's wrong." He looked Adam up and down, and motioned toward the neckerchief tied around Adam's upper thigh. "What's that?"

"Nothing." Adam tugged at Joe's arm, but Joe held his ground and Adam sighed. "Fine. If it will get you moving, I'll tell you. While I was in the middle of dragging your dead weight to the lake, one of those braves caught up to us."

Joe stared at him. "And what happened?"

Adam shrugged and bent to pull a wicked-looking knife from his boot. He held it up for Joe to see, then replaced the knife and straightened. "At least we got a weapon out of it. Let's go."

A knife. Joe looked pointedly at the smear of blood on Adam's pants. "How bad is it?"

Adam looked at Joe and sighed impatiently. "Not bad. I'm still here. He's not. Now, come on."

Joe started to argue, but stopped himself. Adam's face had taken on that hard look that meant a man could argue all day long if he wanted; it still wouldn't do any good. Adam had said all he was going to. Besides, he spoke the truth. If they were going to live, they had to move.

Joe looked down at the sodden stretch of shoreline as Adam pushed him forward. It was easy to see where Adam had dragged him away from the hole after the Indians had left; a swath of weeds crushed into the mud clearly led back to where they had lain hidden.

Joe shook his head, staring at the crevice under the rock shelf. "How the heck did you get us both in that little bitty hole?"

Adam flashed him a grin. "It wasn't easy. Good thing it was you and not Hoss I had to squash in there, or we'd never have fit."

Joe laughed, and was caught by surprise. After days of glowering at his brother, being able to laugh with him was oddly freeing. He cut the laugh off short, both because of the physical pain the action caused and because he was suddenly uncomfortable. Hannigan's horse suddenly seemed a million miles away, but their argument over it was still tight under Joe's skin. It was just one more disagreement among hundreds where Joe felt Adam had emerged triumphant and his own opinion had been dismissed as if he were nothing more than an untried greenhorn.

The significance of the dispute had paled in light of the day's events, and yet Joe couldn't quite bring himself to let go of it. His stinging pride wouldn't let him.

He turned his attention toward hobbling along at Adam's side, throwing a quick glance back at the hole as they went. He didn't know how Adam had managed to get the two of them to the lake's edge and into that hollow, but he knew it had to have cost Adam something. Even with his own injury making his progress stiff and sluggish, he could feel the jerkiness of Adam's movements, and knew his brother was hurting regardless of his attempts to hide it.

They stumbled through the trees for almost an hour, moving as fast as they could. Adam was soon limping, and the limp was quickly growing more pronounced. After awhile, Joe wasn't sure who was supporting whom. He grimaced as they crashed against a young sapling, snapping off one of the branches.

"We're leaving a trail a drunk could follow," he muttered, gesturing at the broken branch and the ruby droplets of blood sparkling on the ground behind them, and Adam nodded, leaning against him and breathing heavily. Joe stared at the paleness of his brother's face, starkly white in the shadow of the heavy pine growth. "Adam, you look...let's stop," he said abruptly, suddenly more afraid than ever and not sure why.

"We can't. If we stop they're going to catch us. We've got to keep moving." Adam jerked his arm from Joe's grasp and lurched forward—and fell face forward onto the thick bed of pine needles carpeting the forest floor.

He didn't move again.

"Adam!" Joe staggered forward and dropped to the ground beside him. The smear of blood on Adam's leg had grown into a dark, wet stain that even now was spreading across the side of his left thigh. Joe placed his hand against the stain, and his palm came back red with blood, his hand shaking as he stared at it.

He swore softly and bent over Adam's leg. The neckerchief Adam had tied over the wound had loosened. There was a tear in the center of the blood-drenched fabric of Adam's pants leg, and Joe pulled at the edges of the tear, ripping it further apart. He sat back in dismay at what was revealed.

"My God, Adam," he whispered. A three-inch cut, dangerously deep and bleeding freely, gaped up at him like a leering beast.

The implications had Joe reeling. They were in more trouble than they could handle, both of them hurt and bleeding, pinned between a band of scalp-seeking Paiutes and the oncoming chill of what was sure to be a desperate night.

His own pain clawed up his side again, but he pushed it back down, trying to keep his head clear. He looked back again at the trail they'd left; it was only through sheer luck or God's good mercy that they hadn't been found already. Apparently the Paiutes had been searching in all the wrong places, but it was only a matter of time before they came across such a glaringly obvious trail.

When he looked back at Adam's still face, Joe's priorities began to fall into place through sheer hard need. If he didn't get the bleeding stopped, his brother wouldn't last long enough for the Indians to find.

Hands shaking with cold and pain and fear, he hurried to untie the neckerchief from Adam's leg and re-knotted it, thrusting a stick through the knot in order to twist and tighten it further until the fabric stretched tightly just above the stab wound. Joe gave a relieved sigh as the flow of blood began to ebb. Adam never moved.

Joe froze as he heard a distant shout, very distant, drift from somewhere back toward the lake. The Paiutes. They were back, and unless he missed his guess, they'd just discovered Adam's hole at the lakeside.

"Figuring out how you tricked them isn't likely to improve their disposition any," he murmured as though Adam could hear him. "What do we do now, brother?" But of course Adam couldn't hear him.

Joe didn't know how, but they had to hide again. They sure wouldn't be able to run.

He stood up to more carefully survey their surroundings. The pine timber was heavy here, interspersed with a few slender aspens and wagon-sized boulders. He stared at the rocks scattered up the mountainside, considering.

"If we could get up there into those rocks, we might be able to throw them off the trail, at least for awhile," he said, still speaking as though Adam was capable of hearing. He looked down at his brother and then back up at the rocks. What should be an almost unnoticeable climb seemed to tower over him.

He knew he was capable of carrying his brother...on a good day, which this definitely was not. His own wound was sapping his energy, making him lightheaded and queasy; he was barely able to move himself along. He wouldn't be able to wait for Adam to come around, though; there was no time to spare for that. He shrugged; there was nothing to do but try, and he bent toward the effort with everything he had.

The climb up into the rocks was long and tortuous. He half-carried, half-dragged Adam along, and every few yards he had to stop to lower him to the ground and stand gasping to get his breath back. The hole the arrow had left in his side was steadily seeping blood, but it couldn't be helped. He kept moving.

He climbed steadily on until they were as high into the rocks as he thought he could make it. Then he carefully laid his brother down and propped himself against a rock, looking back at the path they'd taken. He'd have to go back and cover the marks they'd left as best he could.

Adam moaned, and Joe quickly went down on his haunches beside him.

"Adam?"

But Adam didn't respond, even after Joe called his name twice more. Joe's brows scrunched in worry as he regarded his brother. Adam's face was the color of a trout's underbelly, and he was shivering. Joe shucked out of his jacket, ignoring the frigidity of the mountain breeze running across his shoulders, and draped it across Adam before removing his tourniquet once more.

He reached out and gently touched the stab wound. It was no longer bleeding, but it was slightly red and warm to the touch. Infection was already raising its ugly head.

"Got yourself stuck good this time, didn't you, brother?" Joe whispered, and he found himself wishing the Indians had attacked before he and Adam had left the logging camp. At least they would've been able to hole up in the tiny cabin there, and they would've had food, ammunition—and medical supplies.

He shook his head. No use wishing for what wasn't. He slid the

Indian brave's knife from Adam's boot and moved over to an aspen tree. Using the sharp blade, he peeled several hunks of the white bark from the tree and carried it back over to his brother. He stared at the woody pieces of bark for a moment, considering. From what he had been told, it really should be brewed into a tea, but that wasn't possible under the circumstances.

He shrugged and put a chunk of bark into his mouth and chewed, pulling a face at the bitter taste. When the bark was a mushy mess in his mouth, he spit it out into one hand, and then chewed on another piece. He kept on chewing and spitting until he had a good-sized pile of wet, spongy bark collected.

He plastered the entire pulpy mess across Adam's wound and wrinkled his nose at the unappetizing mound. "You might not approve of the treatment, brother," he murmured. "I'm not sure I'd want you spittin' pieces of chewed up bark on me, either. It's not exactly something that Doc Martin would do, I don't reckon. 'Course, since you ain't awake to argue about it, you'll have to take it up with me later." He retied the tourniquet to hold the wet, mushy bark snugly against the wound.

He sat down to cut a strip off the bottom of his own pants leg to use as another bandage for his side; he couldn't afford to leave more of his own blood to lead the Indians back to them, and he hoped the fabric would continue to absorb long enough to let him finish covering signs of their passing. He changed the blood-soaked neckerchief out with the strip from his pants leg, and then stood to hover once more over Adam's pale, shivering form. "I've got to go cover our trail, Adam. I'll be back," he said, but then he hesitated. Leaving his brother lying alone ripped at his gut, and yet he knew it had to be done. Murmuring a prayer that Adam would be watched over, he turned and scrambled over the rocks and headed back down the slope.

Backtracking along their trail ended up taking more time than he had been gambling on. Blood from both him and Adam was sprinkled liberally across the ground; Joe had to stop and painstakingly sift dirt and pine needles across every spot he saw, praying to God he didn't miss any and being careful not to leave any new droplets behind. Where tufts of needles had been disturbed by their awkward passage, he stopped and soothed and fluffed. When he came to the sapling they had damaged, he took a stone and scraped bark from the trunk. With any luck, if the Indians came across it they would think a buck had done it while rubbing its antlers. Or so he hoped.

He kept going until he came to a small creek. He crossed to the other side, and then he very deliberately tramped his boots solidly along the damp bank, removing his makeshift bandage from his side and letting the blood drip steadily onto the ground as he moved along.

He listened for more sounds from the Paiutes, but heard none. That was to be expected; if the braves thought they were closing in on their prey, they would be prone to keeping quiet. The very silence made his nerves clang.

He walked for a half mile or so downstream, and then stepped back into the icy water and began to wade back upstream as fast as he could. He knew his pace was slow, but his injury was making him stiff and clumsy. Several times he stumbled and fell, and the frigid water left him gasping.

Still a considerable distance from where he had first crossed the stream, the earthen bank gave way to a steep cascade of fallen rock; there he climbed out of the water and started to climb, careful to clamp the bandage, now cold and wet, tightly against his side.

The position of the sun told him he'd been gone from Adam for at least a couple of hours. His arms and legs shook as he climbed, and he knew it wasn't just from the cold. He was tired, and he was weakening. Night would be coming on soon, and he had no idea what to do next. And beyond all that, he was afraid for his brother, afraid of what he would find when he finally made it back to him. A vision of Adam's dead body stiffening in the rocks wedged its way into his mind, and bile rose into his throat. He stopped and leaned against a boulder, inwardly cursing at his inability to move faster. Giving his head an angry shake, he wiped the back of his hand over his eyes as if to clear away the bitter image.

"Just stop thinking," he muttered to himself, and continued in his diagonal climb across the rocky face of the mountain.

When he finally made it back to where he had left Adam, the first thing he saw was his brother sitting propped against a rock and gazing steadily back at him. The relief of it brought hot tears to sting the back of Joe's eyelids.

He collapsed in a heap at Adam's feet and tried to regain his breath.

"Where you been, kid?"

Adam's nonchalant tone made Joe raise his head off the ground to stare incredulously at him. "Where've I been?" he squeaked. "I've been running myself ragged trying to save your hide, that's where I've been!" Too late, he saw the edges of Adam's grin sneak along his face and realized that his older brother had gotten the reaction he was looking for. He rolled up onto his side and looked at Adam, offering him a reluctant grin of his own. "How're you feeling?" he asked softly.

Adam shrugged. "Lightheaded. Sick. Cold. Guess that brave got his knife in a little deeper than I thought." He stared at Joe and shook his head. "I can't believe you got me up here." His eyes narrowed as he looked at Joe more closely and noticed his damp hair and clothing. "What the hell -have you been swimming?"

Joe rolled his eyes and sat up. "Yeah. I got so hot lugging you up here that I thought I'd cool off after I went back to cover our trail." He wrapped his arms around his knees. Now that he had stopped moving, he was starting to shiver again.

Adam's lips tightened. "We're going to have to get your clothes dry or you'll be dead of pneumonia by this time tomorrow."

"How? Even if we had time to wait, we can't build a fire. The smoke would give us away."

"It'll be dark soon. Maybe we could get a fire going then—"

"No." Joe shook his head. "We can't spare the time. As soon as you feel up to it, we've got to move again. The Paiutes must've swung back in our direction; I heard them back down by the lake earlier."

Adam's eyes fell shut and he leaned his head back against the rock. He whispered something that could've been either a curse or a prayer; Joe couldn't quite make it out.

"I set up a decoy trail," Joe offered.

Immediately Adam raised his head again, his expression intent. "Tell me," he prodded, so Joe did. When he finished, Adam's eyes glinted with new hope. "It might give us some time."

"Some, maybe," Joe allowed. "Not much. They'll figure it out eventually. We'll rest up, let you try to get some strength back, and then we've got to get out of here."

Adam nodded in resignation, knowing they had no choice. "Probably best if we wait until nightfall, and then make a run for it. Less chance of them spotting our trail that way."

Less chance of him and Adam seeing the Indians sneak up behind them, too, Joe thought, but he didn't say it. Instead he leaned against a rock and slid down to sit on the ground. Despite his relief, he was suddenly feeling a lot worse now that Adam was awake and alert again. Joe's head ached, his stomach was roiling, and the fire had come back to stake its claim on his side with new-found force. It was as if now that he was once again in the company of the brother who always knew what to do, his own mind was telling his body to just let go. While he had been hurrying to hide their trail, he had barely been aware of how bad he felt; now it was all he could think of.

Joe watched his brother chew thoughtfully on his bottom lip, and he knew Adam was thinking hard to find a way to get them both out of danger. Joe found himself taking a childlike comfort in the knowledge, and he leaned his head back and shut his eyes. He didn't want to think any more; he was happy to let Adam make the decisions. Whatever his oldest brother decided, he'd go with it.

"Joe? What was this stuff you put on my leg?"

Joe opened his eyes and grinned. "Nasty looking, isn't it?"

Adam smiled back and nodded. "Pretty nasty. It seems to be working real well at taking some of the heat out of the cut, though. What is it?" he asked again.

"Aspen bark. Indians use it for fever and infection," Joe explained, wanting to laugh at the incredulous look on Adam's face.

There was a moment's silence. "You learned that from Blue Wolf, I take it?"

Mention of his former Apache friend pulled the smile from Joe's face. Joe's relationship with the Indian had never set well with Adam, and Joe himself had a confusing mixture of both bitter and pleasant memories from it. Their friendship had ended with murder and heartbreak; he had never been able to talk to Adam about what had happened, and he had no desire to try now. He simply nodded and shut his eyes again.

More silence. Then, "Joe...Hannigan's stud. I want you to know—"

"For heaven's sakes, do you have to bring that up?" Joe snapped. He opened his eyes once more to glare at Adam. "You can stop worrying about that darn horse. I'm done fighting you over it."

"Joe—"

"You don't have to keep telling me—I know I don't know as much about horses as you do, Adam. Hell, I don't know as much about anything as you do, and I never will. I know it, you know it, and Pa knows it, so you can stop rubbing it in," he sighed. He shut his eyes once more and reached up to pull his hat down over his face.

Adam didn't take the hint to drop the subject. "That's not what I mean, and you know we don't believe that. You're angry over—"

Joe didn't bother to raise his hat. "You're wrong, Adam," he murmured. "I'm not angry at all. I really don't care about it any more." As he drifted off to sleep, he realized that he spoke the truth. He was so dog-gone tired and felt so blasted sick that he had no energy left to spend on being mad.

It was a sure sign of just how bad off he was.

HE WASN'T SURE how long he dozed, but he awoke to Adam gently shaking his shoulder.

"Come on, Joe. Time to head out."

Joe blinked his eyes open, and saw pinpoints of light fluttering over his head. Awfully cold out for fireflies—no, they were stars. Only they didn't behave as stars ought to, swirling around like that.

"Joe? Are you alright?"

The concern in Adam's voice pulled his attention off the wandering stars and onto his brother's face, barely visible in the darkness. Heavy, thick darkness. Lots of nervous stars, but no moon to light the earth. Blue Wolf had sworn to him that Apaches could see in the dark; Joe had laughed at him, but now he wondered abruptly if it was true, and if it was a trait shared by Paiutes as well.

"Joe?"

Joe blinked again. "What?"

"Are you alright?" The concern in Adam's voice was growing, and Joe shook himself.

"Yeah. Yeah, I'm fine." He was stiff with cold, even though he suddenly realized that his jacket had been draped back around his shoulders while he slept. He struggled into a sitting position and shrugged his way into the jacket, managing to bite back the hiss of pain that the movement caused. He looked up at Adam's silhouette standing dark against the night sky. "Good to see you on your feet again, Adam. Can you walk?" Joe asked the question matter-of-factly, but inside he was already worrying, wondering how he would ever be able to conjure up the strength to carry his brother any further.

But Adam nodded. "Yeah, I can walk, more or less. While you were asleep I made myself a crutch from a pine branch. I can lean on that. Hopefully it'll help me keep up the pace a little." He bent low over Joe again as if to peer into his eyes. "How's the arrow wound?"

"Hardly feel anything at all," Joe lied, and he was glad the darkness kept Adam from seeing the fib on his face. Adam was in as bad or worse shape than Joe was, and it would do no good to worry him. In removing the arrowhead, Adam had already done everything he could do, anyway.

With an effort, Joe got his feet back under him and stood up. The ground pitched, and he steadied himself against a rock, again thankful for the cover of darkness. For a moment he thought he might retch, but he gritted his teeth and the moment passed. When he was sure he could speak without giving himself away, he asked, "Which way do we go?"

"North across the slope, I think, and then east. I heard a shout off to the west just as the sun set. I'm pretty sure they were following that trail you set." Adam paused. "It was good thinking, Joe, setting that false trail. Likely saved our lives."

Joe couldn't help smiling in self-conscious pleasure. His oldest brother didn't normally go around handing out compliments, so one from him was like gold. Joe dropped the smile then and shrugged. "Our lives aren't saved yet, brother. In case you haven't noticed, we're huddled in the middle of a bunch of rocks with a band of murdering Paiutes on our tail. Seems to me we're both still in danger of losing our hair."

The dim starlight was enough for him to catch the flash of Adam's grin. "Then let's make sure that doesn't happen. Come on."

FOR THE NEXT hour, they moved in the direction Adam had indicated, their progress painfully slow. With every step he took,

Adam let out a tiny grunt of pain, and Joe began to have serious doubts about just how much longer his brother would be able to go on. Just as he had said to Adam, they were a long way from safety.

Maybe rescue was on its way. Joe clutched Adam's arm to help him over a rough section of trail. "Do you think Hoss and Pa are looking for us yet?" Joe asked hopefully.

"Most likely. If not, they will be soon. It's a long ride up here, though. We can't depend on them to get to us before the Paiutes do. And we're so far off the main trail that they'll have to hunt for us once they get here."

"Shouldn't we try to get back to the main trail, then?"

Adam grunted again as he maneuvered his way over loose rock with Joe close behind him. "We can try to get closer, but we'll have to be careful. The Paiutes may be expecting us; if they do, they'll have guards posted on the wagon trail. We'll have to— damn!" The curse came out as a harsh whisper, and Adam backed up, bumping into Joe.

"What is it?"

"They must've figured out we're up here somewhere," Adam whispered. "They're down there on the other side of this ridge." He sat down, breathing heavily. "We're cut off."

Joe joined him on the ground. "Do we veer south?"

Adam shook his head. "We'll run straight into Marble Bluff. No way to climb up it, and we'll be out in the open. They'll reach us before we can get around it."

"North, then?"

"North will bring us back down to the wagon trail. If they know we're here, they'll be expecting us to try to move that direction."

Joe sighed in exasperation. "Well, we can't head west."

"We have to. It's the only way out of these rocks."

"The only way out—you can't be serious! If we head west, we'll run right back down to the lake."

"I realize that."

The defeat in Adam's voice set Joe's heart to pumping. "Then what do we do?" Joe asked urgently, and moved close enough to see Adam's face in the starlight.

Adam heaved a sigh and shook his head. "Joe—I don't know what to do. We're trapped."

I don't know what to do. The words chilled Joe down to his very bones. In all his life, he didn't think he had ever heard his oldest brother utter those words, and the fact that he heard them now threw his entire world out of kilter.

"What do mean, you don't know what to do?" he blurted. "We've got to do *something.*"

"I mean *I—don't—know!*" The last three words were ground out and emphatically spaced, and, coming from Adam, undeniably angry. They hung in the air like stones, and Adam dropped his head for a moment. Then he looked back at Joe, staring through the darkness at him as though searching for something. "I don't know," he said again, very softly this time and with shame tingeing the words. "We're in trouble, Little Joe."

Joe sat back, flabbergasted. He was suddenly put in mind of the time when, as a child, he had snuck downstairs on Christmas Eve, determined to catch Saint Nicholas in the act of putting gifts in their stockings. He had caught Pa instead. The disillusionment he had felt at that moment was strikingly close to what he was feeling now.

Adam, the brother who always knew what to say, what to do, was stumped. He was the one who always had all the answers, and now he was telling Joe he had none. The revelation sapped the remainder of Joe's energy. Even in the dark he could see the tired, discouraged set of Adam's shoulders.

Joe's head pounded. He ran his sleeve over his forehead to wipe away the perspiration, and then stood up, even though the pain in his side bade him stay where he was. Carefully, he clambered up to the point where Adam had seen the Paiutes at the bottom of the ridge. The landscape was a muffled blur of black and grey, and at first he saw nothing that resembled another human being. Then he saw movement down to his right, and his breath caught. "Oh, hell, here we go," he breathed.

"What?"

Joe was already moving, grasping Adam by his arm and heading him down the slope out of the rocks. "They know we're up here, alright. They're coming up," he said.

Adam didn't waste time asking more questions. He lurched along beside Joe as they scrambled down, skidding and stumbling as they went. They leaned on one another for support; three times Adam went down, taking Joe with him.

By the time they reached the bottom, they were both gasping for breath. "Which way?" Adam asked.

"You said it yourself. West is the only option. Let's go."

They struggled along in the dark, Adam still letting out a soft, tight grunt with every step he pushed his left leg to make. Adam's involuntary admittance of pain was hard to take; Joe did his best to block out the sounds, with little success. When the sound of triumphant Paiutes began to drift up behind them, he tried to block that out as well.

Adam heard it, too. "They're on us," he noted grimly. Joe didn't bother to answer. He was too busy trying to stay on his feet. The ground seemed to be swaying beneath him, and he had the uneasy feeling that he was starting to lean on Adam much harder than Adam was leaning on him.

Suddenly the quiet surface of the lake was looming before them, shining like dull, dark pewter in the starlight. They stopped at the shoreline and stared out at the water, then back into the timber where the Indians' cries were growing ever louder.

"It must be true; they can track even in the dark," Joe murmured.

"What?"

"Nothing." He stared down the shoreline as it stretched away from them on both sides. "Should we try to head around the lake?"

"We'll never make it." Adam's voice was quiet.

"I know." But they turned and started along the rocky beach anyway, hurrying as fast as they were able.

Adam stopped suddenly and pointed out at the water. Some distance out from shore was the dark shape of a tiny island, a jumble of jagged rocks rising from the water, with four or five scraggly pines standing sentinel.

"Could you swim out there, do you think?"

Joe looked, considering. He bent to put one hand in the water; it was so cold it hurt.

"Joe, I need an answer," Adam barked. "Can you swim to that island or not?"

Joe stared at the dark pile of rocks marring the lake's smooth surface. "I think I'd rather die by drowning than by having some Paiute brave sawing on my forehead," he admitted.

A loud shout rang out as the Paiutes burst out of the timber only a few hundred yards away.

Joe looked at Adam expectantly. Adam looked out at the tiny island, then back at Joe, and then he shook his head regretfully. "You're a strong swimmer. I think you can make it—but I can't. My leg won't give me the kicking power I'll need to get across." He hesitated. "You go. I'll take off around the lake. Take your boots off." He ignored Joe's protests, pushing him down into a sitting position and tugging at his boots himself.

Swimming out to the island was a long shot, Joe knew, but staying pinned against the shore was sure suicide. If Adam couldn't swim, he was finished.

The Indians were running toward them; Adam was pushing him into the water, pulling his jacket from him at the same time.

"It won't do you any good wet, and it'll only weigh you down," Adam said, flinging the jacket toward shore. He walked into the water himself, continuing to push at Joe.

Joe felt the sting of the icy water against his legs. "Adam, you can't—" But then Adam was already moving away, galloping along the water's edge with a lopsided lurch that would've made

Joe laugh had the circumstances been different.

Something tore loose inside Joe's chest. The burden and bless-ing of his entire existence was based on the fact that everything he'd ever done, everything he'd ever tried, had been done under the watchful eyes of his pa and brothers. It seemed that he had spent his whole life working to either struggle up to their level of manhood, or climb out from under their shadow, Adam's in particular. In this moment, a moment when death moved toward them with terrifying swiftness, Joe watched as Adam played the role of protector one last time. The Indians would see Adam running; they'd be too busy running him down to notice Joe in the water. Joe's path was being ripped away from his brother's against his will, and he knew without a doubt that he'd never see him again.

He glanced toward the island. Could he make it? He thought he could.

But he wouldn't.

If Joe had to die tonight, it would be at the side of the man he'd often fought and argued bitterly against—and yet loved all his life.

He splashed back out onto shore and quickly caught up to Adam, who threw him an astonished glance and skidded to a stop.

"What the hell are you doing?" Adam was infuriated.

Joe grabbed his arm and began to pull him along. "Shut up and run, Adam."

But Adam was having none of it. "You damn fool! If you don't make a try for that island, you're going to die. Don't you under-stand that?"

"I understand perfectly." Joe's words were quiet but unwaver-ing.

Understanding and sick resignation crossed Adam's face. "You're insisting on staying with me." It was a flat statement, not a question. Adam shut his eyes briefly, and then painfully lowered himself to the ground and started to pull off his boots.

Now it was Joe's turn to be astounded. "Adam—what are you doing? They're coming!"

Adam flung his boots to the side, threw off his coat and waded into the water, still holding onto the crutch. "You'd better come on, then."

Joe shut his mouth and splashed out to his brother. "I thought you said you couldn't kick—"

"We'll do the best we can, Joe. Both of us. Nobody can ask more."

Joe swallowed and nodded. Side by side, they waded quickly out into the icy water. By the time it lapped at their waists, they were both shivering violently.

Then Adam grabbed his arm to stop him. "Joe. I want to tell you something. Hannigan's horse—"

Joe's eyes widened in disbelief. "You're bringing that up now? Oh, for crying out loud, Adam—"

"No. I want you to know—" Adam shook his head. "I need you to know. The reason I didn't want the horse—"

"Adam, we don't have time for this. Tell me later, after we make it to that island. Because we are going to make it." Joe pulled away, but Adam grabbed his arm in a grip so tight it hurt.

"No. I'm telling you now." Adam's tone was hard and determined. He took a big breath and his eyes were large and dark as they stared into Joe's. "The reason I was against buying Hannigan's stud was because you were so determined to tame the thing. I wanted him for the herd as badly as you did, but I was so afraid that you'd get yourself killed on him that I decided it wasn't worth the risk." Adam loosened his grip, and his voice faded until it was almost too soft for Joe to hear. "You're fearless, Joe, and it scares me to death. Every time you climb onto the back of some jugheaded bronc, every time you take on some drunken cowboy in the saloon—hell, every time you walk out the front door and fly headlong into whatever chaos you happen to be chasing that day, you act as though nothing could possibly go wrong. One of these days your luck is going to run out, and you're going to—" Adam sighed. "I didn't want to lose you to some fool horse. I didn't want to watch Pa go through that kind of suffering again...." He looked back up at him. "You're not invincible, Joe."

Joe stared at him, and then a lopsided grin spread across his face. Even though they could both very well be breathing their last, Joe's heart was suddenly light. Somehow, things were right again between him and Adam, and that alone was enough. Joe reached for the reckless courage with which he faced every dilemma, hopeless or not. "And you're not always right, older brother," he said, still grinning. "I reckon now's as good a time as any to see what wins out—your philosophizing or my luck. I'm putting my money on my luck. Ready?"

Adam stared at him, and then gave him an answering grin. "Ready."

"All right, then. Let's find out just how bad a bunch of Paiutes want to catch a couple of skinny cowboys." With that, Joe dove forward into the water.

The cold was stunning in its power. It took his breath away and shocked him into total numbness. He floundered and sank before finally forcing his limbs to move, and hard kicks thrust him back to the surface.

He sucked in air and looked around for Adam just as his brother's head broke the surface beside him.

"God—it's—cold!" Adam gasped. He grabbed the crutch floating beside him and held on.

"Yeah." Joe could hardly force the word up out of his throat as he made a concentrated effort to keep treading water. His insides seemed to be as paralyzed as his outside.

"Start—swimming. It'll help—keep the blood—pumping," Adam panted, striking out for the dark lines of the island—an island which suddenly seemed impossibly far away. Joe followed his lead. They didn't talk any more; they couldn't afford the energy, and anyway, their violent shivering made it hard to form words. Instead of speaking, they put everything they had into pulling stroke after stroke.

Surprisingly, they heard no sounds of splashing Indians behind them. Joe spared a second to look over his shoulder, and could just make out a line of braves standing shoulder to shoulder along the shoreline, laughing and pointing toward them.

Damn Paiutes. They thought they were watching a couple of idiots trying to drown themselves. No reason to get cold and wet doing what dark lake water was sure to do anyway. Anger surged through Joe's veins, and he struck out with new determination.

They swam on, and the Indians' whoops grew fainter behind them. The island grew slowly larger. So slowly. Using the crutch to help stay afloat, Adam kicked and swam the best he could; several times Joe had to stop swimming and tread water so as not to get too far ahead of him. Joe had no idea how long they'd been in the water. It felt like hours. He was aware that the water no longer seemed quite as cold, and he wondered how that could be.

He tried to keep his concentration on the rocky outline of the island. They were going to make it; he refused to entertain any other conclusion. He turned his head to shout a word of encouragement to Adam—and watched his brother's head slip beneath the black surface.

"Adam!"

He swam back to where he'd seen his brother disappear and dove under at the spot where the pine branch bobbed on top of the water. Once under, however, he could see nothing but inky blackness. He came back up and cried out his brother's name again, spinning around and frantically wiping away the water streaming over his eyes.

Suddenly Adam's head broke the surface. Joe threw out an arm, grasping wildly for his brother and missing entirely. Adam went down again. Joe dove, reaching out—and his hand brushed against his brother's hair. He clenched his fist, feeling the wet locks twining around his fingers, and he jerked upwards with all his strength, kicking hard for the surface at the same time.

Adam came coughing and gasping into his arms, and Joe held

on to him for all he was worth.

"I've got you, Adam. Just hold on. It's not much further."

"I'm finished, Joe," Adam choked out. His teeth were knocking together so hard that Joe could barely make out the words. "You've got to let me go. You'll never make it otherwise."

Joe didn't bother answering. He wrapped one arm around Adam and struck out through the water with the other.

He swam on, and time lost all meaning. He thought of nothing other than telling himself to swim, to swim, to swim. It was as though his entire body had forgotten how to do things on its own. He had to keep sending mental messages to his legs to keep kicking, to his left arm to keep stroking, to his lungs to keep pulling in air. The only part of him that didn't need to be told what to do was his right arm; it curved around his brother's body with a fierceness that made his bicep bunch and cramp.

Several times he went under, choking and sputtering along with Adam when he managed to fight his way back up to the surface. Every time Adam demanded that Joe let go of him. Joe ignored him, even when his brother swore at him.

And then Adam stopped speaking completely. Joe looked at his face once and then refused to allow himself to do so again; Adam's eyes were closed, his face white, and the sight of it frightened Joe so badly that he found it even harder to breathe. He kept kicking and kept paddling with his left arm over and over again, his mind blank and his eyes fixed on the black water in front of him.

When his foot finally brushed against gravel, he was so exhausted that it didn't register. He swam until he was able to crawl out, heaving Adam along beside him. Pulling his brother from the water took the last bit of his strength, and he collapsed beside him, trembling from fatigue.

Again he thought about how odd it was that he was no longer all that cold. But his shivering brother obviously was, and he needed a fire. There was nothing to do for it, however; even if Joe could manage to get a fire started, the tiny island would provide little in the way of dry fuel.

He sighed and scrunched up on the rocks next to his brother's body, trying to provide what little warmth his own body had to offer. He pillowed his head on Adam's chest, and the last thing he was aware of was the faint thumping of his brother's heart against his cheek.

HE THOUGHT HE heard Adam calling to him, but he couldn't even begin to pull himself out of sleep...restless sleep, disturbed by odd dreams...such odd dreams. Gunshots echoing like distant thunder. Adam calling his name again, then the voices of Pa and Hoss looming over Adam's. The blessed warmth of someone's coat being wrapped around him before he was lifted and carried. The faint sensation of being rocked like a baby in a cradle, with noises of creaking wood and splashing water sounding dimly in his ears.

Adam calling his name again.

Then the jangle of a team's harness, more creaking wood, and the rumble of wagon wheels. Men talking in clipped, urgent tones. Pa, then Hoss, then Pa again, hovering over him, speaking to him, even though he couldn't make himself concentrate enough to figure out what they were saying.

And over it all, Adam's voice again, agitated and fearful, calling his name out over and over and over.

Time stretched out endlessly before and behind Joe, and then all sound ceased.

IT WAS SO quiet. He was hot, and everything hurt—his throat, his chest, his side. Blankets were piled on top of him, and he wanted to push them away, but couldn't seem to garner the strength to do it. Even trying to open his eyes didn't seem worth the effort.

He thought he heard someone speaking, and he tried to listen, but he slid back into sleep before he could even decide who was there.

"Joe!"

He jerked awake, gasping. "Adam?" He forced his eyes open, but couldn't focus. His vision swam with blurred lights and shadows. Someone—Pa?—murmured something to him and placed a cool hand on his brow.

"Don't do it...Joe, come back!"

It *was* Adam—and something was wrong. Adam's voice was muffled and sounded far off, but there was no mistaking his fear. Joe tried to sit up, his heart slamming hard in his chest. "Adam!"

The Paiutes—were they coming? He struggled to get his bearings, blinking his eyes hard. The shapes around him shimmered and merged and parted again. The face hovering over him coalesced slowly into view. Pa. And beyond Pa's anxious face, the familiar trappings of Joe's bedroom.

"Joseph, it's all right, son." Pa's voice, soothing yet troubled. He pushed Joe gently back down onto the pillow. "Shh, just take it easy now."

"Pa?" Joe whispered.

Then Adam's shouts came again, louder, more insistent, and more frightened, and Joe's head whirled with confusion and fear.

"Adam?" He fought his way up off the pillow and tried to swing his legs off the bed. "Adam!" He struggled, but Pa held tight to him and began to shout for Hoss.

He continued to try to fight his way free. Couldn't Pa hear that Adam was in trouble?

Hoss's big form filled the doorway, and his appearance distracted Pa just long enough for Joe to push past him; he plowed off the bed, only to land in an undignified heap on the floor. Hoss was immediately bending over him, picking him up and placing him back on the bed as easily as if he were a child. Hoss and Pa were both calling to him, but Joe didn't want to listen. Tears of frustration sprang to his eyes; he had nothing left in him—he couldn't even summon the strength to speak, and Adam was still calling his name in that frightened, awful voice.

Pa was pulling the blankets back up to his chin. Against his will, Joe's eyes began to drift closed. Adam's pleading calls continued to come, and one hot, bitter tear of defeat escaped to slip down Joe's cheek.

"Joe...son, it's all right," Pa insisted, but his voice shook, and Joe was left with the rare consternation of wondering whether his father's words were true.

"Ben! I need one of you in here!" With a start, Joe recognized Doc Martin's voice. Usually calm and matter-of-fact, his voice was strained as it rang from the other room.

"Stay with Joe, Hoss." Pa's voice was rough and weary. "I'll go help Doc Martin with Adam."

"Are you sure, Pa? Adam, he's—"

Adam was...what? Adam was what? Joe struggled to open his eyes to ask the question, but couldn't manage to do it. Pa gave brusque instructions to Hoss.

"Doc and I can handle Adam for a few minutes. The laudanum is bound to be taking effect soon. Just stay with Joe. And for God's sake, let's keep the doors closed until they're both asleep."

Joe heard the click of the latch as the door to his room was drawn closed. A few seconds later he heard the soft thump of another closing door, then the muffled voices of Pa and Doc Martin. Beside him, Hoss gave a long, shaky sigh, and then started talking to him softly about such mundane matters as the weather and how many new calves they'd had this week—talk calculated, Joe knew, to calm him as he drifted back off to sleep. In the background, behind Hoss's low voice, the November wind blustered through the trees and against the window pane.

And still, rising above it all, was the terror-stricken sound of Adam calling for him.

As Joe relinquished himself to sleep, he knew it was a sound he'd hear in his nightmares for years to come.

JOE CAME AWAKE to the sound of sparrows trilling outside his window. Foolish birds; they sounded deliriously happy. Didn't they know spring was still a long way off?

Joe sighed and rolled over. He knew he'd overslept—again. These days nobody seemed inclined to complain about it, though. His family was still worried about him pushing too much, too fast.

"It's not just the wound from the arrow—pneumonia is nothing to trifle with, young man," Doc had told him sternly. "You'll have to watch yourself for some time or you'll suffer a setback; mark my words. You may be young and strong, but you're not invincible..."

You're not invincible.

The bittersweet memory of Adam saying the exact same thing came to mind, and Joe immediately sat up and put his bare feet onto the floor. The events of that day weren't anything he cared to dwell on.

He quickly dressed and began to make his way downstairs, pausing when he heard Hoss and Pa conversing quietly at the table.

Hoss was shaking his head. "Are you sure this is such a good idea, Pa?"

"No, I'm not at all sure. As a matter of fact, I think it might be a huge mistake," Pa grumbled. He sat back in his chair and sighed. "But it's what Adam wanted."

Hearing that, Joe continued down the stairs and stood at the end of the table. "What did Adam want?" he asked. The looks Hoss and Pa threw each other made him think they weren't going to tell him.

"What did Adam want?" he repeated.

Joe watched Pa's eyes soften as they fell on him. He stared at his father's face, taking in the newly etched lines webbing around the corners of his eyes. The last couple of months had been rough on Ben Cartwright. They hadn't been easy on any of them.

"Sit down and have some breakfast, Joseph," Pa said gently, and Joe chafed at having his question left unanswered. But he dutifully sat down and began to fill his plate. His appetite had finally picked up over the last few weeks, and with it his strength had begun to come back as well. He dug in earnestly, only to slow down when he realized that Pa and Hoss were watching him. He looked from one to the other, unable to discern what they were thinking.

"What?" he mumbled through a mouthful of eggs, earning him a momentary look of disapproval from Pa.

Hoss shot a look at Pa, and shrugged at Joe. "Nothin', Joe, nothin' at all. Don't mind us. You just keep on with your breakfast."

Joe stared at his brother. A smile twitched at the corners of Hoss's mouth; he looked as if he could barely contain himself. A quick glance at his pa caught the same smile, although Ben quickly tried to hide it.

Joe put his fork down. "All right, what's goin' on?"

Before either of them could answer, a knock sounded on the front door. Joe pushed his chair back, but Ben waved him back down. "I'll get it."

The voice at the door belonged to one of the hands. "We need some help out at the barn, Mr. Cartwright. That mare is trying to foal."

"Oh, yes—right. Get your coats, boys."

Joe groaned, thinking about the heavy mantle of snow that lay over the yard outside. He had always loved winter, but he had been cold almost continuously over the past two months, almost as if he might never be warm again. The thought of tramping through the snow to get to the barn didn't appeal to him at all.

He sighed. He should be thankful. While he'd been snoozing in a warm bed, Hoss had most likely been out to the barn a dozen times already, taking care of both Joe's chores and his own.

Resolutely, Joe stood and moved toward the door. Hoss and Ben already had their coats on, and Hoss grabbed Joe's off the hook and tossed it at him. Joe put it on, looking down to button it up as he followed Pa out the door. He didn't dare leave the coat hanging open as he normally would have—Pa would have a conniption fit.

"Why do they always pick the coldest mornings to foal?" Joe grumbled, fussing with a contrary button. "Just like that heifer the other night during the blizzard—why can't it ever be easy?"

"I reckon that's because nothin' worthwhile is ever easy, Joe," Hoss said.

"Hoss is right. Nothing worthwhile is ever easy."

Joe jerked his head up. Adam stood in the middle of the snow-covered yard, dimples framing a wide grin. He held a lead rope in his hand, and at the end of the rope stood Ted Hannigan's big chestnut stud.

Joe stared at the horse, then at Adam, then at Hoss and Pa, who both simply grinned back at him. He turned again to Adam and found that, for once, he could think of nothing to say.

"Ain't you gonna say somethin', Joe?" Hoss asked. "You keep standing there with your mouth open and you're liable to let your tongue get frost-bit."

They all laughed at that, Pa, Adam, Hoss, the row of grinning ranch hands standing off to the side. Everyone but Joe.

"I...I don't understand," he whispered.

Hoss moved up beside him. "Well, uh...see, it's a horse, Little Joe."

This time Hoss's wisecrack earned him a hefty wallop in the arm. "I know what it is, you muleheaded..." Joe sighed and looked back at Adam, who still smiled as he watched him. Joe walked slowly through the snow until he stood face to face with his oldest brother.

"I don't understand," he said again, and he searched his brother's face.

Adam shrugged. "It's a good horse," he said.

"Yeah. A really good horse. But that didn't matter back in November," Joe said quietly. "What changed your mind?"

Adam glanced down at the snow and rubbed one hand over his mouth. Then he looked back up at Joe. "A lot of things," he said. "You. Me." He cleared his throat and turned his head slightly to look up at the mountaintop where the new logging camp sat. "You handled yourself real well out there, Joe."

Joe fidgeted, suddenly uncomfortable. "All I did was try to save our hides. And you were right there beside me." Just as he'd always been, Joe thought. "I'd be dead right now if you hadn't killed that brave."

Adam nodded, still looking out at the mountaintop. "I take my responsibilities seriously, Joe."

Joe frowned, unsure of what his brother was getting at. He looked back at Pa and Hoss for answers, but they looked as perplexed as he was.

Adam continued, speaking slowly as if even he weren't quite sure of what he was trying to say. "When you were a little kid, you were like a small cyclone, always charging off in a thousand different directions. It took all of us to keep tabs on you. By the time you were thirteen, you were pulling stunts that had Pa tearing his hair out. I did my best to help him by keeping you out of as much trouble as I could."

Joe blushed; he knew very well what stunts his brother was talking about. Why, though, was he talking about all that now?

"By the time you were fifteen," Adam went on, "we began to seriously wonder if you'd live long enough to make it to manhood."

Some of the hands chuckled, but Joe kept his eyes glued on Adam, who still stared up at the mountain.

"You were always rash and foolhardy, and again, I did my best to try to make sure that you stayed alive long enough to become a man." Adam paused. "While you and I were up on that mountain, I thought I had failed you. I thought I had protected you from a rogue horse only to lose you to a scalping. Then, when I woke up on that hellish iceberg of an island, and you were so cold, so still..." He shook his head. "I didn't know what else to do to keep you in this world, so I just kept calling to you. I called as long as I could, until I lost consciousness again." He glanced at Hoss and Pa. "I'm told that I still called during all those days when I was out of my head with fever." He sighed and stared down at the snow. "I remember dreaming about you. Terrible things, things I couldn't protect you from no matter how hard I tried..."

The anguish in Adam's voice was as fresh as if he had just awakened from one of those dreams. No one said a word, but the look Ben gave Adam said that he knew what those dreams, those feelings, were like. Wanting to protect the ones you love and being helpless to do so. Joe, too, could understand the terror to be found in that.

Adam swung his gaze back up to Joe. "When I finally woke up, and they told me you would be all right, it finally occurred to me—my job is done. Has been for some time. You are a man, in every sense of the word—the kind of man I'm proud and glad to have at my side regardless of the situation we're in."

At a loss for words, Joe simply kept looking at him, his throat working. Finally he smiled and asked softly, "Does this mean you're through trying to tell me what to do?"

Adam smiled back. "Absolutely not. You may be a man, but you're still a rash and foolhardy one."

Joe laughed, and suddenly everything was bright and fresh and new. The sun broke through the clouds, sending a million sparkling diamonds skittering across the snow.

Grinning, Joe turned toward the horse. "How'd you get him to stand so nice on the halter?"

Adam rolled his eyes. "Hours and hours of hard work and frustration, that's how. I thought for sure one of us, either me or the horse, wasn't going to make it."

"Nothing worthwhile is ever easy." Joe repeated his brothers' words and moved near the horse to rub its neck.

"I worked him up to the halter, but the rest of it is up to you,

Joe. I know horseflesh, but you—you're the one who's got the instincts and the ability to turn him into something."

Another compliment from Adam; another pearl. Joe tucked it away along with the others, where it could be taken out and polished and admired when he was alone. When he could trust his voice, he asked, "What's his name, anyway? I never asked Ted."

Adam chuckled. "Well, Ted called him a lot of things, none of which Pa would appreciate being hollered out across the yard. So I took the initiative of naming him."

"Well, what is it?" Hoss asked. He and Pa had moved close, faces full of the peaceful joy that comes from almost losing something precious and having it handed back.

Adam patted the horse's nose, but his eyes were on Joe. "His name is Invincible." He smiled and shared a look with Joe that only they understood.

"Mighty high-falutin' name for a horse, if you ask me," Hoss grumbled. He stroked the horse's sleek side. "I'll be callin' him Vince if it's all the same to you two."

Joe moved to stand in front of Adam once more. "Thanks, Adam," he said softly, and then he threw his arms around him in the same exuberant way he had done since he was a small child, breaking through Adam's natural reticence as he always did, causing the horse to snort and throw his head back in nervous reaction. His kid brother in his arms, Adam relinquished the rope to Hoss.

Pressed chest to chest, Adam and Joe pounded each other hard on the back, exulting in the kind of boisterous, turbulent love that only men can delight in, and through the noise and laughter and Vince's nervous snorts, neither one was aware of the steady, sure synchronization of their hearts falling into step with one another once again.

Destiny and Mud

by Kelli Marie Patchin

This story features characters created in the epsiode "The Wooing of Abigail Jones", written by Norman Lessing.

Abigail pushed a loose strand of hair out of her eyes as she marked the last paper. She absentmindedly set the quill down and glanced out the window. The sun was just beginning to set and if she did not hurry she would be walking home in the dark. She hadn't intended to stay at the schoolhouse this late but her mind was simply not on the task at hand. *He would be returning tomorrow.* It had been four long years since she had feasted her eyes upon him. Four years since she had seen his powerful stride as he made his way determinedly into the school room to fetch his brother. Four years since she had looked upon his handsome face and stared into his dark brooding eyes.

Abigail shivered just thinking of his strong muscular arms. She hummed slightly off-key as she gathered her papers and wrapped her shawl around her slender shoulders. As she made her way out the door she thought back to the first time she had met him.

Abigail and her mother had moved to Virginia City shortly after her father's death. Abigail had graduated from one of the finest finishing schools a few years before and had returned home anxiously awaiting the day she would wed. Of course, she had yet to find the proper suitor and after a few years of searching decided the best course of action would be to find some type of employment to pass the time. It was upon attaining her teaching license that the news of her father's passing had come. After a year of mourning, her mother decided, with the help of some rather eccentric friends, that she and her daughter needed to seek adventure elsewhere.

The two had made some inquires and within the month Abigail found herself on a stagecoach headed west, a teaching job awaiting her arrival. It had only taken her mother a week to fit in to small town life, as if she had always lived in such states. Abigail found the west to be even more romantic and adventurous than she had hoped. Why in the first week she and her mother had witnessed two shootouts and a shotgun wedding. Of course not everything was like the dime novels she secretly read during the nights prior to their trip. The novels failed to mentioned the insufferable heat, dust, or lack of indoor washrooms. Abigail had been appalled at the condition of their lodging. Fortunately, her mother had acquired a great deal of wealth during her marriage and the two were staying at the boarding house while improvements were being made in their home.

Teaching in itself was an adventure. Abigail had not known what to expect at first but within the week many of the students had already found a place in her heart. She enjoyed training their young minds and the satisfaction that came when their eyes lit up in understanding. Of course, there were times when she wasn't sure what she had been thinking when she agreed to teach out

West. It was on one of these days that she first met him.

"Seth! Little Joe! What is the meaning of this?" Abigail yelled, quickly making her way down the steps after school.

She roughly pulled the two apart. This was the second fight today between Joseph and another student. With Joseph's older brother, Hoss, finishing his schooling the year before and his not being there to defend or control his little brother, Joe had had a lot to prove. Abigail understood standing up for oneself but she was not about to abide fighting. She had a lot to prove herself in this town and she wasn't about to let two eleven-year-old boys ruin that for her.

"Both of you head over to that pump and wash up and then meet me in the school house," she ordered, shaking both boys a little.

She had just entered the school once again when she heard the commotion outside. A quick glance out the window revealed Joe and Seth were once again rolling on the ground. Sighing in frustration, Abigail quickly exited the building.

"Joseph! Seth! Stop this at once!" she ordered making her way towards the pump and the boys.

The boys paid her no mind and continued to roll around on the ground, occasionally throwing punches. Abigail was not one to give up easily nor did she like her orders to be ignored. Reaching down, she made a grab for Seth who was currently sitting on top of Joe appearing to be winning the fight. However, she misjudged Little Joe's stamina and just as she was grabbing Seth's shoulder, Little Joe gave a mighty heave and threw himself atop Seth. The ground was quite wet under the pump and before Abigail could even let out a squeal she found herself landing none to softly on her backside in the mud. If that small event in itself did not stop the fight, the voice coming from behind Abigail most certainly did.

"Joseph Francis Cartwright! What is going on here?" the voice bellowed.

Abigail could clearly see Joe's face for it was inches from her own and the fear that crossed it caused her to temporarily forget her own circumstances and turn to see who the voice belonged to. As far as she could tell only Ben Cartwright had such an effect on one Joe Cartwright. What she saw when she turned around temporarily left her speechless. A tall man, dark haired and muscular, stood with his hand held out, looking down on her in concern. She found herself smiling up at this stranger despite the fact her best dress was covered in mud, mud that was currently seeping into her petticoats and causing her much discomfort.

"Are you okay, ma'am? Let me help you up," the man said, pulling her up from the ground.

Abigail nodded slightly and did not realize she was still clutching his hand until he cleared his throat and gently yanked his hand away. He quickly turned his glare on the students standing in the schoolyard and one by one they scrambled to their horses and made their way home.

"It's not what you think, Adam," Joe said scrambling up off the ground, successfully regaining Adam and his teacher's attention.

"Not what I think! So you were not fighting, at school no less, ignoring your teacher's instructions and causing her to fall on the ground?"

"Well...uh..." Joe replied looking frantically to Seth for help.

"It was just an accident, Adam," Seth added, inching towards his horse.

"Hold it right there, young man," Abigail commanded. Now fully recovered from her shock, she was quick to realize that her first meeting with Adam was on her backside, in the mud, at the expense of these two boys—something they would not be getting away with.

Seth froze. "Yes, Miss Jones?" he asked innocently as Little Joe continued to stare at Adam with wide eyes.

"I believe I asked you and Joseph to meet me in the school house, did I not?" she asked glaring at the boy, daring him to defy her.

"Yes ma'am," Seth replied quickly heading towards the school-

house making a large circle around Adam.

"I suggest you join him," Adam ordered Little Joe, nodding towards Seth. "I will wait for you out here."

Little Joe nodded and made an even larger circle around Adam heading towards the school building.

Adam turned to Abigail. "I apologize, ma'am for my brother's behavior. I assure you our Pa has taught us the proper way to treat a lady and how to behave in school. I am sure he will remind Joe of what is expected when we return home."

Abigail looked up at Adam admiring his amazing eyes and enjoying the fact he had just referred to her as a lady. Adam waited patiently for a reply and taking her silence for anger, he attempted to apologize again.

Abigail quickly snapped out of her reverie when he placed his hand on her shoulder. "Oh no, um, Mr. Cartwright. I am quite all right. Really just a little mud," she said, quickly trying to reassure him. She was fine, as a matter of fact she was more than fine. She had just found the man she would allow to court her. "I am Abigail Jones and I take it you are Joseph's older brother?"

"Yes, I have been away on a cattle run, so I haven't had the pleasure of making your acquaintance. I just returned a few days ago," Adam added, tipping his hat.

Abigail was not at all sure why cattle would need days to run but she was sure it was an important job and there would be plenty of time for Adam to explain all of this when they were wed.

"Excuse me?" Adam asked, looking slightly bewildered. "Did you just say...no never mind, I must have been hearing things. It has been a long couple of weeks."

"Ahh, yes, I am sure it has," Abigail agreed, embarrassed she had spoken aloud.

"Well, I am sure Seth and Joe are waiting anxiously for you," Adam said nodding towards the schoolhouse.

"Yes, I am sure they are," Abigail replied, smiling up at Adam.

"So, I guess I will just go wait by the wagon," Adam replied when Abigail made no attempt to leave. "Um, it was nice meeting

you, Miss Jones."

"Please, call me Abigail," Miss Jones replied still beaming at him and subconsciously taking a step towards him.

"Oh ok, I will," Adam replied, taking a quick step backwards. "Good day," he added over his shoulder as he walked rather swiftly to the wagon.

Abigail waved and admired the view a little longer before turning and entering the schoolhouse to deal with the boys.

"YOU GOING TO come inside the house or stand outside all night wool-gathering?" Mrs Jones asked, waving her hand in front of her daughter's face.

Abigail jumped back with a small squeal. "Oh sorry, mother. I was just thinking."

"Humph, well come on in. Dinner is almost ready," she replied, turning on her heel and shuffling inside.

Abigail sighed. How could one possibly eat when their mind was on greater matters, matters of the heart? Her Adam was returning tomorrow. She sighed in contentment. Tomorrow was Saturday and the Cartwrights being God-fearing men would be attending church that Sunday. She could hardly contain her excitement as she raced inside after her mother to assist in dinner. Sunday everything would fall into place. She just knew it.

"THAT WAS A marvelous sermon, Pastor. Thank you," Abigail said, shaking the elderly man's hand affectionately. The pastor was one man in Virginia City who actually saw her worth and always treated her with utmost respect. Abigail knew she was an excellent Sunday school teacher, never mind the fact she was the only person willing to teach the youngsters. She knew she had been chosen because of her Biblical understanding and guidance.

After greeting a few more friends, Abigail scanned the congregation for one face. The Cartwrights had not been in attendance at the beginning of the church service but Abigail knew immediately when they had entered the church building for every female in the room had turned her head to gawk. Abigail made herself not glance back for she did not want to appear too eager nor ruin their reunion.

She scanned the yard one more time when suddenly, she saw him. He was standing beside his brother, Hoss, laughing at something another friend had said. His strong arm draped around Hoss' shoulder as the two doubled over laughing. Abigail found herself smiling, almost laughing with them as if she could hear the joke. Her Adam looked different, more relaxed, more mature. His shoulders had broadened and city life had not lessened his muscular physique as she had feared it might. His hair was a little shorter than she remembered but when he smiled again at his brother she immediately recognized his slight dimple and her breath caught in her throat. He was beautiful, a Greek god. There was no other way to describe this man who had captured her heart so quickly. The man she would soon marry. The mere thought made her weak in the knees. She sighed again and then quickly composed herself and made her way towards him.

Just inches away from her destination, Abigail felt a hand on her arm. She looked up in surprise to see Widow Moore glaring down at her. "Watch where you are going, little missy," she snapped, shaking her cane a little at Abigail.

Abigail mumbled an apology and quickly moved around the Widow, for her Adam was walking back towards the church building with Hoss. She rushed after him, attempting to look nonchalant but failing miserably. She stopped just inside the church entryway to catch her breath when she heard her name.

"So, what about Abigail, uh, Miss Jones, Hoss? Did she finally marry?" Adam asked his brother as the two stood just inside the church searching the pew for Hoss' lost handkerchief.

"Well, older brother, I do believe she hasn't found the right man yet. Waiting, I do believe," Hoss replied, elbowing his brother in the side, with a wink, before bending down and retrieving the lost handkerchief from behind a pew bench.

Abigail gasped. He did love her. He was concerned she had found someone else while he was away. Silly man. Did he really think she would forget his love so quickly? Wait, was that a groan? No, couldn't be. She must have imagined that. She was sure that was a sigh of satisfaction she heard coming from her future spouse. She smiled happily to herself.

Well it was now or never. Abigail quickly fluffed her hair and entered the church building. She smiled at the shock on Adam's face. Poor dear, she thought, he must be afraid she had over-heard his conversation.

"Hello, Adam," Abigail said, holding out her hand.

"Uh, hello Miss Jones," Adam replied taking her hand and looking to Hoss for help.

"Adam, please, close friends would not be so formal," she said squeezing his hand. "You must call me Abigail."

"Yes, right then. Abigail. You are looking well," Adam replied, trying to free his hand.

Before Abigail could reply the group was interrupted. "Hoss! Adam! Pa says to hurry it up if we are going to go on this picnic. I want to get some fishing in so get a move on it," Little Joe yelled into the church house, then spotting his teacher he added, "And hello, Miss Jones. Sorry to interrupt."

"That's quite all right, Joseph," Abigail said smiling at the boy. Joseph, at first, had been the one draw back to her affection for Adam, but since the boy's sixteenth birthday, Abigail was sur-prised to find she quite enjoyed his company.

"I do love picnics. What you say I join you and your family and then Adam and I could finish this conversation?"

Joe quickly looked at Adam in surprise, but he couldn't very well tell his teacher no. He shrugged his shoulders. "Okay. Let me check with Pa," he added, exiting the building as quickly as he had entered it.

Abigail took Adam and Hoss' silence for approval and turned to get her wrap and Bible.

Adam slowly turned to Hoss. "Did she really just invite...I mean...is Abigail coming on a picnic with us?"

"Afraid so," Hoss said, then breaking into a huge smile, he hit his brother on the arm. "Welcome back brother!"

ABIGAIL SMILED POLITELY at Mr. Cartwright as he explained once again how one goes about branding a cow. At least she thought it was a cow. She regretted ever asking such a question, but since their arrival Adam had been strangely quiet and someone had to carry on the conversation. She could not understand why he didn't suggest they go for a walk where they could discuss much more intimate things then the burning of an animal's flesh. Of course she supposed he must have felt it would be rude to leave his father so soon after his return. She inwardly sighed. It would once again be up to her to get the ball rolling. Forget politeness, she simply did not have time! She turned towards Adam, once Ben had finished his description of course, and gave him an encouraging smile.

"Adam, would you please accompany me on a small stroll? Perhaps we could check to see if Little Joe and Hoss have caught anything?"

Adam quickly looked to his father, his eyes large. If Abigail didn't know any better she would of sworn a look of fear had crossed his features. Then again, maybe being alone with her did make the poor man nervous. She did often have that affect on men.

"I would hate to leave Pa here alone, Miss Jones, ah, I mean Abigail," he replied, wiping his palm against his pant leg.

Before Abigail could insist, Joe came running up. "Pa, come quick! Excuse me, Miss Jones," he added tipping his hat at her, then turning once again to his father. "Hoss has caught the biggest fish. It just might be the granddaddy we let go last year. You gotta come see. I was gonna bring it to you but Hoss said that wouldn't be something Miss Jones here would want to see. So come on. Adam can keep Miss Jones company."

Abigail almost clapped her hands in delight when Ben agreed and followed Joseph towards the lake. Once the two were out of sight she inched closer to Adam and placed her hand on his. She was just about to announce her decision to allow Adam to court her when he quickly jumped up, almost causing her to fall over.

"Maybe we should take that walk now," he said quickly helping Abigail to her feet.

"Of course Adam," Abigail replied not letting go of his hand as he led her along the lake's bank. The two walked in silence. She waited patiently for Adam to bring up the subject of courting but a girl could only wait so long.

"Adam, dear, I have something to say. Something I know will make us both happy. But first I must explain something to you," Abigail said, stopping them both and turning Adam's face towards her with her free hand.

"Abigail, I don't think now is..." Adam began fighting the urge to jerk his head away.

"Shhh," Abigail said, placing her fingers over his mouth. She was so shocked by the tingle of excitement that small act gave her she temporarily forgot to take her hand from his mouth. It was not until Adam pulled her hand down that she remembered she was about to tell him something important.

"Adam, please let me speak my piece. I have waited four long years to tell you this. Surely you know by now how I feel," she replied, taking his other hand into hers.

"Miss Jones, please, I beg you..." Adam tried again, prying his hands free.

"Adam, there is nothing to be ashamed of. It is as obvious to everyone else as it is to me how you feel. Honestly, Adam, I am not blind," Abigail replied, once again taking his hands into hers.

"It is time we did something about these feelings. We must speak the truth!"

"You know what, Miss Jones, you are absolutely correct. It is time to be honest with each other," Adam agreed, firmly yanking free of Abigail's grasp.

Abigail could not believe her ears. It was finally happening. The Adam Cartwright, the man in black, the man that had dominated her thoughts and dreams for the past five years was about to confess his undying love for her. She blinked back tears.

"Yes, Adam, please. Tell me the truth," she said a little breathlessly.

She closed her eyes and sighed happily. This was exactly how she had always pictured this moment. The sound of birds chirping in the distance, a cool breeze coming off the pond and actually wait, no, this was not perfect. She suddenly realized she was facing Adam. This would not do. She looked better in this particular dress from the side and one should always look their best when being proposed to. She turned her self quickly around.

Unfortunately, Abigail had forgotten to open her eyes and in her haste her left boot connected with Adam's right ankle. The intense and unexpected pain caused Adam to double over and his chin to connect rather roughly with Abigail's shoulder. Abigail yelled out in pain, most unladylike she was sad to admit, causing Adam to jerk back quickly. Once again, the forces of nature were against them for a small rock that Adam had been standing on chose that moment to shift, causing Adam to slide. There was nothing for him to grab a hold of but poor Abigail's dress. Fortunately Abigail was an excellent seamstress and the fabric did not rip. It did, however, pull Abigail down with Adam.

The two landed in a heap at the edge of the lake. Abigail found herself lying face first on Adam's muscular chest. Seeing as how she rather enjoyed lying there she was in no hurry to get up. Adam tried desperately to stand back up, but it was at that exact moment that Adam learned just exactly how much fabric went into a woman's dress, petticoats, and undergarments. The more he struggled and the less Abigail tried to help, the more tangled he got. If Ben had not found the two a minute later there was no telling how long Adam would have been helplessly trapped under one Miss Abigail Jones and her dress.

After untangling and helping the two to their feet, Ben demanded to know what was going on. Adam tried to sputter an answer but could not form a complete sentence. He finally gave up and quickly walked away, mumbling something about confounded women. Abigail was sure she had heard wrong for her Adam would never use such an uneducated word as 'confounded' or refer to women in such a derogatory fashion. She shook her head and wondered what it was about that man that always caused her to end up on her backside in the mud.

She graciously accepted Ben's invitation to take her home and followed him to the buggy. She supposed that tomorrow would be just as good as any for her to tell Adam how she felt. After all she had waited five years, what was one more day! No one could fight destiny.

Love You, Joe

by Meghan A. Kenworthy

"I don't want ta get mad at ya, Joe, but by thunder I sure will be if ya don't tell me what the tarnation is goin' on!"

"Hoss, I told you it ain't any of your business. Now keep yer nose out of it!" seven-year-old Joe snapped back at his brother, making sure that Hoss couldn't see what he held behind his back.

"Joe, I've about had enough of this silliness, now show me what's behind yer back!" Hoss lunged at Joe, who tried to dart away, but Hoss' hand was clamped on his arm. The two boys began to struggle with each other, Joe still refusing to show the object he had in his hand. The sound of ripping paper brought them to a halt as both of them stared at the torn piece of paper in Joe's hand. Tears stung Joe's eyes and he looked at Hoss, his green eyes snapping. Angrily, he flung the paper at his big brother.

"There! Look at it! I don't care! It's ruined now! Go ahead and laugh at it!" He turned on his heel and dashed out of the room. His throat tightening, Hoss looked down at the ripped piece of paper and bent to pick it up. He turned it over and looked. It was a picture of two people standing with their arms, at least he thought they were arms, around each other. One tall, the other short. The wild, curly squiggles atop the short person made him easy to identify. The other was a little more difficult, but the red shirt, black vest and blue jeans, and the dark hazel eyes that were colored brown in the picture gave him away. There was some writing on the bottom and Hoss squinted to read it. "To the best big brother in the whole world from Joe with lots o' love."

Tears stung Hoss' own eyes and he eased himself onto Joe's bed, the paper trembling in his big hands. Insurmountable guilt filled him and he lifted his eyes to the door through which Joe had disappeared only moments before. He stood and walked out the door, still clutching the precious piece of paper.

As he passed Adam's room, he heard soft sniffles and stopped to listen. His forehead crinkling, he put his hand on the door and quietly pushed it open. Joe was sitting on Adam's bed, his knees tucked under his chin, wiping his tears away on the back of his hand. He lifted his head as Hoss stepped in, then quickly lowered it again, even more fervently wiping his face. "W-what do you want?" he asked, bitterly.

Hoss didn't answer. He crossed over to sit on the edge of the bed. He looked at the picture, then raised his eyes to see Joe staring accusingly at him. "Why'd you try ta hide it, Joe?"

"'Cause it weren't any of yer business, that's why," Joe mumbled, looking down at his knees. "I was gonna send it to him next time Pa had us write 'im letters but..." His voice quivered and Hoss saw more tears well up in the young boy's eyes. He looked at the picture again.

"Ya did a good job," he said, softly.

"Don't matter now. It's ripped." Joe reached over and took the picture from Hoss. He stretched his legs out, placed the paper on his knees and stared at it, a small sigh escaping him. "Don't think

I'd be able ta do another one as good, neither." The two brothers sat like that a long while, both thinking on their big brother across the country. Then Hoss raised his head and patted his little brother's arm with the back of his hand.

"Hey, tell ya what. I'll fix it, and then I'll help ya send it to him."

Joe looked up at him, hope glimmering in his eyes. "Ya think ya can fix it?"

"It won't look as nice maybe, but Adam wouldn't care." Hoss grinned at Joe, excited at the prospect that he might be able to make things right. Joe looked down at the picture then he nodded.

"Okay." He carefully took the picture in his hand and scooted to the far end of the bed. He slipped off then left the room, Hoss behind him. Both boys ran down the stairs.

"Whoa, there now, where you boys off to?" They halted on their way to the desk and looked at their Pa. Joe held up his picture.

"Hoss is gonna try and fix my picture so I can send it to Adam," he explained. Ben raised his eyebrow and looked at Hoss who blushed.

"I accidentally ripped it...Say, Pa, do we have any paste?"

Ben's forehead puckered as he thought a moment then he nodded. "Yes, I think Hop Sing has a jar of it in the pantry."

"Come on, Joe." Hoss took his little brother's arm and they darted off for the kitchen. When they came back out, the jar of paste under Hoss' arm, they headed for Ben's desk. There, Hoss took out a piece of paper. Joe watched carefully as his brother cut a wide strip from it then dabbed some paste onto it. "Okay, give me the picture." Joe handed it to him and looked up as Ben came to stand beside him.

His tongue sticking out of the side of his mouth in concentration, Hoss carefully put the picture together and put the pasted strip along the rip. He gently smoothed it then carefully flipped the picture over. The faintest of lines showed down the middle, but other than that, the picture looked as it had when Joe drew it. Hoss looked up and grinned. "There!" Joe grinned back at him and Ben reached over to clap his middle son on the shoulder.

"Good job, Son."

Hoss set the picture down then looked at Joe. "It'll have ta dry a while, then ya can send it."

Joe skirted the desk and wrapped his arms around his brother.

"Thanks, Hoss." Hoss smiled sheepishly and put one arm around his baby brother.

"Anytime, Short Shanks."

A COUPLE MONTHS later...

"Joe! Come here, Son!"

Joe winced at the sound of his father's voice and began to frantically recollect anything naughty he'd done lately. Worrying that his father had somehow found out about the cookies he'd snitched from the cookie jar, Joe tentatively walked into the great room. His father was seated at his desk, an envelope in his hand and a smile on his face.

"Yes, Pa?"

"A letter arrived for you. It's from Cambridge," Ben said, softly. Joe's eyes widened and he hurried to stand in front of the desk. His hands shook as he took the letter from his father and read the return address on the front.

"A.S. Cartwright, Cambridge, Mass."

He started to open it when the door opened. He looked up and saw Hoss walk in. His brother took one glance at his face then at the letter. Hoss' face lit up and his sky blue eyes twinkled. "Ya got a letter from Adam!" he whooped, dashing over to stand by his brother. Joe nodded and bowed his head. Carefully, he opened it. Clearing his throat, he unfolded the piece of paper he'd pulled out and began to read.

Hoss fidgeted then said, "Can't ya read it out loud?"

"Hoss." Ben shook his head. Joe looked up.

"No, it's okay, Pa." He looked down at the letter and again cleared his throat, trying to get rid of the tightness in it.

"Dear Joe,

Thank you for the wonderful picture you sent me. I was very pleased when I got it and it now hangs from the side of my bedroom mirror so that I can look at it every day and think of you.

I have sent you something in return that I drew in my art class. It can't compare to your picture, but I hope you will like it anyway.

I sure miss you, Little Joe..." Joe's voice caught as tears stung his eyes. He blinked them back and went on. *"Give Pa and Hoss my love.*

Love you, Joe. Your affectionate big brother,

Adam."

Joe stared at the letter when his Pa said, "This came with the letter." He looked up and saw Pa holding out a small paper package. Resting the letter on the desk, Joe took it and shakily opened it. He bit his lip as the paper fell away to reveal a hand size portrait of his older brother. Hoss looked over his shoulder and Ben stepped around to stand by Joe to see. They gazed at the strong, handsome, young face, memories flashing through each of their minds. Ben slipped his arm around Joe's shoulders and squeezed them slightly. "He did a good job, didn't he?"

Joe, unable to speak, nodded. "Y-yeah," he finally choked out. Then he looked up at his Pa. "Think I'll go hang it up in my room now." Ben smiled and patted his shoulder, nodding. Without a word, Joe picked up Adam's letter, cradling the picture in his other hand. Then he turned and walked towards the staircase.

Winter

by Krystyna Woollon

Nothing was worse than winter upon its first arrival. Somehow this particular winter was worse than usual as it had leap frogged autumn and jumped straight into a bitterly cold season of relentless northerly winds and torrential rain.

Grey skies like lead. Rain that teemed down like bullets. Wind that lashed the rain horizontally and drove the breath out of one's lungs. The earth turned to molasses as the rain churned it into thick mud and the horses' hooves made a further morass of the ground as they walked upon it. No wonder the riders were wading through wet, cloying mud that sucked at their boots and made going everywhere twice as difficult as normal.

Everyone was in a bad humour. Hop Sing was nearly dancing with anger every time the door opened and closed and another Cartwright entered the house with half the yard on his boots to be deposited upon the floor.

Hoss complained that, being the biggest, he got to become the wettest because more rain fell upon him that anyone else. Joe groaned that, being the smallest, he was most likely to be blown away by the wind. Adam said that with Joe being the smallest and nearest to the ground he was also in the most danger of being drowned. Ben just complained—of his aching bones, the rain that poured down his neck and trickled down his back and seemed to end in puddles in his boots; of cold bedrooms and draughty floorboards, at food being cold by the time it reached the table, and at Hop Sing for being unreasonable when he complained to him about the cold food.

"Dangblast it, Pa, this here egg's colder now than when it went into the pan," Hoss groaned as he lifted the offending congealed object onto the tines of his fork for all to see.

"Hasn't stopped you from eating them before," Joe observed as he stabbed at a piece of ham. "When will it ever stop raining?" he asked no one in particular as he stared out of the window at an obscured view due to the rain that lashed at the windows.

"Just hurry up and eat; we've work to do," Ben growled as he hastily swallowed his breakfast and washed it down with coffee. "Where's Adam?"

"You mean you've only just noticed he isn't here?" Joe chortled, "We've been sitting at the table for half an hour, and you've only just noticed he isn't here, waxing lyrical about the season and adding his complaints to ours?"

"That's enough," Ben scowled at his youngest and then glanced again at the empty chair.

"He left early. I heard him pass my door about four o'clock this morning." Hoss yawned, "Pa, how about we take the day off? We could treat ourselves to a holiday, huh?" and he looked hopefully at his father with his blue eyes wide and, he thought, appealing.

(Well, it always worked with Joe.)

"Don't be so ridiculous," Ben snapped and rose to his feet away from the table, casting down his napkin. The whole idea of taking the day off was oh-so-tempting, but there was work to be done and if he expected the hands to get on with it, then he, and the boys, should be there setting an example.

The thought of going out in the rain didn't propel them from their seats with the same alacrity as their father, but eventually Hoss and Joe managed it. The putting on of gun belts, hats and jackets took twice as long as usual and was accompanied by sighs and groans and mumbles under the breath. Ben cast thoughtful glances in the direction of his desk and tried to recall whether or not there was some urgent bookwork that needed some attention.

Just as Ben reached out to unlatch the door, it was pushed open and Hank stepped inside. He coughed and stood for a moment in silence as rain water tipped from his hat brim onto the floor as though from a gully. It streamed from his tarpaulin slicker and puddled the floor. He looked, with red-rimmed eyes, at Ben.

"Bad news," he mumbled.

"Shucks," Hoss frowned, realizing there no way was he going to be able to coax his family into staying home now.

"Just knew there had to be—" Joe sighed, looking at his brother's face with resignation.

"What is it?" Ben prompted, as Hank didn't seem in too much of a hurry to divulge the information.

"The bridge is down on the Mill Road. It's flooded over and broken up. We—"

"We?" Ben frowned, mentally anticipating the reply.

"Adam and me—"

"Adam was with you?"

"Yes, Mr Cartwright. I was up early and so rode along with him. He said how he wanted to check on the state of the river as it was so high yesterday. Anyhows, the bridge there was all shattered up so we rode on along some to where the river widens out for the bridge crossing onto the road to town. Adam reckons on it just about holding but not for much longer if this weather carries on. He was mighty concerned about the folk at the Box G. Wondered if'n we oughta go along and check on 'em."

Joe looked at his father's face and then at Hoss'. If the bridge wasn't there they would be cut off from any help if there was any severe flooding onto their land. Ben caught his son's glance and nodded.

"Best if Joe and Hoss go along and check them out. Where's Adam now?"

"Keeping a check on the bridge. I just come back to grab me some tools—"

Ben nodded. It was bad enough that the bridge at the Mill Road had collapsed, but the bridge that spanned the river close to the Box G was a vital link for the Box G as well as themselves. It served as an alternative route to the town as well as to the homesteaders on the borders of the Ponderosa.

"You two had best go and check on the Chapmans. Make sure they're quite safe and provided for should there be an emergency. And—" he grabbed at Joe's arm as the younger man made a hurried move to leave, "don't take any unnecessary risks."

"Sure thing, Pa." Hoss nodded reassuringly, and placed a firm hand upon his brother's shoulder as though to reinforce their father's request.

Ben frowned thoughtfully as he thought of all the homesteaders, ranchers and farmers who would be dependent on the Box G Bridge remaining open. It was a curse indeed, this wretched rain, with the threat of flood, and the links to town destroyed. He firmed down his hat upon his head and looked at Hank.

"Let's go."

ADAM CARTWRIGHT RODE his horse slowly along the swollen banks of the river. With his hat lowered to shield his eyes from the worst of the rain, his view of the river was somewhat restricted, but he could see only too well the debris that was hurtling through the swollen, engorged, frenzied waters. Broken trees that had worked loose from so much rain after weeks of drought were tumbling down river as though mere straws. Clumps of muddied reeds from the river banks had been pulled free to turn over and over in the currents to eventually be deposited elsewhere, at which site they would eventually re-establish roots for regrowth. Adam watched as several branches snagged together, twirling around and around before breaking free again. He shook his head thoughtfully knowing that this boded no good. There was a danger of the branches locking together to form a dam further downstream, and that would escalate the threat of flood in this particular locality.

Adam wheeled his horse around and returned slowly back towards the bridge. It had always stood firm against any weather in the past, and only that summer Hoss had busied himself by reinforcing any weak spots. Thank goodness for it, Adam mentally noted, it gave some hope that the structure would withstand this storm.

"What the—" the words came from his mouth as an involuntary gasp of amazement as he noticed the wagon that had rolled onto the bridge and was carefully making its way towards his side of the bank.

He raised a hand as though in an attempt to stop the wagon from proceeding any further. Surely, the man could see that the whole venture was a risk. Surely, he could see that he was putting himself and his people in danger as the waters surged muddily and greedily beneath the planks; every so often, the structure would resound with the thud of some debris striking against it. Even now, a large branch was snagged between the planks and sides with the current pulling at it one way and the bridge holding it fast at the other.

The horses pulling the wagon were nervous as they felt the planks shaking beneath their hooves. Inch by inch, they moved further along; second by second, the horses became more and more jittery. The man pushed the reins into the hands of another man and clambered down from the wagon seat to walk to the head of the horses. The wind blew against him, and he had to bend double to fight against it, holding onto his hat with one hand as he did so. As he neared the trapped branch, he kicked against it with a strength and violence that succeeded in setting it free to be carried away downstream.

Adam watched the man's progress with concern while at the same time urging Sport towards the bridge, for he knew only too well that the man would be requiring some help before long. His hand reached out for his lariat, ensuring that it was free and ready for use.

The man reached the horses and grabbed at their harness. At the same time, a heavy swell hit against the bridge which rocked violently upon its footings. The horses reared up their heads, squealing in panic as the boards beneath their feet proved themselves unsteady. The man was pushed against the side of the bridge but held on grimly, shouting at the animals and pulling at the lead horse's head in an attempt to make them move onwards.

"Hey, you!" he yelled over at Adam who was now much closer to the bridge. "Don't just sit there, come and give us a hand."

"Take the wagon back while you can—" Adam shouted back. "The horses want to back up, man, don't fight them."

"We need to cross the bridge. Are you going to give us some help or waste your breath shouting orders at me?"

The man was wrestling with the horses now as the bridge continued to shake and tremble. His attempts to move them forwards was not giving them confidence in him, and certainly not compelling them to move on. They backed up against one another, pushing the wagon into the railings that ran along the sides of the bridge.

The man with the reins was leaning into the wagon now and yelling to whoever was inside. It seemed certain that the more panic stricken the horses became the more they would push the wagon back, but as it stood now at an angle it was not going to go onto the bank of the river, but hard against the bridge rails with all probability of smashing through them. The outcome would eventually be the wagon going over the side and into the river.

Whether the man realised his wagon was in such danger was not obvious, but the older man on the wagon seat seemed aware of it and was now clambering down. Once on the bridge, he turned and raised his arms as though in supplication to those still within.

Adam had now reached the bridge and had dismounted. One end of his lariat he had tied to the pommel of his saddle, while he held the rest in his hand, feeding it out slowly as he ran with head lowered along the bridge. He could feel the wooden structure trembling as though it were a living sentient being in fear of being destroyed by the greater force that was waged against it.

When he raised his eyes to check on the progress of the wagon, he saw running towards him a woman holding the hand of a child. They were a mere few feet from him and within minutes he had them by the hand and had led them across the bridge to stand beneath the shelter of a tree by which his horse was standing. Then he retraced his footsteps and ran towards the wagon.

SARAH MORGAN CRINGED against the sturdy trunk of the tree against which the stranger had positioned her. Her child, Laura, clung to her skirts, her face white with fear, mute with terror. It seemed to Sarah as though after so many dangers and tribulations all their efforts were to be dashed, quite literally dashed, to pieces just as they were on the threshold of nearing their goal.

Her lips moved in silent prayer although her heart was breaking within her breast. She watched with fever bright eyes as the stranger joined with her husband to fight the horses, to steady them enough to gain the confidence they needed to move forward and to inch the wagon away from the danger of going over the bridge's side.

Her hand remained resting upon her daughter's head, and gently she turned the child to face her. She looked down into the trusting but ashen little face, bereft now of freckles and sunny smiles just as the sky was barren of sun and sunlight.

"Don't be frightened, sweetheart, it'll be alright," she consoled and drew the child closer. "It'll be alright," she repeated as though now she needed to console herself.

"Where's Liam, Mummy?"

Sarah now turned stricken eyes back to the wagon and her mouth framed the one word, a name, Liam. The colour and strength drained from her body, and without a sound she slid onto the ground with her child sobbing over her.

The horses were calming slowly. The stranger who had come to them had a deep resonant voice that encouraged them to be still, vastly different from the strident curses and yells from their owner. Behind the wagon, the other man struggled to straighten the vehicle, putting all his weight against the back wheel which had lodged itself against the railings.

At last there was a return of some confidence in the beasts. Perhaps they had sight of the sturdy chestnut horse standing at the far end of the bridge dutifully awaiting the return of his master. Whatever it was, the two horses seemed to have decided to do their master and the stranger some justice and pulled the wagon forward.

The wagon lurched and rolled. The bridge shuddered as the wheel continued locked in the side railings. Adam hurried round the wagon to where the other man was struggling to free the wheel and, realizing the problem, he put his hands on the spokes and added his strength to that of the other. Together they heaved against the wagon, against the wheel striving to force it free.

"Daddy..."

The child's voice was a mere whimper, and Adam glanced up to see the infant's face with the quivering bottom lip and the large eyes pooling with tears. The other man turned also, looked at the child and straightened his back.

"It's alright, son, Daddy's here. Just be still now like a good boy."

But the child had no idea of what he should or should not do. He was frightened, he was alone in the wagon, and he needed his father. He reached out, and he leaned forward into the man's arms. It seemed to Adam as though he were transported back in time to when he himself had trusted more in the safety of his father's arms than in anything or anywhere else. How many times had he turned to the man who had always been there for him, who had, like this man, taken him into the enduring comfort of his arms when fear had so overwhelmed him? No child thought of a father having fear, no child knew nor wanted any other reassurance but that of his father's presence.

It was at that moment the horses in front pulled together, and the wagon righted itself, steadied, and turned. It was at that moment that man and child were cast over the railings into the surging waters of the river. The brown brackish waters covered their heads immediately. There was no cry, no shrill scream to mark their passing...just a silence and where they had once stood, nothingness.

ADAM STILL HAD the rope end in his hand. Unconsciously, he had not for a moment loosened his grip upon it, and now as he threw himself into the river he wondered if God in his mercy would grant him the strength to use it for the benefit of the three of them.

The strength of the current was fiercely uncompromising. He found himself cast into a maelstrom of eddying currents that pushed him under, hurled him upwards and spun him around. He searched wildly for sight of the man and boy when he was above the surface of the water and then grappled for his own life when sucked back under once again.

His body was numb within seconds of being in the water. His eyes were nearly blinded by the volume of force that struck against his face; yet still he held onto the rope in his hand. He looked for sight of the others who, he felt, had less chance to survive than he, for he knew the man would not release his hold on the child unless the river snatched him away from him.

Now he could see the man's head bobbing close to him. Now he knew was the time to strike out and fight for their lives against the currents and to pray that strength beyond what was normal would be provided for their safe being.

Ben and Hank dismounted with a haste that almost propelled them both into the river, but gaining their feet they ran to where the taut rope held fast to Sport's saddle horn. Ben was about to cast himself into the river, but Hank's hand grabbed at his arm and forced him to exercise some self-control even though they could see that Adam was fighting not just for his life, for now he had reached the other man.

"Take the boy."

The man's scream was high above the sounds of the river, and the wind blew them into Adam's hearing.

"Take the rope, man," Adam replied. "Take the rope. Both of you can be hauled into the bank."

"No strength left—" the man cried even as he was pulled beneath the water yet still held his child aloft.

"Hold fast, man, hold fast." Adam yelled, and cast the loop of the rope over the wrist of the hapless fellow.

"No strength. Save yourself. Save my boy," cried the man as he resurfaced. "Save him."

The current pulled them along. Adam felt the rope become taut, even as he went beneath the surface. His hands groped, felt and held fast to the man's body and together they resurfaced. The rope was still taut and the man's arm was now victim to another battle as Hank and Ben hauled at it from the bridge. Adam reached up, grabbed at the rope, while at the same time his other arm encircled the body of the man.

Using their feet both men pushed themselves against the strength of the river. Morgan, one arm still enfolded around his child, had now a firm grip upon the rope. Above Morgan's hand, Adam's fingers also gripped the rope so that all three were now totally dependent upon the two men hauling the rope in.

Neither of them could see through their eyes now blinded by the waters rushing against their faces. They pushed with their feet and held tightly to the rope. Morgan clung to his child, and Adam clung to Morgan. It took all of Hank and Ben's strength to haul them in, aided by Sport who maintained a loyal and steady stance upon the bridge.

It seemed as though their battle through the waters was interminable. On and on it lasted as one moment they were pulled under, only then to be forced up. Never once did Morgan loosen his grip on his child, nor on the rope. It was Adam Cartwright who found himself weakening, unable to maintain his hold on the man, his fingers too numb to continue his grip on the rope.

He didn't hear his father's cry, his name being called aloud. He only saw a brief glimpse of the leaden sky, felt the rain splatter against his face and then the strange sickening lurch of his body as the water engulfed him and pulled him down into its murky mud laden bottom.

He didn't feel the strong arms that gathered him up and brought him to the surface, for he was unaware of his two brothers seeing his danger and of Hoss throwing himself into the water. He didn't hear their voices as they assured him he would be alright, really, he would be alright.

SARAH MORGAN DREW closer to the fire. Tentatively, she held out her hands to the flames and felt their warmth. She had thought she would never feel warm again, nor dry. From somewhere the kind gentleman had found clothes for her and a dry child's nightshirt for Laura. Now they sat in the big room with the roaring fire while the Chinese gentleman fussed around making coffee and soup and freshly baked bread.

She shivered now, not from the cold for she was no longer cold, but from guilt. She knew even as she sat there, safe and warm, that in the room above the young man who had come to help them was fighting for his life.

She drew the shawl closer around her shoulders and forced a smile on her lips for Laura's sake as the child sidled up to her mother and crouched beside her, rested her head upon her mother's lap and gazed into the flames.

Peter Morgan thanked Hop Sing for the bowl of soup and hugged it to his body. Like his wife, he felt a myriad of contrasting emotions as he rejoiced for his own life and that of his son, but he knew that another life could well have been the cost of them both. He looked over at Joe who was talking in a low voice to his brother, the big man who had dived in to save the man they knew to be Adam Cartwright.

Howard Morgan drank his coffee and watched his brother and sister-in-law. It had been a risky venture right from the time they had signed up at St. Josephs, Missouri. But there was no help for it; plans had been arranged, negotiated and concluded for them to take over a property that bordered the Ponderosa. As the weather had worsened, they knew without doubt that if they did not make a push for it they would be trapped in the mountain passes and probably perish. Instead, they had risked everything and almost died anyway. He sighed heavily and approached the two Cartwright brothers.

"Has someone sent for the doctor? I presume there is a doctor in town, isn't there?"

"We can't get to Virginia City. It's flooded and the bridge is down," Hoss muttered, and he looked at Howard as though just realizing that the man was there. "Don't worry, though, one of our men is heading for Carson City and getting the doctor from there."

"At least it's stopped raining," Howard muttered and then

wished he hadn't said something so inane, but Hoss seemed to understand for he allowed a brief smile to cross his face and he nodded.

"Yeah, that's some relief anyway."

Howard moved away to sit close to his family. Liam Morgan, aged nearly three, slept soundly. Wrapped in a blanket and cradled in his mother's arms, he was now oblivious to what had happened. Perhaps in time to come he would have dreams and nightmares that he would not understand the meaning of, fears of things the origin of which he would not recall. At the present time, he slept, having been clothed, fed and cosseted. In his world, he was safe once more.

Now there was just that sudden quietness that often happens when an event has arisen that snatches one away from the normality of life. Each and everyone of the adults there waited for news of the one who had been brought home as though dead and who now fought for his own life as desperately as he had fought for theirs.

The flames of the fire chased themselves up the chimney. Hop Sing bustled among them with an admirable calmness about him, bringing with him a new confidence and hope of a good life ahead in this new world. The child, Liam, lay in his mother's arms and she, holding him tenderly, sat mutely by the fire, now staring down at the beloved face—no, not staring, more rightly to say, devouring—the little face, with the sweet pursed lips and the long curled lashes upon porcelain cheeks.

"How is he?"

She looked up and saw Joe's face; the anxious strained look in the young man's face was not, she knew, just for her and Liam. She forced a smile.

"He's much better. He's a strong little boy."

"That's good," Joe leaned forward and gently held back a fold of the blanket to reveal the child's face. "There's more colour in his cheeks now, isn't there?"

She only nodded but said nothing. She pulled the blanket

back, closing it around her infant as though to trap within its folds every last amount of warmth.

There was the heavy tread of a footstep upon the stairs. They looked up in a movement that indicated their concern as the rancher came down the stairs, one by one, each step leaden as though weighed down by his sorrows. He paused at the bottom step, raised his dark eyes and realized he had guests who had gone through their own sufferings. He straightened his shoulders and forced himself to smile.

"The rain has stopped."

They looked at him as though bewildered. Joe stood up and stepped forward, a question on his lips but knew now it was better not to ask, not in front of these strangers. Hoss licked his lips and turned away; his eyes fell upon the coffee pot, and he promptly poured out some coffee for his father, a normal action on an abnormal day.

"Here, Pa, guess you could be doing with some of this inside of you." Hoss passed the cup into his father's hands, and as he looked deeply into his father's eyes he knew he was being told, "No change. "

Peter Morgan stood up and approached Ben, his hand outstretched.

"Thank you again, Mr Cartwright. I can't thank you enough for all the help you've given to us. Your son—" his eyes flickered nervously to the stairs, "saved our lives. You all did. I'm just so sorry that it has caused you all so much—" he swallowed the word, for he found he couldn't bring himself to say it.

"Winter's a dangerous season, Mr. Morgan. Not the time to be venturing out on journeys such as yours," Ben replied, and if there was a hint of remonstrance within his words he did not mean them, for he was a man himself who had undertaken just such ventures in the past.

"We were delayed in the hills." Howard Morgan spoke up, a trite defensively, "My wife—she was ill for a while which further delayed us. We would have been here sooner, before winter came.

We knew it was a risk, but it was important to reach our new home as soon as we could, for we have commitments here."

Ben nodded in understanding. There was no point in anyone referring to the fact that there was but one woman there present. Mrs. Howard Morgan had been ill, and her death had no doubt contributed to their delay.

"Howard has a position in Virginia City to take up; he was due to take it up at the end of last month. He—we—didn't want to risk his losing it after all the difficulties we had endured on this journey." Peter Morgan made haste to speak up in defense of his brother. Although no accusation had been levelled against him, he felt the need to justify what had already been said.

"Well, I think the best thing would be to take one day at a time," Ben suggested, and he settled down into his big red chair and drank some coffee. Then he glanced up to the ceiling as though his love for his son would enable him to see through the floor boards into the room above where Adam now lay.

The clock ticked away the minutes, seemingly louder than usual as it marched the time away from their lives. The flames seemed to crackle and snap more loudly. The rain had stopped, and now a straggling watery sun sparkled upon the raindrops on the windows.

It was Peter Morgan who broke the silence now. He looked around the room, and his eyes met those of his wife.

"Mr. Cartwright, we have taken up so much of your time, and—and caused you anxieties enough. I can only thank you on our behalf for everything." He bit his bottom lip and struggled to find the words, so that Sarah, standing up with the child still in her arms, was the one to now speak.

"While the weather holds fine, we should be getting to where we should be and not filling your house with strangers when you have things to deal with of such a personal and necessary kind. I thank you with all my heart for what you have done for us today, and when it is possible we shall come and thank Adam personally for his courage and bravery."

She placed a gentle hand upon that of the rancher who rose to his feet and with a smile covered her hand with his own.

"Take care, Mrs. Morgan. You know there's always a welcome here for you at the Ponderosa."

She nodded and turned away, with little Laura behind her still clutching at her mother's skirts. The child raised her eyes and looked into Ben's face. It seemed to her that he looked sad but she couldn't exactly work out why. Everyone seemed sad. She sighed and allowed herself to be picked up by her Uncle Howard.

Outside the sun sparkled upon puddles and raindrops. The air was calm; the clouds had folded themselves up like Bedouin tents and stolen away. The Cartwrights stood on the porch and watched as the Morgans clambered back into the wagon, turned it around and rolled away.

"An odd start for them—" Ben muttered, as he turned to re-enter the house.

"They'll survive. We did," Hoss replied, closing the door behind him before pushing his hands into the pockets of his pants.

Ben sighed, the heavy weary sigh of a tortured man. He put his arm across Hoss' shoulders and said softly, "Well, I guess we had to..."

IT SEEMED TO Adam Cartwright that everywhere he turned there was water, dark, black water. The coldness of it made him shiver, and his teeth chattered. He could feel drops of water trickling down his face, irritatingly slow. Wave upon wave crashed into him, so that his chest tightened as though a band was buckled around him and was being pulled tighter and tighter, crushing his ribs and making it impossible to breathe. He knew he had to push the water away in order to reach the surface, and yet no matter how hard he pushed some force still held him down. There was no doubt about it: he was going to drown.

Hoss looked up over his shoulder and his blue eyes widened in frantic appeal as he continued to hold down the blankets that Adam was continually pushing away.

"Shucks, Pa, ain't that doctor ever going to git here?" he hissed through clenched teeth. "If Adam keeps this up he'll be too exhausted to fight the fever when it gets worser'n this."

"Do you think it can get worse?" Joe asked as he wrung out the cloth and carefully wiped around his brother's face and throat.

"I hope not," Hoss sighed and turned to his father who had just entered the room. "Was that the Doc?"

"No. It was Hank to say that the bridge was secured and the river levels are already going down. The Morgans reached their place safely. How is he?" Even as he asked the question, Ben was striding over to his son's bedside, looking down anxiously at the sick man in the bed.

"What do you think, Pa?" Joe whispered anxiously. "Do you think he'll be alright?"

Ben could say nothing. He placed his hand upon his son's arm and just sighed before he drew nearer to Adam. From experience, he could tell that his son was in critical condition; he needed no doctor to tell him, for he knew the signs well enough by now. The pulse beat was too rapid, the breathing too shallow, the lips too dry. He leaned closer towards his son and noticed how the eyelids fluttered, sometimes partly opened to reveal the whites of the eyes, and the perspiration spiked the dark hair, collecting in a pool at his throat, while the dry lips twitched in silent conversation.

"Surely the doc should be here by now?" Joe cried, his voice having the shrill edge to it that came to him when under stress.

"Who knows what the roads are like from Carson City, Joe?" Hoss said soothingly. "Could be that he won't be able to git here." He straightened the covers over the sick man once again and then bit his bottom lip as he concentrated on thinking what else he could do to help.

"Pa?"

The sick man's voice cracked as he spoke, but the eyes opened and rolled to gaze upwards at the dark-eyed man leaning over the bed. Immediately, Ben took hold of one of Adam's hands and reassured him that he was there, he'd always be there.

"Pa? "

"What is it, son?"

The lips twitched, words were formed in silence and never uttered before, with a sigh, Adam gave a shudder and closed his eyes.

How strange, Adam thought, that he could be feeling so hot. So hot and no respite from it. The water, once so cold, was now a foaming cauldron of steam and heat in which he writhed in torment. If only someone could add just a few little icebergs that could float towards him and cool him. And the child—wasn't there a child somewhere?

"The boy—"

Ben glanced up at Joe and Hoss as the cry rang out as a sound of despair. He waited for Adam to say more, but there was no further sound. It seemed as though Adam were just slipping slowly away.

THEY HAD NEVER met the Doctor before—a balding man with a straight back and an intelligent face. He looked reassuringly much as one expected a doctor should look, even one consigned the dubious responsibilities of caring for the people so far from the sophisticates of the East.

He followed Ben Cartwright up the stairs and passed into the patient's room without a word, leaving Hoss and Joe to pace the floor in the big room downstairs. He had often heard mention of the Ponderosa and the Cartwrights. He had often wondered what the big ranch house would look like and what he would do were he to be called out to treat any one of them. Well, now here he was, and he was discovering that there was not so much different about the Cartwrights and other mortals after all.

The man in the bed lay very still. The darkness of his skin was emphasized by the pristine whiteness of the striped nightshirt he wore. He sighed and looked over at the father, Ben Cartwright.

"Has he been like this all the time?"

"No. Only for the past hour."

He nodded and stepped nearer to the bed. He placed the small trumpet shaped instrument upon Adam's chest and listened to the heartbeat, then to the lungs. He pursed his lips and sighed. He peered into the man's eyes and then gently lowered the hooded eyelids. He felt for the pulse at the neck and wrist. Then he ran his hands along the body, gently fingering the ribcage, the spine, the base of the skull. He put his hand upon the young man's brow and stood there for a moment, staring at the far wall and thinking whatever it is that doctors think when everything they do indicates the worst possible news.

Joe and Hoss stood up as though to attention as the doctor, followed by their father, descended the stairs.

"Adam is a very sick boy, Ben. There's no point in hiding the truth: it's out of my hands."

The brothers exchanged looks, gazed anxiously at their father who gave a cry of protest, before asking the doctor exactly what it was he meant.

"He'll reach the point of crisis tonight. If he passes it, all well and good. If not—" he paused, sighed, "Stay close to him, Ben." There was a slight shrug of the shoulders as he turned to leave. "I'll stop by in the morning."

There was a slight hesitation as the three Cartwrights seemed to need the time to catch their breaths; Ben murmured thanks to the doctor even as the man closed the door behind him.

"Pa, Hoss and I'll take turns sitting by him—"

"Yeah, Pa." Hoss nodded in agreement, although he could barely raise his head to meet his father's eyes. "Pa, he's going to pull through this, he'll be alright, don't you worry. You go up and get some rest, we don't want you to be sick, too."

"No," Ben shook his head, pushed their caring hands away.

"No, you boys get some sleep. I'll sit with him."

IT WAS A long silent vigil. The man in the bed was so still, so composed and to all appearances already dead. Occasionally, there would be moments of rapid shallow breathing, the struggle to force one breath through laboured tortured lungs after the other. Sometimes, there was soft whispering as though he were talking to someone else in the room, someone other than Ben who sat beside the bed.

He sat for some while with Elizabeth's picture in his hand, remembering the time he had married her, the tussle with Captain Stoddard over becoming a shop owner instead of the proud owner of his own ship. Oh, he could hear that strident voice now. "What! Captain Abel Morgan Stoddard a shop assistant!" and Ben smiled at the irony that Abel's middle name had been Morgan, the name of the family that had led them into this crisis today—no, yesterday.

Captain Abel Morgan Stoddard. Oh obstinate, stubborn fellow! Even on the day Adam was born, Stoddard had courted trouble and a fight. Always the same, always.

He picked up the book Elizabeth had loved. 'Paradise Lost'. He wanted to read it, to drift back to that time when they had shared a picnic in the summer and read poetry together, when they had first realized they were in love. Love, oh sweet tenderness of love, how perfect when young, sweet and chaste. Elizabeth, Elizabeth.

She had made him promise to pursue his dream. "Our dream," he had said. "Our dream." But how often had that dream turned into a nightmare. Wasn't this more of the same? He lowered the book and gazed at his son. "He'll be like you," she had said, and Ben smiled at the memory of her saying it. "As tall and straight as the trees among which he stands." And he leaned towards the bed and took his son by the hand, a proud tree indeed, and stricken down in its prime, he thought.

Again, he picked up the book and turned the pages, forcing his eyes to dwell upon the words—"The world was all before them..."

How quiet the room was, not even the ticking of a clock to relieve the silence. Soundless. In the bed, the young man lay without moving. Up and down went the covers on the bed as they were raised by his shallow breathing.

"WHEN THINGS GET really tough," the old man narrowed his eyes and looked deep into the near black eyes of the younger man sitting opposite him, "yer just gotta keep tight hold of what goals yer got. Keep it right up thar in front of yer, like a beacon shining bright on the horizon of your future."

Ben remembered the voice; he remembered the time all those years ago when he was pursuing that dream Elizabeth had made him promise to pursue. He recalled the old man sitting by his side in the gutter of that town far away. Adam had been sleeping in his arms, and this old down and out had sat by his side to offer him more hope and encouragement than any of the other upright citizens in the brand new settlement that was growing all around them.

No doubt about it, he had been tired. Exhausted. The dream he and Elizabeth had conceived together seemed to be fading more and more with every waking hour. Now his child was ill, and he had found the townsfolk of this settlement too busy to pay any heed to their needs. He was just another itinerant passing through...

So there he had been, sitting in the gutter with his child in his arms nestled in the natural cradle of his lap. The old man had come and sat down beside them and asked him where he was headed and all of Ben's misery had poured out like a dam bursting. When he had stopped, the old man, his name was Billy, had stayed silent for awhile and asked him once again, "Where are you headed fer, young un?"

Ben could recall it as clearly as though it were yesterday. The old man with the stubble on his face, the blue eyes glazed from too much drink and little else besides. But he had told the old man, told him about their dream. Two men sitting in the gutter with a sleeping child. Busy housewives had hurried past them, scowled at them, tut-tutted at them. Harassed businessmen and shopkeepers, ranchers and farmers, looked over at them and had shaken their heads. No one offered help or counsel. There had been no hand providing food, shelter or hospitality. Only a rheumy-eyed old man who had listened patiently to Ben's dream.

"Now, son," Billy had said as he had placed his hand upon Ben's arm, "hope can be like a lighthouse far out there in the distance. At times, it gits shrouded by fog and mist and the storms of the sea, and the light gits pretty dim. But if'n you know anything about lighthouses then yer know that yer have to keep everything inside bright and shining so as to reflect as much light as possible. Then, when the mists clear, and the storm bates down some, that thar light grows big and strong agin and leads yer to a safe haven. Now, ain't I right?"

"You're right, old timer. I should know having been a sailor for some time."

"Thought as much by the roll of your gait. Don't let anything rob yer of thet dream of your'n."

Ben had glanced down at the child asleep in his arms and frowned. He had opened his mouth to speak when Billy once again had stopped him.

"Guess yer ain't got no funds, huh? The little feller needs some food inside of him and some medicine too, I should reckon, seein' how flushed his cheeks are."

"Yes, but—"

Billy had raised a hand in protest and pulled a small leather pouch from his pocket and placed it firmly in Ben's hand. When Ben had opened his mouth to protest Billy raised his hand once again for silence.

"You know what they say: never judge a book by its cover. Yer look at me and think I'm a poor old man, too drunk to rub two dimes together. But the fact is, I struck pay dirt some time back and can afford to be generous to folk like yerself. I had a dream once, son, but I let it slip through my fingers. Now I got me the money, I ain't got the health and strength to go with it." He had smiled then, a furtive secretive little smile and had folded Ben's fingers over the pouch with a firmness that belied his claim to ill health and made Ben doubt the truth of his story. "Take this, get the boy seen to and get some grub inside of yourselves. Then follow that thar dream of your'n and the little missus. Give that boy a future."

Ben had mumbled a thank you, stammered a little, for the cold reception of the townsfolk had not prepared him for the generosity of the one who appeared least able to give. When Billy had rounded the corner and disappeared, Ben opened the neck of the pouch and peered inside and then hurriedly retied it. Billy had been right. He had been right then, just as he was now. One should never judge a book by its cover.

Ben sighed and picked up Elizabeth's picture once again. He reached over to the bed and once again placed his hand upon his son's arm. *Give that boy a future,* old Billy had said, and Ben felt the tears knot in his throat.

"Is this the only kind of future I've given you, son?" he whispered.

Downstairs the clock chimed, but he couldn't count the hours. Daylight was stealing over the windowsill. The man in the bed stirred and opened his eyes. For a moment, he stared up at the ceiling as he struggled to emerge from his dreams into reality. By his bedside, Ben opened his eyes, realized he had drifted into sleep and leaned towards his son.

"Pa?" A whimsical smile played about Adam's mouth as he looked at his father's tousled hair and heavy eyes. "Was it a long night?" he asked.

"Not too long," Ben replied, glancing down at the portrait in

451

his hands and smiling. "I had company and memories."

Adam smiled and watched Ben replace the picture. He folded one arm behind his head and stared up at the ceiling.

"I had memories too, kind of mixed up in a dream. I was on a clipper ship on a dark black sea and suddenly the sun came up. Guess it was from all those stories you told me as a boy, huh?" he turned towards his father and smiled.

Ben gave a small sigh and nodded.

"Memories and dreams are precious things, Adam. They're always there when you need them most."

It seemed to Adam as though his father wished to say more but before he could do so the door opened. Hoss and Joe came into the room, rather hesitantly, looking anxiously at their brother and then at their father.

"How is he, Pa?" Joe asked in a hollow sounding voice. He was answered when his brother raised a hand in greeting. Now the tension slipped from their shoulders and, more eagerly, they approached the bed to pause for a moment at the realization of how easily it could have been so different.

Hoss smiled his gentle smile, and his eyes filled with that feeling of joyous relief when one realizes danger has at last passed.

"Howdy, Adam," he mumbled. "Welcome home."

Grateful thanks to Anthony Lawrence, the author of "Elizabeth, My Love."

To Wake a Sleeping Beauty

by Patina

The Cartwrights had sat down to supper even though Adam wasn't home yet. The sixteen-year-old had spent the week breaking horses and then helping to deliver them to the Army. Ben knew his son would be home sometime this evening.

"How come we ain't waitin' on Adam?" asked Little Joe.

"Because Hop Sing doesn't want supper to get cold," answered Marie.

"He shore is missin' a great meal," said Hoss as he cut up a large slice of the pork roast on his plate.

The door opened and Adam walked in, dust covering his

clothes and boots. He hung up his hat and walked towards the staircase.

"Sit down and eat, Son, before you fall down," said Ben.

"I'd like to wash up first."

"Non, your père is right. Come and eat. Then you may wash up," said Marie.

Going to his chair, Adam heavily plopped himself down. Marie went to the kitchen and came back with a plate for her stepson. As he reached for the mashed potatoes, Ben cut off a slab of the pork roast and put it on Adam's plate. Hoss poured his older brother a glass of water. Little Joe didn't think it was fair that he had to be clean before supper but Adam was allowed to sit at the table covered in dirt.

"How did the delivery of those horses go?" asked Ben.

"Just fine, Pa. We had no problems." Suddenly remembering the bank draft in his boot, he pushed back from the table and bent over to retrieve it.

Curious, Little Joe bent sideways and peeked under the table. Seeing Adam pull the bank draft out of his boot, Little Joe now knew where his brother hid things. The boy thought he could hide stuff he didn't want anyone else to see in his brother's boots from now on.

Sitting up, Adam handed the draft to his father. Ben placed it in his shirt pocket for now. He'd have to wait until Monday to take the draft to the bank for deposit. With a harrumph, he got Little Joe's attention and the boy popped back up, head above the table.

"Didja have fun with the horsies?" Little Joe asked.

"Sure did, Buddy," said Adam with an indulgent smile.

"When kin I go on a trip like that, Pa?" asked Hoss.

"When you're much older," replied Ben.

"How much older?" asked Hoss. Since he was big for his age, he hoped that he would be allowed to take that kind of trip soon.

"I wants ta ride buckin' horsies," said Little Joe with excitement. "I won't never get tossed off neither."

"It'll be a long while before you're doing that, young man," said Ben to his youngest.

"In two or three years?" asked Little Joe with green eyes sparkling. That was a long time in his mind.

"Oh no, mon fils," replied Marie. "You are limited to your pony until your père and I decide otherwise."

"But, Mama..." he started to whine.

"Non. Hoss is not allowed to ride the broncos yet and he's ten."

"So how old has I gots ta be, then?"

Ben was going to answer, but a gesture from Marie caught his eye. Looking over to Adam, he saw that his oldest had fallen asleep, a fork-full of mashed potatoes just above his plate. All Ben could do was smile warmly. The boy must be completely exhausted. Good thing he hadn't gotten in the bath, thought Ben.

Seeing his parents looking at Adam, Little Joe looked hard across the table and then rubbed his eyes. Nope, Adam was definitely sleeping. That just wasn't fair. Not only did he have to be clean, he wasn't allowed to sleep at the table.

"He must be so tired from all of the work this week. You shouldn't work him so hard, Mon Cher."

"Adam works hard by choice, Darling."

"I've just never seen him like this, though. A mother worries about her children growing up too fast."

"Good thing he fell asleep here instead of on his horse," said Hoss.

Ben laughed at that. "What's so funny?" asked Hoss.

"There was one time, when Adam was five, he fell asleep almost like this. The wagon train had stopped at a small lake for a couple of days to rest and water the stock. Adam and some of the other boys spent the first day chasing locusts in the tall grass. Everyone was amused by their antics until the boys started putting locusts down the backs of girls' dresses. We got our sons all sorted out and back to their mothers. During supper, Adam fell asleep with a spoonful of stew halfway to his mouth. Inger and I got him to bed, where he slept soundly through the second day. When he woke up, we were on the move again."

Marie smiled fondly, imagining Adam as a boy about Joseph's age, carefree and having fun.

"Adam played with bugs?" Little Joe asked in awe. Hoss was usually the one who helped him collect crickets and lightning bugs.

"My Ma took really good care of Adam, huh?" asked Hoss.

Ben looked across the table and saw tears in Marie's eyes. "Yes, Son, your Ma did and now Mama takes good care of Adam." The thank you in Marie's eyes nearly melted Ben. He knew Hoss hadn't meant to be insensitive. All the boy knew about his mother came from his father or Adam. Plus, after Ben married Marie, Adam constantly compared her mothering skills to Inger's.

Standing, Ben said, "I'd better get this sleeping beauty to bed." Marie and Hoss giggled. Little Joe looked at Adam in confusion.

Gently, Ben removed the fork from his son's hand and sat it on the plate. "Do you need help getting him into a nightshirt?" asked Marie.

"No, I'm just going to take his boots off. He can sleep dressed."

"But what about the dirt?" she asked.

"It'll wash out of the sheets."

Little Joe again thought how unfair things were. He was never allowed to go to bed dirty and he had to wear a nightshirt. Maybe he could go to bed dirty and sleep in his clothes when he got older.

Ben had picked Adam up and was heading for the stairs. Adam's head hung back and his arms and legs hung limply. Even though muscular, Adam's frame hadn't filled out yet and he was gangly. Little Joe watched their progress carefully. Adam must be in a deep sleep, the boy thought.

Coming back downstairs, Ben brushed the dust from his clothes. He went back to the table to finish supper. "You boys be quiet this evening so Adam doesn't wake up," said Ben, gesturing to Hoss and Little Joe with his fork. "Especially when you go upstairs for bed."

"Yes, sir," they both replied.

When they went up for bed, Hoss and Little Joe decided to check in on Adam. Surely Pa didn't put Adam in bed fully dressed. Hoss held the lamp while they peeked in the room. Adam was lying on his back, the covers pulled up to his chest. His arms were above the quilts and his hands were one on top of the other on his stomach. His shirt was still on, because the tan sleeves covered his arms. Hoss pulled back the covers at the foot of the bed, exposing one leg of Adam's jeans. As Hoss put the covers back over Adam's leg, he and Little Joe looked at each other in surprise. Pa had put their brother to bed fully dressed. Adam's boots were on the floor at the foot of the bed. Quietly, the two boys left Adam's room and headed for their own rooms. They certainly didn't want to get caught disturbing their older brother.

In the morning, Little Joe got up, dressed, and headed for the stairs. On an impulse, he decided to peek into Adam's room. The boy was shocked to see Adam still in bed. What was more shocking to Little Joe was that Adam hadn't moved since he and Hoss had checked last night.

Now scared, the four-year-old went to his parents' room in the hopes of finding his mother or father. Marie was gathering up clothes that needed to be laundered. She glanced up to see her youngest looking frightened.

"What's wrong, Mon Petit?"

"Is Adam dead?"

"Why would you ask that?"

"He don't look like he's breathin'."

"Hush. Adam is just sleeping. It's alright."

"But it's mornin'. Everyone's woked."

"Your frère is just trés tired from all of the work, Mon Fils. He'll wake up when he's not tired anymore."

"When?"

"Probably in a couple of hours. Until then, play quietly."

"But what if he's really dead?"

Marie picked up her hand-mirror and took Little Joe by the hand. They quietly went into Adam's room, where she held the mirror's surface below Adam's nose. Little Joe saw the mirror fog up. Marie then took Little Joe back to her room. "You see the fog on the mirror, Mon Petit?" Little Joe just nodded his head. "That's from Adam's breath. He's just sleeping." She put the mirror back on her dressing table. Shooing Little Joe out of the room with a smile, she said, "You'd better go downstairs and eat some breakfast."

Arriving downstairs, Little Joe wasn't surprised to be eating alone. Papa was probably working and Hoss was doing chores. He probably had to do Adam's too. The boy piled eggs and bacon on his plate as Hop Sing came out of the kitchen with a glass of milk.

As Little Joe ate, Hoss came in the house. He hung up his hat and came over to the table. Picking up a piece of bacon, he said, "Pa says I can play the rest of the day. You wanna go fishin'?"

Little Joe looked up at his older brother and said, with complete seriousness, "I think Adam's under a spell. That's why he ain't woked."

"Huh?"

"You heard Papa call him sleepin' beauty. A witch musta used a spell on him ta make him sleep."

"He's jes' sleepin'. You saw how tired he was last night."

"Uh-uh. I saw Adam put his finger in his boot. He fell asleep while eatin'."

"Adam had the bank draft in his boot fer safe keepin'. That was all that was in there."

"The witch musta put the spell on that, then."

"But Pa touched that bank draft, too. He's out in the barn right now workin'."

"Then it musta been somethin' else in his boot. When he

touched it, it poked his finger and he fell asleep."

"You're not makin' sense, Shortshanks."

Marie came downstairs and interrupted the conversation. "Hoss, you've already had breakfast. Let your frère eat. If there is anything left, you may have it."

"Yes, Ma'am," answered Hoss.

Their mother went over to the sideboard and picked up her sun hat. Tying the ribbon under her chin, she said, "I'll be in my flower garden. You boys be quiet if you stay inside."

"Yes, Ma'am," they replied in unison. After Marie went outside, Little Joe and Hoss resumed their conversation.

"I can prove Adam's under a spell," announced Little Joe.

"How?"

"Wait here." Little Joe got off of his chair and went into the kitchen. Hop Sing was preparing vegetables to make stew for lunch. Standing on tippy-toes, Little Joe tried to see what was being cut up on the work table.

"What boy want?" Hop Sing asked.

"Can I have a pea?"

"Peas not cooked yet. You wait until lunch."

"No, I need one that's not cooked."

"What boy need raw pea for?"

Trying to think fast, Little Joe replied, "Hoss an' me are playin' marbles and we's one short." Fixing the cook with his green eyes, Little Joe raised his eyebrows in a pleading manner.

Unable to resist, Hop Sing went to the sack that held the peas. Pulling out a pod, he shelled the peas and handed them to Little Joe. "I only need one," the boy said.

"Take all. You might need. Now, outta kitchen."

Returning to the big room with his prize, Little Joe waved for Hoss to follow him up the stairs. The boys crept into Adam's room. Whispering, Little Joe said, "We gots ta put the peas under Adam. If he ain't under a spell, he'll wake up."

Little Joe's little hand slid under Adam's back with the peas. Adam didn't even stir. Sliding his hand back, Little Joe and Hoss waited. Nothing happened.

"Now what?" whispered Hoss.

"He shoulda woke up. That witch musta used a strong spell."

Leaving the room, the pair headed down the stairs. Marie walked in with some fresh-cut flowers for the table. "What were you boys doing upstairs?"

"Nothin'," said Little Joe.

She fixed the two with a look and said, "You two should play outside." Marie then took the flowers into the kitchen to put them in a vase.

Going outside, Little Joe and Hoss stood on the front porch, wondering how to break the spell Adam was under. "Maybe we should make him look like a princess in a story."

"But Adam's a boy," said Hoss.

"Yeah, but in the stories, the witch always puts a princess to sleep. Maybe the witch couldn't see too good."

"Hmph," was Hoss' only answer.

"Dontcha see?" asked Little Joe. "The princess can't sleep when a pea is under her back. Adam didn't wake up and we used three of 'em."

"But in the story, the pea goes between two mattresses. You jes' put it under his back."

"He didn't wake up, Hoss."

"That just proves he ain't a princess."

"It means that he's under a real strong spell. What do the princesses in the stories have?"

"Long hair?" asked Hoss, trying to be helpful.

"No. Flowers," replied Little Joe. "We gots ta put some flowers on him."

"Then what?"

"The smell of the flowers will wake him up."

"I don't think that's the way the stories go," advised Hoss.

"It gots ta work," said Little Joe. He then led the way into Marie's flower garden. "Get some of those daisies, Hoss," the younger boy said. Hoss pulled up a big clump, roots and all.

"What're we gonna do with these?" he asked.

"Make a crown."

"And then what?"

"I dunno."

While Hoss was standing there with a clump of daisies in hand, Ben approached the house. "What are you boys doing in your mother's flower garden?"

"Pickin' some flowers for Mama," replied Little Joe.

Ben was surprised to see a whole clump of daisies in Hoss' hand, but he didn't want to fuss too much at the boys. After all, they were trying to do something nice for their mother.

"Can you cut us some roses, Papa?" asked Little Joe.

"I don't know, boys," answered Ben. "Your mother prizes this rose bush."

"That means she'll really like it when we gives her some flowers from it," said Little Joe.

"No, boys. The daisies should be enough." Ben could always order more daisy seed. Rose bushes were harder to come by. He then headed for the house. "You boys coming?"

"In a minute," said Little Joe. "You gots your knife?" he asked his older brother.

"Yeah. Why?"

"Cut off one a those branches," Little Joe instructed, pointing to the rose bush.

"You heard what Pa said," answered Hoss.

"It's just one branch. Mama won't know."

Hoss handed the daisies to Little Joe and pulled out his pocket knife. He reached for a branch and then pulled his hand back. "Those thorns hurt."

"Then scrape 'em off," advised Little Joe.

Running the knife blade against the cane, Hoss got the thorns off. He then began to saw through the cane. Finally slicing through the stem, Hoss pulled the cutting to himself. This particular cane had half a dozen roses blooming on it.

"Now what?" Hoss asked.

Little Joe led the way to the door and then gestured for Hoss to be quiet. They opened and shut the door quietly, tip-toed over to the stairs, and went up. Going into Hoss's room, the two sat on the floor and pulled the daisy stems from the clump. Little Joe's nimble fingers began to weave the stems into a circlet. Finishing, the boy held it up for Hoss's approval.

"Let's go put it on Adam," suggested Little Joe.

Coming out of Hoss's room, the boys ran into their father. Hoss put the roses behind his back. "What are you two doing up here?" His eye was then caught by the circlet of daisies. "Is that for Mama?"

Hoss looked startled while Little Joe's mind leapt into action. "Yup. We's gonna s'prise her. You won't tell, huh?" The boy fixed his father with a puppy look. Unable to resist, Ben smiled and put a finger to his lips. With that, he went into his own room.

Deciding to act fast, Little Joe and Hoss went into Adam's room. Hoss placed the circlet of daisies on Adam's head and then slid the roses under Adam's hands. The two boys took a step back to admire their handiwork. A giggle started to escape Little Joe, so Hoss clamped a hand over his little brother's mouth and hauled him downstairs.

Reaching the first floor, they were surprised to see Hop Sing setting the table for lunch. "How marble game go?" he asked, fixing Little Joe with a look.

"Good," answered the boy. "I won."

Hop Sing shot Little Joe a skeptical look, finished the place settings, and then went back to the kitchen. Hoss noticed that there wasn't a setting for Adam. He mentioned that to Little Joe.

"Hop Sing must know about the spell."

"How come?"

"Adam ain't got a plate."

Marie came out of the kitchen with a tureen full of stew. "You boys go wash up. Lunch is ready."

The two quickly washed up and returned to the table to join their parents. "Do you think we should wake Adam, Mon Cher?"

"No. Let him sleep. He's earned it. Besides, I once slept for two days after returning from a sea voyage to Europe with Captain Stoddard."

"Two whole days?" Little Joe asked in awe.

"That's right. The only reason I know that is because I missed a meeting with Adam's mother. She took her time in forgiving me."

"How could she have stayed mad at you, Mon Cher?" Marie asked teasingly. "I'm sure you charmed your way back into her good graces."

"Took more than charm," replied Ben, blushing at the memory. "I took her on a picnic. Liz fell asleep after we ate. She looked so beautiful lying under that elm tree. I couldn't help myself and I kissed her. She woke with a start and nearly punched me in the eye." Both Ben and Marie laughed. "All was forgiven when I gave her that music box and proposed."

Marie cherished the few memories Ben shared of his youth. She felt that hearing of his relationship with Elizabeth would help her to better understand Adam. Plus, she liked to imagine her husband as a dashing young sailor on the high seas.

Little Joe quickly realized that the only way to wake Adam would be with a kiss. But who could they find to do the job?

When they finished lunch, Marie told the boys to go outside and play. She hoped that Hoss would tire Little Joe out so he would take a nap.

Out in the yard, Little Joe told Hoss, "We gots ta find a girl to kiss Adam. Then he'll wake up."

"Where are we gonna find a girl?" asked Hoss, wrinkling up his nose.

"I dunno. Ain't there a girl in school who'd do it?"

"How would we get to town? Pa ain't gonna let us go on our own."

With a snap of his fingers, Little Joe had the solution. "A frog!"

"A frog?"

"Yeah. If the frog kisses Adam, he'll wake up."

"But in the stories, a girl kisses a frog and it turns into a prince. 'Sides, how can a frog kiss Adam?"

"Let's go catch one an' I'll show ya."

The boys headed for a nearby pond. They each grabbed a frog, just in case. On their way back, they heard their mother scream, "BEN!!"

Peeking around the corner of the house, they saw Mama standing in her flower garden in front of her rose. Ben raced from the barn, fearing the worst. Marie only called him Ben when she was frightened or extremely angry. He hoped it was just that rat snake again.

Reaching the flower garden, Marie turned to him and pointed at her rose bush. "How did this happen?!?"

"The boys wanted to cut a flower for you, but I told them not to."

"Didn't you tell them to stay out of the flowers?!?"

"I told them to leave the rose bush alone. They had already pulled up a clump of daisies." Ben immediately realized he'd said the wrong thing as his wife's face turned a deeper red.

"This rose bush came all the way from New Orleans. Where will I get another if this dies?"

"San Francisco?" Ben asked, trying to be helpful.

Seeing that Marie's temper was about to get out of hand, he told her, "Keep your voice down. Adam's still asleep."

Hoss and Little Joe saw Mama take a deep breath. Then they heard her begin to count in French. Little Joe knew she must really be mad because Mama usually only did that when he did something really bad. Deciding to sneak inside with their frogs, the boys quickly went around to the front door and let themselves in.

Creeping upstairs, they went in Adam's room. Adam was still lying there. With a nod from his little brother, the larger boy touched his frog's mouth to Adam's cheek. Nothing happened. Hoss did it again. Adam still slept. "Hold on," said Little Joe as he

put his frog in his pocket.

Little Joe went to his parents' room and took the hand-mirror off of his mother's dressing table. Re-entering Adam's room, Little Joe gave the hand-mirror to Hoss and whispered for him to hold it under Adam's nose. Hoss did as told and showed the fog on the mirror's surface to his little brother.

At a nod from Little Joe, Hoss touched the frog to Adam's cheek again. Nothing happened. Little Joe pulled his frog out of his pocket. He touched his frog's mouth to Adam's cheek, but nothing happened.

"These frogs ain't workin'," whispered Hoss. "Now what?"

"I dunno. That witch made a strong spell."

They were so engrossed with touching the frogs to Adam's cheek that they didn't hear their mother come upstairs. She peeked in her oldest son's room since Ben was worried that her tirade might have awakened the boy. "What are you doing, Mes Fils?"

Little Joe and Hoss practically jumped out of their boots. Hoss turned scarlet while Little Joe put his frog behind his back. Marie was shocked at Adam's appearance—a circlet of flowers on his head and roses under his hands. She might have laughed if it wasn't for her sons' disobedience. Those two had butchered her rose bush and were not leaving Adam alone.

Marie quietly entered Adam's room and steered the two younger boys by the shoulders out into the hall and then into her room. Sitting them on the bed, she asked, "What are you doing with those frogs in the house?" Before they could answer, she asked, "What are you doing to your frère?"

Little Joe and Hoss looked at each other helplessly. "I'm wait-ing for an explanation," she said.

The words came tumbling out of Little Joe's mouth. "A witch gave Adam a sleepin' spell. The spell started when he put his hand in his boot last night. Hoss an' me thought it was that bank paper, but the spell didn't do nothin' to Papa. We puts peas under him to wake him up but it didn't work. Then we made him look like a princess in the stories, but he's still sleepin'. That's why we's usin' frogs."

"And what do frogs have to do with sleeping?" she asked.

"Nothin'. But if a girl kisses a frog it becomes a prince. If a frog kisses Adam, he'll wake up."

Marie had no idea why Little Joe's logic led him to this conclusion. There were times the boy reminded her of her Oncle Henri. People were easily exasperated by him, too.

Turning the conversation back to their actions, Marie asked, "Why did you cut my rose when your père said not to?"

"Papa never said not to," answered Little Joe.

Marie looked at Hoss. She wanted the truth and she knew Hoss wouldn't make up a wild story.

Hoss crumbled under her gaze. "Pa told us you really like that rose bush. Little Joe said we had to have the roses fer Adam. But they didn't work."

"Why didn't you boys leave Adam alone like we told you?"

"'Cause he's under a spell!" insisted Little Joe.

"That's enough, Mon Petit."

"But he's still sleepin', Mama," persisted Little Joe. "We can't break the spell."

"Adam is just tired. He's not under a spell. Let's go downstairs and wait for supper. Bring the frogs."

Steering the boys downstairs, Marie saw them to the door. As the boys went out with their frogs, their father came in the house. Ben asked, "What are those two up to?"

"I'm sorry about earlier, Mon Cher," said Marie with a kiss to her husband's cheek. With her finger, she gestured for Ben to follow her. With great curiosity, he followed his wife up the stairs. Instead of going to their room, however, they headed for Adam's.

Peering in, Ben was shocked at the sight that met his eyes. "What have those two done?" Ben whispered.

Pulling Ben back into the hall, Marie explained Little Joe's insistence that Adam was under a spell. "Whatever gave him that idea?" Ben asked incredulously.

"You, Mon Cher."

"Me? How?"

"You called Adam sleeping beauty. Petit Joseph already thought Adam had been enchanted because he was sleeping at the table."

"That's ridiculous," said Ben with a snort.

"I tried to tell the boys that, but you may have better luck."

The couple went downstairs as Little Joe and Hoss came back inside. "Boys," said Ben, "your brother is not under a spell. He's just tired from all of the work he did this week."

Hoss and Little Joe weren't completely convinced. "How come he ain't hungry?" Hoss asked. Hunger sometimes woke the boy during the night.

"Because his body is too tired to care about food. Now, go to the kitchen and wash up for supper."

Little Joe and Hoss went into the kitchen. "How can Adam not be hungry? He ain't ate all day."

"Must be part of the spell," replied Little Joe.

Hop Sing gave each boy a dish to carry out to the table. When all of the food was on the table, the Cartwrights sat down to eat. Little Joe noticed that there was no place setting at Adam's spot.

Upstairs, Adam's eyelids began to flutter. He opened his eyes to muted oranges and yellows. Must be morning, he thought. His body felt very stiff and sore as he moved his feet under the covers to stretch out his legs. When he decided to move his fingers, he felt something in his hands. Craning his neck, he saw wilted roses under his hands. He didn't know what to make of that. Noticing his shirt sleeves, he thought Marie would be upset with him for going to bed dressed.

When he sat up, the circlet of daisies fell onto the floor. Swinging his legs over the side of the bed, Adam was surprised to see his jeans covering his legs. He could understand leaving on his shirt, but his jeans? His feet were covered by his socks. At least he'd taken off his boots.

Getting up, Adam placed one hand behind his back, stretched up, and then leaned back a bit. His hand encountered something smushy. Turning, he looked at the bed and saw what appeared to be smashed peas. He hoped he hadn't been eating in bed.

Going over to the washstand, he poured some water into the basin and then dipped in his hands. He splashed his face several times and then reached for the towel to wipe off the water.

Still feeling groggy, he changed into clean clothes. The toes of his left foot encountered something in his boot. Pulling it off, he shook the boot upside down. A marble, a checker, and a bird's feather fell out onto the floor. He just raised his eyebrows and then put the boot on.

Once dressed, he decided to go downstairs. He must be the first one up. There were no breakfast smells. Before he left his room, he picked up the circlet of daisies.

Coming downstairs, Adam was surprised to see everyone at the table. And it appeared they were eating supper.

Hearing footsteps on the stairs, the rest of the family looked over. Excited to see Adam awake, Little Joe jumped up from the table and ran to his oldest brother. The boy yelled, "We broke the spell, Hoss!!" Adam was almost knocked over by his youngest brother's hug.

Even though his body ached, Adam picked up Little Joe and carried him to the table. "What spell?" he asked.

Before either Ben or Marie could speak, Little Joe launched into an explanation about a witch, the boot, how Adam fell asleep at the table, how he and Hoss had tried to break the spell with peas, flowers, and frogs, and how nothing worked. Adam was even more confused.

"You mean I've slept all day? Why didn't anyone wake me up?"

"Son, you needed to sleep. You wore your body out with those horses. Besides, we took care of everything around here today."

"It wasn't for a lack of trying that you remained asleep, Mon Fils," said Marie. "Your frères tried everything they could think of and you stayed asleep."

"Yeah, because the witch used a sleepin' spell."

"What witch?" Adam asked, really confused.

"The one who put somethin' in your boot."

"All that was in my boot was a bank draft from the Army." Adam started to get up, afraid that he had forgotten to give the draft to his father.

"You gave me that draft last night, Son."

Adam was relieved that he had remembered to do that.

"That was the only thing in my boot last night, Buddy." Remembering the stuff in his boot this evening, Adam pulled the marble, checker, and feather from his pocket. "These were in there tonight. Any idea how they got there?"

"Uh-uh," the little boy replied. "That witch put somethin' in your boot yesterday because Papa didn't go to sleep when he touched the bank paper."

"Your brother was exhausted, Joseph, from working all week. There was no spell."

"But ya called him sleepin' beauty," said Little Joe insistently.

"That doesn't mean there was a spell, Son. Adam was just really tired."

"All the stories say a witch uses a spell and then the princess sleeps 'til someone wakes her up," said Hoss. "Me an' Joe went over some of the stories this mornin' to make sure."

"In case you two haven't noticed, I'm not a princess," said Adam with a raised eyebrow.

"We know," said Little Joe. "We tried ever'thin' in the stories but nothin' worked. That's why we knows it was a strong spell."

"There is no witch," said Marie. "Let's not hear any more of this nonsense."

Thinking quickly, Adam looked at his younger brothers and said, "Now that I think on it, there was a witch. She had long flowing brown hair and the biggest brown eyes I've ever seen. And the size of her teeth! You just wouldn't believe it."

Ben steepled his fingers and watched the boys over them. Marie hoped this story didn't lead to bad dreams for Joseph.

"Did the witch have a name?" Little Joe squeaked out.

Taking a sip of water, Adam paused for dramatic effect. "Her name was Dumpling and she could fly like the wind."

Little Joe gasped. He knew it! There had been a witch.

"But Dumplin's a horse," said Hoss with disappointment.

"And I fell under her spell," replied Adam. "Pa, I convinced Captain Howson to let me keep her since her temperament is too sweet for a cavalry horse."

"Whatcha gonna do with her?" asked Hoss. No one had noticed how disappointed Little Joe looked to find out there had been no real witch after all.

"If it's okay with you," Adam said as he looked between Pa and Marie, "I thought I'd give her to Hoss."

Ben and Marie looked at each other. They would have to discuss this. Hoss had outgrown his pony and they knew they'd need a horse for him to ride to and from school.

"So there was never no witch?" Little Joe asked.

"Nope," replied Adam. Putting the circlet of daisies on his head he added, "And don't confuse me with a princess again."

Little Joe giggled at the sight of Adam wearing the daisies and Hoss made kissing noises at his older brother. Ben rolled his eyes while Marie hoped that Little Joe would forget about witches.

After the boys retired for the evening, Ben and Marie talked about letting Hoss have Dumpling. On their way upstairs to bed, Marie asked, "Perhaps I could be sleeping beauty and you could awaken me with a kiss?" She added a come-hither smile.

"I'm afraid you'd never get any sleep, my beauty," replied Ben, kissing her on the lips, cheek, and neck.

Slack Reins

by Dbird

They found him too late or just in time, depending on how you looked at it.

For days, they'd taken turns sitting beside his bed, simply waiting. None of them actually talked about what they were waiting for. Ben stayed during the day when Adam and Hoss went to work, but in the evenings, they all sat together in Joe's room. Hop Sing brought up their supper on a tray, and they ate beside him. They'd never seen Joe lie so still. He'd always been a boy who needed to keep moving. His brothers wondered privately if he was sleeping or if he really wasn't there any more. They would not say anything like that to their pa.

To pass those long nights, they told stories. This particular night was no exception. First, they shared about their day, peppering the conversation with details they thought Joe might appreciate, if he happened to be listening. After a while, Ben talked about his years at sea, and Adam told Hoss stories of crossing the plains in a wagon train. Hoss never got tired of hearing about their journey west, so those stories seemed to go on the longest.

There was much sadness, cold, and loss on that trip west, including things they never really talked about. Folks said that one out of every seventeen emigrants was buried alongside the Oregon Trail. There were plenty of terrible stories Adam could have told, stories his pa hadn't been able to protect him from knowing about. Children caught and crushed under wagon wheels. Epidemics. Snake bites and stampedes. Skirmishes with the Indians. The terrible day that Inger died in their pa's arms. But they didn't want Joe to overhear those kinds of stories. Who would want to come back to a world where children died from a momentary oversight and mothers didn't live to nurse their newborns?

Instead, Adam told Hoss about dramatic prairie storms and fording rivers with the oxen and horses. Adam could remember pretending he was in his pa's clipper when his own wagon made its successful crossing. Who could have been scared with Ben Cartwright at the helm? He told Hoss about playing games with the other children after supper and about sitting around a campfire, staring at more stars in one night sky than he'd ever seen since. They hadn't had much, but the food they did have tasted better back then. Dried buffalo meat, beans, and camp-baked bread. They slept together under blankets, all huddled together. They could hear each other breathing all night. It was always cold once the sun went down, even in the middle of the summer. Ben and Adam shivered just talking about it but then remembered the present. It was too sad sitting there in that quiet room, thinking about the cold. So they kept talking.

They talked about Hoss as a baby. He had been a huge and healthy baby, robust and a solid eater. They didn't bring up the fact that the infant might not have survived the journey if he hadn't been so strong. Surely, Joe wouldn't have made it if he'd been the one born on the trail...he had been too small and a poor eater. Adam carried Hoss everywhere, even though his arms ached at the end of the day. After all, he'd only been six years old, himself. Sometimes, he got so tired. Adam recalled the evening he climbed into a neighbor's wagon with his newborn baby brother and took a nap, curled into the corner. It was so rare for Adam to not be where he supposed to be that the entire party was in a panic searching for the missing children, certain that somehow they'd been lost on the trail.

"We'd thought we lost both of you that day," Ben mused with a soft smile, his eyes not drifting from Joe's face. "Looked everywhere."

"Was that before or after Ma died?" Hoss asked. He was sitting on the edge of his chair, wanting to be as close to his little brother as he could, but not knowing how to do it without hurting him. Cautiously, he rested his hand on Joe's unbroken knee.

"After," Ben and Adam chorused. They smiled at each other with some amusement and longstanding regret.

Adam explained. "Inger never let you out of her sight. She kept a pretty good eye on me as well. She'd have known where we were sleeping, even if no one else had even seen us leave the wagon."

"I reckon that's how it is with ma's," Hoss said, also smiling at the idea.

"Was Marie protective like that?" Adam asked, as he finished off the last of his roast pork and gravy. "I don't remember her following Little Joe around."

Ben stroked his youngest son's arm. "Marie knew that Little Joe needed a little more freedom to explore than other little boys. She never could bring herself to keep him under a tight rein. She said it might break his spirit."

Adam shook his head. "Maybe that's how it started. I can't help thinking that this didn't have to happen."

"Adam—" Hoss chided, but Ben shook his head.

"It's all right," he said. "Say what you mean, Adam."

Adam looked like he was tamping down something close to anger. Then he leaned against the wall, as if trying to control himself. "I don't know what I mean, Pa. But I just can't stop thinking about the way Joe rides a horse...I don't know how he got so hurt, but I do know he was riding too fast. Shouldn't we have learned something from what happened to Marie? Why didn't we ever try to stop him? There are so many things we let him get away with..."

Hoss snorted. "You're just forgettin', big brother. We did stop him. Plenty of times. We been keepin' him from getting himself killed every day of his life. We'd have 'bout as much chance stoppin' Little Joe from riding a fast horse as a one-legged man would have in a kicking contest."

Ben had to laugh at the truth of that, despite the seriousness of the situation, but Adam refused to smile. He stared down at his little brother. Each was well aware of the fact that Little Joe was apt to do what he was going to do, no matter what anyone had to say about it. Adam hadn't been able to stop thinking of Marie and that terrible day when she died in front of the house, her neck snapped after her horse rolled over on her. Marie had always done as she wanted. *Never mind the consequences,* Adam thought to himself, even as his own bitterness surprised him. *Why did she have to ride so damn fast that day?*

"Did you ever try to stop *her?*" Adam turned to his father. "Marie and the crazy way she used to ride?"

Ben sighed and rubbed his eyes. He was tired. This vigil with Joseph was taking a toll on his body and spirits, and here they were, still waiting on either a miracle or the unthinkable. And yet, Adam was also waiting for an answer. The stories about the wagon train had reminded Ben how much tragedy his oldest son had known as a boy. The things he had seen. Adam's closest friend on the trail had died of cholera. It had happened only a few days after Inger had been killed in front of them. No wonder

Adam was always trying to find a way to control his life. Ben tried to ignore the accusation in his son's question. His poor boy had never known his own mother, but he'd watched two others die. He couldn't help but grieve wild-hearted Marie who heedlessly loved to ride a horse as fast as the wind. Ben could hardly begin to remember the terrible day that she died. No wonder Adam was thinking of Marie. It was so tragically similar.

Ben gazed down at Marie's son. They'd always looked so much alike, and never so much as in their sleep. Now, there was even more that bound them. Joe's poor body was a mirror of his mother's broken body the day they'd brought her in the house. The same violent bruising, the crushed leg, so much blood they didn't know where it was coming from. Marie's neck had been broken, but Joseph was still breathing. Marie had never opened her eyes again. Never said goodbye. How they'd both loved to ride fast. Was there something he should have done differently? Could Ben have stopped this from happening, if he'd kept a firmer hold on the reins?

His older boys were waiting for an answer. Ben rested his head against Joe's headboard and stroked his son's cheek with an ache he could hardly hold in. How could he explain? His sons had never been married. They'd never raised children. They didn't know how little in life a man could control. Ben's entire life had been a study in taking control and giving it back again, and never more than with this youngest son. Joe had kept him humble, even from the start. Even as he kept his touch light and gentle against Joe's face, he could swear he could almost see his son's smile under all that swelling. Ben wondered if his boy was dreaming about riding that blasted horse. Go figure. It was the way Joe lived his life. There was sorrow and pain but there was great exuberance as well. It all came bound up together.

"Keeping Marie from that horse would have been like stopping water from running downhill," Ben said at last. He hoped that was a good enough answer for Adam. He hoped it was a good enough answer for himself.

After a quiet moment, Hoss asked, "Pa, do you reckon there's such a thing as second chances?"

"Of course, I believe in second chances." Ben regarded his son with real curiosity. "We've seen our share of people who've made mistakes and then turned their lives around afterward. I'm surprised you would ask that, Hoss."

Then Ben saw it on Hoss's face—the grief of a man who had never known guile. Gently, he asked, "What are you really asking me, son?"

Hoss scrunched up his face, staring miserably at his little brother. "I reckon it just don't make sense. First his ma and then Little Joe both getting hurt in the same way. Don't you think God owes us a second chance?"

Adam asked, "A second chance for what?"

"Don't know. Getting it right, I reckon."

"Saving Joe?" Adam asked.

Hoss shrugged. "Maybe we could have done it different somehow."

Ben knew exactly what his son meant. Tragedy always carried hard questions. *Could I have stopped this? Is there anything I could have done that would have made a difference? If it is possible, let this cup pass from me....*

As always, Adam seemed to be watching him.

"Is it worth it?" Adam's voice caught on the question. "Having to go through this again and again?"

Ben couldn't bring himself to answer. Love was always worth it, but the pain it sometimes brought was something else altogether. How many men his age had grown bitter as the losses mounted? Ben had not grown bitter, but all the same, he couldn't help but cast yet another prayer in Heaven's direction—for second chances, slack reins, and eighteen-year-old boys who didn't wake up, even after days and days and days of waiting.

It was already late. They began gathering up the dishes to take downstairs, when they heard it. A low moan, sheets rustling. Life. Was it possible to hear a second chance? Almost dropping the dishes on the floor, they crowded back to the bed. Joe's eyes were barely open, but already he had something to say. They all leaned in, touching him where they could and trying to get close enough. Joseph hardly had a voice, but that didn't matter. They could hear him, loud and clear.

"Is my horse all right?"

It hadn't been the first time Ben had heard that question from his boy, but he had never been so glad to hear it before. His own voice was thick with what he couldn't say. "Your horse made it home just fine, son."

"Knew he would." Joe was already falling asleep again. He could hardly turn his head, but he managed a smile for Adam. *Is it worth it?* They had forgotten to choose their words carefully, forgetting that he could be listening. "It's always worth it, brother," he mumbled, before his eyes started to close of their own accord. "Best ride I ever had...."

17458421R00262

Printed in Great Britain
by Amazon